RICH MEN, DEAD MEN

MICHAEL DYLAN

RICH MEN, DEAD MEN.

by

Michael Dylan

1

Detective Inspector Simon Wise held out his hand, desperate to stop a murder. 'Give me the gun. Please — think of your wife. Your kids.'

The gunman stared back at him with wild eyes, sweat pouring down his face, pistol shaking in his hands. 'I can't do that.'

They were on the roof of the Maywood estate in Peckham. It was still hot despite it being 11 p.m., the June heat stored deep in the concrete. The surrounding buildings overlooked the unfolding drama, all washed blue by the flashing lights of the army of emergency vehicles below.

There were two others on the roof with Wise and the gunman.

Derrick Morris, the star witness in a gangland murder trial that was due to start in the morning, was on his knees. Barefoot and shirtless, he looked like he'd been dragged out of his bed and hauled up onto the roof. He had his arms around his girlfriend, Tasha Simcocks, who was also on her knees next to him, wearing only her nightdress. Both were crying, eyes fixed on Wise with the desperate hope that he could keep them alive just a little bit longer.

The trouble was Wise didn't know if he could because the other person on the roof, the man Wise was pleading with, had his gun pointed at Morris and Simcocks' heads. If Wise couldn't find the right words to stop him, he was going to murder the pair of them.

It was a bad situation made far worse because the gunman was a police officer, a Detective Sergeant in one of the Metropolitan Police's Murder Investigation Teams. He was a man Wise knew better than almost anyone else in his life, and seeing him there with a gun and intending to kill a witness made no sense at all.

Andy Davidson was his partner, after all. They'd risen through the ranks together, helped each other, supported each other, and did a damn lot of good together. Not only that, Andy had been Wise's best man at his wedding, godfather to his kids, and whom he'd been drinking beer with only hours before.

There was no one he knew better — except Wise didn't know Andy at all.

'Please, Andy. Before Armed Response gets here. Give me the gun.' Wise took a step towards his partner, hand still out.

'Don't come any closer,' Andy cried, his eyes wide and bulging, burning cocaine bright. Sweat glistened across his face and soaked his t-shirt. He pressed the revolver against Morris' head, but Wise could see the shaking in his hand. Was that a sign of his resolve weakening or just his desperation? 'Another step and I'll shoot him.'

'Mate, please,' Wise said. 'I don't know why you're doing this, but we can sort it out. We can fix it — whatever it is — if you give me the gun. You're not a murderer.'

'You don't know what I am!' Andy screamed. He wiped his free hand across his face, rubbing the snot from his nose, blinking tears away. 'I have to do this.'

A red dot danced across Andy's shoulders, seeking his head, finding its spot, stopping on his temple, dead still. An ARO in one of the neighbouring buildings had Andy in his sights, the laser targeting locked on a kill shot.

'No!' Wise shouted. He thrust both hands up in the air, turning, trying to see where the sniper was, trying to block his line of sight. 'Don't shoot! Don't shoot.'

Time stopped as Wise waited for the crack of a shot and the sight of Andy's brains punched from his skull. But no shot came. No order given to terminate his friend. Someone still hoped Wise could stop this without bloodshed — for now. The clock was ticking, though. The order would come soon enough. No one would risk Andy killing their star witness.

He turned back to his friend. 'The AROs have got you in their sights, Andy. Please give me the gun before it's too late. Think of Debs. Think of Katie and Mark.' Think of me, he wanted to say. He'd already lost his actual brother, he couldn't cope with losing Andy too. 'Please, mate.'

'If I don't do this,' Andy said, 'he told me he'd kill them.'

'Who did?' Wise took another step forward. 'If someone's threatening you or your family, we can stop them. You just have to trust me and give me the gun.'

The two men stared at each other. Twenty years of history being relived in their eyes. Their friendship. Their bond. Surely, he'd give up. Andy was no killer.

'Please mate.'

Andy shook his head. 'I'm sorry, Si. I'm sorry for ev—'

Something punched Andy off his feet a heartbeat before Wise heard the crack of the gun. Time slowed as Andy tumbled forward, red mist leading the way, his brains and blood already splattered across the rooftop. He landed on the concrete with a wet thud and lay unmoving, his eyes open and fixed on Wise, a hole in the side of his temple where the red dot had been.

Wise couldn't move. His mind couldn't take in what his eyes told him, refusing to accept it.

'ARMED POLICE! ARMED POLICE! NO ONE MOVE!' The AROs ran out onto the rooftop, all dressed in black, balaclavas covering their faces, bulletproof helmets on top of those, goggles covering their eyes, Heckler and Koch MP5 machine guns in the ready position, shouting orders, looking for more threats, making sure Andy was dead.

They got Morris and Simcocks to their feet and bundled them away to the stairs, down to safety, to medical help. One snatched up Andy's gun, made it safe, and bagged it. Another checked Andy and shouted that the target was dead.

Then an ARO was saying something to Wise, but Wise couldn't understand him, couldn't reply, couldn't move. All he could see was the jerk in Andy's head as the bullet struck him, the shape of his mouth as his last breath left his body, and the look in his eyes as he fell, accusing Wise.

More people rushed out onto the roof. More police. An ambulance crew.

Someone put a tinfoil blanket over Wise's shoulders. Said more words he couldn't understand. Some of Wise's team were on the roof, too. Madge appeared, hand over her mouth, staring at her dead colleague, her dead friend, then at Wise.

Wise felt the judgement in her eyes. Their condemnation. He was their leader. He should've stopped this from happening.

Wise couldn't comfort her, couldn't say anything that would make this horror any better. He couldn't even blink.

All he could see was Andy dying.

Andy dead.

Dear God.

Tuesday, 13th September

2

Mark Hassleman leaned over the coffee table and sprinkled more cocaine onto the glass surface. He let a nice little pile fall from the little plastic bag — but not too much. There wasn't much left, and he'd already had more than enough Charlie for the night. More than enough to last a lifetime if truth be told, but Mark tried not to think about that too much. After all, what was the point of being a tech multi-millionaire if he couldn't enjoy the simple little pleasures in life?

Not that a five hundred pound a day cocaine habit was a simple pleasure. It was a hard-earned extravagance. What was it Robin Williams had said? Cocaine was God's way of letting you know you had too much money? He'd been damn right about that.

Back in Hassleman's college days, he'd thought only movie stars and rock singers did cocaine. Not people like him. Not the nerds, geeks, and the socially awkward. What would his friends from back then say now if they saw him like this? Hunched over a table of powder, a half drunk bottle of whisky by his side, shut off from the world with the curtains drawn. They'd not think he was living the dream. They'd be unimpressed. Disappointed. Shocked.

From *Wired* to wired.

But who cared? He didn't. Hassleman was a million miles away from them. He wasn't just living in a different world; he was in a different stratosphere. He was the rich and famous now. And he was only too aware of the irony that his fame, his fortune, had come from an app designed to get people laid, created by a man who once upon a time couldn't get lucky to save his life.

Hassleman laughed at that. Necessity was the mother of invention, after all.

Hassleman picked up his black AmEx card and began delicately shaping the powder into lines. Small, sensible, thin ones because he was going to make this pile last the rest of the night. He certainly wouldn't finish the rest of the bag. He definitely wouldn't call for more. Hassleman had told Ivan as much when he'd dropped off the last delivery. Told him not to come back that day even if Hassleman called. Not even if he begged. Hassleman had to have some self-control left, prove to himself that he wasn't an addict, that he was doing all the blow for fun, not need.

His hand carved and re-carved the lines, already making the sensible lines into something more ... impressive. Bigger. Bolder. Not too much, but enough. To do less was a waste of time.

Soon, his sensible little lines had merged into three long train tracks but Hassleman pretended not to notice, still believing he was going to make it last, that what was on the table was all he'd have and no more. Believing his own lies. Fooling himself.

He rolled up the hundred-dollar bill he kept just for snorting coke with, stuck it in his nostril and bent down once more, breathing in, racing along one line, then swapped the note to his other nostril and went to work on the second line, struggling a bit more this time, his nostril already clogged with everything he'd stuffed up it earlier, but he preserved.

God, it stung. He squeezed his nose together, making sure he didn't sneeze as he felt the drip run down the back of his throat, felt the coke kick in, a dull thump instead of the roar it'd been at eleven that morning when he'd started. All because he'd been bored.

Not that he needed much of an excuse these days.

He leaned back on the leather sofa, mind racing, going nowhere fast. Should he stay in or should he go out? Maybe make some calls. Call some people. Have some drinks. More drinks. He'd sunk most of a bottle of whisky, as it was. He didn't need more.

Or did he? He was in now. Settled. He wasn't even sure what time it was. The curtains were closed all day, cutting off the world. Just the way he liked it. Who knew what everyone else was up to? They wouldn't be on his wavelength even if he did meet up with them.

Then it would be awkward. Uncomfortable. He certainly didn't need anyone judging him and ruining his high.

Better he stay in. Stay alone. He preferred it that way, anyway.

Porn played on the eighty-inch TV that filled the far wall of the living room. Bodies doing this and that in glorious 4k. Ultra-hard, utterly depraved. Not that it meant anything. Not that it turned him on. He didn't know why he was watching it. If he was watching it. Why did he have it on? When did he turn it on?

He rubbed his face, feeling hot, feeling clammy, then downed his glass of whisky and poured another. He needed the booze to take the edge of the coke, smooth out the jitters, quieten the crazy thoughts.

He muted the porn and turned on some music. Stormzy thundered from the stereo. That was better. The bass was deep and loud. Pulsing through him. Shaking the walls. Pounding in time with his heart. A hundred beats a minute. Heart attack time. Maybe he should turn that down. He didn't want anyone coming around to complain. Not now. Not when he was like this. Feeling good. Feeling electric.

Living the fucking dream.

He bent down and inhaled the third line. His last line. The last of the night. Thank God for that. A few more drinks and he could call it a night. Pop a xanax. Get some sleep. He'd feel better in the morning. Yeah, early night.

How boring did that sound?

The night was just getting started. He was just getting started.

Hassleman looked at the dregs left in the bag. It wasn't a lot. Maybe enough for one more line. A small one. Maybe he should get tomorrow's supply in tonight? Have it ready for when he needed it? Ivan wasn't a morning person, after all. What drug dealer was? It was better to have it and not need it than to need it and not have it. Or something like that.

He picked up his phone, opened WhatsApp, clicked on the conversation with Ivan. It was full of the usual drug dealing drivel. Bad code that wouldn't fool an imbecile, let alone the police. Still, it was how it was done. Expected. Everyone played the game.

He had to focus on the screen and concentrate on what he typed. 'Mate, decided to go to the party after all. Can you drop five VIP tickets off at my place?'

Ivan pinged back two seconds later. 'LOL. I thought you weren't going to call me?'

'How long?' Hassleman messaged back.

'Ten minutes.'

Thank God for that. Hassleman put the phone down and picked the bag up, emptying the last of its contents on the table. He'd made the right call, making the call. Who was he kidding? The night was young, and he was king of the fucking world. Even Zuckerberg hadn't made his first million as quick as he had. Now he was chasing his first billion three years on. After that? Who knows what he could do? What he could achieve?

Maybe he'd be president of the United Fucking States. Make his mom proud of him at last. The bitch.

He sprinkled the last the specks of Charlie over the table, free of the pretence of restraint. Picked up the note. His hundred-dollar bill. Down he went, as quick as he could. One snort and it was gone. That was it.

Finito.

Until Ivan arrived.

Hassleman wiped his nose, sniffing more, aware of flakes falling from his nose, wasting what was there. He tipped his head back, letting gravity help him instead of rob him of his precious drugs.

God, what was he doing? It was madness. Stupid. Why had he done all the coke? Why had he called Ivan for more? He should message him back. Cancel the order. He didn't need it. Didn't want it. He had to have some control. He wasn't an addict after all. It was just fun. Too much fun once. Not enough now. Never enough.

The doorbell rang.

Ivan.

That was quick.

Oh well. Ivan was there now. The drugs were there. He might as well pick them up. It'd be rude not to.

Hassleman jumped to his feet, then needed a moment to steady himself. He blinked, eyes wide, trying to focus, a little voice whispering it was a bad idea while another shouted it was a bloody good one.

It was hard work walking from the living room to the front door. He was drunker than he thought, definitely more wasted. It took him so long, Ivan rang the doorbell again. Impatient bastard. Hassleman thought about keeping him waiting even longer, teach him a lesson, leave him out on his doorstep to show him who was boss, who was in charge.

But who was Hassleman kidding? He wanted Ivan inside, off his doorstep, out of sight of his neighbours and Ivan's drugs out of his pocket and into his nose.

He checked himself in the mirror by the door, making sure he had no cocaine on his face. Nothing to give away what he'd been doing all day, just in case it wasn't Ivan. He didn't want to frighten the neighbours. But who else would it be? Only Ivan. Only his drugs. No one else called.

Sucking his teeth in anticipation, Hassleman opened the big, black front door.

But it wasn't Ivan standing there. It wasn't his drugs.

It was a man wearing a motorbike helmet, and he had a gun pointed at Hassleman's face.

'No,' said Hassleman, putting up his hand, as if that could stop a bullet.

Wednesday, 14th September

3

W ise tried not to yawn as he reached Ladbroke Grove and failed miserably. The last thing he'd needed was a call out at 1:30 in the morning. Not that he'd been asleep. He didn't do much of that anymore. Not since ...

'I'm sorry, Si,' Andy says. 'I'm sorry for ev—'

He blinked the memory away and concentrated on where he was. Ladbroke Grove. It was a place he always associated with The Clash, his dad's favourite band — not that it bore any resemblance to when the punk band had called it home. The working class was long gone, replaced by big money.

That was never more true than in Elgin Crescent. It was one of the most expensive streets to live in London and that was really saying something these days. It certainly wasn't the sort of place where people got murdered.

Police barriers stopped traffic entering or leaving the street under the watchful eye of two uniformed officers. One came over with a clipboard to check Wise's ID card. After noting his details down, the officer went back to move the barrier enough to allow his car through.

There was a row of Georgian terraced houses on one side of the street, some of which were converted into apartments, but each one had to be worth several million pounds each. On the other side, the prices of the detached Georgian mansions had to stretch into the tens of millions.

Wise didn't need to be much of a detective, though, to know where the crime scene was. Flood lights illuminated a white awning over the entrance to one of the mansions two-thirds of the way down on the right-hand side of the street. Scene Of Crime Officers — SOCOs — were going in and out in their white forensics suits, all hooded up, while the road outside the house looked like a police station car park. Wise passed three patrol vehicles, a forensics van, and two unmarked cars before he found a spot to park his knackered old Mondeo, blocking a top-of-the-range Land Rover and a Jag. A quick glance down the rest of the residents' cars confirmed that most of the residents' vehicles had at least a hundred grand price tag attached to them, but it was that kind of neighbourhood.

So very different from where Wise lived.

He sat for a moment, watching the goings on. He spotted DS Roy Hicks on the pavement, head down, shoulders all hunched up in his crumpled raincoat, hands deep in his pockets. Waiting where Andy should've been waiting.

A red dot dances across Andy's shoulders, seeking his head, finding its spot, stopping on his temple, dead still.

Wise closed his eyes and composed himself, fighting the cracks, smothering the pain. He looked in the rear-view mirror and made sure his face gave nothing away. This was no time for memories or ghosts. He had a job to do.

It was all he had left.

His face a mask, he grabbed his suit jacket and phone off the passenger seat and got out. The phone went into his pocket and then he slipped the jacket on, taking a second to smooth the front and button it up. Only then did he walk over to his colleague.

'Hicksy,' Wise said.

'Guv,' Hicksy replied. His voice was so flat he might as well have been addressing a stranger instead of his boss for the past five years. That was another fallout from Andy's betrayal and death. Wise's team had lost all the closeness that had made them so effective, their faith in each other.

If Wise wasn't feeling as out of place as the rest of them, he might've known what to say to repair the damage and bring everyone back together, but he nodded towards the house. 'What happened?'

'Officers responding to a 999 call found a man shot dead on his doorstep at approximately 11:25 this evening,' Hicksy said. His hair was cut so short it barely existed and he had broken his nose so many times that it zigzagged down the middle of his face like a lightning bolt. The shadow cast from his wild eyebrows hid his deep-set eyes, making him look more tired than Wise felt.

'We know who he is?' Wise asked.

'The house belongs to a Mark Hassleman, twenty-eight. Apparently, he's the social media guru who invented the Sparks dating app.'

'I've heard of him. "Britain's Bill Gates."'

Hicksy nodded. 'That's the one, Guv.'

'Anyone else in the house at the time?'

'No, he was alone, as far as we know. The uniforms who responded to the 999 call had a quick look around. There're traces of cocaine on the coffee table and porn's playing on his TV, but that's it.'

'A party for one, then?'

'Looks that way, Guv.'

'Who's the Home Office pathologist on call tonight?'

'Harmet Singh.'

'That's good. Is she here yet?'

'Got here about twenty minutes ago.'

'What about our team?'

'Jono's talking to their neighbours. School Boy's inside having a look around and Sarah's headed to Kennington. She's getting the street CCTV footage requested — not that there's going to be a lot. Cameras only cover the crossroads with Kensington Park Road at one end and Ladbroke Grove at the other. The rest of the street is a blank.'

'Some houses must have cameras — if not all of them.' Wise said. 'Action someone with getting copies of anything they might have filmed.'

'Will do,' Hicksy said. 'I told the rest of the team to be ready for you at 8:30 a.m. for the DMM.' The Daily Management Meeting was the heart of any investigation for Wise. Solving a crime was like putting together a jigsaw puzzle, getting small pieces of information and slotting them together bit by bit, until the overall picture appeared. The DMMs were the place where he assembled that picture from everything he and his team uncovered, where he could create order from chaos.

'Good,' Wise said. 'Now, let's see who got killed.'

At the forensics van, Wise and Hicksy gave a SOCO their IDs to check. In return, the officer gave them each a suit with a hood to put, plus gloves and coveralls for their shoes. The outfits were supposed to be one-size-fits-all, but Wise was a big man, and every time he put one of the suits on, he tested the sizing description to its limits. In fact, on more than one occasion, the suit had ripped apart, much to everyone else's amusement.

Dressed, they moved from the forensics van to the house, where the scene guard signed them into the logbook.

A white tent covered the short path up to the front of the house and treads were in place along the side of the house steps for the officers to walk on to preserve the crime scene and any evidence that the killer might've left behind.

SOCOs were scuttling here and there, looking for anything out of place that might provide a clue to who killed Hassleman. And, of course, there were SOCOs working just inside the doorway, examining the body. Even from the bottom of the steps, Wise could see the bare feet of the victim sticking up and, over the heads of the working SOCOS, the blood and brains that covered the wall behind.

Andy's head jerks as the bullet hits him. Red mist erupts from the other side of his head. His brains hit the concrete roof a heartbeat before Andy's body.

Wise clenched his fists, burying the memory. This wasn't the time. He concentrated on his breathing, forced his legs on, acted like everything was alright. He couldn't let anyone see any weakness. Not Hicksy, not the SOCOs. He was in control.

With a deep breath, Wise went to look at the dead man.

4

As Wise and Hicksy reached the top of the steps to the Georgian mansion, one of the suited figures examining the body looked up, as if sensing they were there.

'Hello, Inspector,' Harmet Singh said. She was a rising star in the forensics world and had never failed to impress Wise when they'd previously worked together. She had a good sense of humour, too, and liked a bit of banter. That was always a good thing. Especially when things were as bad as they often were.

'Doctor,' Wise said. 'What brings you out here tonight?'

'You know me, can't resist a corpse in the middle of the night.' Singh stood up, arching her back slightly. She wasn't much over five feet in height — at least a good foot smaller than Wise — and she was drowning in her one-size-fits-all forensics suit.

Wise nodded at the body. 'He's definitely dead, then?'

'As some of his brains are covering the wall and floor behind him, I'd say so,' Singh said.

Wise ran his eye over the corpse. The man was wearing

dark blue jeans and a black t-shirt with a smiley face on it. His head turned to the left, so the damage by the bullet was out of sight but, as Singh had said, most of his brains lay in a dark red pool of blood behind him and decorated the wall on the other side of the hallway.

He'd died just like Andy.

God, he wanted to be sick. He shouldn't be there, working this case. Shouldn't be working at all. 'How many times was he shot?' he said, trying to focus.

'There are two bullet wounds,' Singh said. 'One to the hand, one to the face. However, we've only recovered one bullet so far.' Singh pointed to the bloody wall. 'From amongst that mess.'

'One bullet, two wounds?'

'He could've put his hand up as they shot him.'

'What? To stop the bullet?'

'It's instinctive. It happens more often than you'd think.'

Wise glanced down the corridor to the main part of the house. The wooden floorboards looked spotless. 'No bloody footprints.'

'It doesn't look like the killer entered the house after they killed the victim,' Singh said. 'But we're checking everything.'

'So the motive wasn't robbery then?' Wise said, more to himself.

'Again, you're the detective, Inspector,' Singh said. 'I'll leave that sort of thing up to you to work out.'

Wise stared at the body. 'Someone rang the doorbell. Hassleman answers it. They shoot him, then walk away. No messing about.' Just like the AROs did with Andy.

'Pissed off boyfriend or husband?' Hicksy suggested. 'Maybe he hooked up with someone he shouldn't have done.'

'Maybe,' Wise said. 'And it's definitely Hassleman who's dead, Doctor? No chance it's a house guest or something like that?'

'He had a driver's licence in his wallet,' Singh said. 'The picture matches.'

'That's something, at least,' Wise said. 'Still, we'll need someone to formally identify him.'

'I'll look into next of kin,' Hicksy said.

'Good. Let's have a nose around inside,' Wise said.

'I'd rather you didn't traipse past here just yet. There's a private garden around the corner, shared by the residents,' Singh said. 'You can access Hassleman's private garden from there and then get into the house via the back door.'

'Thank you, Doctor,' Wise said. 'Let us know when you know anything.'

'I'll be in touch,' Singh said. 'The PM should be first thing in the morning.'

Wise turned around and headed back down the steps, Hicksy following. They both removed the blue foot coverings that prevented their shoes from leaving any marks, then headed to the corner of Kensington Park Road, to the entrance to the private park; a gate set in a row of iron railings.

Wise looked around and quickly spotted the CCTV cameras affixed to the lampposts and traffic lights. 'Good camera coverage here.'

Hicksy nodded. 'Shame they put all the bloody cameras here and not in Elgin Crescent. Could've made our job easier.'

After showing their warrant cards again to the uniforms manning the entrance to the park, they entered the gardens and immediately the world grew darker, away from the street lamps and under the trees. The rear of

Hassleman's was easy to spot, though, illuminated by more police lights.

Another uniform waited under the lights by a smaller gate, set in a low wall. On the other side was a narrow, well-tended garden.

Both put back on the plastic coverings over their shoes and made their way across more metal treads to the back door.

'I wonder why they shot him on the front doorstep?' Hicksy said. 'The killer could've snuck through the back gardens and entered the house this way. No one would've seen them entering. They could've killed Hassleman without fear of interruption and the body would've gone undiscovered for days, depending on when anyone was expecting to see Hassleman next. Plenty of time to get away.'

'From what I could tell, the CCTV had pretty much all the park entrance covered,' Wise said, 'whereas the front of the house is a complete blind spot. That's reason enough. And what if the killer wanted the body found? There's a message in killing a well-known man like Hassleman. Someone who's rich. Successful.'

'A professional hit?'

'Could be. You don't get this sort of money without pissing someone off along the way — or having someone want what you have.'

They entered the house into the kitchen. It was a decent size and well-equipped, but it didn't look like Hassleman was much of a home cook. Empty delivery boxes were piled up next to a full bin and there were several empty pizza boxes lying around on the countertops, along with empty beer cans, wine bottles and whisky bottles.

'Bloody hell. Looks he had a party after all,' Hicksy said.

'Or the cleaner's been on holiday,' Wise said, looking at

the kitchen table covered in unopened mail. 'Maybe his PA too.'

'Maybe he was just a slob,' Hicksy said. 'I've always thought these boffins weren't normal.'

They walked out of the kitchen into the living room. Judging by the smell in the room, Hicksy was probably right about Hassleman being a slob. The room stunk of stale air, mixed with body odour and alcohol.

Someone had paused the porn on the big TV, leaving a still image on the screen of a woman hard at work on her male counterpart. The picture was so bright that Wise had to squint as he tried to look around the room. 'I think we can turn off the television now,' Wise said to the SOCOs in the room. 'We're not immature teenagers, after all.'

'Sorry, Guv.' A SOCO picked up a remote control that was already bagged up and pressed the power button. The screen went dark.

'That's better,' Wise said. There was a black leather sofa positioned to face the TV, with a kidney-shaped, glass coffee table in front of that, covered with the detritus of Hassleman's evening entertainment. There was a near empty bottle of scotch next to a tumbler with a mouthful left in it and a mobile on one side while the other half of the table had smears of white powder next to a rolled up dollar bill, a black American Express card and several, small empty plastic baggies that, no doubt, once were full of cocaine. 'He was really going for it.'

Hicksy nodded. 'Twenty-eight years old with more money than God? I think I might lose the plot too.'

'Such a waste.'

'Maybe his death was a drug deal gone wrong?'

'Maybe,' Wise said. 'I'm not sure, though. Hassleman would've been the best sort of customer — a heavy user with lots of money. He's not going to argue about money or try to stiff his dealer.'

'That amount of coke's enough to send anyone nuts, though,' Hicksy said. 'If he wasn't alone and Hassleman started arguing with whoever he was with ... Things get out of hand. The friend storms out, Hassleman follows, calling them every name under the sun. The friend turns around, pulls a gun and shoots him on the doorstep.'

The rest of the room was sparsely decorated; a couple of uncomfortable armchairs, an arc light dangling over the sofa and table and an expensive-looking rug covering the centre of the floor. Art covered several of the walls. Wise wasn't an expert, but even he recognised some pieces. Either Hassleman had great taste or he had a buyer who knew their stuff. 'Whatever happened, it definitely wasn't a robbery. The art in here has to be worth millions on its own.'

'Guv?'

Wise turned to see DC Callum Chabolah standing in the doorway. He was twenty-three and relatively new to the team, joining a month or two before Andy ... No, Wise didn't want to think about that.

The others called Callum 'School Boy,' on account of the fact he was still a trainee, doing his detective exams, but they just wished they had his energy. The lad was around five foot eight, with a slim build only young people can have and yet not appreciate. He wore dark jeans, a black sweater and a dark green bomber jacket, his hair cut with a fade. 'His office is upstairs, Guv. It's like something out of a spaceship.'

'Show me,' Wise said.

Callum led Wise and Hicksy up the narrow stairs to an equally dark and dingy upstairs. The first room off the stairs was a bedroom that had been converted into an office, but that seemed an inadequate way to describe the room. It looked more like a military command centre with nine monitors stacked in rows of three above the desk, each one bigger than most people's home televisions. A screensaver of a flame spark danced between the screens in a hypnotic pattern. There was an illuminated, curved keyboard on the desk, next to a wireless mouse and a trackpad and pen, plus more signs of white powder. The computer hard drive was in a monstrous tower next to the desk.

'Fucking hell. What did he need all these monitors for?' Hicksy said.

Wise walked over to the window. The shutters hadn't been opened for a long time. 'Get the tech bods on this tomorrow along his phone downstairs. I want to see his emails and messages, who he was talking to and what was being said. The guy was a tech genius, so there's a good chance we'll find a motive and maybe even a suspect in his hardware.'

'Will do, Guv,' Callum said.

'Is the main bedroom next door?' Wise asked.

'Yeah, Guv. It's a bit of a mess, too.' Callum led them back out into the hall and into the next room. It took up the rest of the second floor with windows that overlooked the gardens, but again shutters closed off the view. The bed was king-sized and unmade, with half the sheets lying on the floor, along with a good few days' worth of clothes strewn everywhere.

'Definitely a slob,' Hannah said, wrinkling her nose.

Wise peered into the ensuite bathroom. Towels littered the floor there as well and a tube of toothpaste, squeezed to death, was next to the sink. Wise checked the cabinet above the sink and found at least a dozen prescription pills bottles, some fuller than others. 'Looks like Hassleman liked his prescription drugs, too,' Wise said. 'They're all prescribed by the same doctor — a Doctor Onylil, Harley Street. There's some anxiety meds, and about three different brands of sleeping tablets.'

Hicksy peered over his shoulder. 'How did he get any work done if he was off his head all the time?'

'How many functioning alcoholics have you known over the years?' Wise said. 'Maybe he used these to balance the various drugs out, so he felt whatever he considered normal.'

'Can't be a kosher doctor, though, dishing all these out,' Hicksy said.

'Let's add Doctor Onylil to our list of people to talk to.'

They moved on. The walk-in wardrobe looked like a hurricane had ripped through it. Trainers lay half in and half out of boxes and clothes lay here and there or dangled off shelves; mainly t-shirts of various colours and jeans of every style.

'I don't think you and Hassleman would've gotten on,' Hicksy said. 'Not a suit in sight.'

'I think I'd object to the drugs before I worried about his wardrobe,' Wise said, looking over Hassleman's clothes. It wasn't as if Wise never wore jeans and t-shirts himself, but he could never bring himself to wear them to work. He might not have to wear a uniform anymore, but he found a comfort in having one still. Even more so now. A sharp suit hid the cracks. His dad had taught him that. "Shoes always polished. Shirt always starched. Suit pressed. World's already full of bums. You don't need to be one."

They moved through the rest of the house, but every other room looked unused simply by the fact they were clean and tidy. Hassleman seemed to only use the kitchen and living room downstairs and his office and bedroom upstairs.

It was gone 3 a.m. when Wise called it a night. 'So what do you think?' he asked as they walked outside into the bitter night, a drizzle of rain falling.

'I think Hassleman got rich too quickly,' Hicksy said, 'and if someone hadn't shot him, he'd have been dead of an overdose sooner rather than later — but there's a lot to look at. Who gets his money, first and foremost?'

'Callum?'

'I think maybe it was the drugs,' the lad said. 'He could've found a new dealer and pissed off the old one, or maybe he was trying to buy wholesale instead of retail?'

Wise nodded. He nearly turned around to ask Andy for his opinion before remembering he wasn't there.

Andy tumbles forward, red mist leading the way, his brains and blood already splattered across the rooftop.

'We've certainly got lots to look into — his love life, his finances, his business dealings and his drug habits. Let's pull his life apart and see what drops out. No one this wealthy gets murdered by accident.'

They returned their suits to the forensics van. After saying good night, Hicksy and Callum left Wise standing alone. He stood staring at the front of Hassleman's house, not caring about the rain, picturing Hassleman at the front door, a gun in his face. Did he even know he was about to die?

Had Andy?

He climbed into the Mondeo, feeling exhausted. It'd been a long day, in an already long week of an even longer month. Ever since that night, he was finding it harder and harder to pretend to be the man he used to be.

Slipping the Mondeo into gear, he made his way to the

Ladbroke Grove exit, merged into the night traffic, and headed home. He watched the streets as he drove, London coming more alive as he left the more wealthy, residential areas. There were a good few drunks falling out of clubs, trying to hail cabs or stagger off to somewhere else, eager to carry on despite it being a school night. Then there were the homeless, curled up in shop doorways, trying to sleep or shoot up or drink their way to numbness. Others wandered past on their way home, knackered after a long night's work, caught up in their own worries and ignoring the world. Delivery people dropped off stock for the next morning while the all-night takeaways and cafes blazed neon out into the night, flogging greasy food to the night crowd.

It was strange, but this was the London Wise loved. At night, the city felt more real to him, stripped of the respectability that drew the tourists by the thousands during the day. It brought back memories of running wild with his brother, out after dark when they shouldn't be, getting in trouble, drinking underage, having fights, having laughs, trying to pull, sometimes getting lucky, sometimes not.

He'd not thought about his brother in a while, hadn't spoken to him in even longer, and that had been ... not good. God, he missed him. Missed Tom. Missed what they had back then. They'd been inseparable ever since they'd shared a womb together, together until that night forced them apart. That night and the trial and the prison sentence.

Their relationship wasn't the same after that. Couldn't be, no matter how much Wise had wished it so. But, even now, he wondered if it had to get as bad as it had. They were so different now. Alien to each other. From twins to strangers.

God. His best friend was dead and his brother might as

well be for all the contact they had with each other. No wonder Wise felt like he was barely keeping it together. He must've really pissed someone off in another life to keep getting smashed apart like this.

Wise blinked away the memories as best he could as he tried to force his mind back to the streets, to the now, but that much guilt knew how to hang around. It had its hooks deep into his very soul.

Shit. He needed some sleep. Get his thoughts back in order. Bury the past in the back of his mind as best he could. He had Hassleman to concentrate on. People who needed him.

At least there was a parking spot outside his house for once. Wise reversed the Mondeo into it, but he didn't turn the engine off. He stared at the four-bedroom terrace house, with its red door that he'd once happily painted, and tried to find the courage to go inside.

It was hard enough pretending to the people he worked with that everything was alright but it was all but impossible to fool the people who loved him.

Jean could see it and she wanted to help, but how? All he saw were his failings reflected in her eyes.

And then there were his kids, Ed and Claire. Nine and seven. Little Mister Sensible and Little Miss Chaos. The best parts of him and Jean all mixed into something new. Hopefully something better. The love he felt for them was a burning light against all the darkness, the thing that held him together. Two wonderful little people that he'd do anything for. God, it hurt to see their love for him when he was crying inside.

Wise turned off the engine. Gathering his stuff, he got out of the car, locked it and headed into the house. Everything was so quiet that he felt like an unwelcome intruder, invading his family's tranquility. Even his key in the door lock turning sounded loud enough to wake the street.

Wise had to fight the urge to just turn around, get back in his car, and drive away. But he knew running wouldn't get him anywhere. It'd only make things worse. He'd run that night, from Tom, from they'd done, and he knew only too well the price he'd had to pay for that mistake. A price he was still paying.

Wise opened the door and stepped into the darkness. There was a glow upstairs, from the bathroom light left on and the door half-open, just in case one of the kids woke up and needed the loo.

He checked the time. 3:45. He'd have to leave by 7:45 to get to Kennington in time for the DMM. Factoring in time to shit, shower and shave, he had, maybe, three and a half hours to get some sleep.

Taking his shoes off, he trudged up the stairs. The spare room was to the left, the kids' room was straight ahead and then, after the bathroom, was his and Jean's room.

He stood on the landing, imagining them all asleep, hoping that they were all having happy dreams. He needed to find his way back to them somehow once he'd put all his ghosts to rest.

Wise turned left and headed to the spare room.

Alone.

5

It was nearly 4 a.m. by the time Wise had climbed into bed but, despite being knackered, his dreams had woken him up every half hour or so. All he had to do was close his eyes, and he was back on that rooftop with Andy, Derrick Morris, and his girlfriend, trying to stop a bullet that couldn't be stopped. No matter what Wise tried, the dreams all finished the same way, with that red dot finding the right spot. In the end, it was easier just to give up and get up. At least if he was busy, he could keep his mind on what it was supposed to be doing.

However, to get his brain to work, Wise had to get some decent coffee in him quick or he wouldn't last another hour.

When Wise parked up at Kennington police station, there was still half an hour to go before the DMM. Slipping his suit jacket on, he didn't go inside. As desperate as he was for caffeine, he couldn't face the staff canteen's poison. Instead, he jogged across Kennington Road and nipped into Luigi's Cafe.

The place was busy as always, full of people like him in desperate need of coffees and teas before heading to their day jobs, grabbing pastries and sandwiches to fill their stomachs. Luigi was behind the counter, white apron already smeared with this and that, while his daughters, Sofia and Elena, made the coffees and teas in a fog of steam behind him. Luigi's wife, Maria, worked the till. Wise had noticed that most of the time she just had the cash dispenser open, taking the money and giving back change with nothing actually being rung into the till. After all, no receipts, no records, no tax.

She'd scowl when a customer wanted to pay with a card because that meant she had to do things properly. She'd enter the amount in the till in order to activate the card reader, cursing all the while. Receipts generated records that had to be declared to the taxman and that meant handing over to the Inland Revenue their percentage and Maria didn't like that. Even if it was a fraction of what the cafe actually made.

'Hello, my friend,' Luigi said when Wise reached the counter, a big grin on his face. 'How are you today?' He was a large man with dark, curly hair retreating rapidly back across his skull.

'Good, thanks,' Wise said, even though he felt terrible.

'You look like you need a holiday, my friend. Why don't you take that lovely wife of yours somewhere warm? Relax a little?' Luigi said.

Wise tried not to wince at the mention of his wife. That was the trouble about frequenting the same place every day for years — people got to know things about each other that one day, maybe, they might prefer were still private.

'Double espresso and a large Americano, with a splash of milk,' he said instead.

'Coming right up!' Luigi turned to Sofia, repeated the order, then gave Wise another smile. 'Be right with you.'

Wise glanced over at Maria as she put a five-pound note into the cash tray without ringing it up and handed back some shrapnel in change. 'Luigi,' Wise said. 'You know I'm a police officer, don't you?'

The Italian nodded his head. 'Of course. A very good one too.'

'And you know half the police station come in here to get their food and drinks?'

'Of course. The police are our best customers.'

'Then has anyone told you tax evasion is a crime?' Wise's eyes motioned towards Maria. 'People can go to prison for fiddling their books.'

'I pay my taxes,' Luigi said.

Wise raised his eyebrows. 'All of them?'

'My friend, if someone was to report their false suspicions to HMRC, they would soon find themselves barred from this establishment,' Luigi said. 'Then what would they do? I hear your canteen is not the best.'

'It's terrible.'

'Then, perhaps, one must focus on what's really important, eh?'

Wise smiled. 'Fair enough.' Luigi's coffee was the only thing that kept him going after all.

Wise moved along the counter to Maria and held up his debit card on principle. He might turn a blind eye to their fiddling, but he wouldn't encourage it. His money was going on the books.

At the sight of the card, Maria's scowl deepened as she slapped the card machine down in front of him. Wise gave her a grin back as he tapped the card against the reader.

Sofia shook her head at him as he collected the drinks, as if to let him know he was wasting his time. He shrugged in return and then headed out the door to the nick, with his precious coffee in hand.

A police station had been in Kennington since 1874, but the original building was demolished in 1939, while the fire brigade used the site for emergency water supplies during the blitz. The new station at 49-51 Kennington Road opened to very little fanfare in 1955, a lonely building of red brick and utilitarian design, and it hadn't got any more welcoming since then. Wise doubted the police had spent a penny on the place since then. In fact, it was a wonder the building was still standing. It looked as knackered as he felt.

With all the government cutbacks and layoffs, the front desk had been closed to the public a few years back, and the uniforms sent elsewhere. Now and then, someone would try to walk in, demanding to see someone, but unless they were in a life-threatening state, they were redirected to Brixton nick instead.

Now, Kennington housed one of the Metropolitan Police's Murder Investigation Teams and an army of backroom staff that the Met depended on to keep it running. Most of whom were, according to Wise's boss's boss, Chief Superintendent Walling, 'a bunch of bloody accountants' sent to make his life a misery and their ranks were immune to any of the cuts that everyone else faced. Somehow, in today's Met, they deemed it more important to have calculator skills than detective skills.

As he approached the front door, DC Sarah Choi opened it and came outside, a pack of cigarettes in her hand. 'Morning, Guv.'

'Morning Sarah,' Wise said. 'How are you?'

'Bit tired,' Sarah said. She was short, about five foot three or so, with shoulder length hair and a sharp fringe that sat just above her eyebrows. She ran the Incident Room for the team's investigations. 'I should have all the CCTV footage in soon.'

'Good,' Wise said. 'Be quick with your cigarette. It's nearly time for the DMM.'

'I might have a bit more time,' Sarah said. 'The boss popped into the incident room earlier. She wants to see you in her office first, Guv.'

Great.

Wise sighed. 'Alright. Tell the others we'll start the moment I'm done with her.'

'Good luck,' Sarah said, pulling a cigarette out of the pack.

Wise used his pass to buzz himself in through the front door and headed straight up the stairs to the second floor where his boss, Detective Chief Inspector Anne Roberts, had her office. He passed a few familiar faces walking down the corridor to her room, nodding greetings back as he made his way to Roberts' office.

When he got there, he saw a woman sitting on one of the chairs outside her door. Tall, black, and with her hair tied back tight against her head, she wore a black leather motorbike jacket and there was a helmet on the floor beside her foot. She looked up as he approached and Wise placed her in her early thirties.

'Morning,' he said as he stopped by Roberts' door. 'Are you waiting to see the DCI?'

'I've already seen her, thanks,' she said.

'Right,' Wise said, not sure why she was still sitting outside Roberts' office if that was the case. 'Okay.'

The woman didn't say anymore, adding to the awkwardness. She watched Wise juggle the coffees in his hand so he could knock on the door without spilling his precious caffeine.

'Come in,' Roberts called, and Wise entered her office. It was certainly bigger than his own shoebox, but not by much. She was behind her desk, already smothered in paperwork, reading glasses sitting on top of the pile like an inadequate paperweight. She indicated the chair in front of her desk with a tilt of her chin. 'Have a seat.'

'Boss,' Wise said in greeting. He put his coffees on her desk and sat down.

Roberts had about ten years on him, with short, silver hair that accentuated the lines on her face, hard earned over the years. Her thin lips made her mouth appear to be just another one of those lines, and she certainly didn't do smiles often enough to make a difference. She was a good boss, though. Smart and always to the point. Wise liked her most of the time.

'One of those coffees for me?' she said.

'I'm sorry. They're spoken for,' Wise said. 'And they've got sugar in them, too.'

A lie, but Roberts was notorious for pinching anything hot that crossed her path and only sugar could stop her. 'Shame. I could do with a strong cup right about now.'

'I'll get one of the team to bring you one after the DMM,' Wise said.

'Luigi's?' Roberts made it sound like a question, but Wise knew it was a command. No one with any taste buds and a choice drank the muck the canteen dished out. It was literally the cafe of last resorts.

'Of course.'

'Wonderful.' Roberts smiled. 'I hear you had a late night last night.'

'Yeah. A man was shot on his doorstep over in Elgin Crescent.'

'I heard. A bit of a celebrity, too.'

'Yeah. We think it's Mark Hassleman. Twenty-eight. Internet billionaire. "Britain's Bill Gates" and all that.'

'Even I've heard of him. That means he's the sort of person who's going to get the press all excited when they hear about it.'

'Unfortunately.' After Andy, Wise had had enough of the press to last a lifetime.

'Are you up to that?'

'Yes,' Wise lied.

'You know, if you wanted to take some time off, we'd all understand. You've done nothing but work since ... that night,' Roberts said. 'Being busy is good, but you can have time to grieve. You worked with Andy for a long time.'

Wise kept his face impassive, his back straight. 'I'm fine. We're short-staffed enough as it is.'

'But a case like this? It'll be high profile. And everyone will be watching to see how you do.'

'I'll try to avoid any rooftop shoot-outs, this time,' Wise said, regretting his words the minute the words came out of his mouth. God, he wished he could drink his bloody coffee. 'I'm sorry. I didn't mean to sound disrespectful.'

'It's fine. I understand. It's just ... You can go on stress leave if you need to. No one will think less of you for doing so. We know how close you and Andy were.'

Yeah, they were close. Close enough for more than a few people to think Wise must've been in on all Andy's antics. Close enough to think Wise was a rotten apple, too. But, apparently, not close enough for Wise to have a clue Andy was bent.

Jesus. What sort of detective was he not to have noticed anything?

'You don't know what I am!' Andy shouts across the rooftop, a red dot dancing across his torso.

'Have they made any progress in finding out who Andy was working for?'

Roberts shook her head. 'I've heard nothing. Specialist Crime and Operations Ten are running the investigation now and they're not very good at sharing. I'll keep my ears open, though, and I'll let you know when there's something to report.'

SCO10 were the ones who went after the mobs and the gangs. Wise tried to think if he knew anyone there that he could ask for an update. It'd be against protocols, but maybe someone would update him. He'd seen the text messages on Andy's phone after all, sent by an unknown number from a burner phone.

'If I don't do this,' Andy says, 'he told me he'd kill them.'

Wise wanted to know who destroyed Andy's life. He had to know. Not that he could tell Roberts that. 'Thank you,' he said, instead.

'Well, keep me informed on how the Hassleman investigation goes. Walling will be after updates and I don't want to be blindsided by anything,' Roberts said. 'I've already got the press office preparing a statement about last night's murder, so we're ready when they come knocking. The first hint of this and they'll be all over us like a rash.'

'We haven't formally identified the body yet.'

'Don't worry. We won't go into too many details. I'll have someone from Media Relations join your DMMs as well, so they're up to date on everything.'

'Okay,' Wise said. 'If that's all, I'd best get on.'

'There's just one other thing, Simon,' Roberts said.

'Yes?'

'As you said, you're short-staffed, so I've got you another body for your team. A replacement for Andy.'

'A replacement?'

Andy's head lurches forward a second before Wise hears the gunshot. Red mist blows in the summer night. A look of surprise on his face.

'That's right.'

'I'm not sure the team's ready for a new member,' Wise said, knowing he definitely wasn't. New people had questions. They'd want to know what happened. They'd want to talk about Andy.

'I think a new face is exactly what you need,' Roberts said. 'And DS Markham comes highly recommended.'

'Perhaps in a month or so,' Wise said, trying not to let his frustration get the better of him. 'Once this case is over ...'

'She's already here,' Roberts said. 'DS Markham is sitting outside.'

'Ah.' Bloody wonderful. So that's who the woman was, why she was still waiting outside. Wise couldn't believe it. 'I wish you'd talked to me about this first.'

'You'd have just said no. Now, take her with you on the way out. You don't want to be late to the DMM.' Roberts put on her reading glasses and picked up a piece of paper, her way of dismissing Wise.

Wise glared at the top of her head for a moment before standing up. He collected his coffees and left the office. Markham looked up as he stepped back out into the corridor. He forced a smile that was probably more of a grimace. 'DS Markham? I'm DI Simon Wise. I hear you're joining the team.'

She stood up. She was tall, only a few inches shorter than Wise. 'Thank you for the opportunity.'

'Don't thank me,' Wise said. 'Thank the boss.' It was all her bloody idea, after all.

She glanced at Roberts' door. 'Right. Anyway. I'm really excited to be joining your team.'

Of course she was. Maybe Wise would be too if he'd had time to drink his coffee. Next time, he was necking one the moment he bought it. 'Come on,' Wise said. 'You can meet the others.' He headed back towards the stairs without waiting to see if Markham followed.

———

6

Grabbing her bike helmet, Hannah Markham had to trot after Wise as he set off towards the stairs at quite the pace. He'd not looked too happy to see her either. Quite the opposite, in fact. She only hoped it wasn't the same reasons that had plagued her career so far. She didn't need another a sexist or racist boss in her life.

Her first impressions of the man were quite something, though.

The first thing she'd noticed was his size as he'd ambled down the corridor towards her. He was tall and wide and obviously well-built, but he didn't move with the awkwardness of someone who just humped heavy weights up and down to get massive muscles. Rather, he was light on his feet, like a fighter of some sort. Like he boxed maybe, or did some sort of martial arts. And his hands! Christ, it was easy to imagine him doing some damage if he hit someone with those slabs of meat. It was a good job he was a copper, because Wise looked damned dangerous.

Then, when he got closer, she'd noticed how immaculately dressed he was, with his well-cut black suit, perfect creases pressed in the trouser legs, a white shirt that looked like it was straight out the packet, all matched perfectly with a dark tie and shoes that were polished till they virtually sparkled. His blond hair was cropped short, almost army-style, with not a hair out of place. He was a man who cared about how he looked.

Anyone else of his size would've looked like a gorilla in a suit, but, somehow, Wise carried it well. He looked elegant.

Elegantly dangerous. That was some combination. Not one she was expecting.

'What do you know about us, DS Markham?' Wise asked as they walked up the stairs.

Hannah didn't know how to answer that either. She knew what every officer in the Met and a large number of Joe Public knew about Wise and his team. A month or so earlier, his old DS was shot on a rooftop in Peckham while trying to murder a witness in a gangland murder trial.

There'd been more rumours about why he'd done it, of course. Stories of drugs and prostitutes and bags of cash hidden away in his house. There'd been even more rumours about others being involved. More rotten apples waiting to be found. But Hannah couldn't repeat that to Wise. She was smart enough to keep her mouth shut, after all.

'Just that you head up one of Kennington's Murder Investigation Teams,' Hannah said instead. 'And that you investigate only the most serious crimes.'

'That's right,' Wise said. 'There are fifty officers stationed here, broken into five teams of ten. The number goes up or down by a few here and there, depending on our workloads.' They reached the third floor. 'Our team is based out of Major Incident Room One — or MIR-One, as it's known.' He stopped by a door painted long ago in a battleship grey and tapped the name plaque on the wall next to it. 'This is our home. It's nothing fancy, but it works for us.'

'Right,' Hannah said. She doubted anything in Kennington could be called 'fancy.' From what she'd seen so far, the entire building hadn't been updated in decades. Even the ceiling tiles were still stained brown from back in the day when police officers could smoke inside buildings and they'd banned that nearly twenty years ago.

'What's your first name, by the way?' Wise asked.

'Hannah, sir,' Hannah replied.

'I don't really like being called "sir,"' Wise said. 'Most people call me "Guv" but you can call me Simon if you wish.'

'Guv is fine,' Hannah said. She'd had another boss once who'd insisted she called him by his first name, like they were friends, which was okay until he decided that he'd rather be lovers. When she'd refused, he'd called her "that dyke bitch" to everyone else. She'd not make that mistake again.

'And do you go by Hannah, or is there another name you prefer?'

'Hannah works.'

'And what station were you at before?'

'Brixton.'

'Major crimes?'

She shook her head. 'I was in CID, but it was mainly robberies, rapes and drugs I was dealing with. Occasionally, the odd assault that had gone too far. I only passed my sergeant exams a few months back.'

She'd probably still be there if the vacancy for Wise's team hadn't come up. A vacancy, it would appear, no one else wanted. A vacancy that more than one person told her not to go for. But fortune favoured the bold and all that.

Hannah knew what it was like not to be wanted, to have everyone hoping you'd fail. She'd spent her life with a point to prove. Joining a team in the same boat made sense — or so she hoped.

'That's good,' Wise said. 'It'll be a bit of a change for you but hopefully you can get up to speed quick enough. You've picked a good day to start, anyway. We picked up a murder last night.'

As Wise opened the door to MIR-One, the first-day-of-school feeling that had been bubbling away in Hannah's gut all morning went into overdrive. This is what she'd wanted ever since she was a little girl, watching detective shows on TV. To be on a murder squad, actively involved and not just a pair of hands amongst many. This was why she'd put up with all the snide comments from colleagues and the insults from the public. It was why she'd worked her arse off, double-checking everything she did, being so conscientious all the time, giving no one a chance to find fault in how she did the job.

She followed Wise into the office, noting that describing MIR-One as 'nothing fancy' was giving it more credit than it deserved. Its only concession to modernity were the computers on everyone's desks, but even they looked like they were days away from earning a place in a museum. The walls were the same battleship grey as the door and bore all the marks of some hard wear and tear over the years; chipped here, stained there, and peeling elsewhere.

Three white boards ran the length of one wall, ending by a door to another office. One said, "What do we know?" The second said, "What do we think?" and the third, "What can we prove?" In the middle of the second was a picture of an IC1 male, with the name "Mark Hassleman" written underneath it and his date of birth.

It looked like most of Wise's team were already there, waiting for their governor, standing in little groups, chatting away. Nearly everyone had a mug of tea or coffee in their hands as they waited for the briefing to start. They all turned to see who had entered the room, smiling when they clocked Wise. Their smiles turned to puzzlement when Hannah followed him in.

She was glad to see they weren't all as smartly dressed as Wise. She'd have hated turning up in her jeans, only to walk into a room of people all suited and booted.

'Sorry I'm late, everyone,' Wise said, walking to the front of the room. 'I had to have a quick chat with the boss. Everyone ready to get started?'

There were murmurs of agreement, but everyone still had their eyes on Hannah and she could feel her cheeks colour. She wasn't sure quite what to do either — follow Wise to the front of the room or stop where she was and let Wise have the stage to himself?

In the end, Wise turned to her and pointed to an empty desk near the front. 'That spot's free, Hannah.'

'Thank you.' She walked over to the desk and placed her helmet on it, but didn't sit as everyone else was still on their feet.

Wise put his coffees down on the table near the white boards, took the lid off the smaller cup and downed the contents in one gulp. Obviously a man in need of caffeine.

'Before we get started,' Wise said, 'I just want to introduce Detective Sergeant Hannah Markham, who's joining us from Brixton nick. I know you'll all make her feel welcome.'

Hannah waved self-consciously. 'Hi.'

'For Hannah's benefit, can you all quickly introduce

yourselves?' Wise said. 'Then we'll move onto the real reason we're here. Let's start with you, Hicksy.'

'Right,' a man with a mess for a nose said. His head slouched forward so far it gave the impression that he had no neck and, in contrast to Wise's pristine appearance, he looked like he'd slept in his suit. Even the creases had creases. 'I'm DS Roy Hicks. As you heard from the Guv, most people call me Hicksy.' There was a rasp to his voice that probably came from too much booze. He looked at Hannah with an air of disapproval, something else she was far too used to. It was always the old school coppers that seemed to dislike having a woman, let alone a black woman, around. As far as Hannah was concerned, the sooner they were put out to pasture, the better.

'DS "Jono" Gray,' grunted the man next to him, no more welcoming than his mate. He was overweight with a drinker's nose and had the top of a biro rolling about in his mouth like a cigarette.

A Chinese woman spoke next, watching Hannah intently under her fringe. 'DC Sarah Choi. I mainly run the MIR-One, but the Guv lets me out occasionally.'

'I'm DC Ian "Donut" Vollers,' a tall man said. God only knew why he was called Donut because he was stick thin, almost uncomfortably so. But maybe that was the joke. At least he looked happy to see Markham.

'And I'm trainee DC Callum Chabolah,' a young man with a sharp fade haircut said as he cracked open an energy drink.

'School Boy,' Hicksy and Jono chorused, making Callum's cheeks colour. Of course, it would be those two trying to make the black kid feel uncomfortable. Bloody neanderthals. Still, it was good to see the pair of them were in the minority for once.

'Alright,' Wise said, not sounding impressed either, and Hannah was glad about that too. 'That's enough. We've got a lot to get through.' Wise pointed to the picture of Hassleman on the board and Hannah's first day nerves went into overdrive. This was it. Her first proper murder case. This is what she had worked so hard to do. This was why she'd joined Wise's team.

'Last night, at approximately 11:25 p.m.,' Wise said, 'Mark Hassleman, twenty-eight, was shot on his doorstep of his mansion in Elgin Crescent, by person or persons unknown, killing him instantly.'

Hannah stared at the picture, taken off the internet at some sort of event. Hassleman didn't look like anything special. He wore jeans and sneakers with a sports jacket over the top of a t-shirt, despite everyone else around him wearing black ties and ball gowns. He was round in the face, with dark hair that was a little on the long side and in need of a brush, dark-framed glasses hiding his eyes but not his frown. If that was the 'before' picture, she tried to imagine what he looked like 'after' — shot dead, frown gone. She'd not seen many bodies in her time in CID and most of those were people who'd died of natural causes, overdoses and more than a few stabbings.

'Forensics will confirm if there's any evidence that anyone was with him at the time but, as far as we know,' Wise continued, 'it looks like he was home alone, indulging in an evening of fine whisky, cocaine and porn before he was murdered.'

'He had all the major food groups covered,' Jono said.

Wise ignored the crack. 'The victim is relatively well known. Dubbed "Britain's Bill Gates," Hassleman's personal wealth is in the billions — which, in itself, is a good reason for someone to justify killing him. He earned his wealth by creating the Sparks dating app, which I'm sure a few of you have used, as well as other social media and tech applications.

'Because of his money and profile, this case is going to get us a lot of attention from the press, so we need to move quickly, smartly and effectively on this. Understood?'

'Yes, Guv,' the others replied.

'That also means, as DCI Roberts just reminded me, that we don't go blabbing about the case, whether we're down the pub or on the bus home with anyone else in earshot. Okay?'

'Hicksy better go teetotal till we solve the case, Guv,' Jono called back. 'You know he's like bloody Radio One when he's had a few.'

Hicksy slapped him on the arm. 'You're a fine one to talk.'

'Both of you need to take care,' Wise said. 'For now, we need to build a picture of Hassleman's life — what was he doing when he wasn't doing drugs? Did he have any friends, lovers, or enemies? Who inherits his wealth now he's dead? We need eye witnesses — did anyone actually see the murder take place? There was no sign of anything being stolen, nor that there had been a fight or argument prior to the victim being shot.'

The young lad, Callum, put up his hand. No wonder the others called him School Boy.

'Yes, Callum,' Wise said.

'Well, as you said, the victim is ... was a bit of a celebrity in the right circles, so I looked him up on Wikipedia,' Callum said.

'And?'

Callum read off his phone. 'Hassleman was born and raised in Putney. The only child to parents, Brian and Claire.

They died when he was twelve, though — a drunk driver crashed into the family car. Social Services put him in the care of an uncle, who sent him to boarding school in Wimbledon, then he went onto Trinity College, Oxford, before doing post-graduate studies at MIT in Boston. While there, he claimed that one day he'd be able to create algorithms that could make the impossible possible. A Harish Vasudean then bet him a hundred dollars that he couldn't create a program that could get him laid. So Hassleman created Sparks, got laid and claimed the hundred bucks.

'It launched six years ago and how has over seventy-five million users. The company also has divisions working on Artificial Intelligence, virtual reality and media entertainment. Hassleman owns fifty-one percent of the company and its current value is fifteen billion dollars.'

'Fucking hell,' Jono said. 'No wonder he's off his head on drugs all the time.'

'Vasudean tried to sue Hassleman after Sparks took off, claiming it was his idea to start with, but they threw the case out of court and Vasudean had to pay two million pounds in costs.'

'That's another good motive to whack someone,' Hicksy said.

'Despite the app and his money,' Callum continued. 'Hassleman is apparently single at the moment and known to be a recluse.'

'That's fantastic work, Callum,' Wise said. 'How do you spell "Vasudean?"'

Callum told him, and Wise wrote the name on the board.

'I also checked his other socials,' Callum said. 'Nothing on Facebook. His last post on Instagram was six months ago, and that was a picture of a burger at a place called The Trainer in Finsbury Park. He's been a bit more active on Twitter, but he's mainly spouting nonsense on whatever the day's rage topic is. The man's a bit of a troll on there.'

'So he enjoys winding people up?' Wise said.

'Looks like it,' Callum said.

'Any threats?'

'Plenty, but nothing too serious by the looks of it. It's mainly people calling him names.'

'Go through the comments all the same. Maybe one argument got serious and someone took offence. And let's find out where this Vasudean is now.' Wise said. 'Anyone else?'

'We knocked on a few doors last night as you asked,' Hicksy said. He got his note-book out and flipped it open. 'No one was home at the houses on either side of the victim's, as was the case with over half the other homes in the street. Whether the owners were out for the night, on holiday or live somewhere else in the world will take a bit of digging to find out. Seems like most of London's top properties are empty these days. Owned by foreigners for investments.' Hicksy's tone made it very clear what he thought of that and Markham could feel her dislike of the man growing. 'We spoke to a few people who were home, though. A Mr Ranvick was outraged we had the cheek to disturb him so late at night and he's going to make a personal complaint to the Police Commissioner, who he, apparently, is on first-name terms with. However, a Mrs Fredrick was out walking her dog around a quarter past eleven or thereabouts. She remembered seeing a man on a motorbike parked outside Hassleman's. The man had a helmet on, so she didn't see a face.'

'Did she see the shooting?' Wise asked, a touch of excitement in his voice.

'Nah, she only remembered him because she thought it was too late to be delivering stuff,' Hicksy said. 'We're going back this morning to see if we can talk to a few more people.'

Wise turned to the board and wrote "motorbike messenger?" 'That's something to look out for. Your witness wasn't wrong. It was late for a delivery.' He looked over at Sarah Choi. 'When are we getting the street CCTV?'

'Should be with us this later this morning, Guv,' she replied.

'Let me know what you find when you go through it,' Wise said. 'See if you can spot any motorbike messengers. And I want to know who called 999.'

'Guv,' Hannah said. It felt odd speaking out and, when every eye in the room turned her way, she felt like she'd made a mistake by doing so. She was the new girl, after all. Even the DCs had more experience than her when it came to major crimes.

'Yes, Hannah?' Wise said.

'If it was this messenger, that would mean he drove to Hassleman's house, knocked on his door, shot him and then drove off.'

'That's right,' Wise said.

'So it was pre-planned. Organised. What about if it was a professional hit?'

'It'd be worth your while hiring a hit man if you were going to inherit billions,' said Sarah, glancing Hannah's way and smiling.

'Or a hit woman,' said Donut.

'"Or a hit woman,"' mimicked Sarah, rolling her eyes.

'Send someone on a diversity and inclusion course and they think they know it all.'

'Donut's got a point,' Wise said, raising his voice just enough to quieten everyone else down. 'We all have to have an open mind here. We know nothing yet. It certainly could be a professional hit or it could be a jealous ex-girlfriend or boyfriend who shot him on the doorstep and made it look like a hit.' He pointed at the board. 'Let's dig up the facts. Find out what actually happened. From there, we can develop theories about the who and the why. A man has been murdered. If it is a hit, someone paid serious money for it to happen. That means this was not a crime committed on the spur of the moment. It took serious forethought, planning and organisation. If it's not a professional, we're looking for someone very calm and cold-blooded. So, let's get digging. We need to move quickly on this.'

'Hannah and I will go to Hassleman's head office and chat to whoever is running the show there,' Wise said. 'Find out how they really felt about their boss.'

Hearing her name mentioned threw Hannah for a moment. She wasn't expecting to be paired up with the boss and, judging by some of the others' reactions, they weren't either. Great.

Wise's phone buzzed in his pocket. He pulled it out and looked at the screen, then slipped it back in his pocket. 'Anyone got other suggestions, thoughts or comments they want to share? Anything we've missed so far?'

'We got an initial report in from the SOCOs,' Sarah said. 'They said the scene was one of the cleanest they'd worked — outside, at least.'

'In what way?' Wise asked.

'No footprints, no shell casing, no unexplained marks.

The SOCO I spoke to said it looked like a ghost had killed Hassleman.'

Even Hannah knew that wasn't good before the others started groaning.

'Alright,' Wise said. 'We could hardly expect them to find all the clues waiting for them with a bow on top. This means we just have to earn our salaries. Now, start digging.'

The meeting over, the team all moved into motion.

'One last thing,' Wise called out, stopping them all in their tracks. 'Jono, before you do anything, get the DCI a coffee from Luigi's. She's expecting it. You can get yourself in her good books for a change.'

'Aw, Guv. I got it last time,' Jono moaned.

'That's because you were just as annoying last time as well,' said Callum.

'Piss off, School Boy,' Jono snapped back as everyone else laughed. Even Hannah enjoyed seeing the man's discomfort and she was glad to see Callum giving back as much as he got. Like every copper, Hannah enjoyed a good bit of piss-taking, but there was a line that was so often crossed where a bit of humour became bullying. Jono and Hicksy looked like a pair who would happily go too far, claiming it was just a laugh.

'Hey!' Wise said. 'None of that. Now, get the boss her coffee.'

Jono shook his head. 'I'm not buying it next time.'

'We'll see,' Wise replied. 'Now, get busy, everyone. We've got a killer to catch.'

7

'Hannah?' Wise said, walking over to the new DS. 'Can you get in touch with Hassleman's company and find out who's the most senior person there and get us an appointment as soon as we can?'

Hannah nodded. 'Not a problem.'

'Cheers,' Wise replied. 'I've just got to make a phone call and then we can be on our way.'

Sipping his Americano, Wise returned to his office. He closed the door, then pulled out his phone and unlocked the screen. Jean, his wife, had called him moments before.

He swiped through to the call log but hesitated to hit the dial button by her name, anxiety rising. God, how could ringing his wife frighten him so much? The days of just calling each other to say hello were long gone. The chit chats full of jokes and laughter were history.

Wise stared at her name, thumb poised, not moving. He thought about not calling her back at all. He could always claim something had come up at work. She was used to that excuse, after all. Too damn used to it. But it wouldn't help things between them if he did that. It would be a coward's way out.

With a deep breath, he pressed dial.

'Simon,' she said before the phone had barely a chance to ring. Her voice sounded breathless. Nervous even. 'You're not ignoring me, then?' She did her best to make it sound like a joke, but he knew it wasn't. He had been ignoring her. Hiding from her.

'Hi Jean,' Wise replied, trying to sound cheery himself. 'How are you?'

'I'm good. I'm good. You left early this morning. We missed seeing you at breakfast.'

'Sorry. We picked up a murder case last night. I needed to get in early and I didn't want to wake you.' He paused, trying not to think of his nightmares. 'The kids alright?'

'They're fine. They miss you. Claire got a bit teary when she realised you'd already left for work.' Jean didn't mean to hurt Wise, but her words cut all the same. 'How are you really?'

'I'm fine.' Wise smiled, hoping that it would make his voice sound happier, brighter.

'Are you?' God, Jean knew him so well. Too well. There was no fooling her. Another reason he was avoiding her.

Wise closed his eyes.

He's running up the stairs to the roof, desperate to get there in time, desperate to save Morris, stop Andy.

'I'm doing better, anyway.'

'That's good. That's good ... We miss you.'

'I miss you too.'

'Do you think you'll be home for dinner?'

Wise took a breath. 'Probably not. You know what the first days of a murder are like.'

'Yeah. I do,' Jean said. 'The kids will be disappointed though.'

'I'll make it up to them.'

He thought he could hear Jean cry, just to make it feel even worse. 'Okay,' she said in the end. 'We'll see you when we see you.'

'I'm sorry, Jean.'

'It's okay, Si. You still seeing Doctor Shaw this week?'

'I've got another appointment on Friday,' Wise said. 'Of course, I might not make it. Work's—'

'Make time for yourself, Si,' Jean said. 'It's important that you do. For all of us.'

'I do love you, you know?'

'I know.' Jean's voice cracked.

So did Wise's. 'Give the kids a hug from me. Tell them I love them too.'

'I will.' The line went dead.

Wise put the phone away. He knew he wasn't being fair to Jean or the kids, but it was all he could manage. All he could cope with.

Wise concentrated on his breathing, like Doctor Shaw had told him. Counting to five as he inhaled, holding the breath for five seconds, then counting to five as he exhaled. Thinking about nothing else. Calming himself down. Burying the fear, the memories of that rooftop in Peckham, that pub in Fulham. All his mistakes.

In and out. Regaining control — or the illusion of it, at least. Enough to fool everyone except himself.

Leaving his coffee, Wise straightened his tie, smoothed his jacket, and made sure his face gave nothing away. He just had to concentrate on the job and find Hassleman's killer.

With a final calming breath, he left his office.

Hannah was waiting for him. 'I spoke to Sparks. The

CEO is a woman called Emily Walker. We have an appointment with her in thirty minutes.'

'Good,' Wise said. 'Let's go and see her.' He'd not wanted to partner with her, but he didn't want to inflict her on anyone else either. His team was reeling enough as it was. Dealing with a new person was not what any of them needed. Especially him — but he couldn't cut her out of things either.

Leaving MIR-One, they headed back down the stairs. 'There is a lift,' Wise said, 'but no one in their right mind uses it. You're more than likely to end up spending the day stuck inside it. Unfortunately, it costs too much to fix it, so we walk.'

'That's good to know — and I could do with the exercise anyway,' Hannah said, in a way that only really fit people could.

'Really?' Wise glanced at her. 'I took you for a bit of a runner.'

'Once maybe,' Hannah said. 'I ran a lot when I was at university, but not so much now. The job makes it difficult. And, back when I was in uniform, running was the last thing I wanted to do after a day on my feet.'

'I try to run as often as I can,' Wise said. Running from mistakes and fuck-ups. 'Helps with the stress of the job.'

'I can imagine it can get quite bad.'

'Yeah,' Wise said, in the understatement of the year. 'We're dealing with the worst that London has to offer day in, day out. It's hard to keep the balance right between caring too much and not caring enough.'

'I've heard.'

'I'm sure.' Wise's smile was tight and forced. He wondered what else she had heard. He wasn't an idiot after all. The Met was a gossip factory at the best of times, but what happened to Andy had set everyone talking, especially after the media picked up on the story. It had sent the twenty-four-hour news cycle into a frenzy as they dug up every scandalous detail of Andy's life, not caring about the harm it would do to the dead man's wife, Debs, and the kids. It was bad enough they'd lost a husband and a father without hearing that he was an adulterous, drug addicted criminal.

The press had gone after Wise as well, trying to fling dirt in his direction, hoping it would stick, not realising he had skeletons of his own waiting to be dug up. Somehow, though, they'd not found out about his big, dark secret. They'd not found out about his brother, and Wise was damn glad about that.

'Where's the office?' Wise asked as they stepped outside.

'Rathborne Square,' Hannah said. 'They moved there three years ago, according to the company website, from Covent Garden.'

'Shouldn't take us too long to drive there, even at this time of day,' Wise said, unlocking the Mondeo.

'Might be quicker on the tube.'

'Yeah. I might be a Londoner, but I bloody hate the tube. It's too claustrophobic for me. I'd rather be stuck in traffic than trapped down there.'

Hannah smiled. 'The car it is then.'

'Just don't remind me what I said when we get grid locked and I start cursing, eh?'

'I'll try not to, Guv,' Hannah said, and Wise felt his mood lift just a little. Despite his misgivings, it was nice to have someone around that didn't look at him like he'd fucked everything up.

He drove up through Waterloo, over Westminster Bridge, and up to Trafalgar Square. He'd been wrong about the traffic, though. It was a pain to fight through. It didn't help that they were driving into tourist central. If Hannah thought he was an idiot for driving this way, she, at least, kept those thoughts to herself and spent the time looking up more details about Hassleman and Sparks.

'Hassleman's position was chairperson, visionary and chief happiness officer,' she said.

'Chief happiness officer?' Wise repeated.

'It's that kind of business,' Hannah said. 'Big on the vibes, by the looks of things.'

'Doesn't sound like Hassleman was too hands on.'

'They brought Emily Walker on a year before they moved to Rathborne Square. According to LinkedIn, she did stints working at all the major social networks both here and in the States. She was nominated one of the Top Forty People Under Forty by Marketing Magazine last year. They ranked her at number three.'

'She sounds serious.'

'Lots of posts on Instagram about "it's time to lean in," "loving what I do" and "great work by the team" and so on. Also, there are loads of pictures of her at galas and red carpet affairs.' Hannah continued to scroll. 'Pictures of her with almost every politician you can think of, holidays in the Maldives, meetings in New York and LA. Last week, she did an interview for a podcast about high performance.'

'I'm worn out just listening to that,' Wise said. 'Then again, if I was running a company worth — how much was it again?'

'Fifteen billion dollars.'

'Yeah, for that amount of money, I'd imagine everyone would want to be your friend.'

'Hassleman doesn't sound like he was too popular,

though,' Hannah said. 'Famous for being a recluse and everything.'

'Forensics will tell us more about that,' Wise said. 'Solving his murder will be a lot easier if we find out it was a lover's tiff gone wrong or two mates having a fight after doing too many drugs.'

He headed straight up the Charing Cross Road. The crowds were out, enjoying the September sunshine, darting in and out of the shops as if there was no cost-of-living crisis. Wise felt a pang of jealousy as he watched them, their lives untouched by the darkness that lurked in every nook and cranny of London. A wave of bicycle couriers zipped past, emphasising how slowly they were driving in the all but stationary traffic.

They finally crossed over Oxford Street onto the Tottenham Court Road before turning left onto Stephen Street. The road was narrower here, with people spilling out onto the pavement without looking most of the time. Wise turned right onto Grasse Street and spotted a parking spot on the left. He cut in before a Renault driver could reverse into the spot. The man wasn't pleased with Wise's quick manoeuvrings and hammered his horn, shouting expletives while he did so. He calmed down a bit when he saw Wise climb out the car. There were a few advantages to being six foot one and built like a boxer, after all. The man drove off with a screech of his wheels. Of course, this being London, the Renault driver only charged five yards down the street before he had to stop again because the traffic wasn't moving, making Wise smile.

He caught Hannah watching him. 'Sorry. That was childish.'

She smiled back. 'The Sparks office is this way,' she said, pointing down Rathborne Place.

'Come on then,' Wise said, and they set off down the street, weaving their way between the crowds. Everyone around them seemed to be in a good mood as they bustled here and there. 'Have you had to inform anyone of a death before?'

'Once,' Hannah said. 'A young lad whose mother had thrown herself in front of a train on the way to work. I didn't enjoy it.'

'I don't think anyone does,' Wise said. 'It can be even more difficult for us, though, because we're dealing with victims of violent crimes. One minute they're there, living life, and then they're snatched away, often through no fault of their own. That abruptness of loss makes it even more difficult for their loved ones to deal with it. Some cry, others scream. Many get angry, while a few just shut down.' Like Wise himself. 'Our job is to navigate around those emotions while we try to get the information we need.'

The entrance to Rathbone Square was through a tunnel made of green arches. The first sign that where they were going wasn't like most offices.

The office itself formed a giant U-shape around the square and stretched eight stories high in all its glass-fronted glory. 'It's a little different to Kennington,' Wise said.

'Just slightly,' Hannah replied.

They walked through a ten-foot-high revolving door into the office foyer but, from what Wise could see, it didn't look like any sort of business at all. 'It's more like a university campus,' Wise said, looking around. He was the only person in sight wearing a suit. Everyone else wore very casual clothes — as if for a night out rather than a day's work — and all the men seemed to have artfully crafted beards, whilst competing to see who had the most tattoos.

A woman whizzed past on a scooter while others rushed

along with open laptops in one hand and giant coffees in the other. An enormous poster on one wall proclaimed, "Make Impact!" while another said, "Move Fast and Break Things." Vending machines full of sugar and caffeine were seeing a busy trade, except no money was being used to get the goods. Everything was free. There was even a machine dispensing headphones and power chargers.

As they approached the main reception desk, a very tall woman intercepted them, jet black hair cut short on the sides but teased up high into an elaborate quiff of sorts on top. 'Detective Inspector Wise?' she said in a transatlantic accent.

Wise stopped. 'Yes, that's me.'

The woman smiled and held out a hand. 'I'm Emily Walker. I'm pleased to meet you.' She wore a black top, jeans and black boots, but even Wise could tell the ensemble likely cost more than his monthly salary. Close to Wise in height, she had a physique that appeared as well looked after as her wardrobe. She moved with an elegant grace, as if she was in utter control of herself and her surroundings, but it was her eyes that he noticed most. Ice blue, she looked Wise up and down, evaluating him and, somehow, he felt she was unimpressed by what she saw.

In fact, she reminded Wise of a predator out checking out its supper.

8

Wise shook Emily Walker's offered hand, and the strength of her grip surprised him. 'It's good to meet you. This is Detective Sergeant Markham.'

'Sergeant.' Walker shook Hannah's hand. 'Now, we can chat in the canteen if you want or do you need somewhere more private?'

'Somewhere more private might be better,' Wise said.

'Oh,' said Walker, raising an expertly shaped eyebrow. 'So, it's serious then? I was hoping you were just after a donation to the police fund.'

'I'm afraid not, Ms Walker,' Wise said.

'Shit. That's not good,' Walker said, but there was no actual change in her expression. She turned to face the reception desk. The three people working behind it all looked like models with sharp cheekbones and sharper haircuts. 'Nick, what meeting room is available?'

The man tapped away at a tablet. 'Jagger's free, Emily.'

'Can you book it for me for the next half hour?' she replied.

Nick tapped at the tablet. 'It's all yours. Would you like some refreshments sent to you?'

Walker turned to Wise and Hannah. 'Tea? Coffee?'

'Coffee would be nice,' Wise said. Essential, in fact. He was regretting not drinking the Americano earlier now his nerves had settled once again.

'Cappuccino? Latte? Expresso? Macchiato?' Nick reeled off, suddenly acting like a Starbucks barista.

'Expresso, thanks,' Wise said. 'A double if you can.'

'With pleasure,' Nick replied.

'I'm fine,' Hannah said.

Nick looked disappointed as he tapped only Wise's order into the tablet.

'And I'll have a Soy Decaf Latte, Nick darling,' Walker said.

Nick beamed. 'It'll be with you shortly.'

Walker led Wise and Hannah to an escalator and took them up to the first floor, walking like she owned the place. It was all very casually done, of course. Walked said hello to anyone she passed, and knew most of their names, but half the staff looked like they were about to bow as she passed and the others made damn sure they didn't get in her way.

They passed meeting room after meeting room, full of people hunched around board room tables with laptops open and staring at charts on big, wall-mounted screens. They'd named the brightly coloured rooms after celebrities like Monroe, Beatty, Stewart, Madonna and, of course, Jagger. It was all so desperately trendy.

Walker opened the glass door to the room but allowed Wise and Hannah to enter first. By the time they'd sat down, a woman had arrived bearing a tray with the coffees. She placed the cups on the table, along with a plate of biscuits and napkins, then left.

Walker took a deep breath before speaking, a 'we mean business' smile on her face. 'Now, how may I help you?'

'It's an impressive building you have here,' Wise said.

'Thank you,' Walker replied. 'We like it. It's big, but it still feels intimate — if that makes sense?'

Wise nodded as if it did. 'How many employees work here?'

'There's about six hundred of us in London. And probably about another four thousand spread out across the world.'

'That's quite a workforce.'

'It's what we need. No more, no less. We still run a tight ship despite our success.'

'And you're the chief executive officer?'

'That's right.'

'And what's Mark Hassleman's role in the company? My colleague said he's the chief happiness officer?'

'That's right.' Walker gave Wise a quizzical look. 'Look, what's this all about?'

Wise ignored the question. 'Is Mr Hassleman involved in the day-to-day operations much?'

'No, Mark's a big picture type of guy. He doesn't do details. Running the company bores him. He's better at inspiring the troops.'

'So he stays at home most days?' Wise said.

'Yes.'

'And when did you last speak to Mr Hassleman?'

'Wednesday or Thursday of last week.'

'And how did he appear then?'

'Look. I really don't mean to be rude, but I have little time. Perhaps if you tell me what this is about, I can be of more help,' Walked said, coffee cup in hand.

'A man was killed last night at Mr Hassleman's home, Ms

Walker,' Wise said in a tone that let her know exactly what he thought of her busy schedule.

For a moment, Emily Walker's perfect composure threatened to fall apart. 'Killed? Who ... not Mark?'

'Yes, we believe the victim is Mr Hassleman,' Wise said.

The cup fell from Walker's hand.

9

Hannah watched the cup fall from Walker's hand. It hit the floor, spilling its contents all over the carpet and splashing up Walker's leg. She pushed her chair back, looking at the mess. 'Oh, shit. Shit. Shit.'

Hannah picked up some napkins up from the middle of the table and passed them over to Walker. 'Are you okay?'

Walker snatched the napkins from Hannah's hand and dabbed at her leg furiously. If it was a way of buying time, it was very effective.

Eventually, she had to stop and return her attention to the two detectives. 'I'm sorry. This is such a ... a shock. Oh my God.' She looked from Wise to Hannah, mouth open. 'Are you being serious? He's dead?' She said the word as if it were an impossibility.

'We believe so,' Wise said. His voice was calm and steady. 'Someone needs to identify the body formally, but we're certain it is Mark Hassleman.'

'How did he die?' Walker asked.

'I'm afraid we can't tell you the details, but we're treating his death as suspicious,' Wise said.

'Right. Of course. That's why you're here.' Walker shook her head and Hannah could see her slipping her business mask back on. 'Right. This is awful.'

'Do you know if Mr Hassleman has any family or close friends we should contact?' Wise asked. 'From what we understand, he was an only child.'

'That's right. There was an uncle once, but they weren't close from what I understand, but he died several years ago.'

'Did he have a partner?' Wise asked. 'A girlfriend or boyfriend?'

'God, no,' Walker said. 'Despite what he invented, Mark was quite possibly the most anti-social person you could ever meet. He didn't see why he had to meet anyone in person if he could chat over Zoom instead. And he'd not even want to do that if he could email or text instead.'

'So he didn't come into the office much?' Wise asked. He had a way of talking to Walker that was polite, but to the point. Hannah had heard from others that her own style could be quite impatient and brusque and she knew she'd have to work on it now she was in major crimes. Getting shirty with some street drug dealer wasn't the same as cajoling a reluctant witness into testifying.

'Once in a blue moon,' Walker said. 'Normally for press events if we forced him.' She tried a smile.

'So he wasn't involved in the day to day running of the company?'

'He pays me very well to do that.'

'What was involved in his role as chief happiness officer, then?' Wise asked.

'All he had to do really was stay away from this place,' Walker said. She took a deep breath, adjusting her body so she no longer looked like the CEO, but adopted a much more casual attitude. Her shoulders slumped forward, her back curved as if she was releasing all the tension in her. Even her voice lost its formality. 'Look, I don't want to speak ill of the dead, but Mark's brain wasn't wired for real life. He had no tact, no empathy, no charm. On his day, he could be the rudest man alive — a walking HR nightmare. I've lost count of the times we've had to pay off an employee to stop them suing us for what he'd said or done. He could make all our jobs difficult.'

Wise took a sip of his coffee as he leant forward, as if responding to Walker's change in attitude. 'Were there any such incidents recently?'

'No, thankfully. Mark was happy to do his thing from home. We were all happy for Mark to do his thing from home.'

'Was he that disruptive?'

Walker laughed. 'Get Mark in one of his moods and he could take a flame thrower to every bridge in sight, but we managed him so that he didn't get the opportunity to do that. Mark could be obnoxious, but he was just a big geek at heart. A big, socially inept, maladjusted geek.'

'Were there threats made to Mr Hassleman or the company?'

'None. We get the odd complaint when a date goes wrong, but that's about it.'

'People complain to you about their dates?' Wise clarified.

'Oh God, all the time. They'd rather blame the app for a terrible date instead of themselves, or they think we should know when someone is lying with their details or that they using a picture that's fifteen years out of date,' Walker said. 'Or, heaven forbid, they find one of their matches is married.

Our algorithms are good, but they can't keep track of every married man keen to cheat on his wife.'

Wise glanced at Walker, half-smiling back and shaking his head. 'People are strange.'

'Especially with their love lives,' Walker said.

Wise nodded as if in complete agreement with Walker. Hannah wasn't sure if he was or if it was just his way of putting Walker at ease. 'Any recent firings? Or disgruntled employees?'

'No firings, but we work in tech. Everyone's overworked, overstressed, and prone to overreaction. If they weren't pissed off, then they're not doing their jobs properly.'

'What about Harish Vasudean? We understand he had a grievance against Mr Hassleman.'

Walker waved the name away. 'First of all, I'd like to clarify that Vasudean's claim had no substance to it and courts in the US and here agreed with us. However, we did reach an agreement with him to stop any more time being wasted on his spurious claims. He draws a salary from us of one million dollars a year, a salary we will keep paying until the day he dies — or we go bust.'

'That's quite the pay off,' Wise said.

'It is what it is,' Walker said. 'Unfortunately, the more successful you are, the more people come at you with their hand out wanting a slice.'

'You said you last spoke to Mr Hassleman last week?'

Walker leaned back in her chair and looked around the room for a moment, as if searching her memory. 'I think it was Thursday.'

'You didn't speak that often?'

'It depended really what was going on. We tried not to bother Mark too much.'

'And why did you call him on Thursday?'

'Er ... I didn't actually call him. He rang me.'

'Was that unusual?'

Walker shrugged. 'Yes. No. Mark was always unpredictable.'

'And what prompted this call?'

There was that half-smile again on Walker's face. 'He wanted money — or more money, rather. As I said, everyone wants a slice but, just because the company is valued at fifteen billion pounds, it's very different from us having that cash in the bank. In fact, most of the capital we have is tied up either in our day-to-day operations or in the businesses we're developing.'

Hannah noticed a shift in Wise's posture. 'How much money did Mr Hassleman want?'

Walker shook her head. 'We were already paying him very well, but he needed more cash. I said I couldn't authorise a pay rise by myself and that it would have to go to the board. However, I told him it would be unlikely that they would approve it. We're just not cash rich at the moment.'

'And how did Mr Hassleman take that news?'

'Not well. He got angry. Shouted a lot, said a few things that weren't very nice and threatened to fire me.' Walker shook her head. 'It was all the usual nonsense.'

'Were you worried about your job?'

'No, not at all. Mark needed me far more than I need him. He didn't have the power to fire me and, if he did, I'd walk out of here and find a hundred job offers waiting for me by the time I got home. I told him as much.'

Hannah had to admit that she liked Walker's confidence in herself. She couldn't imagine Walker took any crap from anyone.

'And what was Mr Hassleman's reaction to that comment?' Wise asked.

'He threatened to sell some of his shares. It wouldn't have been ideal, but we are publicly listed, so it was within his rights to do so,' Walker replied.

'I would've thought the founder and major shareholder selling shares might not look that great on the markets?'

'That would be an understatement, but I wasn't worried. Selling shares takes effort and Mark would've most likely have not bothered.'

'Did he say why he needed the extra cash?'

'No. And I didn't ask.'

'And you weren't curious?'

'I don't have the time or the inclination to worry about other people's issues. I only care about the company.'

'Really?' Wise said. 'I would've thought Mr Hassleman's need for money directly affected the company. If he sold his shares, someone else could get ownership of the company or you could have millions wiped off the share value if the market got worried about why he wanted to sell.'

'That wouldn't happen while I'm in charge.' Walker shifted again, her back straightening, her informality gone within a heartbeat.

Wise nodded. 'Understood. Now, we also found evidence of cocaine at his house. A lot of cocaine.'

'Cocaine?' Walker repeated. 'Shit.'

'Does that surprise you?'

'Was it Mark's?

'We don't know yet. The autopsy will confirm that. However, we don't believe anyone else was with him prior to his murder — but again, that's not been confirmed yet.'

'Dear God. What a mess.'

'But you didn't know he might be using drugs?' Wise asked.

'No, not in the slightest,' Walker said. 'We have a very

strict "no drug" policy here. If we'd known — if I'd known — we would've made sure Mark got help for any problem he may have, not just because he was our figurehead, but because we care about everyone's well-being at Sparks.'

'Even someone as difficult as Mr Hassleman?' Wise said.

'He was still Mark Hassleman,' Walker said. 'And his name was worth a lot to us, even with all his ... personal quirks.'

'What about the company? How will Mr Hassleman's death affect all of this?' Wise said, waving a hand towards the outside of the meeting room.

'I don't know,' said Walker. 'We're publicly listed so the shares might take a hit until people realise nothing's changed but other than that? Mark was the majority shareholder. A lot will depend on who he left those to, I suppose.'

'Do you know who the benefactor of Mr Hassleman's will is?' Wise asked.

'To be honest, it'd be typical of Mark not to have a will. But no, I don't know who he'd leave it to if he did,' Walker replied.

'Not you then?'

'I'm just an employee, Inspector. I have — had — no relationship with Mark beyond working for him.'

'You wouldn't know who Mr Hassleman's solicitor is?'

'I'm afraid not. I can check with our company solicitors. Maybe they know.'

'That would be wonderful, thank you.'

'No promises I'll have any answers for you.'

'Of course not.' Wise smiled. 'Well, thank you for your time.'

'Before you go,' Walker said. 'When will you make news of Mark's death public? I need to inform the board and preparations will need to be made to protect the business. Plus, of course, we need to let the staff know.'

'We won't release his name until we're a hundred percent certain there's no one else that needs to be notified first,' Wise said. 'And even then, we'd prefer to keep things out of the public eye while we do our work. Once the press gets wind of these things, it often hinders the investigation.'

'That's good to know,' Walker said. 'But we can't keep this quiet for too long. The markets will see that as a sign that we're worried about what's happened.'

'I'll have our press office get in touch and we can coordinate what's said and when.'

'Right. I'll look forward to hearing from them,' Walker said, rising to her feet. 'Please let me know how you get on and if there's anything else I can do to help you.' She walked over to the meeting room door and opened it, waiting as Wise and Hannah got to their feet.

Wise quickly downed the last of his expresso, then walked over and shook Walker's hand once more. 'Thank you again for your time. We can see ourselves out.'

'Thank you, Inspector,' Walker said. 'This news has been a terrible shock.'

'I'm sure,' Wise replied. 'We'll be in touch if we need to speak to you again.' He then stopped, half-in, half-out of the meeting room door. 'Sorry — just one last question before we leave you.'

'Yes, Inspector?' Walker said.

'Where were you last night around 10:30?'

For the first time, Walker seemed genuinely taken aback. 'Me? Why do you want to know? What's that got to do with anything?'

'Just routine, Ms Walker,' Wise said.

'I was at home, working,' she snapped back.

'Is there anyone that could corroborate that?'

'I live alone — but I had a conference call with LA at 11 p.m. They can confirm I was at home at that time.'

Wise smiled. 'And where do you live?'

'Kensington Gardens.'

'Thank you,' Wise said. 'You've been a big help.'

Wise and Hannah left Walker, heading for the escalator by themselves. Neither spoke as they travelled down to the ground floor and made their way to the revolving doors. They had to stop once to allow a heavily tattooed and artfully bearded man skateboard past, with a laptop open in one hand.

'Bloody kids,' Hannah muttered. 'I'd hate to work in a place like this.'

It was cold when they got outside. The September sunshine might've gifted them with bright, blue skies, but it had little warmth.

'You were quiet in there,' Wise said as they walked back to the car.

'I'm sorry,' Hannah replied. 'I should've asked you what you wanted me to do before we saw her. Some governors preferred to do all the talking.'

'I'm not like that,' Wise said. 'I want my officers to give their opinions and ask questions.'

'Okay,' Hannah said. 'Next time I'll do that.'

'Good. Now, what did you think of Ms Walker?'

'Slick. Very slick. I kind of liked her for most of the time we were with her. I mean, you can see why she's super successful. But I also thought she was very cold underneath that polished exterior. As she said, she only cares about the company. I don't think she gives one jot about Hassleman, except how it would impact the business.'

'Was she being honest with us?'

'I was taught very early on to assume everyone's a liar.'

'She certainly didn't paint a very good picture of her boss.'

'Walker made him sound like a right arsehole. She certainly wasn't too upset that he was dead.'

'Was Walker surprised, though, when we told her he was dead?'

Hannah thought for a moment, remembering the dropped coffee cup. 'I don't know. It was all very dramatic, and she doesn't look like the person who does drama too often.'

Wise said nothing.

'What do you think?' Hannah asked.

They reached Wise's Mondeo. He unlocked the doors, then turned to look at the green tunnel that led to Sparks' building once more. 'I think there's a lot of money at stake to have a temperamental drug addict for a figurehead. Having Hassleman dead solves a lot of problems for them.'

They climbed into the car.

'Walker's smart. Determined. Knows how to get things done,' Wise continued as he put on his seat belt. 'She'd have the money to pay for someone to kill Hassleman as well.'

Hannah sat back in her seat. She found she could easily imagine Walker shooting Hassleman or hiring someone to do it. 'It'd be just another business decision for her.'

'Exactly.'

'So, Ms Walker is on the list?'

'Definitely,' Wise said.

As he turned on the engine, Wise's phone beeped. He looked at the screen. 'They want us at the morgue.'

10

The morgue at the back of King's College Hospital in Camberwell was a thirty-minute drive from Rathbone Square, but it took Wise over three-quarters of an hour to fight his way there through London's traffic from the Sparks headquarters. He spoke little on the way, his mind going over the case and everything they'd learned so far.

Emily Walker was certainly something. He wasn't sure what, if anything, was genuine, though. She was a businesswoman above all else and, as Hannah had said, all she cared about was the business. Hassleman being killed in a tragic murder was a good way of making him a bit of a martyr, rather than a liability. And he could not shake that first impression he'd had of her as a predator.

Hopefully, Singh would have some good news for him, some clues that would propel the investigation forward.

He found a spot in the car park at the back of the hospital and turned off the engine. 'Right. Let's see what the good doctor has for us.'

'Guv? I thought you should know this is my first Post Mortem,' Hannah said, getting out of the car.

'Don't worry too much,' Wise said. 'Most of the cutting will be done by now, so we shouldn't see anything too gruesome. But, if you think you're going to throw up or pass out, don't be a hero — just leave. Pathologists don't like people messing up their workspaces.'

'I'll do my best,' Hannah said.

Wise led her through the car park and into the hospital building. Perhaps he should've confessed to Hannah that he hated PMs himself and just being in the building always put him on edge. It was the antiseptic smell that always set him off. A smell that took him back to his teenage years, back to that moment when everything changed for the worst.

He'd been thirteen when he found out his mother had cancer, an age when he thought he didn't need her, but it turned out it was the time when he needed her the most. He hadn't believed her when she'd first told him, thinking it some poor joke, then he'd got angry when he realised it was true, then sad, then numb as he built walls around his heart, trying to protect himself from the horrible times still to come.

He grew to hate that antiseptic smell as he spent long months waiting in hospitals with her while she underwent treatment, then more time visiting her in the hospice, heart full of dread watching her fade away until finally, he, his brother and his father stood in a funeral home, staring at her corpse. Three people feeling lost, alone and broken-hearted, not knowing how to connect with each other to lessen the pain they all shared.

No wonder he and Tom went off the rails after that. Rushing head long into looking for trouble, doing anything to feel alive, putting their father through more hell.

Embracing violence. Destroying more lives — including their own.

Wise glanced down at his fists, seeing the scars that criss-crossed his knuckles, faded but lingering still. It was easy to remember the blood that used to cover them all too often. The pain he liked to dish out to hide his own.

'DI Wise and DS Markham?'

Wise looked up. A lab assistant approached them, walking quickly down the corridor.

Both showed their IDs. 'We're here to see Doctor Singh. She's expecting us,' Wise said.

'I know. She sent me to find you.' The assistant turned and led the two officers back the way she'd come. 'She's already in the examination suite. You're late.'

'Traffic's bad,' Hannah said in an act of solidarity that Wise appreciated.

'It's always bad,' the assistant replied, with no hint of sympathy or forgiveness.

Wise raised an eyebrow at Hannah, who shrugged back. The assistant took them to a room where they put on gowns and masks. They then went through to the examination suite.

'Took your time getting here, Inspector,' Singh said, without looking in his direction.

Hassleman's body lay opened up on the table, or "canoed," as it was known, when the corpse was opened from neck to navel and the insides hollowed out. A microphone hung over the body, recording Singh's observations while a technician filmed the procedure. Another helped Singh with the body. 'We're just about to stitch things back up here.'

'Traffic was terrible,' Wise said from near the door. The

excuse didn't get a better reaction from Singh, though. In fact, he thought he heard her tut.

'Well, you're here now,' Singh said.

Hannah, despite it being her first visit, moved further into the examination suite. Wise loitered by the door, images of Andy flashing through his mind, of his friend lying on the steel slab with its grooves to drain the mess away so neatly, half his skull missing, his blood sent off for tox reports — just like Hassleman.

'Found anything unusual yet?' he asked, fighting the thoughts.

Singh looked up. 'For goodness' sake, if you were any further away, you'd be back at the police station. Come closer. You can't catch what killed him.'

He could've sworn he heard Hannah stifle a giggle as Wise shuffled closer under Singh's watchful eye. Once he was close enough, Singh returned to her examination. 'Now, our victim was shot once. I can confirm what I mentioned last night as a possibility: the victim put his hand up, no doubt in a defensive gesture, and the bullet went through it, losing some velocity as it did so, before entering the victim's face just below the left eye, killing him instantly.

'There are no other wounds or marks. Certainly no defensive injuries, suggesting the killer surprised the victim. Apart from sticking up a hand, he did nothing to stop the killer.'

'Any DNA or other evidence that could've come from the attacker?' Wise asked, even though he already knew the answer. His earlier hopes of a breakthrough were fading fast.

'Not a thing,' Singh said. 'Another thing to note is the state of the victim's internal organs. Alcohol and drug abuse has enlarged his liver, with high levels of fat, and his heart.

He was an excellent candidate for kidney failure. His nasal septum was also perforated from extreme drug use and close to collapse. If the victim hadn't been shot and had continued with his life style, he would've been dead within a year or two.'

'So the drinking and the drugs weren't a new thing?' Wise asked.

'Not at all,' Singh replied. 'I would say he'd dedicated a lot of time, effort and, no doubt, money to get himself in such a state. We've obviously sent his blood off for analysis and we should get that back tomorrow. That will tell us a lot about the physical state he was in when he was murdered.'

'What about the bullet that killed him?' Hannah asked.

Singh looked over, as if noticing Hannah for the first time. 'I don't think we've met.'

'I'm DS Markham,' Hannah said.

'She joined the team today,' Wise added.

'Right,' Singh said. 'Pleased to meet you and all that. The bullet is a nine millimetre and as about as common as you get.'

'Great,' Wise said. It wasn't as if you could buy a nine millimetre pistol at the local corner shop, but it wasn't far off that. Plenty of guns were going missing from east European or middle eastern war zones only to end up in the UK.

'The only other thing I can tell you,' Singh said, 'the killer used a silencer when they shot the victim. We know this because there is a very focused powder burn on the victim's palm. Silencers, as you know, suppress the gas that leaves the barrel after the gun is fired, smothering much of the noise and the flash of the shot. What does escape is funnelled through the tube of the silencer, so we don't see the same sort of powder spread that we'd see with an unsuppressed shot. I can show you on his hand, if you'd like.'

'Don't worry. I'll take your word for it,' Wise said. Singh had never been wrong about anything before. He certainly wouldn't waste time double-checking her theories.

'I'm sorry, but I've got nothing else for you,' Singh said.

Wise smiled, despite his frustration, but then realised she couldn't see that behind his mask and immediately felt foolish. 'Thanks. Let us know if anything of interest crops up.'

'Oh, I will, Inspector. You have my word on that.' Singh glanced over at Hannah. 'Nice to meet you, Sergeant.'

'And you, Doctor,' Hannah replied.

Wise and Hannah left the examination suite and headed back out to the car, disposing of their medical gowns and masks en route.

'Aargh,' Wise said as he stepped outside. 'That was a waste of time.'

'The killer seems pretty efficient. Single shot. Silencer,' Hannah said.

'Yeah, I don't like that,' Wise said as they walked to the car. 'Most murders are messy affairs. Normally, it's a family member, a friend or acquaintance that's done it, more often in the heat of the moment — during a jealous row or an argument over money or maybe the person's having a mental health episode. When that happens, the murder weapon can be anything that's handy — from a knife to a baseball bat. I once saw someone who died with a biro in the neck.'

'A biro?' Hannah repeated.

'Yep,' Wise said. 'Anyway, with cases like that, we're normally drowning in evidence and we'll make an arrest within the first twenty-four to forty-eight hours. It's the others that are harder, the twenty percent that are committed by a stranger for who knows what reasons. But, even then, the spontaneous killings — the rapes that go too far, the gang fight that gets out of hand — still leave plenty of forensics for us to work with. It might take longer, but we'll track whoever did it down, eventually.'

Wise glanced back at the morgue as he unlocked the car. 'But cases like this are the worst. There's no emotion here. No spontaneity. No mess. Someone's planned this carefully.'

'What do we do next?' Hannah asked.

Wise opened the car door but didn't get in. 'We dig, Hannah. We keep digging until we find the clue that unravels everything. Because it's out there, waiting for us. The perfect murder doesn't exist.'

11

I t was late afternoon by the time Wise and Markham had fought their way back through London's traffic to Kennington, and the sky was dark and cold. Wise resisted the urge to buy another coffee, despite the tired fog in his brain. He needed to sleep that night and it was worth struggling now if he could achieve a good eight hours' kip later.

The incident room was still busy, though, despite the hour. The first twenty-four hours of a murder inquiry were always the most frenetic as everyone tried to gather as much evidence as quickly as possible.

Before Wise had a moment to go to his office, Sarah waved him over the moment she saw him enter with Hannah, with a smile that looked like she'd won the lottery. 'Guv.'

'What you got?' Wise asked as he walked over, feeling a bite of excitement.

'I think I've found our motorbike messenger,' Sarah said. 'Have a look at this.' She clicked on a file and a video opened up on her monitor. It was CCTV footage from the corner of Elgin Crescent and Kensington Park Road. The time stamp said 2318HRS. She pointed to someone on a motorbike in the corner of the frame. 'There they are.'

She hit play, and the frozen frame lurched into life. The motorbike rider was in all black with a plain black helmet. They turned into Elgin Crescent just before the clock changed to 2319HRS.

'We haven't got footage of Elgin Crescent, but keep watching.' The motorbike rider reappeared at 2325HRS, turning right into Kensington Park Road. Sarah hit pause on the video. 'They're in Elgin Crescent for just under six minutes.'

'Enough time to murder Hassleman,' Wise said. 'But enough time for a delivery, too.'

'At that time of night?' Hannah said.

'It's still possible,' Wise replied. 'Do we see where they go?'

'To a point,' Sarah said, clicking play again. The film restarted, and they watched the motorbike rider continue on their way as they moved from one camera's coverage to another. 'The rider keeps to just under the speed limit all the way down Westbourne Grove, then turns left into Queensway before disappearing into the NCP car park.'

'Disappearing?' Wise repeated.

'They don't come out,' Sarah said. She stopped the film again. The time read 2329HRS. 'I've been in touch with the car park, hoping they had CCTV inside, but they had problems with their own cameras that day and nothing's recorded.'

'Did they dump the bike there and leave on foot?' Wise asked, still staring at the screen.

'I asked if there were any unattended or long stay vehicles there, but the manager said no.'

'Let's get someone down there to check it out right now,' Wise said. 'Just in case.'

'What about the bike's number plate?' Hannah said.

'Stolen a month ago from a bike in Pimlico,' Sarah said.

'A month ago?' Wise rolled his neck. 'How long have they been planning this?'

'The bike's a Honda PCX Scooter,' Hannah said. 'It's one of the most popular messenger's bike in London. You see them everywhere.'

'It doesn't look fast,' Wise said.

'Yeah, but it's perfect for London traffic. Nippy enough when it matters and easy to manoeuvre through all sorts of gaps,' Hannah said.

Wise looked up. 'I forgot you were a bike rider. What sort do you have?'

'A Ducati monster,' Hannah replied. 'Expensive. Impractical. I love it.'

Wise wasn't a bike guy, but even her choice impressed him. 'What about before the shooting, Sarah? Have you been able to trace where the bike came from?'

Sarah tapped the video image of the car park. 'Yeah, they come from here. They drive out of the car park at 2310HRS, then they're back nineteen minutes later. But I've found no footage of them prior to that so far. There's no sign of them driving in at all.'

'They had to come from somewhere,' Wise said.

'I know, but I haven't found it. I've put in an ANPR request, so maybe we'll pick it up somewhere else,' Sarah said. Automatic Number Plate Recognition was provided by roadside or mobile cameras on roads and highways. They captured the details of every car that went past them. 'However, there is someone else I want to show you.' She rewound the tape. 'You see this car? The Nissan Maxima?'

She pointed to a black car that turned into Elgin Crescent just before the motorbike rider.

'Yeah ...' Wise said, staring at the screen.

Sarah clicked a few more buttons and another piece of film appeared on the screen. 'This is the other end of Elgin Crescent, where it meets Ladbroke Grove ... and here's our Maxima.' The time stamp said 2329HRS as the Maxima shot into the frame and accelerated down Ladbroke Grove.

'Now, they're in a hurry,' Hannah said.

'Understandable if you've just witnessed a murder,' Wise said. 'Do you think that's our 999 caller?'

'Right time, right place,' Sarah said.

'Please tell me that number plate's not stolen,' Wise said.

'I'm not cruel, Guv.' Sarah clicked away and a mug shot appeared on the screen of a white man with a crew cut and a pissed off stare. 'Meet Ivan Radinsky. He's a bit of a naughty boy. Croatian, but he's been living in the UK for the last ten years. We've nicked him for possession three times, intent to supply twice, and he did a five-year stretch for assault and grievous bodily harm after he took someone's eye out with a dart in a pub fight — but nothing since he got out three years ago.'

Wise leaned in, staring at the mug shot. 'I think we're looking at Hassleman's dealer and our mystery 999 caller.'

Sarah held up a piece of paper. 'And here's his address — over in Bevington Road.'

'That's about ten minutes from the murder scene,' Hannah said.

'Excellent,' Wise said. 'I think we should pay Mr Radinsky a visit early tomorrow morning. People like him like getting up early.'

'Just the two of us?' Hannah said. 'Or do you want to bring friends?'

'I don't think we need to go in heavy just yet,' Wise said. 'The drugs don't matter right now. I'd rather he told us what he saw for now and if we go in mob-handed, he might clam up.'

'And if he doesn't want to talk to us?'

'Then we'll huff and puff and smash his door in,' Wise said. 'Good work, Sarah. Good work indeed.'

'Thanks, Guv,' said Sarah.

'Can you put in a request to see Emily Walker's bank accounts and let's have a look at her phone, too?' Wise said. 'Let's see who she's been chatting to and where she was Tuesday night.'

'That's the CEO of Sparks?' Sarah asked.

'That's right. I know it's a bit of a fishing expedition, but maybe something interesting will show its face. She's certainly got the means to pay for a hit and has a probable motive,' Wise said.

'She's even the right height and size to be the motorbike messenger,' Hannah said.

'Sarah, show us the messenger again,' Wise asked.

Sarah clicked away, and another window popped up on the screen with the CCTV footage. A couple more clicks and there was the bike rider, tall and thin. 'It could be a woman,' Wise said.

'Don't tell me Donut could be right about something,' Sarah muttered. 'I'll never bloody live it down.'

Thursday, 15th September

12

It was 6 a.m. when Wise swung his legs out of the bed in the spare room, his eyes burning from lack of sleep after another long night of bad dreams. Dear God, he wished he could just scrub his mind of what happened with Andy if it meant he could sleep for more than an hour, but then he immediately felt guilty for thinking that. Andy had been a good man once.

The best.

God only knew what had sent him down the dark path he'd found himself on, whose thrall he'd fallen under. Maybe if Wise knew that, he could find some peace. He'd have to chase up SCO10 somehow. Maybe Jono or Hicksy knew someone on the team investigating Andy that they could get some information from.

It'd be against protocols, but, as the days went on, Wise knew he couldn't just let it lie. Once the Hassleman case was over, he'd look into it all the more seriously.

He sat on the edge of the bed, trying to wake up, listening to the rest of the house. It was all quiet. Everyone was still asleep.

Wise had gotten home late again, after spending the evening going over the Hassleman case, aware that he was really just killing time until Jean and the kids would be asleep, so he'd not have to face them. He could fake it at work well enough, but lying to his family was just too much for him. His mask felt too thin to bear their scrutiny, and he didn't want them to see the cracks tearing him apart.

He slipped down the hallway to the bathroom, treading quietly as not to wake anyone, and climbed into the shower. The water was ice cold to start with, but Wise welcomed it, the needles of water on his face lifting some of the fog in his brain. As the water warmed up, Wise concentrated on pulling himself together, washing away the lingering effects of his nightmares, and setting his mind on what he had to do that day.

Even though they now had a possible identity for the 999 caller, it was the professionalism of the killer that had Wise worried. Whoever had done it had put some serious thought into it, and he had to admit, the way the bike had appeared and disappeared into thin air impressed him. With the amount of CCTV in London, it should've been impossible. He got his phone out and sent Sarah a message. *Update me when you hear about the car park. Thks.*

Showered and shaved, Wise dressed in the spare room, picking one of his favourite suits out of the selection he'd put in the wardrobe. Its rich dark blue contrasted nicely with the crisp white shirt and a stripped blue and white tie. Looking in the mirror, he could almost fool himself that everything was normal.

Almost.

There would be no time for coffee from Luigi's, so he filled a flask from home, making it industrial strength, and managed to drink half of it by the time he reached the station at 7. Hannah was waiting for him in the car park, her leather jacket zipped up tight against the morning cold. She'd parked her Ducati, in all its bright red glory, in a spot near the main doors.

'Nice bike,' Wise said as she climbed in.

'Some things are worth spending a bit extra on,' Hannah replied.

'You ready to have a chat with Mr Radinsky?'

'Absolutely. I even put on my best boots for the occasion,' Hannah said with a smile.

'Hopefully, we won't have to give him a kicking.' Unlike him, Hannah looked like she'd had a good eight hours of perfect sleep, and Wise felt a brief pang of jealousy. He couldn't remember when he'd last felt that good. Instead, he took another glug of coffee and set off for Bevington Road.

The one good thing about an early start was the traffic was light, and they arrived outside Radinsky's house twenty minutes later, just as the sun was coming up.

It was a pleasant street, with tree lined pavements and Victorian terraces. The cars parked along either side were all in good condition, mainly SUVs mixing along with the odd salon car. None of them matched the value of the cars in Elgin Crescent, but there was a decent collection of BMWs, Mercedes, Audis and Range Rovers all the same. Not that different from where Wise lived with Jean and the kids. It was a "good area," as estate agents would put it. There was even a primary school opposite Radinsky's that looked more than well maintained.

'Not the sort of place I'd expect to find a drug dealer,' Hannah said. 'It's all a bit middle class.'

'If the rest of his customers are like Hassleman, then they live in areas like this,' Wise said. '*Daily Mail* readers who like to get high at their Saturday night dinner parties.

Not the sort to go down to local street corner or crack den to score.'

'Bloody hypocrites,' Hannah muttered.

They got out of the car. 'You're not a fan of the *Daily Mail* then?'

'Sorry,' Hannah said. 'I went to university with a load of privileged white kids whose mummies and daddies all did something in the city or the media and I hated them all. Most of them just didn't realise how lucky they were and they certainly couldn't give a shit about anyone who wasn't from their social circle, especially not a black girl whose mum was a cleaner.'

'I can imagine,' Wise said. He'd not gone to university himself, but he'd grown up in the London that wasn't all luxury cars and fancy restaurants. His dad had been a grafter, working in Smithfields all days of the week. He'd done alright, but his old man had only earned 'getting by' money and, at the end of every month, there were a lot of tightening belts and counting the days to payday.

The Maxima, that Sarah had clocked on the CCTV, was outside Radinsky's, its bodywork gleaming in the early morning light. Wise peered through the window. The interior was spotless. 'The man takes care of his car.'

'That doesn't make him a good person. You sure we don't need backup?' Hannah asked.

'We've got each other, haven't we?' Wise said. 'Anyway, let's keep it casual. If Radinsky called 999, then that means he wants Hassleman's killer caught.'

'Or he's worried about his own safety.'

'Even more reason to talk to us.' Wise opened the front gate and walked up to the front door. There was a gold knocker and Wise used it, smiling as he hammered away, the sound echoing through the house, loud enough to rouse the dead. Hannah stayed back out in the street, her eyes on the windows above.

A minute passed and there was no answer, so Wise gave the door another good thump with the knocker. He glanced back at Hannah when there was no reaction from the inside. 'Any sign of life?'

'Nothing,' Hannah replied.

'Maybe he's a heavy sleeper,' Wise said, hammering the door again, hoping the dealer was home and not elsewhere.

They both listened to the silence and Wise could feel the frustration build inside, mixing with his tiredness, making him half-tempted to kick the door.

'Curtain twitched,' Hannah called out. 'We have movement inside.'

Wise gave the knocker another good workout on the door. 'Wakey wakey.'

Hannah joined him at the door as they both heard stirrings from inside. Footsteps stomped down the stairs. 'All right. All right.' The man's voice had a heavy accent; Eastern European. 'It better be important.'

The door swung open abruptly and Ivan Radinsky stood scowling before them, wearing boxer shorts and nothing else, all bulging muscles and dodgy tattoos, blinking and growling, unhappy at being woken up. 'What the fuck you want?'

Wise looked him up and down. The man had put in some serious hours down the gym on the heavy weights since they had arrested him last. Maybe backup wasn't such a dumb idea.

13

As the drug dealer loomed over them from his doorstep, Wise held up his warrant card. 'Detective Inspector Wise and Detective Sergeant Markham. Can we ask you a few questions, Mr Radinsky?'

'Police?' Radinsky said, his demeanour not improving at that bit of knowledge.

'Yes, Mr Radinsky,' Wise said. 'Police.'

Radinsky glanced back into the house for a moment, making Wise wonder who or what might be inside before returning his attention back to Wise. 'What do you want?'

'May we come in?' Wise asked instead, smiling, taking the fact Radinsky was no longer swearing as a good sign. He kept his voice calm and as non-threatening as he could make it, even as his own adrenaline kicked in. Right then, he'd put the chances of Radinsky either having a pop or doing a runner at about fifty-fifty. 'We're happy to wait while you put some clothes on.'

This time, Radinsky looked past them out into the street, looking left and right.

'We're on our own,' Wise said.

'Very brave of you.'

'We're not here to arrest you or search the house,' Wise said. 'We just want to talk.'

Radinsky sniffed. 'Just ask questions? About what?'

'Can we talk about this inside, please?' Again, Wise smiled as the Croatian tried to stare him out, doing his best to show there was no threat. Radinsky didn't seem to buy it, though. Maybe the man wished he'd put on some clothes before answering the door. A pair of silky boxer shorts wasn't the best thing to be wearing if he was about to have a fight or do a runner. Then again, Wise didn't want to have a ruck in on a drug dealer's doorstep either, despite a familiar urge tingling inside him. Not in his favourite suit, anyway. Maybe he should've worn something different, too.

Seconds ticked away.

Wise clenched his fists without thinking, getting ready for things to go bad. Even Hannah had tensed up, her hand inside her jacket, making Wise wonder if she had a retractable baton tucked away in there.

Wise and Radinsky were both of equal build, equal height, and Wise let the drug dealer look into his eyes so he could see what lurked behind them. They were two fighters weighing each other up, looking for weakness, working out who would win.

In the end, it was Radinsky who looked away and there was a little part of Wise that was disappointed.

Radinsky stepped back and nodded towards a door off the hallway. 'Wait in there. I put some clothes on.'

Wise stepped into the hallway but stopped as he was passing Radinsky. 'Thank you.'

Radinsky sniffed again. 'You want coffee? I put on coffee.'

'Coffee would be lovely,' Wise said.

Radinsky backed away, keeping his eyes on Wise, until he reached the kitchen. There, he quickly added water to a coffee machine and turned it on. 'Two minutes,' he said and headed up the stairs.

Wise glanced back at Hannah, who had a strange look on her face. 'You okay?'

Hannah stepped into the hallway. 'I hope you don't mind me saying, but you can be a bit scary when you look at people like that,' she said before heading into the living room.

Wise followed her in. 'Sometimes, you need to let people know they can't muck you about.'

Hannah nodded, but said nothing. The silence was awkward and a stark reminder that they both didn't know each other well. Staring out villains was something both he and Andy had done all the time. A little of the right sort of intimidation had saved them plenty of hassle when dealing with hard nuts who fancied themselves in the past but, looking back now, Wise had to wonder pushing the line like that was part of what had allowed Andy to cross it. Maybe he had to rethink how he did things.

Radinsky's living room was surprising in its domesticity. Of course, a giant TV dominated one wall, with a PlayStation Five hooked up underneath it and a smattering of games stacked up alongside the console. A brown sofa faced it, with two armchairs on either side and a coffee table in between, with a smattering of remote controls and a small box of coasters. Like the car, the room was spotless. Radinsky certainly wasn't the cliched drug dealer stereotype, living in squalor surrounded by junkies.

They heard Radinsky pad down the stairs and go into the kitchen.

'You want milk?' he shouted.

'Not for me,' Wise said.

'A splash in mine,' Hannah added, peering around the door so she could watch him work.

Radinsky noticed. 'I make coffee. Not poison.' He carried three mugs into the living room. He'd put on a black t-shirt and some jeans. The clothes were casual, but still expensive. The man wasn't picking up his clothes at Gap. 'Can you get coaster?' he said, indicating the container on the coffee table with his chin.

Wise smiled as Hannah did as Radinsky asked. The man was obviously house proud. Hannah placed three square coasters on the table, upon which Radinsky put the coffees. He sat in one armchair, and Hannah took the other. 'So, what do you want?'

'We want to know what you saw in Elgin Crescent two nights ago, Mr Radinsky,' Wise said, sitting on the sofa next to him. He didn't see any point in dancing around the subject. 'Right before you dialled 999.'

'And that's it? You're not interested in anything else?' Radinsky looked from Wise to Hannah and back again.

'That's it.'

Radinsky rubbed his face as he looked at Wise and Markham. Then he shrugged, as if making up his mind. 'I saw a motorbike messenger pull up outside a house. He gets off his bike, walks up to the door, and rings the bell. A man opens the door and the messenger shoot him in the head. Then he put his gun in a bag, gets on his bike and drives off. So I call police.'

'Why didn't you wait for the police to arrive?' Hannah asked.

'Why you think?' Radinsky laughed, then picked up his coffee and took a gulp. 'I have a ... a cake in my car that police would not like, so I leave.'

'Were you in your car when you witnessed the murder?' Wise asked.

'I had just parked when the motorbike stop but I got out when I saw him go to house,' Radinsky said.

'Why did you get out when you saw where he went?'

'The house he go to. It belong to my customer. He ordered cake from me but I see this man and I think my customer order cake from him too. I want to tell this man to leave my customers alone.'

'So how far away were you from the messenger?'

Radinsky pursed his lips for a moment. 'Maybe halfway across the road. Maybe thirty metres. Maybe less.'

'Did you see the man's face?'

'No. He wear helmet with black visor.'

'How tall was he?'

Radinsky shrugged again. 'Maybe your height. Maybe a bit smaller.'

'So five foot ten to six one?'

'Yeah, maybe.'

'What about build?'

'He was thin. Like a woman. Before he show gun, I think it no problem to tell him to go away.'

'Tell him?' Wise repeated.

'I can ask nice — or not so nice if I have to. No one steals my customers.'

'You said he was thin, "like a woman,"' Hannah said. 'Could it have been a woman?'

'Maybe,' said Radinsky. 'But if it was, it was a woman with balls. To shoot someone like that, so cold, it's not easy thing to do.'

'What about the gun? Did you see what type of gun they used?' Wise asked.

'A gun is a gun. I see one, I go the other way. That's all I know.' Radinsky drank more coffee. 'This one has silencer though.'

'A silencer?'

'Yeah. The gun. It don't make a bang, you know. More of a pfft noise.'

'You were still standing in the road at this point?'

'No. The moment I see the gun, I run back to my car. I'm not getting shot. Not for anything or anyone.'

'Was anything said between Hassleman and the motorbike rider?'

'I don't know. I was running in the opposite direction.'

'And the motorbike messenger didn't see you?'

Radinsky shook his head. 'I watched him through the car windows, keeping my head down. Once he was gone, I call 999 then leave.'

'You didn't check on Mr Hassleman?'

'No. I go over there, I leave evidence, DNA, shoe print, whatever, and you think I did it. Anyway, who survives bullet in head? No one.'

Andy's head lurches forward a second before Wise hears the gunshot. Red mist blows in the summer night.

Wise picked up his coffee and took a sip, aware his hand was shaking. It was well-made, not instant crap, and he was grateful for the caffeine. 'So, why call 999? Why get involved at all?'

'Once, maybe, I was a bit of a gangster. I liked trouble, yes?' Radinsky said.

'Right,' Wise said, thinking of his own youth.

'But now, I'm a businessman. I don't want trouble and I don't cause trouble if I can help it. I just do my job, come home and play video games. But this man, he messes with my customers. He messes with my business. I don't like that. I don't like that at all.'

'When did you first meet Mr Hassleman?' Hannah asked.

'Some party. Another customer introduce us. That's how these things work.'

'And how long had you been selling ... cake to Mark Hassleman?'

'Two years maybe,' said Radinsky. 'He was a good customer. He like a lot of cake. Hungry man. He wanted more and more each time.'

'You talk to him much?' Hannah said. 'Must've seen him a lot over that time.'

'Sometimes every day, sometimes — but not often — he could go a week without calling,' Radinsky said. 'But we not friends, you know? I don't sit and eat cake with him. I don't eat cake with anyone.'

'You wouldn't know if anyone had threatened him or he thought someone wanted to kill him?'

Radinsky laughed. 'You eat enough cake, you think the world is out to get you, even if it isn't.'

'Was Hassleman like that?' Wise asked.

'Maybe.' There was that shrug of Radinsky's again. 'Look, normally I knock on door, give him cake, get my money and leave. We don't discuss the weather. Maybe he tell me this is the last time he eat cake and not to bring him anymore but he never mean it.'

'Before that night,' Wise said, 'how often were you delivering cake to Hassleman?'

'I've been there every night for weeks now. The man ... he had appetite, you know? He was a good customer.'

'How much was he spending a day with you?'

Radinsky smiled and shook his head. 'I can't tell you that. But, as I say, he was good customer. I'll miss him.'

'Was he always alone when you delivered, or did he have people with him?' Hannah asked.

'That man? Friends? No. He just want cake all to himself.' Radinsky shrugged. 'I don't judge.'

'And you didn't notice the motorbike rider on any other occasion? Perhaps parked up somewhere near? Watching?' Wise asked.

'Not that I remember,' Radinsky said. 'But I look out for police — not motorbikes.'

Wise finished his coffee. 'I think that's all we need for now, Mr Radinsky. We'll be in touch if we have any more questions.'

'You know where I am,' Radinsky replied, leaning back and crossing his arms, a big smile across his face.

'We'll show ourselves out,' Hannah said, standing.

Radinsky leered at her. 'Suit yourself.'

By the time Wise had gotten to his feet, Hannah had the front door open and, by the time he was outside, she was waiting by the car.

'You okay?' he asked as he unlocked the Mondeo's doors. 'You left quickly.'

'Sorry,' Hannah said. 'He was just sitting there, so smug. All that nonsense about "cake." It just wound me up. I want to go back there and arrest him.'

'On what grounds?'

'He'll have a stash in there. I guarantee it.'

'But we don't have a search warrant, nor do we have probable cause.'

'How about we bust him for being a smug git and go from there?' Hannah said, but Wise could see her mood lifting.

They both got into the Mondeo. 'What do you think about what he said?'

'There's no doubt that the target was Hassleman,' Hannah said. 'And it confirms the motorbike messenger is our shooter.'

'And we don't know if it's a man or a woman,' Wise said.

'"A woman with balls,"' Hannah said, mimicking Radinsky's accent.

'I don't think he's done on any diversity and inclusion courses.'

'A fitting description for Emily Walker.'

'Not sure that would hold up in court.' Wise got out his phone and checked his messages. There was one from Sarah. *Someone cut the wires to the car park CCTV. ANPR came back as well. No pings on the bike. It appears and disappears like magic.*

Wise showed Hannah the message. 'Let's have a look ourselves at the car park. I want to know how the bike vanished. I don't believe in magic.'

14

Hannah sat back as Wise drove north up Goldborne Road, then took a right onto Elkstone Road before cutting over the Westway on the A4207. It was rush hour now, and the journey was all stop and start, with odd little patches where Wise could put his foot down. She couldn't help but think how much quicker it would be to weave through the near stationary cars on her bike or cut the traffic out completely by getting the tube, but Wise seemed to love being in his car.

He'd not said much since they'd left Radinsky's and Hannah was happy to use the silence to go over the case herself. For her first proper murder enquiry, she couldn't have asked for a more challenging investigation. It was certainly better than what she'd been working on before. If she never had to deal with another burglary again, she'd be happy. Hannah hated the fact that all she was doing was filling in paperwork for insurance claims most of the time, while the victims stood around, hoping she'd get whoever had wrecked their lives. The sad fact was that only five percent of burglaries in London ever got solved. That was five percent out of over fifty thousand reported break-ins each year.

Hannah had joined the police because she'd wanted to make a difference — not to be impotent in the face of ever-increasing crime. Joining a Murder Investigation Team was her way of doing that. It had surprised her when Wise had asked her to partner up with him. She just hoped it wasn't because he thought she wasn't up to the job.

She already regretted telling Wise he looked scary when he was staring out Radinsky and why had she stropped out of that twat of a dealer's place? Hardly the actions of someone feeling confident and comfortable with what she was doing. She had to be smarter than that. The last thing she needed was Wise to kick her off his team.

'Here we are,' Wise said as he turned off Westbourne Grove into Arthur Court. The car park was in a block of flats halfway down Queensway, with a narrow entry that was easy to miss if you weren't looking for it.

There was no barrier, so Wise drove the Mondeo down to the first level of the car park. Unsurprisingly, for the time of day, it was already quite full, and Wise had to continue down to the next level before he saw a smattering of parking spaces. He reversed the car into one of them and turned off the engine.

'Not much of a car park,' Hannah said, looking at the single line up of parked cars, with barely enough room to manoeuvre behind them. 'It'd be a struggle to get two cars down here at the same time, trying to park.'

'No barriers in or out, though,' Wise said. 'No attendants either. Not busy with traffic. It's a good spot if you're up to no good. Now, where are the cameras?'

They both climbed out of the car. The place stunk of petrol fumes, stale air, damp, and just the odd hint of urine. All very London.

Hannah spotted the camera quick enough. It wasn't anything hi-tech. In fact, it looked like a museum piece with more rust than paint on it. 'It's over there,' she said, pointing to the corner near the down ramp. 'It's got a decent view of the lower level, but it's blind to anything coming down the ramp from the floor above.'

'Let's have a look at the floor above.' Wise and Hannah walked up the slope to the higher level. The camera was above the door to the pedestrian exit.

'The camera wouldn't pick someone entering the car park from the street until they were well inside,' Hannah said. She watched Wise walk over to the camera and look up, checking its mounting.

'Our killer walks in here off the street, vandalises the cameras,' Wise said, acting it out by reaching up with an imaginary pair of wire cutters in his hand, 'then returns the next day at some point, and remains totally unseen until they go to kill Hassleman.'

'Pretty damn organised,' Hannah said.

'Yeah,' Wise said. 'But how did they get here? The street cameras should've picked them up, but we don't see the bike come in before the murder or go out again afterwards.'

Hannah looked around the narrow car park again, almost expecting to see the bike in a parking spot, but there were the usual array of luxury cars that this part of London attracted only too well. 'They had to bring the bike here in something else, so it's hidden. A van or a big SUV or something like that?'

Wise walked over to the nearest car. 'It's got a resident's

parking sticker stuck to the inside of the windshield.' He moved onto the next car. 'This one too.' He moved onto the next car and the next. 'Most of these cars belong to people living in Arthur Court. Probably, they all park in the same spots every day. Maybe someone saw the motorbike being unloaded or there was a van in their usual spot.'

'We should get a team to knock on doors,' Hannah said.

'Give Sarah a call and get her to action it.' Wise stood with his hands on his hips, scanning the car park. 'I doubt they'd find anything, though. The killer is too good, too smart, too professional. They would've picked times to come and go when they knew the place wouldn't be busy.'

'They've been planning this for a while,' Hannah said.

'Yup,' Wise said. 'This isn't someone he's just pissed off or had an argument with. This is someone with a long-term grievance with Hassleman. Or they're set to profit from his death.' Wise looked around once more. 'Let's look outside.'

Hannah followed Wise out of the pedestrian exit, up a short flight of steps, and then out into Queensway. After waiting for a bus and taxi to pass, Wise nipped over the road and turned to face the car park. Hannah joined him.

'You're right. It's not much of a car park,' Wise said. 'So why did they pick it?'

'It's close to Elgin Crescent,' Hannah said. 'Five or six minutes on the bike.'

'But there are plenty of other car parks that are probably closer.'

'Maybe they've got better security, attendants, modern cameras?'

Wise nodded, then looked up and down the street, watching the people walk past. 'It's an expensive neighbourhood, even for London.'

Hannah kept quiet, giving Wise time to think.

'The killer either knows the car park already or they've done their research and recced various options until they've found the right one.'

'What if they live in Arthur Court and the bike's in their apartment out of sight?'

'No. I don't think so. That would be reckless for someone so careful. But I think whoever we're dealing with is comfortable in this world.' His eyes watched a woman walk past in a fur coat and sunglasses. 'They fit in.'

'Plenty of motorbike messengers around, though. Most people wouldn't even notice them.'

'But would they risk the bike being spotted by cameras? Especially with stolen number plates?' Wise shook his head. 'No. I think they're invisible because they look like everyone else, drive the same sort of clothes and live in the same sort of neighbourhoods.'

Hannah couldn't argue with that logic. 'That makes sense if it's someone that knows Hassleman.'

'Let's look at the murder scene next. You've not seen it yet and I could do with a look around in daylight,' Wise said.

Within minutes, they were in the Mondeo and heading down Westbourne Park Road. It was all Georgian houses with white pillars outside, cute coffee shops with even cuter names, posh nail salons and a shopping centre full of expensive fashion labels. 'It's all a bit different from where I live,' Hannah said.

'Where's that?' Wise asked.

'I've got a flat off Tooting High Street with my ... partner,' Hannah replied. She'd nearly said "girlfriend" but she certainly didn't know Wise well enough to share that bit of knowledge. He seemed pretty cool about things, but she'd learned very early in her time at the Met to not presume anything, either about the criminals they dealt with or the people she worked alongside.

'Been together long?' Wise said.

'About five years.'

'They in the job?'

Hannah chuckled. 'God, no. They're a teacher at the local Comp.' She glanced sideways at Wise. 'What about you?'

'My wife used to work in the city, but now she looks after the kids,' Wise said. 'We've been married twelve years.' Hannah detected an element of sadness in his voice, as if all was not well. She didn't ask, though. That wasn't the sort of question you came out with to your boss on your second day in the job.

Wise said no more, obviously happy to not continue the conversation. He turned into Elgin Crescent, pulled into a resident's only parking spot, turned off the engine, and unclipped his seat belt. 'Here we are.'

Hannah followed him out of the car. Two uniforms stood guard by Hassleman's house, where blue and white police tape stretched across a big, black door. Wise showed them his warrant card. 'DI Wise and DS Markham. We're just having another look around. Everything okay?'

'We've had a few reporters come down a short while ago, sir,' said one uniform. 'They filmed the front of the house and tried asking us questions.'

'Like what?' Wise asked.

'How was he killed and that sort of stuff. One of them offered us five hundred quid if we let them in to film inside.'

'You better have said no.'

'Of course, I told them to—'

'Inspector Wise!' A woman with red hair ran towards

them, a cameraman in tow. They must've been waiting in one of the parked cars. 'Inspector Wise, is this your case?'

Wise straightened. 'You need to go through the press office.'

'Is it true they shot Mark Hassleman on his doorstep?' The reporter had a microphone in Wise's face, the camera not far behind.

'I really can't comment on any cases,' Wise said, trying to move away.

'Do you know why he was killed?'

'Please,' Wise said a little too sharply, 'speak to the press office. You know how these things work.'

The woman wasn't intimidated, though. If anything, Wise's brusque nature encouraged her. 'Were you surprised to be given such a big case after what happened with your partner? Have they have cleared you of any involvement with Andy Davidson's criminal activity?'

Wise stopped trying to get away from the reporter and, instead, advanced on her, seeming to grow in size. He leaned into her face, fists bunched. 'Now listen here, you b—'

Hannah stepped between them. 'Speak to the press office, eh? We've got work today.'

The reporter looked grateful to step back, so Hannah turned back to face Wise. 'I think we should head back to Kennington.'

Wise's eyes were still locked on the reporter and, for a moment, Hannah thought he was still going to go for her. Suddenly, standing between Wise and the reporter didn't seem like the best idea. Then, it was as if someone had flipped a switch, and Wise shrunk back down to his normal, enormous size. His fists unclenched and the darkness went from his eyes. 'Right,' he managed to say.

Without another word, he stomped back to the Mondeo, climbed in and slammed the door behind him.

Hannah glanced over at the uniforms, who both gave her a look that said, 'What was that about?'

With a shake of her head, she ran after Wise, wondering what the hell had she got herself involved in.

15

W ise was seething as he drove back to Kennington. Who the hell did that reporter think she was to say that to him? He gunned the car when he could, driving aggressively through the London traffic. By God, she was lucky he hadn't rammed that microphone right up her pretty little nostril. Now, that would've made good TV. It would've ruined his career, most likely, however satisfying it would've been.

Hannah said nothing in the seat next to him and he regretted losing his temper like that in front of her — although it was a good thing she'd stepped in the way before he really mucked things up.

And how the hell had they found out what had happened? If someone on his team had talked ...

He took a breath. He had to calm down. Getting angry wouldn't help anyone. The press were bound to find out sooner rather than later. Someone like Hassleman can't get murdered without the entire world wanting to find out about it.

A cyclist cut in front of his car, forcing Wise to slam on

his brakes. 'Wanker,' he shouted, even though the offender was a good half dozen cars ahead of him already.

'That was close,' Hannah said. 'He could've been another bad dent in the car.'

Wise turned to look at Hannah, who gave him an 'I'm on your side' smile.

'I'm sorry,' Wise said.

'What for?' Hannah said. 'The wanker comment or nearly throttling the reporter back there?'

Wise sighed as he inched the car forward. 'Both?'

'It's alright. Both of them deserved it — kind of.'

'I shouldn't have let her rile me like that — especially with a camera around.'

'You would've gone viral for sure if you'd done it.'

'It's just the comments about Andy — DS Davidson — hit a nerve.'

'I can imagine.'

'Of course you've heard all about it?'

Hannah hesitated for a moment. 'Er ... I think the whole Met heard about it. And maybe a good portion of the news watching public.'

'Yeah. It was sensationalist enough for them. Corrupt cop. Drugs. Prostitutes.' Wise shook his head, trying to stop his mind from drifting back to that roof top in June. Failing.

'Please, Andy. Before the AROs get here. Give me the gun.'
Wise takes a step towards his partner, hand out.

He blinked and focused on the road.

'It must've been awful for you and the rest of the team,' Hannah said.

'Yeah. We've all done good work over the years and he put a shadow over all of it — over all of us.' And Wise still didn't know why Andy had done it — or who for.

'It'll be old news s—'

Wise didn't need to ask Hannah what had cut her off. He could see for himself. They were twenty yards away from the nick and, as far as he could see, all the press in London had turned up. There were vans parked up along the side of the road, baring the logos of Sky News, BBC, ITV and Channel Four.

The main entrance by the gate was even worse. There were dozens of reporters, all with phones and cameras ready, trying to muscle past the uniforms on guard duty.

'Shit,' Wise said, slowing down, cursing them, cursing himself. Of course they'd be there. He had to be ready. They couldn't take him by surprise like earlier. He had to be in control. Keep his mask on. Stop the cracks from spreading.

He stopped the car when he reached the wall of reporters. They all had their back to the Mondeo, not caring who they blocked, focused only on trying to get into the station.

God, he was tempted to nudge some of the vultures with his car, but that would only cause more problems. In the end, he put his hand on the horn and held it there as they all jumped in surprise. However, whatever pleasure Wise had gotten out of surprising them soon evaporated as they turned and saw him behind the wheel.

'Inspector Wise! Inspector Wise!' They flowed around his car, banging on the windows, aiming their cameras through the windshield. 'Inspector Wise!'

Surrounded, Wise couldn't move his car without risking knocking someone over.

'Inspector Wise! Are you investigating the Hassleman murder?' a reported shouted through the window.

'Vultures,' Hannah muttered.

Cameras flashed in Wise's face. He blinked, then held up a hand to block off the worst of it. No one moved when he tried the horn again. He was their prey now. He was their story.

Shit. 'Where are the uniforms?' Wise could feel his anger rising and had to swallow it down. He was in control.

He hit the horn again and, this time, the uniforms in their high viz jackets forced their way through the pack. The original two had reinforcements now — another four clearing a space for Wise to drive through, the gate to the car park already up to allow them access.

But the gate being up also allowed the press to follow, shouting through the windows, taking their pictures, filming everything. 'Inspector Wise! Inspector Wise!'

'Keep your head down, say nothing and go straight inside,' Wise said as he parked the Mondeo, steeling himself to do the same.

'I'll do my best,' Hannah said.

The camera flashing seemed to increase a hundredfold as they stepped out of the car.

'Inspector Wise! Inspector Wise!' The shouts came from everywhere as the reporters swarmed towards Wise. 'Inspector Wise!'

'What can you tell us about Mark Hassleman's murder?' bellowed a woman an inch from Wise's face.

'Was it a drug killing?' A man shoved a microphone towards Wise's mouth.

'Who did it, Inspector?' said another, walking backwards to keep Wise in frame of the camera as he struggled to walk towards the station's front doors.

'Was he assassinated?' They shouted question after question, not giving anyone any time to answer, more interested in the optics of the scrum than in information.

It was as if the world had gone mad. The uniforms came

to help but only added to the push and shove as the reporters jostled Wise this way and that.

'Let me through,' he growled.

'Is the murder connected to your former partner? Should you even be running such a high-profile case?'

Wise looked up when he heard the question and more flashes immediately blinded him, making it impossible to see who'd thrown the comments at him. The reporters pushed forward, and Wise had to bring his elbows up to ward them off. 'Get out of my way,' he snarled. 'Let me through.'

He blinked away the flashes, trying to see the path to the station doors, trapped with the pack, as they shouted more questions at him, overlapping each other, creating meaningless noise.

Wise wanted to scream. He wanted to lash out. All his anger, his frustration bubbling away, eager for release, desperate to do something. But he couldn't. Shouldn't.

He closed his eyes. *Stay in control.*

Then, just like that, the pressure eased. The shouts were of protest, not accusation. Wise opened his eyes and saw his team had joined the uniforms, clearing the press away and out of the police station car park.

Wise didn't waste any time and took the clear run to the doors. Hannah held them open for him and, inside, Wise breathed with relief.

Then his phone buzzed. It was a message from Roberts. See me when you get in. 'The boss has summoned me. Update the boards and I'll catch up with you soon.'

'Will do, Guv,' Hannah replied. 'Good luck.'

Wise stopped on the first floor landing and watched Hannah continue up, feeling exhausted by it all. He could feel the cracks working their way through him deep inside.

All the failures and fuck-ups eating away at him. Felt the weight of it all trying to force him to his knees.

He stared out the window at the car park below, the press safely now back outside. They'd love for him to fall apart. What a story that would make. But not a story he'd want his kids to read.

Maybe he should walk away. Give up before he fell apart. But then what?

He'd become a police officer for a reason — to make up for what had happened that night with Tom. No matter what good he'd done over the years, that was a debt he'd never repay but, at least, doing the job let him sleep at night — that was until Andy ...

Shit. The very things that were breaking him apart were why he had to go on.

Wise straightened himself up and headed down the corridor to Roberts' office. Her door was shut, so Wise knocked.

'Come in.' Roberts' voice was sharp and lacking any sort of warmth. Never a good sign. Still, there wasn't much Wise could do about that. He opened the door and walked in. Roberts sat behind her desk and watched him enter, looking over the top of her reading glasses. Paperwork covered her desk. 'Simon. Take a seat.'

'I see the press have found out about Hassleman,' Wise said, taking the seat to the right of Roberts' desk.

'Thanks to an Emily Walker who gave a press conference earlier at Sparks' headquarters,' Roberts said. 'She gave them all the grizzly facts.'

'Ah,' Wise said. 'We spoke to her yesterday.'

'And you didn't tell her to keep her mouth shut?'

'Not in those exact words, no.'

'What words did you use?'

'She asked if we were going to tell the press and I said no. She seemed quite happy with that as she was worried about the effect Hassleman's death would have on the business. I told her we'd get someone from our press team to coordinate things with her. She agreed.'

'Well, she's obviously changed her mind since then. The super wants us to make a statement as well now.'

'Great.' Wise hated press conferences as much as he hated the press.

'And when I say "us,"' Roberts said, 'I mean you.'

'Even better.'

'They're setting up the media room for 3 p.m. for you. The press office will have a statement that you can read but don't answer questions. Just get in and get out as quick as you can.'

'Are you sure you don't want to do it as my commanding officer?' Wise said with a smile, but he was quite serious.

Roberts gave him one of her tight-lipped smiles back. 'I'm much better at announcing arrests. You'll be fine — what with that nice suit of yours.'

'Sure.' Wise was starting to reevaluate his opinion of her.

'Have you made any progress with the case?'

'Some. We have a witness who saw a motorbike messenger walk up and shoot Hassleman — whether that person was a professional hired to kill him or the person who wanted him dead remains to be seen. We tracked the bike from Hassleman's to a car park where it vanished.'

'Vanished?'

'We think they transported the bike to and from the car park in another vehicle, so we're looking for any that could carry the bike without causing suspicion. Other than that, we have no forensic evidence to work on. The murder itself was well-planned and meticulously carried out,' Wise said.

'We're looking into who might want Hassleman dead but, apart from him being an obnoxious drug addict, nothing's really come up. The man appears to have been a recluse with no heirs. Emily Walker is a possible, but that's about it.'

'Why her?' Roberts said, leaning forward.

'She could afford it, for one thing. Walker's the CEO of his company and made it clear Hassleman coming to the office was not a good thing. She claimed not to know about his drug problems but, from what Doctor Singh told us after the post-mortem, Hassleman's body showed signs of long-term alcohol and drug abuse and his dealer — our witness — said he'd been selling cocaine to Hassleman for years, so I doubt very much it was a secret to the people he worked with. If that was the case, maybe she was worried about his drug problems and the effect it would have on the company if it was exposed? Maybe he was just getting in her way of her plans for the company. Maybe she just wanted to get hold of his shares in the company.'

Roberts nodded. 'All good motives. Well done. It'd be great if we can get a quick result on this case, Simon.'

'I've actioned getting a look at her bank and phone details. If there's something there, we'll find it.'

'Keep at it. No one's perfect. She'll have slipped up somewhere.'

'Will do, boss.'

Roberts picked up her papers again, and Wise knew he was dismissed. He stood up and walked out without a word, wondering why Walker had gone to the press first. If she was behind the murder, playing the shell-shocked CEO was a good way of trying to get the suspicion away from her or moulding the narrative in a way she wanted.

It was a ballsy move, if that was the case.

First, he needed to see the press conference. Roberts had

said Walker disclosed all the grizzly facts, but neither Wise nor Hannah had told her anything other than the bare minimum. If Walker had told the press something that only the killer and the police could know, suddenly it was going to be a whole new ball game. One Wise would win.

16

When Wise reached MIR-One, he headed straight to Sarah. 'Can you show me Emily Walker's press conference from earlier?'

Hannah joined them as Sarah tapped away at her keyboard. A YouTube video appeared on screen. 'Here we go,' she said.

They all watched Emily Walker, her black hair more conservatively styled than it had been when she'd met Wise and Hannah. Compared to the previous day's more casual attire, she was wearing a much more traditional business outfit of black jacket and skirt paired with a dark blouse.

'She looks like she got her outfit from CEOs-R-Us,' Hannah said.

Walker was flanked by two older men, both in dark suits and ties. 'And they don't look like they skateboard to meetings,' Wise said.

'Thank you for coming today,' said Walker, addressing the room. 'For the last six months, our founder, chairman and inspiration, Mark Hassleman has been on medical leave from Sparks while he dealt with some personal issues.

While we've missed his presence in the office, Sparks has continued to grow at an even faster rate than ever before, bringing online other innovative apps as well as buying the music streaming service, Waves. We intend to develop our business into an integrated virtual entertainment hub that will embrace music, television, movies and more. The future has in fact never looked brighter. It was a future we were eager to share with Mark once he'd won his battles with his demons.

'Unfortunately, yesterday afternoon, I was informed by officers from the Metropolitan Police that our founder, chairman and inspiration was murdered on his doorstep. This news has left all of us heart-broken and devastated and, while we will mourn Mark's passing, we owe it to him to continue his vision and build Sparks into the total lifestyle experience that enhances the real world with all the virtual world can provide.'

'Ms Walker,' called out a reporter. 'You mentioned that Mark was dealing with "personal issues" and was battling "demons." Normally, they are euphemisms for drug or alcohol addictions. Was Mark an addict?'

Walker conferred briefly with one of the men beside her before answering. 'Yes,' she replied. 'Mark had a cocaine addiction and, while we were understanding of the struggle he was going through, we also have a strict policy at Sparks about such things. He promised to get clean and we agreed he could return to the business when that day arrived. Unfortunately, his ... his murder means he'll never have that ... that chance.' Walker covered her eyes with her hand. 'I'm sorry. I can't ...'

One of the men put his arm around her shoulders while the other stepped forward. 'I'm afraid that's all we can say for now. We ask for your respect and understanding while everyone at Sparks comes to terms with what's happened. Thank you.'

The men then led Walker from the conference room and the recording finished.

'Well, that was something,' Wise said. 'What do you both think?'

'That was a pretty slick performance,' Hannah said. 'But most of it contradicts what she told us yesterday. Hassleman hadn't been on medical leave for six months and yesterday she claimed not to know about his drug issues.'

'We need to know what the truth is,' Wise said. 'If they did know and he was on medical leave, they'll be paperwork to back that up.'

'Could be just the usual PR bullshit,' Sarah said. 'Trying to get ahead of some bad press.'

'But for someone who cares as much about the company as Walker does, having a druggie as a boss is a good motive for wanting him gone,' Wise said.

'She didn't seem like the crying sort yesterday either,' Hannah said. 'Her tears at the drug question seemed a great way to stop any further questions rather than being genuine.'

'I'm just glad she didn't put out a reward for information,' Sarah said. 'That sort of thing only brings out the crazies.'

'But she didn't reveal any details that we didn't tell her yesterday,' Wise said. 'Did we have any luck with her phone and bank records?'

'We have got nothing from her bank yet, but we have her phone details,' Sarah said. 'But it's overwhelming. She's never off the bloody thing. Calls to all parts of the world at all times of the day and night. Hundreds of text messages too.'

'What about around the time Hassleman was killed?'

Sarah picked up a piece of paper. 'The phone was at her house and didn't go anywhere until the following morning. No text messages were sent or calls made but, if she was on a zoom call like she said, then she'd not be using her phone to call anyone else.'

'Or she went out and left her phone at home,' Hannah said.

'Did we have any luck tracking down any next of kin or partners?' Wise asked.

Sarah shook her head. 'It's as we thought yesterday — only child, dead parents, dead uncle. Unmarried. No partner. No friends from what we can see. We got his phone records, and the only person he regularly contacted was his dealer. There's the odd call to Sparks once or twice a week, but that's about it.'

Wise nodded. 'That's actually quite good for us. A big social circle means a big suspect list. Instead, we have a man whose only relationship is with his company, a company that his addictions could put in trouble.'

'What about a random crazy?' Sarah suggested. 'Someone who wants to be famous by killing someone famous like that Mark Chapman bloke who killed John Lennon.'

'This is all too well-planned,' Wise said. 'Too carefully executed. No, this is the work of someone who wanted Hassleman out of the way. Did anyone speak to Harish Vasudean?'

'Donut did,' Sarah said. 'He lives in LA. He wasn't upset to hear Hassleman was dead, but he pretty quickly started worrying about whether Sparks would continue to pay him his salary. Sounds like he had nothing to gain by Hassleman dying and a lot to lose.'

'Which brings us back to Emily Walker,' Hannah said.

'Yeah,' Wise said. I want the pair of you to get Ms Walker in to identify the body formally tomorrow, as we haven't got anyone better. Let her see what a dead man looks like and watch her reaction. Maybe you'll spot some cracks in her performance.'

'I'll call her now,' Hannah said.

'Thank you,' Wise said. 'Now, if you'll excuse me, I've got to get ready for a press conference of my own.'

'Let me know if you need a hand with your hair and makeup, Guv,' Sarah said.

'I think I'll be fine as I am,' Wise said, and headed to his office.

He closed the door and sat down behind his desk, feeling far from fine. He thought about calling Jean and saying hello. The kids would be home from school now and he'd not spoken to them in a while, either. But what would he say? And Jean would be busy sorting out dinner. The last thing she'd need was a call from him.

He'd not spoken to his dad either in a good while. He was someone else Wise was avoiding and felt damn guilty for doing so. But his dad would probably be off somewhere, seeing his friends down the social club or off having a coffee with one of his lady friends. The man had a life after all, despite being long retired.

Christ, Wise was good at coming up with excuses for his own cowardice.

Wise felt little better an hour later, sitting alone behind the desk in Kennington's media room, facing the reporters who'd been surrounding him earlier. Alone except for a press rep who hovered in the corner after giving Wise a statement to read.

At least he had his favourite suit on, looking sharp, looking like he was in control.

The paper shook in his hands so he placed it on the desk, smoothing non-existent creases out, as his stomach churned. He glanced over to the press rep, got a nod to start, but not much else.

'Thank you for coming,' Wise said. 'My name is Detective Inspector Simon Wise. I'd like to make a brief statement today — however, I will not be answering questions afterwards. We will hold a more detailed press conference in due course as the investigation progresses.' He looked up and saw faces and cameras staring back. 'On Tuesday, the eighth of March, at approximately 2325HRS, a man was killed on his doorstep by person or persons unknown. The victim is a twenty-eight-year-old male, however, the body has not yet been formally identified. As a result, we cannot make any further statements about this case. Thank you.'

A wall of noise hit Wise as he stood up. They hurled questions at him from all directions, cameras snapping, flashes popping. It took all his self-control not to run from the room.

His team cheered him when he returned to the incident room. 'They'll have you presenting the ten o'clock news after that performance,' Jono said.

'I'd rather it was Match Of The Day,' Wise said.

He walked over to the whiteboards. The team had been busy, adding a picture of Emily Walker with her name and date of birth, plus the information they'd got from Radinsky earlier about the shooter's height and weight, along with Radinsky's picture and details. There were screen shots of the motorbike messenger alongside a map showing the route to and from the car park to the murder scene.

Someone had cut out various newspaper, magazine and internet articles on Hassleman. Most proclaimed him to be a genius of sorts. A few commented on the fact he was obnoxious to go with it. A profile piece in *The Guardian* even declared he was "A brainiac from hell."

Picking up a pen, Wise wrote 'No forensics' and '9mm bullet' to the board.

It wasn't much, but the investigation was only two days old. They just needed time.

Wise stared at the picture of Hassleman at whatever event he'd been at. His team knew better than to put pictures up of the victim after they were dead. Wise found it more helpful to see the dead when they were still full of life, when they were people and not corpses.

Still, what life did Hassleman have? A recluse who's only contact with the world was with his drug dealer? All that money and he was holed up in a dark room, crouched over a glass table, poisoning himself bit by bit each day, committing slow suicide. No one to mourn him. No one to care.

'Who wanted you dead?' he asked the picture. 'Who gains now you're dead?'

He sensed someone at his shoulder, turned to see Hannah standing next to him. 'Not much, is it?'

'No, Guv. It's not,' she replied.

'It's always the same with cases like these — premeditated, organised. We're scrambling around to find something — anything — to point us in the right direction. The secret is just to keep going, being thorough, being organised ourselves and we'll get there in the end.'

'You ever have any you didn't solve?'

'Yeah. Too many. Did you know that one in five murders in London go unsolved?'

'No, I didn't.'

'It's sad but true, and I hate it when that happens. The thing about murders is that it's not just the victim that's had their life destroyed,' Wise said. 'It's everyone else that's connected to them, the victim's family and friends, colleagues even. They have to go on somehow, trying to deal with someone being ripped from their lives, unexpectedly, violently, undeservedly, trying to make sense of the senseless. The pain they feel will haunt them their entire lives and, perhaps, the only peace they'll know is if we can give them some sort of justice and put their loved one's killer behind bars.'

Images of a rooftop flashed through Wise's mind.

'If I don't do this,' Andy says, 'he told me he'd kill them.'

'Who did?' Wise takes another step forward.

'I'm sorry, Si,' Andy says. 'I'm sorry for ev—'

Who made you do it, Andy?

'By the way, I spoke to Emily Walker, Guv,' Hannah said, snapping him back to the present.

'And?' He blinked away the memories.

'We're meeting her tomorrow at 10 a.m. at the morgue. You sure you don't want to join us?'

'I have somewhere else I have to be,' Wise said. 'But let's keep the pressure on. Let's get some more facts up on these boards. We're not going to let this one become one of the unsolved cases.'

FRIDAY, 16TH SEPTEMBER

Friday, 16th September

17

The morgue at the back of King's College Hospital in Camberwell was only twenty-five minutes away from Hannah's flat in Tooting, but she allowed herself forty to be on the safe side. For once, there were no idiots determined to knock over anyone on a bike, and she only had one near miss with a pedestrian, who crossed the road without looking. As a result, she arrived at the morgue with a quarter of an hour to spare before Emily Walker was due to show up.

Despite that, she saw Sarah Choi was already waiting outside for her, smoking a cigarette the way Wise drank coffee — as if her life depended on it. Hannah parked the Ducati, climbed off, and removed her helmet. 'You got here early.'

'Yeah,' Sarah replied. 'I can't smoke at home, so it's worth standing around in the freezing cold if I can have a ciggy with no one complaining.'

'You don't still live with your parents, do you?' Hannah said, taking out her vape from her pocket.

'Just a neurotic, controlling husband.'

'Sounds wonderful,' Hannah said, before taking a quiet pull on the vape. Immediately, she felt the nicotine hit.

'Sometimes I think I'd be better off living with my parents again. At least I'd be able to smoke in relative peace,' Sarah continued. 'I'd just have to listen to my mum list out the reasons I should've been a doctor or a solicitor instead of joining the police.'

'They don't like the idea of you being a police officer, then?'

'Apparently, they didn't spend their hard-earned money on a private education just for me to become a copper.'

'How's your husband feel about it?'

'He'd rather I was at home having babies.' Sarah dragged furiously at the last remnants of her cigarette, then dropped it to the ground, grinding it out under her boot heel, where there were already several squashed butts. 'Fuck 'em all, I say.'

'Amen to that,' Hannah said.

'What about you?'

'Ah, no one tells me what to do.' Hannah smiled. Emma, her partner, was as about as easy going as someone could get. After a day bossing little kids around, the last thing she wanted to do was to make any decisions once she got home.

Sarah glared at her in mock disgust. 'I hate people like you.'

'That's okay. I'm used to it.'

'Especially in the Met, eh?'

Hannah had another drag on her vape. 'How long have you been on the team?'

'About four years now. They're a good bunch and the Governor treats us right. Respects us, you know?'

'That can be a rare thing in the Met,' Hannah said.

'Spoken with experience, eh?' Sarah said with a

knowing smile. 'I worked over in Hammersmith for a while and, every time I walked into the room, someone would shout out that they wanted the "69 special." Twats.'

Hannah laughed. She quite liked Sarah. Whatever crap she put up with at home, the small woman didn't act like she'd put up with anyone's bullshit at work. 'I had quite a few offers to straighten me out with their magic penises and, when I told them to fuck off, I was told I was a "dyke" or a "carpet muncher."'

Sarah looked up. 'And are you? A carpet muncher?'

'Is that a problem?' Hannah said, regretting sharing so much.

'Only if you want to munch on my carpet — because that's not really my thing,' Sarah said with a wink. 'My husband might be a pain in my arse, but he still knows how to ring my button.'

'No wonder you married him,' Sarah laughed. 'That's a rare gift.'

Sarah looked at her packet of fags, then at her watch. 'Fuck it. Time for one more.'

A black cab drove into the car park, Emily Walker in the back.

'Bugger,' Sarah said, putting her cigarettes away.

'Here we go,' Hannah said.

They watched Walker in a flowing black coat exit the cab and Hannah couldn't help but wonder if this woman was behind Hassleman's death — either as the shooter or as the money behind it. If she was, she seemed pretty damn cool about it all.

'Good morning, Ms Walker,' Hannah said. 'Thank you for coming this morning.'

'Is the inspector on his way?' Walker said, running her eyes over Hannah and Sarah.

'I'm afraid Inspector Wise is needed elsewhere this morning,' Hannah said. 'You just have myself and DC Choi this morning.'

Walker looked Sarah up and down. 'Aren't you too small to be a police officer?'

'We don't have height requirements anymore,' said Sarah, staring back, unfazed by the woman towering over her. 'It was a discriminatory policy.'

'I'm sure the bad guys were happy about that change,' Walker said.

'Perhaps, but not all criminals are men,' Sarah replied. 'Shall we go in?'

'By all means,' Walker said. Whatever charm she had when Hannah and Wise had met her at Sparks' office was gone. Was that because Wise wasn't there and Walker didn't feel the need to impress Hannah or Sarah, or was there another reason? Was this her true personality or was she just upset by everything that had happened? The woman was so hard to read.

They walked quickly and silently to the viewing suite, where everything was already prepared for them. Walker, Hannah and Sarah waited on one side of a window while, on the other, there was a table with Hassleman's covered body on it. An orderly stood nearby, ready to remove the cloth from the corpse's face.

The silence in the room was so acute, Hannah could hear her own heartbeat thumping away in her chest, so loud it surprised her no one else commented on it. The hairs on her arms rose in reaction to the chill in the air as her mouth went dry. She glanced at the covered body and tried to imagine Hassleman beneath it as she tried to steady her nerves. It wasn't natural to be so close to a corpse. It was almost as if every sense of her own had gone into overdrive to remind her she was alive.

'Are you ready, Ms Walker?' Hannah said, forcing the words out. A part of her wished Wise was with them. She was still so new to murder enquiries. What if she misread Walkers' reactions or forgot to ask an important question?

'As much as I'll ever be,' Walker replied, a quiver in her own voice.

Sarah leaned forward, completely unfazed, and pressed the intercom button. 'You can proceed,' she told the orderly.

The orderly had positioned Hassleman's body so that when he lifted the cloth from the corpse, only the right side of the face was visible from the viewing area. The damaged areas, where the bullet had gone in through the left cheek, and the exit wound out the back of the head were out of sight. He looked almost like he was asleep, but not quite. Hannah shivered. How many bodies like this would she need to see before it became normal?

Still, she had a job to do. She forced her eyes away from the body and glanced over at Walker. Sparks' CEO stood rooted to the spot, her eyes fixed on Hassleman, lips tight, face white even under all her makeup. Was that shock at seeing the body or shock at seeing what she'd done? Hannah didn't have a clue. She had no experience with this sort of situation before.

'Is that Mark Hassleman?' Sarah asked.

'I've never seen him looking so still before,' said Walker, her voice a whisper. 'Normally, he'd be talking at a million miles an hour, bursting with ideas and unable to sit still.'

Cocaine had that effect, thought Hannah, but she said nothing.

'Is it him?' Sarah repeated.

'Of course it's him. Of course it's him.' Walker let out a

sob a second before her legs seemed to give way on her. She would've fallen if Hannah hadn't gotten a hold of her. The woman buried her face in Hannah's shoulder and began to cry, her body heaving with each sob.

It felt uncomfortable to be holding the woman, her perfume clogging up Hannah's nostrils, all the while wondering if it was all an act to convince the police officers she had nothing to do with her boss' death. It seemed so out of character with the way she'd behaved when Wise and Hannah had first told her of Hassleman's death. She'd almost seemed glad he was gone, sharing little details of how annoying he was and the trouble he caused. Then there was the performance at the press conference. It was like three completely different people had turned up to each occasion.

When Hannah had held Walker long enough so she could let go without being insensitive, she signalled to Sarah to get the body covered again. Then she lifted Walker off her. 'Why don't you sit down and give yourself a moment to gather yourself? We just need you to sign some forms and then you can get back to other things.'

Walker looked up, her perfect eye shadow now streaked with tears. 'Thank you.'

Hannah guided her over to a row of four plastic chairs that were set against the opposite wall to the viewing window and helped her sit down. She then took a seat next to her as the orderly drew the curtain across the other side of the window, hiding Hassleman's corpse once more.

Once seated, Walker reached into a pocket and produced some tissues so she could dab at her eyes and wipe some of the makeup away. Even so, Hannah could see some of the steel return to the woman.

Sarah brought over a clipboard with the formal

identification documents. 'If you could just sign here and here, confirming the body as Mark Hassleman.'

Walker took the forms, and an offered biro, and duly signed the paperwork.

'Thank you,' Sarah said and left the room, leaving Hannah and Walker alone.

'He's really dead, isn't he?' Walker said, her eyes fixed on the glass. 'He's really fucking dead.'

'I'm afraid so,' Hannah said.

Walker shook her head. 'Typical Mark. Even dead, he's really fucking things up.'

'In what way?' Hannah asked, keeping her voice low. Walker still hadn't looked at her.

'The bloody idiot didn't leave a will. Of course he didn't. He lived like he was the only person in the world. No one else mattered. Only himself. And now, he's still fucking things up.'

'No will?'

'No — because that would be too bloody grown up and responsible.' Walker looked down at the tissues in her hand and shook her head. 'Right. I should get back. Someone needs to sort out this mess.'

'Before you go,' Hannah said, 'can I ask what happens to Mr Hassleman's estate if there's no will?'

Walker turned to face her at last. 'His estate passes to the Crown, of all things. It's called *"bona vacantia"* or some such medieval nonsense, so we're in limbo for now. When they're ready, we'll have to deal with them and try to buy his shares back. Otherwise, they can sell them to who they want when the time comes. The fool's really screwed us over by getting himself killed. Absolutely screwed us.' There was a twitch in her face, of anger perhaps. No matter how matter-of-fact she tried to make things sound, it was obvious this wasn't what she had expected.

'I'm sorry to hear that,' Hannah said. 'Had you ever spoken to him about his estate before?'

'No. More fool me.' Walker stood up and brushed herself down with her hands. 'Anyway, it is what it is. For now, we can carry on as normal, but it makes any expansion plans we had all but impossible to carry out for now. All my hard work just ...'

'Does anyone gain anything by stopping Sparks in its tracks?'

'That list is almost endless,' Walker said. 'Any of the big tech giants. All the small up-and-comers. We're like sharks — if we're not moving forward, then we're dead. Taking us out of the game opens up more opportunity for the rest of them.' She shook her head. 'If any of them were behind Mark's murder, it was a checkmate move.'

'And illegal,' Hannah said, because Walker sounded impressed all of a sudden.

Walker looked at Hannah like she was an idiot. 'A detail that's easy to overlook when there're billions at stake.'

'Of course.' Hannah got to her feet, her mind whirring. If Walker really thought that, she was a serious suspect again. The fact that Hassleman's estate had gone to the crown worked in her favour. The crown would be easier to deal with than an heir to buy the shares from. All Walker had to do was be patient.

'You'll keep me informed of how you get on?'

'We will,' Hannah said. 'Thank you for your time again, Ms Walker. We'll be in touch if we have any more questions.'

Walker nodded, all business again. 'I hope you catch whoever did this. Mark might have been an arse, but he was our arse. He didn't deserve to end up like that.'

Hannah nodded, not convinced Walker meant a word of it. 'I'll show you out.'

When they got outside, Sarah was on the phone. Walker didn't stop, though. She just headed straight out into the street and hailed a black cab as if it were any other day of the week. She was some piece of work all right, but was she a killer?

When Hannah turned back, Sarah was finishing her call. 'Right. We'll be in right away.'

'What is it?' Hannah said when Sarah had hung up.

'The Guv wants us back at Kennington right away.'

18

W ise sat in Doctor Shaw's office, as he had every Friday morning since Andy had died, eyes burning from yet another fitful night's sleep and the warm, orange glow of Shaw's interior lighting was doing little to help his overall fatigue. And it was still dark outside and raining cats and dogs just to add to the mood. At least, he had a large Starbucks in his hand, and a good suit on to cover the cracks.

He glanced at the wall clock. 8 a.m. Sarah and Hannah would be meeting Emily Walker at the morgue right about then. He felt a pang of guilt for not being with them. Instead, he was in his police-appointed psychiatrist's office near Waterloo to chat about his feelings.

'How are you, Simon?' Doctor Shaw asked, her voice like honey. They were both in armchairs in front of her desk, a nice Persian rug underfoot. In her mid-forties, her brown, corkscrew hair with hints of grey fell around her shoulders, accentuating her sharp blue eyes that seemed to see everything in a manner that suggested she wouldn't panic even if the world was about to end. Probably a good thing in her profession. In particular, she worked with a lot of police officers who were breaking or broken. Wise wasn't sure which category he fell into, but then again, neither were good, so he supposed it didn't really matter.

'I'm fine,' Wise said. 'Well, as fine as can be expected.'

'You look tired.'

'We're busy at work.'

Shaw raised an eyebrow in that way of hers that called bullshit on his bullshit. They'd been having these chats ever since Andy had died after all and knew Wise well enough now to not let him get away with most things.

He took a gulp of coffee. 'I've not been sleeping much either.'

'You still having the nightmares?'

'All the time,' Wise said. 'Every night. All night. Even during the day. When I'm on the job. When I'm at home. Driving the car.'

'Andy.' Shaw managed to convey so much sympathy in the way she said his name. It was quite incredible. Wise always thought he had a way of being empathic with people, but Shaw was in a different class altogether.

'Yes. Andy. That night. The roof. The bullet. All of it.'

Andy tumbles forward, red mist leading the way, his brains and blood already splattered across the rooftop.

'It's understandable. It's only been a few months since he died.' Shaw picked up her cup of green tea and took a sip. It had irked Wise at first that she drank something so calming, so tranquil, especially so bloody early in the morning, when he needed electric jump cables fixed to his brain to get going, but he appreciated it now. She was someone who had her shit together, after all. She didn't need the crutches that people like Wise needed.

'Yesterday, I wished I could just forget Andy and get back to normal — whatever normal is,' Wise said.

'How did that make you feel?'

'Guilty as hell. Andy was my friend — my mate. I don't want to forget him. I just want remembering him not to hurt so much.'

Shaw smiled. 'It'll happen. Unfortunately, it takes time, though. There's no switch you can throw. No pill to take. Just time.'

'I know. I've been through this before. But it doesn't make this anymore frustrating to deal with. I mean, I hate feeling like this and what it does to me.'

'What does it do to you?'

Wise sighed and placed his Starbucks on the side table next to his chair. He needed his hands free. 'It distracts me. It upsets me. It makes me angry. It makes me push everyone that loves me away. It makes me hide from them. It makes me feel weak.'

'There's nothing wrong with feeling weak,' Shaw said. 'It tells us we're human, that we care. It's a good thing.'

'Maybe in your profession. Not mine.'

'We are more than our jobs, Simon,' Shaw said. 'How we earn our living should only be a small part of what makes us who we are.'

'It's all I have. It's all I am.'

'Really.' Once again, the eyebrow popped up to signal "bullshit detected." 'What about the other roles you have? Husband, father, son, brother, friend, teacher — the list goes on. They're all important. They all matter.'

Wise shook his head, then realised he was clenching his fists. He forced them open and picked up the white Starbucks cup again. 'I'm not a brother anymore.'

'I thought you said you had a twin — Tom, wasn't it?'

'I do, but we don't speak anymore — or rather, he doesn't speak to me anymore. We fell out. Twenty years ago.'

'What over?'

'Nothing. Everything.' Death. Betrayal. Prison. All the good stuff. Wise took another gulp of coffee and winced at how bitter it suddenly was.

At least Shaw's eyebrows stayed level. 'Have you tried to reconcile things with him?'

'A long time ago. It didn't end well.'

'This is your fault. You did this. You bastard!' Tom shouts as the prison guards haul him back, hate in his eyes.

'Perhaps it's time to try again? Time—'

'—won't make a difference. Some wounds are just too deep.'

'You still miss him, though.'

Wise laughed. 'Of course I do. Every day. More so now since ...' Wise's voice trailed off.

Andy lands on the concrete with a wet thud and lies unmoving, his eyes open and fixed on Wise, a hole in the side of his temple where the red dot had been.

'We shared a womb, for God's sake. We did everything together growing up. Everything. It was us against the world when our mum died. Until it wasn't.'

'Was Andy a replacement for Tom?' Shaw asked.

'I don't know. No. Yes. Maybe.' Wise rolled his neck, feeling uncomfortable. He hated talking about Tom. The memories of that night were far worse than what had happened to Andy. After all, with Andy, he'd been trying to stop things. With Tom, he'd been involved. More than involved. And he'd loved it.

He glanced at his watch. How long had he been here now? How long before he could leave?

'We've still got some time left,' Shaw said. 'Don't worry.'

'Sorry, but I have a lot on at work. I should get back to the nick.'

Shaw leaned forward. 'Simon, burying things instead of dealing with them might work for a while. Keeping yourself busy might help you not think about them for a while. But our minds know what we're doing and they fight back. It might be with feelings of guilt, or sadness or anger. It might be through dreams and memories.' The eyebrow popped up again. 'Our minds fight back until we stop running and avoiding and pretending. It's only when we acknowledge what's upsetting us and start doing something about it we can heal.'

'I think you might have mentioned that once or twice,' Wise said.

'And I will keep mentioning it until you hear me.' Shaw smiled. 'You'll be much happier once you do. I promise you that.'

Wise nodded. 'We've got a new detective on the team. A replacement for Andy. She joined on Wednesday.'

'And how do you feel about that?'

'Resentful at first. My boss didn't ask me if I wanted the help.'

'Why was that?'

'Because I would've said no.'

'Why would you do that?'

Wise smiled. Shaw reminded him of his kids when they were at the age where every answer was met by another question. It used to drive him mad then. Now he kind of missed when they thought he knew all the answers. 'Replacing Andy feels like we're admitting his gone, that we're not coping without him.'

Up went the eyebrow. 'But he is gone. You're not coping.'

'I don't want the team to know that.'

'Have you thought that, perhaps, a new person joining the team will help you all move on?' Shaw said.

'What if I don't want to move on?' Wise replied.

'How's that working out for you so far?'

'Not good.'

Shaw smiled. Wise knew it wasn't because she was amused by what he said. Instead, it was a smile full of kindness, of care, lacking judgement. It made him want to cry.

The clock tinged. The hour was up. Both Wise and Shaw rose together.

'Thank you for your time,' Wise said, grateful to be getting away. Talking to her made him feel better, and he wasn't ready for that. He didn't deserve it. There was still a price he had to pay for what happened.

'Be kind to yourself, Simon,' Shaw said.

Wise smiled. 'I'll try.'

Doctor Shaw's office was near Waterloo station and a ten-minute walk from Kennington. The rain had eased enough, so Wise didn't bother trying to get a cab. Instead, pulling the collar of his raincoat up high around his neck, he crossed over Waterloo Road by the Old Vic and headed down by the Millennium Gardens, along Baylis Road towards Lambeth North tube.

He always liked this part of London. There was nothing really to attract the tourists and most of the office buildings went up in the Seventies when function was all anyone cared about. Tower blocks and terraced housing rubbed up against building sites and unpretentious, more modern structures. There was certainly nothing in sight that would trouble any architecture awards.

The sky was a mottled bruise, spitting down the type of rain that didn't really get you wet but could irritate you if you let it. People hustled by as they rushed to work or to catch trains or tubes, hunkered down under umbrellas, uncaring of who might be in their way. Wise weaved his way through, trying to avoid getting his eyes poked out, thinking of what Doctor Shaw had said.

The situation with Tom would never be fixed, no matter how much he might want it to be. It had been twenty years, after all. Wise had to accept that and move on.

Shaw had been right about Andy, too. He had been his replacement brother in so many ways and his betrayal of all that they believed in hurt, but it was the fact that Andy hadn't come to Wise for help that really cut deep. If he had, they could've fixed things together long before a sniper's bullet put a stop to everything.

He pulled out his phone and dialled Jono.

'Guv?' Jono answered.

'Yeah. Quick one. Do you know anyone in SCO10?' Wise asked.

'SCO10?'

'Yeah.'

'Hmmm.' Wise could hear Jono sucking on his lips. 'Didn't Brendan Murray work for that mob?'

'From Kilburn?'

'Yeah, that's the one. He reckons he looks like Richard Gere if you squint hard enough.' Jono chuckled.

'Good. Do you know him well enough to ask a favour?' Wise asked.

Jono paused for just a moment. 'Depends what type of favour it is,' he said, his voice full of caution.

'They're investigating who was behind trying to get Derrick Morris whacked, and I want to know how they're getting on.'

'That was Andy, Guv.'

'Yeah, but Andy was working for someone. That's who they're after. That's who I want to know about.'

There was another pause. Wise passed a Costa and resisted the urge to get another coffee. The rain on his face was doing a good enough job of waking him up. He jogged across the street and turned left down Kennington Road and past the Hercules pub.

'I'll make the call, Guv,' Jono said eventually.

'Cheers, mate. I'll see you soon.' Wise ended the call.

He was nearly at the station when his phone rang again. He looked at the screen, but the caller had withheld their number. 'DI Wise,' he said on answering.

'Oh, hi,' a man said with a thick Yorkshire accent said. 'This is DCI Barry Samson, from up at the Embankment.'

Wise stopped walking, all his attention on the voice in his ear. The Embankment was New Scotland Yard. 'How can I help you?'

'I hear you're investigating that shooting on Elgin Crescent. Of that tech guy?'

'Yeah, that's right. Mark Hassleman.'

'I was just passed the details and I think we should probably chat.'

'Sure,' Wise said, 'but do you mind telling me why?'

'Because I'm investigating a similar murder that took place three days before yours,' Samson said. 'Someone posing as a motorbike messenger shot a billionaire on his doorstep in Eaton Square.'

Wise felt a surge of adrenaline. 'When can we talk?'

19

R oberts came with Wise to the Embankment. 'Always good to have someone of equal rank there, Simon,' she'd said, and Wise couldn't argue with that. Every visit to the Embankment was political and Roberts thrived in those situations.

It took ten minutes to navigate their way through security before they were sitting with DCI Barry Samson in a dark, windowless meeting room. The DCI was a small, squat man with thick glasses, thinning grey hair and a strong Yorkshire accent and looked close to retirement age. There was a stain on his tie that could've come from an egg and his shirt had sweat marks under the armpit. To say the man was unimpressive was an understatement. However, the thick folder in front of him kept drawing Wise's attention.

'Nice to meet you both,' Samson said. 'Hopefully, I haven't dragged you down for nought.' He ran his eyes up and down Wise as if measuring him up. It was something that had become more and more common since Andy had died. As Hannah had said, everyone knew what had happened and everyone had an opinion — for good or bad. It made him wonder what side Samson fell on.

'It didn't sound like it was nothing on the phone,' Wise said, eager to get the meeting going and onto what was in the man's folder.

'I read the report that was passed to me,' Samson said, 'but do you mind going over your murder first? Just so I'm clear on what you're dealing with.'

Wise would rather have heard about Samson's case first, but he dutifully went over where they were with the Hassleman investigation.

Samson leaned back in his chair. 'Have you uncovered any connection between the victim and Russia?'

'Russia?' Roberts said. 'What's that got to do with anything?'

Samson pursed his lips. 'Could be nothing. Could be everything.'

'I'm sorry, but you might have to be less cryptic,' Wise said.

'Have you heard of Yuri Andronovitch?' Samson asked.

'The name's familiar,' Roberts said, 'but that's all.'

'No,' Wise said.

'Yuri Andronovitch was born in Russia but moved to London in 2005. He became a UK citizen in 2012,' Samson said, removing a photograph from the folder. It showed a Caucasian man with a squat neck, deep-set eyes and a widow's peak for hair. He looked to be in his late sixties. 'His exact net worth is unknown, but it is rumoured to be around the three billion dollar mark. He made his money in oil and steel, following the breakup of the Soviet Union when, if you believe the tabloids, he was Putin's best friend from his

KGB days. Since then, he's dabbled in everything from basketball teams in the States to TV stations in Turkey. He avoided sanctions after Russia's invasion of Ukraine, but that was most likely because he has friends in very high places.'

'How high?' Wise asked.

'About as high as you can go.'

Wise glanced at Roberts. 'Right — but how does he connect to our case?'

'Six days ago, Andronovitch was at his home in Eaton Square, alone, when someone knocked on his door,' Samson said. 'When he answered it, he was shot in the head at point blank range.' He removed another photograph, taken on a pathologist's metal examination table. The eyes were now shut and there was a bullet entry point near the man's hairline.

'Shit,' Wise said.

'Exactly. Now watch this.' Samson turned on the TV that was mounted to the wall. A distorted image appeared that showed a point-of-view from high up, overlooking a front doorstep and the road behind. A time stamp in the top corner said 22:30. 'This is from Andronovitch's security camera, covering the front door.'

Samson hit play, and the scene came to life. Nothing happened for a few moments and then a motorbike pulled up outside the house.

Wise sat forward, feeling excitement nibble away in his gut. It looked like the same bike and rider from the CCTV footage from the corner of Elgin Crescent and Kensington Park Road.

The person driving wore all black, with a plain black helmet. They got off the bike and walked up to the front door. From what Wise could see, the rider was of similar height and build to their suspect. A black messenger bag was slung over the rider's shoulder, resting on his left hip.

The messenger stopped, with their helmet obscuring most of the camera's viewpoint. The clock said 22:33.

'Now, I presume the messenger knew the camera was there,' Samson said. 'And he's blocking the camera on purpose.'

The messenger moved, the helmet coming more fully into frame again and, a second later, there was a brief flash.

'That's when they shot Andronovitch,' Samson said. The messenger bent down out of frame, then straightened before returning to their bike and driving off. The clock said 22:35 by the time it was all over. 'All over and done within five minutes. And, like you, we didn't find any shell casing, and the killer left no forensic evidence whatsoever.'

Wise couldn't believe what he'd just watched. 'Can you replay that again?'

'Sure,' Samson said and hit play.

'And this was on Sunday night?' Wise said, with no doubt they were watching the same killer at work.

'Yep,' Samson said.

'Is it the same bike?' Roberts asked, her face grim.

'Honda PCX Scooter like yours. Different number plate but stolen like yours,' Samson said.

Wise couldn't take his eyes off the screen. 'Do you know where they go next?'

'To a point,' Samson said. 'We tracked the rider along Lower Belgrave Street into Ebury Street and into the Victoria car park. They had vandalised the CCTV inside the car park earlier that day, so we have no footage of the rider from that point — where the bike and rider simply disappear.'

Samson turned off the TV. 'And there you have it. Same MO. Same bike. Same escape.'

'What calibre bullet?' Roberts asked.

'Nine millimetre,' Samson replied. 'The same.'

'Any idea of motive?' Wise asked.

Samson rolled his neck. 'Well, that's why I asked you about Russia. You see, on the surface, this case looks pretty cut and dried. Russian billionaire living in London, a one-time friend of Putin's, gets shot in a well-planned, professional assassination. He's obviously pissed off his mate, Vladimir, or someone connected to him and then it's bye bye Vienna.'

'Do you think this was a political assassination?' Roberts asked.

'It's not so far-fetched. There have been over fourteen suspected murders of prominent Russians or people who worked with Russia in the UK over the last ten years. Most of the time, it's made to look like an accident. They fall out of windows or jump in front of trains — things like that. A few have been poisoned. Hardly anyone has ever been shot, but it's happened,' Samson said. 'The Andronovitch has all the hallmarks of a being one of those — until you turned up with this other murder. Obviously, this complicates things.'

'How?' Wise asked.

Samson scratched his belly and smoothed his tie. 'Can I be honest with both of you?'

'Of course,' Wise said. Somehow, he knew he wouldn't like what he heard next.

'And I'll deny what I'm going to tell you if you repeat it outside of these four walls,' Samson added, just to confirm this wouldn't be good news.

'Go on,' Roberts said with a sigh.

'I head up a team that specialises in political killings in

this country,' Samson said. 'It's a very small team — of me, myself and I.'

'What?' Wise said, confused. 'How can you get anything done?'

'Easily — because my job isn't to solve any crimes. What I do is brush everything under the carpet and put whatever else I find into a big folder marked "unsolved." That's then shut away in a filing cabinet until it's forgotten about,' Samson said. 'The official government position is that there are no political murders in the UK. If some Russian banker gets thrown out of a window, then they fell by accident or committed suicide. If a dissident gets run over by a car, then they stepped out in front of the car and certainly weren't pushed. It's better for all concerned that way.'

'How can that be better?' Wise said.

'Look, normally the assassin is in and out of the country within twenty-four hours. Once they're back in Moscow, then they're safe. Anything we try after that point is just embarrassing for all concerned,' Samson said. 'Sometimes, Putin makes a very public statement, like in the Skripal case, where he gets out some poison or a radioactive isotope to bump off whoever he's had enough of and then something has to be said. With the attempt on Skripal, Theresa May made us name the killers to show we weren't completely useless and the next day, Putin had them on TV talking about how they merely wanted to go sightseeing in Salisbury, openly taking the piss out of us and making it clear he didn't give a shit what we say or do.'

'But we imposed sanctions after that attack,' Roberts said.

'All huff and puff,' said Samson. 'The reality is that Russian money has been pumped into the UK for so long now we can't survive without it. Even when they interfere in our elections, we just shrug and deny it ever happened.'

'That's fucking ridiculous,' Wise said.

Samson held up his hands. 'I'm just telling you the facts of life.'

'So where does that leave us now?' Wise said.

'If Putin is behind Hassleman's death, I'll take over your investigation,' Samson said.

'Close it down, you mean,' Wise snapped back, all his excitement from earlier gone in a puff of smoke.

'Oi,' Samson said, pointing a stubby finger at Wise. 'Reel your neck in, son. We all have the same bosses. Don't be naïve about all this. I didn't say I was any happier than you are about any of this — so don't get shirty with me.'

Roberts put a hand on Wise's arm before he could reply. 'And if Putin's not behind the killings?'

'You can take over the Andronovitch case with my blessing.'

'Which you've done no work on for the last six days,' Wise said. 'If my team takes it over, we'll be starting from scratch almost, sniffing around a trail long gone cold.' He shook his head, thinking about all the evidence that could've been lost in that time.

'Simon,' Roberts warned. 'We're all on the same side here.'

Wise said nothing. It was better that way.

'So,' Roberts said. 'Back to my original question — do you think these murders are Putin's work?'

'They could be,' Samson said, 'but the gun bothers me.'

'In what way?'

'As I said, normally people he doesn't like have "accidents." Easier to deny the Russians have murdered them. Then we have the exotic poisonings of course, but Putin's boys haven't shot anyone in the UK before. Perhaps, Andronovitch was hard to kill any other way but Hassleman? By the sounds of it, the killer could've gone around his house, given him a big brick of dodgy cocaine and that would've been it. No one would've blinked an eyelid at a rich druggy dying of an overdose.'

'Whoever did this wanted to make a statement by making both deaths public,' Roberts said.

'But why? If Andronovitch had fallen out of his bedroom window, everyone who mattered would've known it was no accident but Hassleman? He ran an online dating site,' Samson said. 'From the googling I did before I called you, he's not outspoken about politics, especially Russian politics. He just enjoys winding people up on Twitter and doing drugs — so why kill him? Then, there's the timings of the killings.'

'Timings?' Wise said.

'Yeah, timings,' Samson repeated. 'Putin could've sent one hitman to kill both men, but why wait the three days between murders? Why not bump them off the same night and get the hell out of Dodge? Why risk hanging around? It makes little sense.'

Wise couldn't deny the man had a point. 'But there has to be a connection between the two men. It's too much of a connection to believe two separate people didn't hire the same hitman to kill Andronovitch and Hassleman in the same week. At the most, there's one client, one killer.'

'Which brings us back to Putin,' Samson said.

Wise rubbed his face, feeling ever so tired. 'Can we at least have access to what you have on Andronovitch for now so we can start digging for connections between the two men?'

Samson shook his head. 'Don't hate me, but you can take the CCTV footage and PM reports, but that's it. No bank records. No phone records. Nothing to do with his business dealings or relationships. They certainly don't want anyone being interviewed about what Andronovitch might or might not have been up to with them.'

'You have got to be joking?' Wise spat the words out, feeling his anger turn to fury. They might as well tie his hands together and blindfold him as well. 'Even if we prove these killings have nothing to do with Russia?'

'I don't like it either, but there's no way anyone is going to let you ask a former Prime Minister if he knows of any reason someone would want Andronovitch dead. And even if you talked to him, he'd only lie to you.'

'What about Andronovitch's family?' Wise asked.

'The wife and children are in Moscow. They were visiting family when Yuri was killed,' Samson said.

'So who can we talk to? This is rid—'

Roberts put a hand on Wise's arm before he could say any more, ever the politician. 'We understand,' she said. 'And we appreciate you being so candid with us.'

Wise sat back, not appreciating anything, and concentrated on his breathing. Losing his temper wasn't going to help anyone.

'It was the least I could do,' Samson said. 'And I have your word that if you find a Russian connection, you'll pass your case over to me?'

'You do.' Roberts stood up. 'We'd best be off. We've taken up enough of your time.'

Both Samson and Wise got to their feet. Samson shook Roberts' hand first then turned to Wise, holding out his hand. 'I didn't mean to be an arse.'

Wise shook it. 'It is what it is.'

Wise and Roberts left the meeting room and weaved their way back through the building to the street.

'Thank you for not causing a scene back there,' Roberts said as they made their way down an escalator. 'After everything that happened with Andy, we need friends.'

'I know,' Wise said. 'It's just frustrating.'

'It's just politics.'

'I've never been good at playing that game.'

'This other murder changes things though, doesn't it?' They walked over to the security desk and returned their visitor passes.

Wise nodded. 'The connection between Andronovitch and Hassleman is everything now. I could see Hassleman being killed for business reasons easily enough, but Andronovitch, as far as we know, has no involvement in Sparks — unless he's an investor of sorts. I'll get the team looking at that straight away.'

'You've got to admire the confidence of the killer, though, the efficiency,' Roberts said as they stepped outside. The London Eye stared at them from the other side of the Thames, next to the curve of County Hall. A sharp wind rippled the surface of the river and they could hear the excited chatter of tourists waiting to board their river cruises. 'It makes you think it might well be the work of a real professional.'

'A Russian James Bond, you mean?' Wise said. 'God, I hope not. I really hope not. I don't want to hand this over to Samson to drop in his desk drawer and forget about it all. Hassleman, for all his faults and failings, deserves some justice.'

They walked towards Westminster Bridge and the Houses of Parliament, old London in all its glory. 'It might be better for us if it is,' Roberts said, nodding towards the old buildings. 'The sort of friends Andronovitch has will only make our jobs harder. They'll want progress and they want it quickly.'

'I don't care,' Wise said. 'I'm not giving up.'

20

I t was a full house in MIR-One. Roberts sat on one side while Wise showed the CCTV footage of Andronovitch being murdered.

'Bloody hell,' Hicksy said when the clip finished. 'It's identical to ours.'

'That's right,' Wise said. 'A billionaire shot in the head by a motorbike messenger late at night. The bullet is a nine millimetre like the one used in Hassleman's murder. Let's get forensics to confirm the same gun fired them.'

'I'll see to that,' Sarah said.

'Good. I also want you checking the CCTV footage around the Victoria car park on Ebury Street. Our killer did another disappearing act again, so we need to find vehicles that can carry the bike in the back without it being seen. Now we have two locations, hopefully we can spot the same vehicle at both car parks. Donut can help you.'

'Great,' Sarah said, sounding less than enthused.

'Callum,' Wise said next. 'Let's dig up what we can on Andronovitch. He donated a lot of money to the Conservative party and wined and dined with the upper echelons so we've been told not to go asking questions about his business dealings and with the Tories in particular …'

'That's bullshit,' Jono said.

Wise held up a hand. 'It is what it is. But someone this rich won't be invisible. There'll be stuff online we can find out. Let's crawl through what there is and build a picture of his life and who he interacts with. In particular, I want to see if there's any connection between Hassleman and Andronovitch or Sparks and Andronovitch. Is he an investor in the company, for example? Or an investor in a rival company? Someone wanted these two men out of the way. Why? Who profits from their deaths?'

'Guv,' Hannah said. 'We spoke to Emily Walker earlier at the morgue when she formally identified Hassleman's body. She said Hassleman had no will and no heirs, so everything he owns goes to the government, including his shares in Sparks and it's really screwed things up for the company. It really pissed her off. I spoke to Hassleman's solicitors, and they confirmed what she said. The government will sell his shares eventually, but it'll be up for auction. Anyone could buy them.'

'She seemed really upset when she saw her boss' body as well,' Sarah added. 'I don't think she's behind this.'

Wise nodded. 'All the same, let's see if Emily Walker knows Andronovitch and check where she was the night of the murder. And let's look into her financials. Paying for one hit is expensive, let alone paying for two.

'And if Hassleman's shares go up for auction, who would buy them? Let's find out who the interested parties will be and let's see if we can connect them to Andronovitch, too.

'We also need to see if Hassleman has pissed anyone off in Russia itself. Find out his position on the Ukraine war for instance. In his online trolling, was he having a pop at Putin? We need anything that links these two men together.'

Wise looked into the eyes of all his team. 'This is a tough case. Make no mistake about it. We're dealing with two very well-planned and executed killings here. But now we have two murders to investigate, we have to find the connection points.' He drew a Venn diagram on the whiteboard and wrote Andronovitch's name above one circle and Hassleman's name over the other. He tapped the pen against the over-lapping parts of the circles. 'Whatever fits here will guide us to our killer.'

There was a buzz of excitement amongst the team.

'Now, let's get to work.'

The meeting broke up. Roberts gave him a nod. 'Well done. Keep me updated with your progress.'

'Will do, boss.' Wise turned and saw Jono motioning him over.

'What have you got?' He asked, joining the other detective by his desk.

'About the other business, Guv,' Jono said. 'I made a call to Brendan.'

'And?'

'I'm not saying he told me to fuck off but he might as well have done. I even offered to buy him a drink or two and he got really arsey with me.' Jono glanced around as if he worried anyone might overhear the conversation. 'Whatever they are working on, they have it locked up tight.'

'Alright,' Wise said, disappointed but not surprised. 'Thanks for trying anyway.'

'Sorry, Guv.'

Wise patted Jono on the shoulder. 'Cheers anyway.' He left the detective and headed over to Hannah. 'Fancy a ride out to Eaton Square? I'd like to take a look at the murder scene.'

'Sure.' She jumped up from her desk and Wise wondered when he'd last been that keen.

It took just over twenty minutes to drive the two and a half miles to Eaton Square in the heart of Belgravia, a place that was a million miles from Kennington's grime and grit. There were no working class homes tucked around the corner here, no dodgy bookies or all-night off-licenses. Even the air smelt of money.

'Back in 2016,' Hannah read off her phone, 'this was dubbed "the most expensive place to buy property in Britain." The average house is over twenty million quid.'

'Bloody hell,' Wise said.

'Wikipedia actually has a list of which rich person lives in which house. Even Andronovitch's place is listed,' Hannah read on. 'I don't even think he's the wealthiest person in the street if this is accurate — nor the only Russian.' She read off some of the names, a mix of royalty, celebrities and well-known political figures. 'The first block was built in 1827 by the Grosvenor family and named after their manor house in Cheshire.'

Looking around, it was easy to see not much had changed since then. If it wasn't for the cars parked along the side of the streets, Wise and Hannah could have travelled back in time. He half expected to see a horse and trap turn around the corner. Large gardens formed the centre of the square, one of which included a full-size tennis court.

The houses were white, Georgian, three-stories high, with pillars evenly spaced along the front of the terrace and protected by black, iron railings. The trees from the garden that over-hung the pavement on the opposite side of the road were shedding their leaves in the autumn wind, leaving a mushy carpet of yellow underfoot.

Even the street lamps were from a century long gone.

Wise found Andronovitch's house and slipped the Mondeo into a parking spot. Getting out, he ignored the parking metre and headed over to the house, Hannah following on.

A uniform police officer was stationed outside and Wise showed her his warrant card. 'You all alone?' he asked.

'Yes, sir,' replied the officer. 'And today's my last day here. DCI Samson wanted someone here to keep an eye on anyone who came for a look-see.'

'Well, you can tell him I came for a look-see,' Wise said with a smile. He nodded towards the door. 'I don't suppose you have the keys to the inside.'

'No, sir. I don't.' She glanced back at the black door. 'I'm not sure if any of our lot do either. I've never seen it open. Even when the SOCOs were here.'

'Really?' Wise said. That was odd. Normally, searching the inside of a victim's home would be the first thing detectives would do at a murder scene.

Hannah pointed to a small, round black globe fixed above the door. It was only slightly bigger than a tennis ball. 'That's the camera.'

'Pretty hard to spot if you're just walking by,' Wise said. He looked up and down the street. There were no pedestrians in sight. 'Quiet around here. No real foot traffic.'

He walked away from the uniform and crossed over the road to the garden-side pavement, then turned to look at the house.

'What are you thinking?' Hannah said, joining him.

'Our killer is prepared. Organised. They stole the motorbike number plates a month ago. They did their disappearing acts in car parks after disabling the CCTV in them.' Wise pointed to the camera — or rather where they knew it to be as they couldn't see it from their position ten yards away. 'They knew the camera was there and that Andronovitch was alone in the house. That means they staked the place out and did their research. Nothing was left to chance.'

'Easy enough to do if you're dressed up as a messenger,' Hannah said.

'Perhaps. But the same messenger turning up time and time again? That would get people suspicious. I would imagine the residents of this street are all very security aware.'

'What if they came here in different guises each time?'

'Yeah — or they fit in this world and no one would bat an eyelid if they saw them walking by.'

'You think one of Andronovitch's neighbours killed him?' Hannah said.

'Maybe not someone who lives in this street, but I think they're very comfortable in this world,' Wise said. 'They belong here.'

21

It might be late, but Sir Harry Clarke was damn glad he'd flown back from New York instead of staying on another night. There wasn't a hotel in the world that could compare to the simple pleasures of being home and sleeping in his own bed.

He had a feeling he'd be in a minority, but Harry had loved being locked down during the pandemic. No trips. No days lost travelling to and from airports, packing and unpacking here, there and everywhere, explaining to people how to make the perfect cup of tea and no, he didn't want cream in it or a slice of bloody lemon.

Once Sabine, his PA, had shown him how to do video conferences, he'd taken to it like a duck to water, an old dog with a new trick that he was damn proud of. It was a shame it was all over and things were going back to the old ways of meet and greets, fine wines and racking up the air miles. A dream life, some might think, but not him. Not Harry. At seventy-two, he'd had his fill and now it was all just a ball ache.

Especially this last trip.

As his limousine made its way into central London from the M4, Harry leaned back in his seat in the rear of the car and closed his eyes. It'd been a brutal three days in New York, battling jet lag as he ran from one meeting to the next, from the moment he'd landed on Tuesday morning until it was time to leave that morning. At least the day flight on the way back had gotten him into Heathrow at 9:30 p.m. and now he was nearly home.

Harry glanced at his watch. He'd be home by 11, time for a cheeky scotch, shower and in bed by 11:30. Maybe topped off with a sleeping tablet so he could get a good eight or nine hours' sleep before anyone bothered him in the morning.

A part of him regretted agreeing to lunch with Laura, David and the grandkids. Another meal out and the kids making a dreadful racket was the last thing he needed, but at least they were eating at San Frediano's. Their Pollo Milanese would make getting up and out of the house worthwhile.

Then again, the way things were with David, maybe it wasn't such a good idea. It'd been a mistake giving his son-in-law such a prominent position in the firm, but Laura had insisted and he'd never been able to say no to his daughter. Harry had done his best to guide the man, but David always thought he knew best and never wanted to listen. In the end, Harry had to act in the best interests of the company, no matter how upset Laura would get.

Harry glanced out the window at the rain-soaked streets of London. They were on the Cromwell Road now, five or ten minutes from home. Maybe tomorrow he could pop over to Harrods, pick up some little bits and pieces from the Food Hall. After a week of giant American meals, he quite fancied snacking his way through the weekend.

His phone chirped from inside his suit jacket. Harry pulled it out and saw David's name on the caller ID. What the hell was he doing calling at that time of night? God, he hoped nothing had happened to Laura or the kids.

'David,' he said on answering. 'Everything okay?'

'Hi, Harry.' His son-in-law's voice sounded muffled. 'Just wanted to check that you'd got back with no problems.'

Harry sighed. 'I thought you were ringing because something had happened to Laura or the kids.'

'No, no, they're fine. They're all excited to see you tomorrow.'

'That's good. I'm looking forward to seeing them too.' Harry saw Harrods up ahead as the driver turned into Hans Place. Harry could see his house up ahead, almost taste the whisky that waited inside. 'Where are you calling from? You sound like you've got your hand over your mouth.'

'Sorry. I'm in the study,' David said. 'It must be the line.'

'Well, it's late. I'm tired. I'll see you and the kids tomorrow.' Harry cut the call, knowing he was being rude, but he was too exhausted to care about polite small talk. He put the phone down on the seat next to him and closed his eyes again. God, he needed that whiskey.

'We're here, sir,' Samir, his driver, said.

Harry opened his eyes again. Thank God for that. The car passed a motorbike messenger parked in the spot next to Harry's house, slid to a halt next to the kerb and he was home.

'Thanks, Samir,' said Harry to the driver as he opened Harry's passenger door. 'Apologies for the late pick up.'

'Always a pleasure, Sir Harry,' said Samir. 'Let me get your bags for you.'

Harry waited while Samir opened the boot. It was still desperately trying to rain — little spits of water that weren't worthy of an umbrella — but Harry didn't care. He'd be inside soon. He hoped Nadeeka, his housekeeper, had put the heating on for him.

He glanced around. The motorbike messenger seemed to be watching him, so Harry gave him a glare back. Hopefully, it'd get the messenger to clear off. His street wasn't a car park, after all.

Samir hauled Harry's two suitcases up to the front door. 'Would you like me to carry inside?'

'No, no,' said Harry. 'I'm old, but I'm not that old. I can manage.' He passed a folded twenty pound note to the driver in that time-honoured fashion of tipping everywhere that was both subtle and obvious at the same time. He didn't normally bother, but he appreciated he'd dragged the man away from his family on a Friday night.

Samir took it without looking, gave a polite nod, and slipped it in his pocket. 'Have a good evening, Sir Harry.'

'Give my best to your family,' said Harry. 'I'll see you on Monday morning.'

'Thank you, sir.' Samir tipped his hat and headed back to the car.

Alone, Harry dug around in his carry-on bag for the house keys. If David hadn't called, he would have found them while he was still in the car.

His fingers touched the keys, and he hooked them out of his bag. He fumbled through the keys and selected the Chubb first. As he fitted it into the lock, he sensed someone approaching. He turned to see the motorbike messenger coming up the steps.

'Yes? Can I help you?' said Harry.

Then he saw the gun in the man's hand.

22

It was cold on the roof of the Maywood estate in Peckham and the spits of rain falling from the sky threatened a far worse downpour to come.

'What am I doing up here?' Wise muttered to himself. It was nearly midnight and he should've been home hours ago. He could've had dinner with Jean and the kids, put Ed and Claire to bed, read them stories and kissed them good night. All the good stuff.

Instead, he'd worked late, then driven over to Peckham almost without thinking and wandered up to the roof where Andy had died.

He tried to tell himself he was there because of the session with Doctor Shaw that morning, but that was a lie. Andy was with him constantly. A ghost on his shoulder, replaying memories of that night over and over again in his mind.

He'd hoped going up to the roof, the spot where he died, might bring some peace, but all it had done was make things worse.

Wise could hear his voice in the wind, as useless now as it was then.

'Give me the gun, Andy. Please — think of your wife. Your kids.'

He could see the strobing blue lights crawl up the surrounding buildings, hear the wail of the sirens, feel the fear flutter in his heart.

He wondered what Derrick Morris and his girlfriend were doing. With the trial over and Selmani convicted, they were free to do what they wanted. Were they making the most of the second chance they'd got? Did they appreciate life that little more?

A red dot dances across Andy's shoulders, seeking his head, finding its spot, stops on his temple, dead still.

Wise tried blinking the memory away, but it was impossible. He had to get away from there. Leave this place and its ghosts. Go home.

With nausea rising in his throat, Wise ran to the door to the stairs. He stumbled through, into the stairwell and headed straight down, as fast as he could, using the railing to stop himself from falling, jumping the last few steps down to the landing, then on again, down, down, down. Floor after floor. Lights flickering overhead, graffiti-covered walls blurring as he moved past. Ignoring the stink of piss in his nose.

He just had to get out of there.

Down and down he went, as fast as he could. Down, down, down. He needed air. He needed to escape. Past the fifth floor, past the fourth.

The sound of his feet echoed through the stairwell, a drumbeat of despair. Gravity pulling him, ghosts chasing him.

The jerk in Andy's head as the bullet strikes him, the shape of his mouth as his last breath leaves his body and the look in his eyes as he falls, accusing Wise.

'Why did you let me die? Why? Why? Why?'

Wise reached the third floor, heart pounding, then the second, moving so fast with his head down that he didn't see the three men coming up in the other direction until he was nearly upon them.

'Hey Bruv,' one of them shouted. 'Watch out!'

Wise halted himself just before he would have clattered into them. 'Shit. Sorry.' He tried to catch his breath and blinked the sweat from his eyes, trying to focus past his ghosts and see the real world.

Dressed like wannabe gangsters, they cast a surly, half-stoned look over Wise.

'Well, well, well, Bruv. Where you goin' in such a hurry, dressed up so nice?' the one on the left said, an Adidas tracksuit zipped up tight to his neck, eyes red from weed.

'I think he be up to no good, man,' the one in the middle said, eyes glinting in the shadow of his baseball cap. 'Maybe he doing a bit of thievin'.'

'You a bad boy, Bruv?' the third one said, his hood pulled up over his head. 'Or maybe you just lost? Maybe you be in a hurry to get home to your baby mama?'

'Excuse me,' Wise said between gulps of air. 'I'm just in a hurry.' This was the last thing he needed.

'Excuse me?' said Hoodie. 'How about "fuck you?"'

'I don't want any trouble,' Wise said, but he knew it was coming. He'd grown up around people like this, eager to start a fight over nothing, doing their best to look tough, feeling invincible in their little gang. Hell, he'd even been one of them once. He knew the dance too well. He'd been a master of it once.

'You scared, Big Man?' said Tracksuit. 'Scared some brother going to fuck you up?'

Four steps separated them.

'I'm in a hurry,' Wise said. 'That's all.' He kept his voice calm, his tone polite, still hoping things wouldn't go the way he knew they would. Hoping there wouldn't be a fight, even though his fists were clenched. Even though he could feel the urge to strike.

Baseball Cap moved up a step closer and made a dramatic sniff as his eyes ran up and down Wise. 'You ain't that big, Bruv. Not for the three of us. But we don't want no trouble, neither.'

'That's good,' Wise said, not believing a word. These men wanted nothing but trouble.

Baseball cap smiled, took another step up, a knife suddenly in his hand. It was a little triangle of a blade, made for punching with. 'So, how's about you give us all your bread and we can all be on our way?'

Most people would do what they said, but Wise knew there was still a good chance they'd try to stab him all the same. There were really only two choices — the most basic: fight or flight. And Wise had never run from a fight.

He thought about his warrant card in his pocket, but getting out would only be a distraction and a delay. Most likely, they'd try to kill him the moment they saw it. Anyway, Wise didn't feel much like a police officer right then. Deep down, he was glad he'd met these three fools. Because he wanted trouble too.

'Just let me pass and we can forget all about this,' Wise said all the same, giving them one last opportunity to walk away unhurt.

But Baseball Cap laughed as if Wise was the funniest man in the world. Then he let his face go blank. Trying to look dangerous. 'Fuck you, Bruv. Now, pay up or start bleedin'. I'm not messin'.'

Two steps separated them. Baseball Cap was a big lad, but the two steps added another fourteen inches to Wise's height. If he'd had any sense, Baseball Cap would have made way for Wise to go past and then attack when Wise was in the middle of them all. If they did that, then it would be a close call on who would win. The tight space, the knife, and their numbers would give them the advantage, and Wise couldn't let that happen.

Maybe Baseball Cap worked that all out too, because he glanced over his shoulder to check on Hoodie's position, and that was when Wise moved.

He threw a punch as he stepped down, using height, momentum and all his weight to strike Baseball Cap on the bridge of his nose. The man dropped instantly, blood spurting, already unconscious, knife falling over the edge of the stairs. He fell back into the others, knocking them off balance as Wise waded into them, happy to trample over Baseball Cap's body on the way down, not wasting a second to give any of them time to react.

Hoodie got Wise's right elbow in the jaw and the force of the blow sent his skull bouncing off the graffiti-strewn wall. Wise brought his left up into Tracksuit's chin, snapping his head back and sending him falling back. He bounced down the last few steps to the next landing and lay there, not moving.

Hoodie was the only one barely conscious, so Wise bent down and grabbed him by the neck so he could look into Wise's eyes. 'Don't even think about coming after me again because I'll put you all in the fucking hospital if you do.'

'Ugh,' was all Hoodie said.

Wise dropped him and carried on his way down the

stairs, taking his time, flexing his fingers, breathing heavy once more but in a good way. The panic was gone. The fear with it.

Wise was nearly at the Mondeo when he realised how calm he felt about it all. There was no racing heartbeat, no shakes, no feeling of sickness in his gut. Apart from the slight throb around his knuckles, he felt no different from what he normally did.

No, that wasn't right. He felt awake. Alive! The tiredness that dragged him down constantly was gone. It was like he'd had a dozen expressos. In fact, he felt bloody good. Too good.

Part of him was tempted to go back and hurt them some more or find some other fools to beat up. Go on the hunt like Tom and he used to do, back in the day. Saturday night was for fucking and fighting and they didn't really care which one they got to do. Hurting the world because they couldn't admit they were hurting themselves.

That's how they'd ended up in that pub, the Bishop's Crown, two Chelsea fans down Tottenham way. Standing proudly in their blue shirts as four Spurs fans tried to beat them up. Back to back with Tom as they fought, shouting insults, laughing, kicking and punching whoever was near. It was bloody mayhem and the Wise brothers loved it.

Wise didn't even notice that Tom had carried on booting some lad after knocking him down. Didn't notice the kid had stopped moving.

It was the sirens that broke the blood lust. The blue lights flashing through the window.

They'd run then. Or at least, Wise ran because the police caught Tom, while he was still kicking the lad on the floor.

Brian Sellers was his name. Dead at nineteen just for

wearing the wrong shirt, drinking in the wrong pub and meeting the wrong people. As simple as that.

They charged Tom with manslaughter, put him on trial, put him in prison.

But no one charged Wise.

Tom had said he didn't know who the other bloke in the fight was. He'd said his brother had been at home alone, the boring bastard.

And Wise had let him do that. Let him take the blame. Let him take the prison time.

A choice by both of them that shattered the bond they'd shared since the womb.

The memories came back, so vivid, so sharp, echoing across the years, more painful than anything that had happened to Andy, packed full of shame and guilt.

A second later, bile rushed up Wise's throat. He bent over and threw up over the litter-strewn concrete. Burning his throat, twisting his gut, eyes streaming.

Shit.

Wise had sworn then not to be that person anymore, to follow the rules, to help not harm. With Tom banged up, Wise had caged the beast inside him. He'd gone back to school, got his exams, joined up, walked the beat. His life was about discipline, procedure, order, trying to right a wrong that could never be fixed, to bring justice to all the other Brian Sellers in the world, who were in the wrong place at the wrong time. Twenty years of doing good to make up for one night of being bad.

That's why it worked — or had worked. It was all unravelling a bit too quick these days. Andy had set that in motion.

'Why did you let me die? Why? Why? Why?' Andy's ghost shouts.

'I hate you,' Tom says. 'I fucking hate you.'

More bile came up and out all over the floor. A knot in his gut got tighter and tighter, making it hard to breathe, the guilt making it hard to live.

Wise staggered back and leaned against the Mondeo, a car as damaged as he was, and unbuttoned his top button and loosened his tie, gulping in air. Christ, he had to get a grip. He wasn't getting better. He was getting worse. Maybe he should take stress leave. Maybe he should—

His phone rang. It took Wise a moment to recognise the sound, another moment to get the damn thing out of his pocket.

It was Hicksy.

11:45 p.m. and Hicksy was ringing him. Shit.

'Yeah,' Wise said, straightening up. He wiped the sick from his mouth.

'Guv, there's been another murder.'

23

In the car park of the Maywood estate, Wise closed his eyes, his heart sinking. 'Where?'

'Hans Place,' Hicksy said. 'The victim is a Sir Harry Clarke, an ex-Tory MP. They killed him just after 11.'

'I'll be there as quick as I can,' Wise said. 'In the meantime, get squad cars going around all the local car parks and tell them to look out for anyone with a Honda PCX Scooter. We're probably too late, but maybe we'll get lucky.'

'Will do, Guv,' Hicksy said.

'See you in a bit,' Wise said, and ended the call.

A third victim? Every time he thought they were getting somewhere with the case, everything changed yet again.

Wise opened the car door. There was a half-drunk bottle of water in the side pocket that had been there for God only knew how long. He took a gulp, swished the stale tasting liquid around in his mouth, then spat it out. He couldn't go to a crime scene stinking of vomit.

Then he saw his hands. His knuckles were blood-stained and already swelling and bruised. Wise poured some more of the water over them to get rid of the claret as best he could, smearing more than he could remove, but it was the best he could do. Hopefully, no one would notice. There was a body to look at, after all.

With a few more deep breaths, he got in the car and started the engine. It was time to go to work. Time to forget the past.

He sped away from the estate, blue lighting it, hands tight on the steering wheel, trying to get his mind back on the job as he drove up through Camberwell, past Kennington and over Vauxhall Bridge.

Even he'd heard of Sir Harry Clarke. He was one of the old school Conservatives who'd served with the real Thatcher and hated the dressed-up pretend versions that were in government today. He'd not been afraid to tell the revolving door of Prime Ministers what he thought of them and their general incompetence. It was easy to imagine there'd been an enormous sigh of relief when he'd finally retired.

Not that he'd been out of the public eye since he'd stepped down. A multitude of companies sought a man of his connections — connections that could fast-track them to fortunes, especially during the pandemic. Every time there was a contract for hundreds of millions finalised, Clarke seemed to standing behind the person signing the deal.

The Guardian had run a story about Clarke called "Sir Twenty Per Cent" if Wise remembered rightly. A story that had gotten plenty of people all riled up with its hints of corruption and cronyism. Riled up enough to kill him, though?

And what did an ex-Tory MP have in common with a Russian oligarch and a tech entrepreneur?

Wise drove around the back of Westminster to Belgravia

and into Hans Place. Another billionaire's neighbourhood encircling another Georgian-era communal garden. It always amazed him that no one had sold off such prime plots of land, especially a site that was a stone's throw from Harrods. He knew they were historical conservation sites, but even so. Enough money could normally get over such hurdles.

Then again, there obviously wasn't enough money to stop these billionaires from getting killed when death knocked at their door.

The circus was already up and running around Clarke's house. Blue lights washed over the terraced houses while SOCOs scuttled back and forth from the big white tent that covered one of the house's entrances and a good part of the surrounding street.

As Wise parked up, he spotted Markham's Ducati among the vehicles. She'd made it to the scene in good time. With one last look at his knuckles, Wise got out of the car. He shouldn't have hit those thugs. What a stupid, bloody idiot he was. Wise by name, always so bloody dumb by nature.

He pulled his raincoat tight around him as the cold night air did its best to make everything so much more miserable. He spotted Hannah and Hicksy by the forensics van and headed over. Neither of them looked happy to be there or with each other, judging by the social distancing between them.

'Guv,' Hannah said with a nod.

'You all right, Guv?' Hicksy asked. 'You look a bit rough.'

'Just tired. I might have a bit of a cold coming,' Wise said, sticking his bruised hands into his pockets. 'What happened here?'

'Sir Harry had just returned from New York, where he'd

been on business,' Hannah said. 'His driver dropped him off as normal at his front door around 11 p.m. He was two streets away when he noticed his boss had left his phone in the back of the car, so he turned round. When he got back, he found Sir Harry dead on the doorstep with his brains blown out.'

'When we questioned him,' Hicksy said, 'he said there had been a motorbike messenger parked up outside his house and he had to manoeuvre around him to park himself.'

'And the description of the rider and bike match our guy,' Hannah added.

'So, they were waiting for Clarke to arrive?' Wise said.

'Looks like it, Guv,' Hicksy said.

'Who knew he was getting back at this time?' Wise said.

'The driver said he'd arranged the pick-up though Clarke's PA,' Hannah said. 'But other than that, we know nothing else. I presume his movements are pretty common knowledge if you know where to look.'

'We got a name for this PA?'

'All he knows is her first name — Sabine, but he gave us her number.'

'What about the car parks?' Wise said.

'We've got cars going around them, Guv,' Hicksy said, 'but there are at least twenty in a two-mile radius from here, including the one he used after killing the Russkie.'

Great. There wasn't much hope of getting lucky there. 'What about next of kin?'

'His wife died three years ago, but he has a daughter, Laura, married with three kids, according to Google. I did a DVLC check and they live a few streets away from here in Cadogan Gardens,' Hannah said.

'We were wondering if we should send someone around

to talk to them, Guv,' Hicksy said. 'But it's never good waking up someone with this sort of news.'

'It's needs to be done though. I'll go with Hannah after I've seen the body,' Wise said, and noticed Hicksy's scowl in response. Was he upset at not being taken along? 'Can you let the team know we need them in tomorrow?'

'I've messaged most of them already,' Hicksy grunted.

'Good,' Wise said, already dreading calling Jean to say he wouldn't be around over the weekend, despite the fact he'd been avoiding them all week. Then again, with the state he was in, maybe it was a good thing he could hide in his work. 'Message the boss too. Let her know we've got a third murder on our hands.'

'Wouldn't that be better coming from you, Guv?' Hicksy said.

'You're a big boy. I think you can manage telling her the bad news,' Wise said, too tired to deal with anyone's nonsense. 'Now, let's see the body.'

Leaving Hicksy, Wise and Hannah signed in with the Crime Scene Manager.

'Everything all right with you and Hicksy?' Wise asked as they dressed in their protective suits.

'Nothing I can't handle,' Hannah said.

'Yeah?' By the look on her face, it wasn't nothing at all.

'Yeah.'

'Okay,' Wise said, pulling his hood up. 'I'm here if you need to talk about it.'

Hannah nodded. 'Thanks.'

They made their way under the awning, and Wise got his first view of Sir Harry Clarke.

'We're still waiting for Doctor Singh to get here, Guv,' Hannah said, pointing to the body. 'But the cause of death is pretty obvious.'

Clarke's crumpled corpse lay against his front door, a smear of blood and brains all over it. A suitcase sat next to the body with its handle still extended and a smaller travel carry-on bag next to that. The door keys dangled from the top lock.

'He didn't even have time to open the door,' Wise said. He walked closer, Hannah following, using the SOCOs' metal treads, so he didn't contaminate the crime scene.

'The bullet went in by the right temple,' Hannah said.

'He must've been turning,' Wise said. 'Maybe the motorbike messenger called out to him?' Wise stared at the dead man. One minute he'd been living a life that most people would dream of and the next he was meat waiting for the slab.

'Pretty cold,' Hannah said. 'To sit and wait for Clarke to turn up, then walk straight up like that and pop him.'

'The thing that really worries me, Hannah, is I've got a horrible feeling that we've been looking at this all wrong.'

'Why?'

'Well, first of all, we were looking at reasons anyone would want Hassleman dead. Then, we find out about Andronovitch, so we started looking for connections between the two of them but, now we have this murder.'

'Yeah ...'

'What if this isn't about getting hold of their money or their business or Russia?' Wise almost didn't want to say the words, as if voicing his fear would make it a reality. 'It's the timing. Andronovitch was six days ago. Hassleman three days ago and now this. A three-day cycle.'

Wise looked over at Hannah. Her eyes were fixed on him.

'What if we're dealing with a serial killer?' Wise said. 'What if someone else is going to die three days from now?'

Saturday, 17th September

24

It was nearly 2 a.m. and Wise was running on fumes. They'd had to wait for Doctor Singh to turn up and sign off on the corpse, plus Wise had wanted to check on the SOCOs initial progress, just on the off chance they found something useful but, as before, the killer had left nothing.

Wise's concerns about the case were growing by the minute. Was it a serial killer? Was it a hit man working through a specific list of targets? They needed something — anything — to help move the case along because each new murder wiped out whatever progress they were making and set them back to the beginning again.

Still, there was one job left to do before he could call it a night, to notify the next of kin. Wise and Hannah headed over to the house of Clarke's daughter, Laura.

Cadogan Gardens was like a smaller version of Hans Place; all red brick, Georgian terrace houses with black railings whose exteriors probably hadn't changed at all in the couple of hundred years since the buildings had gone up. It was easy to imagine street traders walking up and down the road back in the day, singing songs about sweet, red roses like in that *Oliver* film Wise used to watch as a kid at Christmas. The house itself had six floors with big bay windows overlooking the green patch of land that gave the street its name.

'What a hovel,' Hannah muttered as they approached the house.

Wise glanced back. 'You wouldn't want to live here then?'

She smiled. 'You could force me, I suppose, but somehow I don't think too many police officers live down this street. Besides, I'm not sure what I'd do with all the rooms.'

Wise thought of his own home. It had felt massive when they bought it, full of giddy happiness and big plans for the future. Now, it felt fit to burst with all the stuff that accumulates over twelve years of marriage and two kids. Full of wonderful memories, laughter, and only the odd moment of tears. Maybe that was why he was scared to go there? He didn't want to infect it with his misery — or, at least, more than he had. Stupid, really. Maybe what he really needed was to be with his family. Maybe they could show him what happy was again.

Stifling a yawn, Wise pressed the door buzzer. Just like the killer had done at Hassleman's house and Andronovitch's. Dressed as a messenger, a sight so common people don't even notice them anymore. What did they feel as they waited for someone to answer? Excited? Scared? Aroused? It was no small thing to kill a person in such cold blood. Andronovitch would've been the hardest. The first always is. How easy had it been to kill Clarke? Had they rung the buzzer only to find the house empty, or did they know he was on his way back from the airport?

Wise pressed the buzzer a second time.

'Light's gone on upstairs,' Hannah said from behind him. 'We've woken someone up.'

Another few minutes passed before a bleary man's voice came over the intercom. 'Yes? What do you want?'

Wise held up his warrant card to the camera next to the intercom. 'We're the police, sir. We need to speak to Laura Smythe.'

'Police?' the man repeated.

'Yes, sir,' Wise said.

Bolts cranked back, and a key turned in a heavy lock before the door finally opened to reveal a dishevelled looking man in a brown dressing gown. He was about Wise's height but thin as a rake, with hair thinning on top. He squinted at Wise and Hannah, confused and still half asleep. 'Has something happened?'

'Can we come in please, sir?' Hannah said.

'I'm sorry,' the man replied, stepping to one side. 'Please, come in.'

Wise and Hannah entered the house. White and black chequered tiles led down a hallway, past the stairs, to a dark room at the rear.

'I'm Detective Inspector Simon Wise,' Wise said, 'and this is my colleague, Detective Sergeant Hannah Markham.'

'And you want to see my wife?' the man asked.

'And you are?' Wise said.

'Oh sorry. I'm ... I'm David Smythe.' He glanced up at the ceiling. 'Laura's asleep. I can ... I can wake her, but she takes a sleeping tablet at about nine every night. Zonks her right out.'

'We'd be grateful if you could please try to wake her,' Wise said.

'And you can't tell me what it's about?'

'No, sir.'

Smythe rubbed his face and blinked rapidly, as if trying to wake himself up. 'Right. Er ... You can ... You can wait in the dining room, I suppose.' He pointed to a doorway off the hallway. 'It's in there.'

'Thank you, sir,' Hannah said.

They watched Smythe trudge back upstairs, and then Hannah opened the door to the dining room and turned on the light. If the street outside was like stepping back in time, the Smythes had mirrored that effect in the dining room too. A long, antique oak table filled the room with twelve high-backed chairs running around it, while a crystal chandelier hung above it. There was a long serving table on one side with a silver tray on top and several crystal wine glasses, above which was an oil portrait of a grey-haired man in a ruffled shirt and a hunting jacket that looked a couple of hundred years old.

'He looks a fun chap,' Hannah whispered.

'He probably was back then,' Wise whispered back.

Neither sat as they waited for the Smythes to reappear. Wise did his best to stifle a yawn, but his tiredness was back with a vengeance and, somehow, he doubted he was about to be offered a cup of tea or coffee. Markham, though, looked fine — as if it was the start of a normal day and not the middle of the night.

When David Smythe reappeared, in jeans and a blue, long-sleeved shirt and his hair carefully combed across his head like Bobby Charlton. 'Sorry to keep you waiting. Laura will be down in one minute.'

'No need to apologise,' Wise said.

Smythe smiled. 'Laura's always telling me off for saying sorry too much. It's a habit I guess.'

'Worse ones to have,' Hannah said.

'Depends who you ask,' Smythe said.

An awkward silence followed, then they all heard footsteps coming down the stairs. A red-haired woman appeared in the doorway, eyes wide and worried. She wore an oversized jumper that went almost down to her knees and black trousers. She appeared to be in her mid-forties, but there was a stillness to her face that suggested she'd had some work done, so Wise's estimation could've been out by at least ten years.

'Ah, here she is,' Smythe said, stepping to one side with an awkward smile.

The woman shot her husband a look that told him exactly what she thought of that introduction, then forced a smile of her own onto her face as she held out a hand to Wise. 'I'm Laura Smythe-Clarke.'

Wise shook her hand and introduced himself and Hannah. 'Perhaps you'd like to sit down, Mrs Smythe-Clarke.' Wise gestured to one of the dining room chairs.

'That serious, is it?' Smythe-Clarke said as she took the seat.

Wise and Hannah both sat opposite her. 'I'm afraid it is,' Wise said. 'It's about your father.'

Smythe-Clarke's hand went to her mouth. 'What's happened to him?'

'I'm afraid someone shot your father this evening just as he arrived home from the airport,' Wise said. 'He died instantly.'

Smythe-Clarke's eyes went wide in disbelief and then narrowed as she started shaking her head. 'No. You're wrong. You've got the wrong person. Whoever's dead is ... is not my father.'

'Your father's driver found his body and identified him,' Wise said.

'No. No. No. You are wrong.' Smythe-Clarke snapped the words out, then turned to her husband. 'Get my phone. I'm calling father now. He can clear this ... this ... this outrage up.'

David Smythe went over to his wife and put his hands on her shoulders. 'Darling, I don't think the police make this sort of mistake.'

Smythe-Clarke shrugged her husband's hands away. 'GET MY PHONE,' she roared instead.

'Yes. Sorry. Give me a minute.' Her husband all but ran from the room and went back up the stairs. Alone, Smythe-Clarke glared at Wise and Hannah. 'I can't believe you've made a mistake like this. I'm going to have your jobs for this.'

Wise glanced at Hannah, but neither said anything while they waited for David Smythe to return. They waited in awkward silence as Smythe-Clarke glared at them. Two minutes later, they heard his feet thumping down the stairs and he entered the room, clutching a Samsung smart phone. His wife snatched it from his hand, unlocked it and swiped through her contacts before dialling her father's phone.

They could all hear it ring, and then a man's voice answered.

A jolt of happiness ran through Smythe-Clarke. 'Daddy! Thank—'

The man on the other end interrupted must have her because the smile fell from Smythe-Thomas's face just as quickly as it had appeared. Her eyes darted around the room as she listened to what they said. Again, there was a little shake of her head. Her hand went to her mouth as she tried to hold a sob in. Then tears appeared as she finally nodded to whatever was said.

'Thank you, Sergeant.' Smythe-Clarke disconnected the call and looked up at Wise and Hannah. 'That was one of your men. He — he said Daddy's dead.'

'I'm sorry,' Wise said again.

It was as if they watched Smythe-Clarke shatter before them. Her lip quivered first as her eyes darted from Wise to Hannah, then her head drooped. Her shoulders shuddered, quickly followed by a whoop of a sob. Smythe-Clarke tried to hold it back, but there was no stopping it. The tears fell fast and furious, Smythe-Clarke's whole body shaking as she wailed.

Wise's eyes drifted over to her husband, expecting him to go over and comfort his wife, but Smythe remained standing near the door, just watching his wife cry, like he was a servant waiting for a command rather than a loving husband.

In the end, Smythe-Clarke waved a hand towards her husband. 'Tissues.'

Again, he disappeared from the room, only to return with a box of Kleenex in his hand. He placed it on the table next to his wife and she snatched a tissue immediately to dab at her eyes. Slowly, she composed herself; her back straightening, her breathing controlled, and a hardness set across her face. 'I'm sorry. That was unbecoming of me,' she said with one last dab of her eyes. 'Tell me what happened.'

'There's not much we can say at the moment,' Wise said. 'They shot him on his doorstep and death was instantaneous.'

'Do you know who did it?' Smythe-Clarke asked.

'Not yet,' Wise said. 'I know this isn't an ideal time, but do you feel strong enough for us to ask some questions?'

'Yes,' Smythe-Clarke said.

'Had your father had any problems recently? People threatening him?'

'Not that I know of,' Smythe-Clarke said. 'My husband works with my father, though. Perhaps he knows of something.'

Wise and Hannah looked towards Smythe standing by the door. He looked shocked to be invited to answer a question. 'Oh sorry. Er ... No ... I ... Er ... I don't know of anyone, really. There was that nonsense during the pandemic, of course — people complaining about Harry making a commission on PPE contracts and stuff — but that all died down pretty quickly. A storm in a teacup, really.'

It was an interesting way to describe something that was all over the papers and TV for weeks and became a topic of conversation in parliament. 'I seem to remember there were protests going on outside your offices,' Wise said.

Smythe waved the comment away. 'Just leftie loons making a bit of noise for a few days.'

'That nonsense was all David's doing anyway — not Daddy's,' Smythe-Clarke said. 'He just let Daddy take all the blame.'

'Er ... it wasn't quite like that, darling,' Smythe said.

'Of course it bloody was. Daddy was furious with you.'

Smythe shook his head behind his wife's head and mouthed, 'She's wrong.'

'What business was Sir Harry involved in?' Hannah asked.

'Mainly property,' Smythe said. 'But sometimes he'd connect people to others that could help each other. He knew everyone there was to know.'

'Did he do business in Russia?' Wise asked.

'God, no,' Smythe-Clarke said. 'He thought they were the enemy — like anyone of his generation that grew up during the cold war. Russia's growing influence was one reason why he retired from politics. He said Maggie would've been spinning in her grave at some things that were going on with the current lot in charge. And, of course, with everything that's happened with Ukraine, he was very happy to tell people he was right.'

'What sort of people?' Wise asked.

Smythe-Clarke wiped her nose with a tissue. 'No one important. Mainly us when we had dinner together. Maybe his friends down the golf club.'

'What about investments in technology?' Wise said.

'Er ... No ... We talked about it, but Harry liked sticking with what worked,' replied David Smythe. 'Sorry.'

'Stop bloody apologising,' hissed his wife through clenched teeth without looking at her husband.

'Just one last question,' Wise said before things escalated into a fight between the pair of them. 'Was your father still active with the Conservative party?'

'Of course he was,' Smythe-Clarke said. 'He might not like the buffoons running it now, but Daddy's blood was blue through and through. He ... He ...' Smythe-Thomas's voice broke, and she reached for another tissue as she gazed down at her phone. Wise noted that the lock screen image was one of Smythe-Clarke, her children and her father, a very clear statement on who she considered important in her life.

He nodded at Hannah, who closed her notebook. 'We'll leave you alone for now. We'll be in touch later about a formal identification of your father's body but, until then, try to get some rest. A family liaison officer will help you through the coming days.'

'We don't need help,' Smythe-Clarke said as she stared at the phone in her hand. Even when Wise and Hannah stood up, she didn't move. Her husband mouthed 'sorry' at them, then gestured to the door. The detectives followed him out into the hallway and to the front door. 'Laura and Harry were very close,' Smythe said as he opened the door. 'She's the only child. His pride and joy.'

'Understandable,' Wise said. 'How long have you worked with Sir Harry?'

'Oh ... Let's see,' Smythe said. 'It was after I got made redundant by Goldman and Partners — the bankers. So, it's been two years or so. Maybe a bit more than that.'

'What do you do in the company?'

'This and that. Mainly shadowing Harry so he could retire someday and not have to close the business when he did. I also look for new ways to diversify the business. Property's been good to us but so much of our capital is tied up in commercial property and, during the pandemic, people realised they didn't need massive, expensive office space anymore.'

'That's a lot of responsibility,' Wise said.

'It's actually a lot easier than it seems. It's mainly schmoozing with people and knowing what wine to order,' Smythe said.

'I'm sure there's a lot more to it than that,' Wise said. 'Thank you again for your time.'

'I hope you catch whoever did this,' Smythe said.

'Oh, one last thing,' Wise said. 'Just out of curiosity, you didn't know Mark Hassleman by any chance? Perhaps do business with him.'

Smythe looked puzzled for a moment. 'Where have I heard that name before? Oh, wasn't he that man that got killed the other day?'

Wise nodded. 'I thought perhaps you might mix in the same circles.'

Smythe laughed. 'Not every rich person knows every other rich person in London.'

'Of course,' Wise said as he stepped outside. 'I just thought I'd ask.'

'You don't think Harry's death has anything to do with the other one, do you?'

Wise gave a half-shake of his head. 'We'll look into every possibility.' He produced a business card from his pocket and offered it to Smythe. 'If you think of anything that might be of use, don't hesitate to call.'

Smythe took the card. 'I will, Inspector.' He watched them from the doorway until they reached Wise's Mondeo, and then he shut the door.

'What did you think of Mr and Mrs Smythe-Clarke?' Wise asked once they were inside the car.

'He seemed nice enough. A bit wet, perhaps. But the wife ... Well, I know she was upset, but she seemed a bit of a handful to me. She enjoyed ordering her husband around.'

'There certainly wasn't much love between them,' Wise said. 'It was interesting what she said about the PPE scandal — that it was all her husband's idea. I imagine that could cause a fair bit of tension between them all.'

'She seemed pretty clear about her father's dislike of Russia, though.'

Wise looked at his watch. It was 3 a.m. 'I'll drop you back at your bike. You might as well get some sleep before we start the day again.'

'What about you?' Hannah said.

'I'll probably grab some breakfast somewhere and some coffee and head straight over to Kennington,' Wise said. 'I won't sleep now and I'll only disturb the wife and kids if I go home.'

'How many kids have you got?'

'Two. Ed and Claire. Nine and seven. They're good kids.' Wise felt another pang of guilt. They were good kids whom he was avoiding.

'Must be tough on them with the hours you do.'

'It's not easy.' Wise turned on the ignition and set off back towards Hans Place. 'What about you?'

'No kids and no real interest in having any,' Hannah said, looking out the window. 'My girlfriend is the broody one in the relationship.'

'Girlfriend?'

'Yeah, Emma.' Hannah turned to look at Wise. 'Is that a problem?'

'Well, if Emma wants kids and you don't, it might be one.'

'I didn't mean that. I meant, is it a problem me being gay?'

'Not with me, it's not,' Wise said. 'After doing this job for twenty-odd years, I figure anything that makes you happy — that's legal — is alright by me.'

'Not everyone on the force feels like that,' Hannah said.

'Unfortunately, the Met's full of meat heads. I find it best to just ignore them.'

'Yeah? How do you deal with Hicksy, then?'

'Ah.' Wise smiled. 'What's he said?'

'He said I was a diversity hire, and the team didn't need anymore as it was already the United Nations.'

'Shit. I'm sorry. I'll speak to him.'

'No need. I can handle him. More importantly, where are you going to get breakfast?'

'There's a place just off the Elephant and Castle,' Wise said. 'Does a fry up that can give you heart failure on a good day.'

'Let me get my bike and I'll follow you there,' Hannah

said. 'I'm not going to be able to sleep now, anyway. We might as well get started on the day. It's not as if we haven't got enough shit to deal with.'

'Emma won't mind?'

'She won't even notice I'm not there. She doesn't wake up until midday at the weekends.'

'Alright then,' Wise said. 'Breakfast it is — I'll even treat you.'

Half an hour, they were sitting in a cafe called Terry's. It was as old school as a place could get. The tables and chairs could've been from the seventies and not in a good way, with Formica surfaces that were all scratched, cracked and stained. The cushioning in the seats was non-existent. Each table had a red squeezy bottle of ketchup, a bottle of vinegar and salt and pepper pots. Net curtains covered the lower half of the windows that overlooked Butcher's Lane, stained yellow from the days when smoking inside wasn't just allowed, but encouraged. A counter ran one length of the cafe at the back, behind which a man with short, curly hair and a red face worked. Above his head, Sky News played silently on a wide-screen TV.

Club kids with bug eyes and sweat-soaked clothes filled two tables, laughing and joking over glasses of water and the odd cup of tea, while four huge men in butcher's aprons sat around another table by the front door, shovelling bacon and sausage and egg into their mouths. 'You come here often?' Hannah asked, not looking impressed.

'Only if I can't sleep.' Wise didn't say that was most nights.

The owner came over. Not Terry whose name was above the door, but Terry's grandson, Bobby, who looked ancient enough to go with the decor. He had a cheeky face with a perpetual smile that almost stopped you looking at the state of his apron that was once white, but was now stained with all the major food groups. 'Alright, Wisey. How are you?'

'Alright, Bob. You keeping well?' Wise said.

'Oh, you know me. Shouldn't complain — but I do.' He looked over at Hannah. 'Who's this then?'

'Detective Sergeant Hannah Markham,' Wise said.

'Pleased to meet you, luv,' said Bobby. 'I hope they're paying you lots to put up with this miserable bastard.'

'Not enough,' Hannah said with a wink. 'Not nearly enough.'

'Tell me about it.' Bobby laughed. 'Story of my life.'

'I'll have the usual, Bob,' Wise said. 'Hannah?'

'Bacon sandwich with HP,' Hannah said. 'And a big cup of tea.'

'Large coffee for me, Bob,' Wise added.

'Of course. I'll get you the extra strong stuff, eh? Be right back with your scrambled eggs and bacon butty.' Bobby ambled back to the other side of the counter and started cracking eggs and dropping bacon onto the grill.

'Scrambled eggs? Not a full English?' Hannah said.

'I like to look after myself if I can,' Wise said.

'The Job can do that to you.'

Wise nodded. The Job could kill you in more ways than one.

Andy's head lurches forward a second before Wise hears the gunshot. Red mist blows in the summer night.

Wise shook the thought away, then dropped his bruised hands under the table. He had a job to do.

'Instead, we've—' The words caught in Wise's throat as he saw a new story come up on the TV.

He recognised the reporter, Claire Martin — known for the big stories — but it was where she stood that captured his attention. She was outside Kennington Police Station, and he immediately knew she was talking about his case. When the words "Killer strikes again" ran along the bottom of the screen, his worst fears were confirmed. 'Shit.'

Hannah turned to look at what had caught his attention. 'Shit,' she said as well.

'Bobby,' Wise called. 'Can you turn the TV up?'

As Bobby fumbled with the remote control, pictures of Yuri Andronvitch, Mark Hassleman and Sir Harry Clarke appeared on screen.

'... Clarke is the third wealthy person to be murdered in six days ...'

25

'Someone on your team bloody talked and I want to know who!' DCI Roberts was red in the face and was as angry as Wise had ever seen her. She'd arrived at the station about half an hour after Wise and Hannah, who'd abandoned their breakfast, and about ten minutes before the full force of the press had descended on the station. She wore a black roll-neck and jeans but, even so, she looked like she'd been dragged through a bush backwards.

'I'm as pissed off as you are about it,' Wise said, 'but it's done now and we need to get on with this case — not go chasing blabbermouths.'

'For Christ's sake, Simon — Clarke was only murdered last night and that bitch on *Sky News* had it on air by 4 a.m. this morning. That didn't happen by accident,' Roberts snapped back. 'And we agreed to keep Andronvitch's death a secret.'

'It could've been one of the SOCOs at the scene last night,' he replied, too tired to put up with any bullshit. 'It could've been anyone. We don't need this distraction.'

'Please tell me you had, at least, notified Clarke's family before his murder made the news.'

'Hannah and I spoke to them around 2 a.m. this morning.'

'That's something, at least,' Roberts said, sitting down behind her desk. 'The last thing we need is for them to sue us for emotional distress. Did you tell them you thought it's connected to the other murders?'

'No. We kept everything vague when we could.'

'Then you find who talked, Simon. Find them and I'll have them on charges right after I've cut their balls off. This sort of fuck up can't be forgiven or forgotten. Not now. Not after Andy. I'm not having my career derailed because everyone on your team is bent.'

'My team's not bent,' Wise said. 'Andy was a rotten apple, but not the rest of them.'

'Really? You seriously believe that?' Roberts said. 'Then you're a bloody idiot. No wonder Andy could do everything he did without you noticing. That says a lot about your detective abilities.'

'That's uncalled for,' Wise said, his temper rising. 'Andy fooled all of us.'

Roberts jabbed a finger in his direction. 'Except you were his bloody partner.'

Christ. He had had enough of this. 'If you can't trust me, I'll put in an application today to be transferred off your team,' Wise said. It frightened him just how much he wanted her to tell him to do it.

Roberts shook her head. 'Oh, stop being so bloody melodramatic. I just need you to solve this case, Simon, and quickly. Before anyone else gets killed.'

'Don't you think I know that?'

Roberts' desk phone rang before she could reply. She picked it up. 'DCI Roberts.'

Wise watched her as she listened to whatever was said, the colour draining from her face. 'Yes, sir,' she said finally. 'I'll be ready.'

Roberts put down the phone and looked up at Wise. 'The Chief's been summoned to Number Ten. Apparently, the Prime Minister is unhappy that an ex-Conservative MP and one of the party's biggest donors were both murdered in the space of a week. He's taking me along to share the experience. Is there any progress we can give before we're torn a new one?'

'No, boss,' Wise said. 'Not after last night.'

'Let's hope that changes quickly, for both our sakes,' Roberts said. 'You can go now. I need to get my uniform on. I like to look smart when I'm being smacked about.'

'You'll tell Samson that we're taking the Andronovitch case?'

'I will. Now clear off.'

Wise headed up to MIR-One, exhausted and demoralised. Everything about this case was just making things harder and harder. Bodies piling up without any clues, some dickhead blabbing to the press and now Downing Street's attention was only going to pile on even more pressure. It would be a nightmare at the best of times, but Wise knew he was far from his best.

The fight with those jobs last night was a testament to that. All those cracks he was carefully trying to hide were just getting bigger and bigger. Each day, it was getting more and more difficult to pretend everything was alright in his world.

A shower and a shave would help. Some clean clothes. Some sleep. The list went on.

He had to remind himself they were only three days into a murder enquiry. That was nothing in real terms. In many ways, more bodies were a good thing for the investigation. There had to be similarities between the cases, connections, maybe even some forensics — anything they could use to reduce the size of the haystack Wise and his team had to search. He had to hope that because he had nothing so far except a mysterious motorbike rider to go on.

Despite it being just after 9 on a Saturday morning, everyone was in. For a moment, Wise stood in the doorway and looked from one detective to another. Who was it who'd bloody talked to the press? Jono? Hicksy? Sarah? There was a time he'd trusted them all implicitly. But that was before Andy had fucked it up for all of them.

And Roberts was right. Wise hadn't suspected a thing. It had completely blindsided him. Even now, he didn't know how long Andy had been on the take or who'd been paying him.

'You don't know what I am!' Andy shouts across the rooftop, a red dot dancing across his torso.

With a deep breath, Wise walked through the room to the white boards. Sarah had been busy, adding a picture of Clarke to the ones of Hassleman and Andronovitch. There were more CCTV shots of the motorbike man from each murder scene — for all the good it did them. The number plates were different each time but always stolen. The only good thing was it was obvious it was the same person on the same bike.

He picked up a pen and wrote under Andronovitch's picture "Russian" and "Tory Donor." Under Clarke's picture, he wrote "ex-Tory MP." Then, above them all, he noted, "What's the link?"

The Venn diagram was still there also, so Wise added a

third interconnecting circle for Clarke. The centre of which was still glaringly empty.

'Guv?' Hannah by his side. He turned and realised the room had gone silent. His team's eyes were all on him.

'Thanks for coming in, all of you,' he said. 'In the last twenty-four hours, what was a challenging murder case has become three times harder. Six days ago, our motorbike rider shot Yuri Andronovitch. Three days ago, they murdered Mark Hassleman, and, last night, they put a bullet in the brain of Sir Harry Clarke, the ex-Tory MP.'

Wise looked around the room at the tired faces. 'Following this pattern, I believe there's a good possibility we'll have another murder three days from now — on Monday night. I don't have to tell you we need to stop that from happening.'

'So, we all need to do some serious detective work between now and then. Cancel any plans you might've had. We're here now and we need to put in some serious graft. Let's find out why these three men were targeted. There has to be a connection and that connection will link us back to our motorbike messenger. Why would anyone want to kill an oligarch, a tech head and a property developer? Not the normal profile of victims for a serial killer.'

'Plenty of people hate the rich,' Hannah said. 'Especially now.'

'Over sixty billionaires live in London,' Sarah said. 'That's quite a hit list, if that's the case.'

'Enough to go to these lengths to kill them?' Wise said.

'Maybe it's a way of getting some power back? Showing that the killer can touch the untouchable?' Callum said. 'I was doing some reading, and this article said serial killing was an act of dominance over the victims — like Shipman playing God with his patients or some lonely bloke getting revenge on the women who have rejected him his whole life.'

Under the "What do we think?" section of the whiteboard, Wise wrote, "Targeted for wealth?"

'It is definitely a possibility. These victims are all incredibly rich, but why pick them specifically? We know both Hassleman and Clarke were in the news lately, but was Andronovitch?'

'His name was mentioned a few times after the war in Ukraine broke out and every Russian with a few bob was being sanctioned,' Sarah said, 'but otherwise, he was a very private man. His daughter was living the high life on Instagram for a while, but she stopped posting the moment Putin invaded Ukraine.'

'Probably Daddy told her to stop,' Donut said.

'What about the Tories, Guv?' Hicksy said. 'Clarke was one of them and the Russian donated to them. Plenty of people hate the Tories, don't they?'

'Again, it's a possibility — but Hassleman has no connection that we know of so far. So let's chase up that angle. Maybe he was part of some secret cabal that we don't know about yet.' Wise wrote "Tories" up on the board.

'Let's chase up Digital Forensics. We need to go through their emails, their calendars and their files. I know they promised us information early next week, but we can't wait any longer for us to fit them in. Cutbacks or not, we need them to prioritise this investigation. Put a rocket up their arses and if they give you any trouble, tell them we'll set the Chief Super on them,' Wise said. 'And let's keep going through their lives. If the connection's not the Tories, then what is it? Were they featured in an article somewhere? Do they shop in the same supermarket? Eat in the same restaurant? Whatever it is, we must find it and quickly.'

'What if it's not a serial killer, Guv?' Hannah said. 'When it was just Hassleman, we were looking at who could profit from his death. What if it is just the three of them? What if this is all a big business move still?'

'Good point, Hannah,' Wise said. 'So let's comb through their business dealings and see if there is a link between them. Perhaps there was some deal or other they were involved in that now someone else is going to profit from.'

Hicksy held up his hand. 'I've got Emily Walker's bank details — or as much as I could find.'

'And?' Wise asked.

'She's pretty damn wealthy in her own right. She's getting paid thirty grand a month from Sparks after tax, but there are no unusual payments going out. Just stuff like mortgage, gym memberships, beauty salons, clothes — she likes clothes shopping a lot.'

'She was out last night in town with some friends,' Callum said. 'According to what she was posting on Instagram. Dinner in Soho, drinks at a private members' club and then more drinks at that fancy burlesque club in Covent Garden.'

'That means she's not our messenger,' Wise said, 'but she could still be behind hiring the shooter. Keep digging, Hicksy, and see if she's got other accounts tucked away. Maybe off-shore?'

'Will do, Guv,' Hicksy said.

'Right,' Wise said. 'The upside about the press going berserk about these murders is that we can now be direct in our questioning with friends and associates. So let's chase down everything.'

People started to move but Wise wasn't done yet.

'Right — before we get busy,' Wise said, raising his voice. 'We need to talk about why the press are going berserk outside. They are here because someone told them about our three murders within hours of the last one happening — despite us all agreeing to keep Andronovitch's murder a secret. I only hope that it wasn't someone in this room who sold out their colleagues for a few pounds because DCI Roberts wants whoever was responsible on bloody charges. Now, maybe someone blabbed because they had a bloody electricity bill to pay or something life-destroying like that, but it's not good enough. We have the world watching us and expecting us to fail quite frankly, so we better pray it wasn't someone in this room who let the rest of us down. And so help me, if it happens again ... then whoever it is will feel all my goddamn wrath before Roberts gets to charge you with behaviour unbecoming of a police officer and whatever else she can think of. After Andy, we have to be better than perfect. Do I make myself clear?'

A few muttered 'Yes, Guv' but most of the team just looked awkward.

'I said — do I make myself clear?' snarled Wise through gritted teeth.

This time, everyone replied.

'Good. Now get busy.' As Wise turned to go to his office, his phone buzzed. He pulled it out of his pocket and saw it was Jean.

Shit. He'd forgotten to call her. Shit. Shit.

He answered the call, heading to his office. 'Jean. I'm sorry.'

'Sorry? Just where the hell are you?' His wife didn't even attempt to hide her fury.

'I'm at the station. There was another murder last—'

'I do not care!' Jean said, raising her voice, as Wise entered his office. 'You are supposed to be here now. The kids are waiting for you.'

'The kids—'

'Harry's got his football match today. You promised you'd watch him play.' Her words were calmer yet crueller, stabbing into his heart.

'Oh God, I forgot,' Wise said. 'Shit.'

'If you'd come home last night, you'd have seen the note he left you.'

'I've been working all night.' Even to his ears, it sounded pathetic. It was the truth, but without the actual reality of it all.

He heard Jean take a deep breath. When she spoke again, her voice was more measured. 'I'm not going to fight with you. You can still get here in time for the game like you promised, or maybe we'll have to have a hard conversation about whether you still want to be a part of this family.'

'Jean, please, I'm dealing with three murders here — the last of which happened twelve hours ago. I can't walk out now.'

'I understand you're going through stuff at the moment, Simon. I really do, but the kids don't. They don't understand why their daddy doesn't want to see them.'

'I am sorry. I really am.'

'You need to decide whether you care more about the dead than you do about your family.'

'That's not true, Jean. My family's the most important thing in my life.'

'And yet, everything else is a priority. Even your dad rang up, wanting to know if you were okay. You've not spoken to him in an age either.'

'Shit. I know. I've just been—'

'Don't say it,' Jean said, cutting him off. 'We've all been very understanding, but enough's enough. Goodbye, Simon.

If you're not back here by 10 a.m., don't bother coming home tonight.'

The line went dead.

'Fuck!' Wise threw his phone down on the desk. 'Fuck. Fuck. Fuck.'

He could see Harry and Claire sitting there, at home, waiting for him. Maybe they were by the window, watching the road, looking for his car to turn the corner, ready to spend the day with him. He'd promised them McDonalds after the game and a movie and then bowling after that. All their favourite things, trying to win their hearts back, and all he was doing was breaking them instead.

He looked at his watch. If he left now, he could make it to the house, to the kids. There was still time to smooth things over. But how could he walk out on the team now, abandon his job? There was still a chance they could crack the case and stop someone else from dying.

What a choice. He was damned whatever he did.

There was a knock at his door.

'Come in,' Wise said.

It was Hannah. 'Guv, David Smythe called. He said his wife is too upset to identify his father-in-law's body, but he'll do it. He'd going to be at the morgue in an hour. Do you want to be there or should I take Sarah?'

Wise sighed. 'I'll come with you.'

His kids would have to understand. He'd make it up to them next time.

26

Hannah tried to stifle a yawn. By God, she was fit to drop. Her eyes burned and she was running on fumes. In fact, while they'd been waiting for the body to be prepared, it'd been all a bit too quiet in the viewing room and she'd nearly nodded off. Luckily, she'd caught herself just in time. She doubted Wise would've been impressed with her if she had.

The DI was now standing next to David Smythe, waiting for the curtain to pull back and reveal Clarke's corpse, and still looking immaculate in his suit. No one would've guessed he'd been up all night just by looking at him. His shirt was all buttoned up once more, his tie straight.

Hannah had no idea how he did it. Granted she'd seen him drink about a dozen cups of coffee but even so, his stamina was impressive. In fact, she'd been pretty damn impressed by everything Wise did. Even the way he'd handled the press leak had been admirable. Most bosses she'd had would've gone on a mad, shouting tirade, demanding someone confess there and then.

Smythe, on the other hand, was about as different to

Wise as a person could be and not in a good way. The two men were of a similar height but that was all they had in common. Where Wise had that boxer's build of his and calm confidence, Smythe was just … what?

She had to be careful in how she assessed him because he seemed to be the personification of so much of what she disliked.

For a start, the man was dressed in that bloody city casual uniform of chinos with razor-sharp creases, a check shirt and brown brogues. On top of all that, he'd come in wearing one of those green wax jackets the toffs loved, the sight of which got Hannah's goat just at the sight of them. Immediately she could picture him with a bunch of Hooray Henrys quaffing about, acting all superior.

Her university had been full of pretentious wankers like that, intent on only having a good time rather than making the most of the great opportunity they'd been given and rubbing their families' wealth in the face of anyone they considered 'common.' People like her. They'd done their best to make her life a misery, mocking her for her accent, her skin colour, her parents' jobs and just about anything that didn't fit in their white mock-upper class lives.

Christ, she'd graduated six years ago now and the memories still triggered all the rage she'd felt back then.

And Smythe's wife was right to be annoyed by the amount of times the man said sorry. He'd only been at the morgue for about fifteen minutes and he must have apologised about thirty times. Hannah could only imagine how bloody grating it would be to be married to the man. No wonder his wife had shouted at him. Hannah was pretty close to doing it herself. She wouldn't mind but it never came across as genuine. It was just a word to say, a bad habit that he wasn't even aware of or even just something he thought he should say rather than actually mean.

There was something else too that she couldn't quite put her finger on. It was as if the man was distracted somehow, his mind on anything but what he was there to do. Maybe it was grief or he was worried about the future or global warming or something but, whatever it was, it came across as odd to her.

At least when the curtain pulled back, he didn't break down like Emily Walker had done. Smythe simply leaned forward until his nose all but touched the glass.

'It's him,' David Smythe said the moment the sheet was lifted off to reveal Sir Harry Clarke's face.

Hannah pressed the intercom button and thanked the morgue assistant on the other side of the viewing glass. The man nodded and replaced the cloth. The curtains then automatically closed over the windows, cutting the body off from view.

'Thank you for doing that,' Wise said. 'I know it must be difficult.'

'It's certainly not something you do every day,' Smythe replied.

Hannah handed the clipboard with the formal documentation to Smythe. 'If you could just sign these, we can let you get back to your family.'

Smythe flicked through the forms. 'I'm sorry but do you have a pen?' He mimed signing the form as if Hannah had no idea what a pen was used for.

As much as Hannah wanted to tell him what she really thought, she produced her pen from her pocket and offered it to him. 'There you go.'

'Thanks.' Smythe took it from her with his left hand and signed each form with a flourish, his signature large and elaborate, like he was some rock star handing out autographs for fans, rather than a man notarising the death of his father-in-law. Once each form was duly signed, Smythe passed the forms and the pen back to Hannah.

Eager to be gone from the viewing room, Hannah was about to open the door and show Smythe out when he spoke.

'Is it true what the TV's saying, that Harry was killed by this mad man?' Smythe said.

'We can't talk too much about the case I'm afraid,' Wise said.

'Ah, right. Of course. How silly of me,' Smythe said. 'Sorry.'

'But did your father-in-law know Mark Hassleman?' Wise asked, his voice casual.

Smythe pursed his lips as if thinking. 'I don't recall him mentioning the name.'

'And what about Yuri Andronovitch?'

'Definitely not.'

'Are you sure? He wasn't investing in tech companies or doing deals in Russia or acting as a go-between for someone.'

Smythe shook his head. 'Sorry. Nothing like that.'

Hannah ground her teeth together. She indicated the exit. 'This way, sir.' She set off, not wanting anyone to dally, and opened the doors for Wise and Smythe to walk through.

'You said you were shadowing Sir Harry earlier,' Wise said as they stepped into the corridor and headed towards the main exit, 'so he could retire one day. Does that mean you'll be running his company now?'

Smythe pulled on his wax jacket. 'Gosh. I hadn't thought about that. I suppose, yes, yes I will. I mean Laura inherits everything so she'll own the company but I presume I'll take over the running of it all. The wife doesn't really like that side of things.'

'What side is that?' Wise asked.

'The business side. I think Laura feels it's all a bit beneath her — she never really approved of her father getting his hands dirty, doing deals. She was much happier with Harry when he was an MP, "doing his bit" and all that. Maybe that's why Laura likes all her charity work.' Smythe chuckled. 'If you can call organising boring dinners with expensive raffles "charity work."' He did the air quote thing as he said it — another thing that got on Hannah's nerves.

'How did your wife feel about the whole "Sir Twenty Per Cent" scandal during the pandemic?' Wise asked. 'She seemed to think that was your doing?'

'Oh God,' Smythe said, looking aghast. 'She was positively mortified, poor thing. Laura didn't even want to do the school run because of all the gossip. She ended up sending the nanny most days to drop the kids off and pick them up.'

'But was it your project?' Wise said.

'Only as far as I saw an opportunity and suggested to Harry that we could do some good in a terrible time. What's the point of having connections if you don't use them when the country is in trouble? Perhaps, with hindsight, we shouldn't have charged so much commission, but we put so much work into it, we didn't think anyone could possibly object to us being paid a little for our time.'

'Who else would've known about Sir Harry's schedule?' Wise asked, holding open the door to outside. Bright light rushed into the corridor, making Hannah blink suddenly. Plenty of cold air came with it, sharp enough to wake her up.

'His plans weren't a secret,' Smythe said, stepping

outside. 'In fact, his itinerary was distributed to quite a few people — everyone he was meeting in New York had it, his team here, his drivers and so on. I'm sure even his cleaner had it so she could get his house ready for his return.'

'Would you be able to get us a list of those names?' Wise said. 'Just so we can eliminate them from our inquiries.'

'I don't think Harry's cleaner shot him,' Smythe said with a chuckle.

'No, but she may have seen someone hanging about outside his home or perhaps someone knocked on the door asking questions about when he'd be back.'

'Sorry. I hadn't thought about that. Gosh, this is all terribly upsetting isn't it?' Smythe zipped up his jacket. 'What a mess.'

'We'll find who did it,' Wise said. 'I promise you.'

Smythe nodded. 'I hope you do. Anyway, I'd best be off. Let me know if there is anything else you need.'

'Thank you, sir,' Wise said.

They watched Smythe climb behind the wheel of a white Porsche Macan and drive off.

'What a wanker,' Hannah said as they walked over to the Mondeo.

'Not a fan then?' Wise said, unlocking the door.

'The man's got a silver spoon stuck so far up his arse, he doesn't even know it's there anymore,' Hannah said, then took a breath. 'I'm sorry. Men like him made my life a misery at university. I shouldn't take it out on him.'

'Well, both he and his wife are a lot richer now though,' Wise said. 'Not a bad motive for murder.'

'But they've got no reason to kill Andronvitch or Hassleman,' Hannah said.

'I know but nothing about this case makes sense,' Wise

said. He opened the door and climbed in. Hannah did the same.

'It's like we're being given too much to look at and yet nothing to work with,' Wise said, making no attempt to start the car. He chewed his lip, thinking. 'It all feels wrong to me.'

'In what way?' Hannah asked.

'Andronovitch was a private person. Rich, yes. Connected. But no one profits from his death. Maybe Putin ordered it but why? He wasn't causing anyone any trouble. Maybe someone was angry at him for being rich but there are plenty of other, more obviously wealthy people to target.

'Same with Hassleman. He was an annoying drug addict but again no one profits from his death. Yes, he was young and wealthy but he was hardly flaunting his cash. He was a recluse whose only interest was cocaine. So why pick him?'

'Sir Harry Clarke was a very public figure and that whole pandemic profiteering thing pissed off a lot of people,' Hannah said.

'I know. But he was out of town for the whole week and yet, somehow, the killer knew he was going to be back at his home at 10:45 or thereabouts on Friday night. The average Joe on the streets wasn't to know that. Only someone who knew him would. Someone like your friend, the wanker, for example, but where do the other murders fit in?'

'What if the deaths aren't connected?'

'Then I'd be pursuing very different lines of enquiry — but the little physical evidence we have shows what appears to be the same person committing each murder and, each time they disappear into a bloody car park never to be seen again.' Wise slammed the steering wheel. 'Shit. I forgot to ask Sarah if she'd made any progress tracking vehicles that could take the motorbike to and from the car parks without being seen.'

'I'll check with her,' Hannah said.

Wise rubbed his face, suddenly looking very tired. There were bruises on his hands that she'd not noticed before, like he'd been in a fight or something. 'Thank you. I appreciate it.' He glanced over at Hannah and smiled. 'I bet you're wishing you'd got an easier case to solve for your first time out with us?'

Hannah winced. 'Does it make me a bad person if I say I'm enjoying it?'

Wise gave a gentle shake of his head. 'No, it makes you a copper.'

'Yeah? Well, in that case, I am. I mean, yeah, a bit of an easier case to start with would've been great but this sort of stuff is why I joined the police.' Hannah paused for a moment, wondering how much she should tell Wise. She didn't want to come across as some sort of glory hunter or a crusader for social justice nut job but she wanted Wise to like her. 'I never really liked being in uniform, dealing with all that petty stuff like nicking someone for shop lifting some nappies or a dealing with idiots having a Friday night punch up. I wanted to do some real good, help people who've really suffered.'

'I get it. I really do,' Wise said. 'My first murder was an eighty-year-old pensioner who'd been killed for about twenty quid's worth of jewellery. She'd been in her flat for a week before the neighbours noticed the smell and called us. There was a half-eaten plate of beans on toast, all covered in mould, on the dinner table next to a half-drunk cup of tea. Some skaghead had broken in while she was having her supper and brained her with an ashtray that she'd probably had since the seventies. I remember thinking that she had no one to even notice she was dead but, from that point on, she had me. I promised her I'd find her killer. I'd find her justice.'

'Did you?'

'Yeah, I did. It was a man called Richard Wilkins, a junkie with a record as long as my arm. He'd made it easy for us to catch him too — fingerprints on the ashtray and on her jewellery box, there was skin under her fingertips where she'd scratched him during a struggle and we had video of him trying to sell the stuff he'd nicked in a pawn shop.'

'So, not like this case?'

'No,' Wise said. 'Not like this case — but I'm still going to get the bastard who's doing this. No matter how clever they think they are.'

27

W ise stared at the whiteboards. There were pictures of all three victims, plus more press clippings about them. Between scrutiny of Andronvitch after the invasion of Ukraine and calls for sanctions against him to Hassleman's tortured genius profiles and Sir Harry's PPE scandals, there was enough information available to write a book or two.

The trouble was, knowing all that didn't help Wise. It didn't help him one bit.

He glanced at the clock. It was gone 7 p.m. and Wise was shattered. Time to call it a night. It had been another fruitless day after all, his team working hard to get nowhere fast, hoping to spot a mistake made by someone who never made any.

Sitting behind the wheel of his car, Wise rubbed his face, trying to get rid of the bleariness that clung to him after thirty odd hours with no sleep. He knew he should head home and get his head down, but he couldn't face it. A row with Jean was the last thing he needed.

The radio came on as Wise started the car. The

presenter was reading out that afternoon's football scores. He smiled when he heard Chelsea had beaten Crystal Palace 3-0. His dad would be happy.

His dad. How long had it been since he'd last seen him?

It had been at the barbecue around at Wise's place. The day Morris had done a runner. The day Andy had died.

Shit. He took a long breath, then another. He couldn't lose it again. Not like he had the night before. He couldn't.

Wise looked at the clock again. His dad would be back from the game by now, probably cooking his dinner, with whatever nonsense was on the BBC playing in the background. Seeing him would make Wise feel better. There'd be no judgement. No criticism. No disappointment.

He turned the car engine on and drove out of the station car park.

His dad still lived in Streatham, in a terraced house he'd bought back in the day for three grand, a fortune in old money, but it was worth at least seven hundred thousand now. Wise had tried to convince his dad to sell the place a few times, cash in on all that equity and enjoy his retirement, but his dad wasn't having it.

'Where would I move to?' he'd said every time. 'All my friends are here. What's the point of having money if I'm lonely?'

Wise couldn't argue with that.

His dad's place was only twenty minutes away, straight down the A3. It wasn't even half past by the time Wise pulled up outside, and he felt another twinge of guilt for not visiting more often.

Wise grabbed his jacket, locked the car up, and headed over to his father's house. He could see the lights on, that warm glow that always used to make him feel safe when he'd been a kid coming home after a night out.

He was about five metres away when the door opened, and a man stepped out.

Wise stopped in his tracks, his breath caught in his throat. He knew who it was, even though he'd not seen the man in decades. The man's features were as recognisable as his own.

He could feel panic stirring in his gut once more. Flashes of memories tearing him up inside.

'See you later,' called out the man as he shut the door behind him. Wise watched as he lit a cigarette in the doorway. The lighter's flame illuminated him enough to confirm the man's identity. He thought about going back to the car, but what if the man spotted him? Wise didn't want to look like he was running away. His only hope was that the man would head off down towards the high street, away from where Wise stood, and not notice him standing there.

But did Wise want that? Wouldn't it be better if they talked? Said hello at least? Should he go up and say something? But what? What could he say?

In the end, the decision was taken out of his hands because the man turned left and walked straight towards Wise. He wore jeans, a white polo shirt buttoned up to the neck and a black bomber jacket, with white Adidas trainers on his feet. A perfect south London casual.

As the man took another drag on his fag, he looked up and saw Wise watching him. He stopped half a metre away. He didn't smile. 'Fucking hell, Si. Wasn't expecting to see you here,' said Tom.

His brother hadn't changed much except there was a hardness to his face, to his eyes that Wise didn't recognise.

'Hello, Tom,' Wise said, forcing the words out. He'd not been expecting this. He wasn't prepared, wasn't ready. It was a miracle his voice held together and didn't break. 'Been a while.'

His brother shrugged as if twenty years was no big deal. 'You look smart. You didn't get dressed up just to see the old man, did you? I know he's got standards, but the suit's a bit too much.'

'I've been at work.'

'Catching bad guys on a Saturday? That's not good.' He grinned. It wasn't a pleasant smile. 'How is police work these days? I hear your partner got his brains blown out. That can't be good.'

'No. It wasn't.' Wise didn't know what else to say. He couldn't tell his brother the truth. The man opposite him was a stranger with twenty years and a lifetime of pain and grudges all stacked up like a wall between them.

'What about you?' Wise said instead. 'Life treating you well?'

'Can't complain.'

'That's good.' Wise didn't know what else to say. They were like a pair of casual acquaintances passing by instead of twin brothers.

Tom obviously felt the same way. There was a slight shake of his head, a curl of a lip that might've been a smile, and he took another long pull of his cigarette. 'Well,' he said, before blowing the smoke out. 'It's been fun catching up, but I've got places to be. Maybe I'll see you in the street again one day.'

He went to walk past, but Wise caught his arm. There was so much he needed to say. 'Tom, I—'

Tom looked at Wise's hand holding him, then turned his gaze up so he was staring into Wise's eyes. 'Nah. We've said all there is to say a long time ago. I've been polite, but don't push your luck. Now, let go.'

'We should talk—'

'About fucking what? How you ran and left me to the filth?' Again, there was the grin. Animalistic. Violent. Nasty. 'How you went and joined them while I was banged up? How you became the enemy?'

Wise released his grip.

Tom laughed. 'I thought fucking not. You never had any balls.' He looked Wise up and down again and shook his head, lip curled in disgust. 'See you again in another twenty years.'

He sauntered off then, like he didn't have a care in the world. Half way down the street, he stopped by a black BMW 5 series and there was a bleep as he unlocked the car, lights flashing. He took another drag of his cigarette, flicked the butt into the gutter, then climbed into the car. The engine roared to life, then Tom pulled away, disappearing into the dark night as if he'd never been there at all.

Wise stood there, staring after him, feeling the hole inside him grow ever bigger. That wasn't the reunion he'd been wishing for, nor was that the brother he missed. He didn't know who it was that he'd just met. Someone whom he shared a face with, but that was it.

Wise missed his brother, it was clear that Tom didn't feel the same. There was no nostalgia pulling at him. No regret at what was lost. There was just the anger and the hate and the blame for what had happened that night.

Rain started to fall, but Wise remained where he was, watching the direction Tom had driven off in, unable to move. His heart broken yet again. Wishing he could turn back time and stop that night, that fight from happening.

He felt sick. He felt broken. If he'd had the energy, Wise would've left and gone to find a hotel or something, but he didn't trust himself behind the wheel anymore. Chances were he'd fall asleep driving. Maybe kill himself or kill someone else.

So he trudged over to his father's house, retracing the steps Tom had just taken, the smell of his cigarette still lingering in the air, mingling with his guilt.

Wise had door keys, but he never felt right using them unless it was some sort of emergency, so he rang the bell and waited. He heard his dad getting up and heading out into the hallway despite the sound of *Strictly* that droned away behind the curtains in the living room.

'You forgot something?' his dad said as he opened the door, then he realised it was Wise standing there. 'Oh, Simon. What are you doing here?'

At least his surprise quickly turned to a smile and Wise felt a bit of the darkness lift from his shoulders. 'It's good to see you, Dad.'

'Come here.' His father pulled him into a hug. 'It's so good to see you too, son.' They held each other, Wise enjoying being in his father's arms, even though the man wasn't the giant he'd been when Wise was a kid. There'd been a time when it felt like his father could've picked him up in one hand and protected him from everything. Now, Wise's arms fit all too easily around the man. Age had turned him from superhero to human and Wise loved him all the more for it.

Then there was the triple pat on the back that always signalled it was time to let go and his dad stepped back. 'You want a cup of tea?'

'That would be great.'

His dad turned and headed back into the house, Wise following, past the door to the lounge, *Strictly* blaring away, and into the kitchen at the back. It was small but always perfectly tidy, his dad's dinner plate already washed and drying in the rack by the sink, a second behind it. Tom's plate, Wise realised.

His father flicked the kettle on and grabbed two mugs out of the cupboard. One had the Chelsea FC badge on it, the other bore the logo of an instant soup brand. Both were worn and faded, dating back to when Wise and his brother were young. His dad never saw the point in replacing something that still did its job well enough.

'How are the kids?' his dad asked.

Angry with me, thought Wise. Let down. 'They're fine,' he said instead as he took off his suit jacket.

Obviously not convincingly though, as his dad turned, eyebrow raised. 'Something wrong?'

'It's all good, Dad,' Wise said, but his dad didn't move. He just looked at his son, tea bags still in his hands, hovering over the tea mugs, with a look of love that would've broken the hardest of criminals into confessing. Wise sighed, pulled out a chair by the kitchen table, put his jacket over the back of it and sat down. 'It's all pretty crap, Dad.'

His dad nodded and went back to making the tea. 'Problems with Jean?'

'I've pissed her off. Let the kids down too.'

'Oh.' The kettle boiled, puffing out steam, and the button clicked off at its base. His father picked it up and poured it into the mugs. 'I must admit she didn't sound too happy when I spoke to her this morning.'

'Well, I'd not been home — there was a murder last night — and I was supposed to watch Harry play football. He had a match on today.'

'I know. He won. 4-2. Jean said he played well.' His dad squeezed the tea bags with a spoon, then fished them out and dropped them in the bin. 'She said you've been struggling with things since Andy died.'

'Yeah. I have. I can't get what happened out of my head.'

His dad took out a half full container of milk from the fridge and splashed some into the tea. 'No sugar, right?'

'No sugar,' Wise said. His dad passed him the cup with the soup brand logo and then spooned some sugar into the Chelsea mug.

'I thought you were going to give it up,' Wise said.

'I'm seventy-one, son,' his dad said, patting the slight paunch around his belly. 'Bit late for worrying about sugar in my tea. Besides, a man's got to have some vices.' He pulled out a chair and sat down next to Wise. 'Andy dying wasn't your fault. You do know that, don't you?'

'Knowing it and believing it are two different things.'

His dad gave him another knowing look. 'Have you eaten? I can rustle up some egg and chips, if you want?'

Wise smiled, grateful for his dad's care. 'That'd be lovely.'

'The spare room's all made up too, if you want to stay here the night. You look proper knackered.'

'I've not been sleeping well and the case I'm on is ... difficult.'

'Not that rich man thing I saw on the news?' his dad said. He delved into the tiny freezer above the fridge and pulled out a pack of ready fries.

'Yeah, that one.'

'Bloody hell. I don't know how you can do your job. Dealing with dead bodies and sickos all day long. It's no wonder you don't sleep well at night.' He shook some chips out onto a baking tray and stuck it in the oven.

'Someone's got to do it.'

His father returned to his seat and took a slurp of tea. 'Yeah — but does it have to be you? If it's costing you your marriage, is it worth it? You're a smart lad. I'm sure you could find something else a bit more ... normal.'

'You know why I do it. Why I have to do it.'

There was a little shake of his father's head. 'Simon, that happened over twenty years ago. You've done more than enough to make up for it. Heavens knows we've all paid a price for it. Some more than others.'

The image of Brian Sellers lying dead on the floor of the Bishop's Crown pub flashed into Wise's mind as if he was there right then and not sitting in his dad's kitchen two decades later.

'I saw Tom leaving,' Wise said, trying not to remember what it felt like to kick and punch Sellers to the ground. The utter joy in the violence. The same joy he'd felt the night before.

'You did?' His dad looked up, like a kid caught with his hand in the biscuit tin.

'Yeah. We said hello, but that was it.'

'Saying hello is progress, isn't it?'

As sad as it was, Wise had to admit that was true. 'He just pop around to see you?'

'We went to see the Chels together. Donnie couldn't make the match, so I offered him the spare ticket.'

'You could've asked me,' Wise said.

'Yeah, I could've and you would've said yes, then not turned up. Jean and the kids aren't the only ones who get pushed aside for your job.'

That hurt. 'I'm sorry, Dad.'

'It doesn't bother me. I still love you no matter how unreliable you are,' his dad said with a chuckle.

'Tom looked well.'

'Yeah. He is, I think. Making a bit of money. Still flitting between loads of women like a dog on heat.' His dad got up, checked the chips in the oven, gave them a bit of a shake, and then went to the fridge to get some eggs. 'He certainly seems a lot more relaxed these days. Less ... angry.'

'I don't think he could get more angry, Dad.'

'He was only sixteen when he went inside. Two years in the juvenile centre, then off to the Scrubs for another ten years. There are bloody hard men in there. It would've been tough on him.' His dad cracked the eggs into the frying pan and they immediately sizzled.

'He ever talk about what it was like?'

His dad laughed. 'Tom doesn't talk about anything serious. It's his way of coping.'

'He was always like that,' Wise said.

'And you've always carried the weight of the world on your shoulders. Still do.' The eggs were ready, so his dad slipped them out of the pan and onto a plate, then took the chips from the oven and dished those up, too. 'There you go. Tuck in.'

'Thanks, Dad.' Wise looked down at the plate and wondered how many times had his dad made him that exact meal in that kitchen? Too many to count, but he'd never get sick of it. His dad might not be much of a chef, but he put all his love into cooking for his sons. 'Tom say what he's doing for work? I saw his motor and they don't come cheap.'

'Tell me about it. Bloody lovely, it is too. It's like a spaceship inside. It'd be wasted on me, though. I wouldn't even know how to turn it on, let alone drive it. He's pretty proud of it and so he should be.'

'So, what is he doing?' Wise forked a spoonful of egg into his mouth.

'I asked him and he just tapped his nose and said "don't ask" so I left it. Whatever it is, it pays well, and it makes him happy, so that's good enough for me.'

'Above board though?'

His dad shrugged. 'You know Tom.'

Probably not then. Wise ate more of his dinner, even though the talk of Tom and all those stirred up memories had spoiled his appetite. He moved the conversation onto the game. A much safer conversation for all concerned. Chelsea blue ran through all the Wise men, going back generations. Some of Wise's earliest memories were of going to the match with Tom, his dad and his grandad, feeling all grown up amongst a crowd of men — and in those days it was only men — who all smelt of cheap cigarettes and stale beer, laughing at all the swearing, joining in with the singing and chants, and eating chocolate wagon wheels at half-time or a burger if they were lucky.

Wise finished his dinner and his tea.

'Go sit in the front room,' his dad said. 'I'll be back in a minute.'

Wise nodded and went through and plonked himself down on the sofa. *Strictly* had finished, and a show with B list celebrities doing challenges was on instead.

His dad appeared a minute later with a sweatshirt in his hands. 'Change out of your shirt and put this on. It should fit. Get comfortable.'

'Cheers, Dad.' Wise took off his shirt and slipped on the sweatshirt.

'Give that to me,' his dad said, taking the shirt. 'I'll pop it into the wash.'

'There's no need,' Wise said, but his dad was already back in the kitchen and Wise knew better than to argue.

He settled down on the sofa again and watched some pop singer from the eighties eat something disgusting while being cheered on by other famous people Wise didn't recognise.

The next thing Wise knew, it was dark, and he was alone in the living room, a duvet thrown over him. He looked at the clock and saw that it was nearly five in the morning. He'd slept for over seven hours on the sofa.

Wise stood up and tried to stretch the kinks out of his back, amazed at how good he felt despite the aches and pains. For the first time in an age, he'd woken up without a brain fog, feeling almost like his old self.

His shirt was on a hanger hooked on the door frame, washed, dried and ironed, looking as good as new. His old man must've stayed up half the night to get that done. He'd even given his shoes a shine. Even after all these years, the man had standards.

Dressed, Wise scribbled a quick note to his dad, thanking him for dinner, the laundry service and his company, and left the house. It was dark and cold still outside, the promise of winter in the air, and Wise pulled his coat tight around him, not wanting to lose the good feelings he'd woken up with.

As he climbed into his knackered old Mondeo, he couldn't help but think of his brother's BMW. God, he hoped his brother wasn't doing anything stupid to pay for such a nice car. Trouble was, Wise couldn't think of too many legal ways an ex-convict with no education could earn that sort of money.

He turned the ignition, and the engine grumbled to life. On went the heater next, blasting away to remove the condensation on the inside of the windscreen so he could see enough to drive. Then it would be back to the estate, shower and change and then onto the nick and maybe forty-five hours to stop another murder.

Nothing too impossible then.

Sunday, 18th September

28

Wise stood at attention in Detective Chief Superintendent Walling's office on the top floor of Kennington nick. Roberts was with him, but Walling had offered her a seat, so that told him exactly whose side everyone was on. The fact she wouldn't even meet his eyes when he'd turned up was even more telling.

The chief wasn't sitting down either. He fixed his eyes on Wise with the same sort of warmth Tom had dished out the night before. 'Have you ever been to Number Ten, Wise?'

'No, sir,' Wise replied.

'Well, funnily enough, I hadn't either — until yesterday,' Walling snarled. 'But dear God, I've seen it now. I even got to meet the prime minister in his private chambers. What an experience that was.'

Obviously, it wasn't a good one, but Wise said nothing.

'I always thought the prime minister was a quiet man, but it appears he has quite the temper when he's unhappy.' Walling paced from one side of his desk to the other, his cheeks growing redder and redder. 'And when his friends and colleagues are getting murdered, he gets very unhappy indeed.'

Wise said nothing. He'd learnt very early in his career that sometimes you just had to stand and take a bollocking no matter how unfair you thought it was.

'He thinks we're incompetent. He thinks we're bloody useless. He thinks we couldn't catch a cold.' Walling was a big man, his gut barely contained in his uniform, and the thought crossed Wise's mind that, if he carried on the way he was going, he'd have a heart attack before he finished his diatribe and that might not be a bad thing.

At least Wise had had a good night's sleep for once. And a coffee. He might not be so tolerant otherwise. If this had happened yesterday, there would have been more than a good chance Wise would've decked the bastard.

'I've promised the PM progress, Inspector. I've promised we'll arrest the killer before anyone else dies,' Walling shouted, 'and I will not have you make me out to be a liar. Do I make myself clear?'

'Yes, sir,' replied Wise. 'We're working around the clock, pursuing every lead.'

'Really? Or are you not capable of seeing the clues?' Walling roared back. 'We all know you failed to spot a bloody criminal working right next to you.'

Wise stiffened. 'No one in this room suspected Andy of any wrongdoing until it was too late, sir.' He put as much venom as he could in the honorific. Andy had fooled everyone, not just him.

Walling stopped his pacing and leaned over his desk, jabbing a finger at Wise. 'You better take care, Inspector. You're standing on very thin ice indeed.'

'As I said to Detective Chief Inspector Roberts, if you don't think I can run this investigation, then I'll happily step aside for someone you have faith in,' Wise said as calmly as he could muster.

'Believe me, I'm looking into that right now,' Walling said. 'The clock's ticking for you, Inspector — in more ways than one. Now, get out of here and get to work.'

'Yes, sir.' Wise didn't bother saluting despite Walling expected it. Instead, he turned on his heels and left the office, doing his best to squash his own temper.

They were five days into the investigation, for God's sake. Five bloody days. It was no time at all as far as investigations of this nature went — especially with all the cutbacks to staffing and resources. And now the man wanted a miracle done.

'Simon.' It was Roberts.

He turned and watched Roberts clomp down the stairs after him. 'Yes, ma'am?' There was no respect in his voice. No nicety.

'Come on. There's no need for that,' Roberts said.

'No?'

'What did you think he was going to say to you? The PM ripped us both a new one yesterday over these murders.'

'And, like any good leader, he passed the bollocking on.'

'That's how these things work,' hissed Roberts.

'Well, I appreciated your support.'

Roberts shook her head. 'Listen — you're still the SIO. I've backed you one hundred percent so far and made it very clear to Walling that I believe in you — but even I can't hold him back forever.'

'I can't just manufacture evidence out of thin air,' Wise said. 'Everyone's working as hard as they can.'

'I know and I've asked for more personnel to help you. They'll be here tomorrow morning.'

That was something, at least. 'Good.'

'Come on. I'll join you for the DMM. Put on a united front for the troops.'

Wise nodded. 'They're already waiting.'

The incident room was quiet when they entered. The entire team knew the pressure they were all under.

Roberts perched herself on a desk to one side while Wise went and stood in front of the whiteboards. Someone had cut and pasted the Sunday papers' headlines on to the board. One proclaimed, "Rich Men, Dead Men" while another asked, "Will The Motorbike Killer Strike Again?" while a third demanded to know, "Who's Killing The 1%?"

It was all sensationalist rubbish, but what else could they expect?

'Happy Sunday,' Wise said. 'Thank you again for coming in over your weekend. We're on day five of our investigation and it's day two since Sir Harry Clarke was murdered. If our killer keeps to his three-day schedule, we can expect another murder tomorrow night. Needless to say, the entire world is watching us.' He glanced over at Roberts. 'So, who's got some good news to add to the board?'

'Ballistics have been in touch, Guv,' Sarah said. 'They confirm it was the same gun that killed all three men.'

'I've got a bit of a Russia connection to the weapon,' Donut said. 'I followed up with Organised Crime and they said it's the Russian mafia who are bringing most of the weapons into London these days. In fact, I was told that victim number one, Yuri Andronovitch, was one of the suspected heads of the Odessa crime family.'

'That's interesting,' Wise said. 'Could he have supplied the gun to our killer, and that's why he was killed?'

'They also said that the Redfellas, as they call them, are so good at bringing guns in that the market is pretty saturated. Apparently, you can pick up anything from an

AK47 to a Mac 10 if you go looking in the right pub,' Donut said.

'That's not such good news,' Wise said. 'Anyone else with anything to add?'

'I've been following up how the killer is magically appearing and disappearing from the car parks,' Sarah said. 'So I'm going through the CCTV again around the car parks, looking for vehicles big enough to conceal the bike that arrive before the murder and leave after. There are about six possibles from the Hassleman murder. I'm just about to start on the Andronovitch car park next.'

'Great going, Sarah. Obviously, prioritise any that appear at all three car parks,' Wise said. 'Any luck with the banks, Jono?'

'We're getting stonewalled over Andronovitch's money,' Jono said. 'DCI Samson rang us yesterday and told us there was no way we'd get that information.'

Wise turned to Roberts. 'Can you speak to them? Surely, they can be of more help to us, especially after your meeting yesterday.'

Roberts nodded. 'I'll see what I can do.'

'Thank you,' Wise said. 'Any joy with Hassleman's bank, Jono?'

'For a rich bloke, he led a bloody boring life, Guv,' Jono said. 'He bought most of his groceries and all his booze online. In fact, the only time he definitely went outside was once in a while to get cash from the bank machine in Ladbroke Grove.'

'His drug money,' Wise said.

'Five hundred quid a day, on average,' Hicksy said. 'There were also in-branch withdrawals of at least a couple of grand once or twice a week.'

'And no one wondered what he was doing with all this cash?' Wise asked.

'We spoke to someone down at the bank and, apparently, they all suspected he was a druggie, but it was his cash he was taking out and he wasn't breaking any laws in the bank,' Hicksy said. 'He turned up the worse for wear a few times, but they just laughed at him behind his back after giving him his money.'

'No wonder Radinsky didn't want anyone else selling him drugs,' Hannah said. 'He was putting serious cash in that man's pocket.'

Wise nodded. 'Let's pass that information on to the drugs squad, eh?'

'Will do,' Hannah said.

'He went out last month, though. Six weeks before his murder,' Jono said. 'On Saturday, the fourteenth, there's two Uber charges on his credit card — one at 7:36 p.m. and another at 11:48 p.m. — but nothing in between, so we don't know where he went. If it was a dinner or a bar, he didn't pay any bills with his card.'

'Maybe he used his cash,' Donut said.

'No, I don't think so,' Wise said. 'That money was for his cocaine. Try to find out where he went and let's check Andronovitch and Clarke's whereabouts on that date. Maybe they were at the same event. Maybe that's our connection.'

'I'll call Smythe and check,' Hannah said.

'No. Let's track down Clarke's PA and ask her. What was her name?'

'Sabine,' Hannah said, checking her notebook.

'You and Sarah go have a chat with her. See if everything was as perfect in her boss' world as his son-in-law makes out,' Wise said. 'Remember — our killer didn't find out

Clarke's travel schedule by following him around. That took inside knowledge — unless they posted it online somewhere and our killer googled it.'

Donut held up a hand. 'I checked and there are a few articles about him in New York during the week, but there's no mention of when he was coming back and there's definitely nothing about his schedule online.'

'He could've rung Sir Harry's office and found out that way,' Sarah said.

'Okay. Check with the PA if that's the sort of information that they would give out over the phone,' Wise said. 'Our killer could've pretended to be a member of the press or a family member or something, but I hope they are more security aware than that though. Because if the information is confidential and known to only a few people, it gives us a list of suspects and, if we can link that person to our other murders somehow, then we could have our killer.'

Wise looked around the room and saw excitement on his team's faces. Maybe this was the slip up they were looking for, the thread they could pull to unravel everything. A lead at last.

29

B y the time Hannah had tracked down Sabine Cricheaux and made it over to her home in Wimbledon with Sarah, it was mid-afternoon and storm clouds were filling the sky once more. Cars packed the small terraced street on both sides of the road, and Sarah had to drive around several times until she found a spot two streets over, next to a park. A sign said "residents only" but Sarah ignored it. 'Traffic wardens don't work Sundays.'

'You better hope so,' Hannah said as they headed back to Latimer Road, but Sarah wasn't listening. She was already lighting up without breaking stride, inhaling deeply as if her life depended on it. Markham shook her head. 'Have you ever thought you might have a bit of a problem?'

Sarah blew out a lungful of smoke. 'The only problem I have is not being able to smoke as much as I'd like.'

They walked along the terrace houses, checking the numbers. The one they were looking for had a B next to it, so it was probably a property that had been converted into flats.

'This is ours.' Hannah said halfway along the street, pointing to a house with two front doors.

Sarah rang the doorbell for the upstairs apartment. Almost immediately, they heard footsteps, and the door opened. 'Are you the police?' asked the woman. Tall and thin, she spoke with the barest hint of a French accent. Her skin had a light olive tone that helped hide some of the redness around her eyes where she had been crying. She had a shoulder-length bob with a fringe that brushed her eyebrows.

'I'm Detective Constable Sarah Choi and this is Detective Sergeant Hannah Markham,' Sarah said, holding up her warrant card. 'Sabine Cricheaux?'

'Oui,' the woman said. 'Come in.' She led them up the stairs, into her apartment and to a combined living room/kitchen at the rear, walking with a sway that reminded Hannah of a fashion model on the catwalk. She'd decorated the flat in a very modern style. A laptop lay open on a white marble kitchen island, a black Hermes Birkin handbag next to it.

'Nice bag,' Sarah said. 'I don't think I've ever seen one of these in real life. Victoria Beckham has loads of them, right?'

'Harry bought it for me a few years back,' Sabine said. 'He called it a bonus because the company was doing well. I'm almost too scared to use it.' She looked up. 'To be honest, I'd have preferred the money.'

Hannah knew nothing about handbags. 'How much does one of those cost?'

'About twenty thousand pounds,' Sabine said.

'Wow.' Hannah didn't know what else to say. She couldn't imagine spending that sort of money on anything that didn't have moving parts and required petrol. 'Couldn't you sell it?'

'Harry wouldn't like that.' Sabine's hand went to her mouth. 'I'm sorry.' She shook her head. 'Would you like some coffee?'

'I'm fine,' Sarah said.

'Not for me either,' Hannah said.

'Well, I need coffee,' Sabine said. 'Please sit.' She indicated the small table under the window at the rear of the kitchen, then popped a dark red pod into a coffee machine. Thirty seconds later, it hummed into life and filled a small expresso cup. With the cup in hand, she turned to face the officers once more. Even with her red eyes, she was quite beautiful.

'How can I help you?'

'We just need to ask you a few questions about Sir Harry Clarke,' Hannah said. 'If that's okay?'

Sabine's cup shook ever so slightly in her hand. 'I still can't believe it.'

'Were you close?' Hannah asked.

'Oui. Harry is ... was a great man. A kind man.' There was a slight crack in her voice. 'I'm sorry. This has been so hard to take in — to accept. I spoke to him just before he got on his flight home and I just can't believe ... he's dead. You must think me very silly.'

'Not at all,' Hannah said with a smile. 'Just take your time.'

Sabine nodded. 'Thank you. We were close. We worked together for many, many years and he was a friend as well as my employer. After his wife died, he would joke that at least he still had me, his work wife. I started helping him when he was still an MP, then I moved with him when he set up his business.'

'You were Sir Harry's PA?'

'He never really liked that title, you know, the knighthood,' Sabine said. 'It was useful for business — the Americans loved it — but he was always Harry to the rest of us. Despite his success, he was a very modest man.'

'What did you do for him?'

'Everything. From organising his day to making sure he had transport to and from his meetings. I filtered any request to see him, handled all his correspondence. I even made sure he had food in his fridge at home.'

'That's a lot of responsibility,' Hannah said.

'We were a good team.'

'I'm sure you were,' Hannah said. 'Behind every successful man, there's a strong woman.'

'I just did what I could to help.'

'Did he ever mention a Yuri Andronovitch?' Hannah asked.

Sabine sipped her coffee. Only her eyes peeked over the rim of the cup. 'That was one of the other men killed?'

'Yes, that's right.'

'I don't remember Harry having any appointments with him. They could've met somewhere, perhaps. At a function or a fundraiser or something like that. Let me check his diary.' She put the cup down and went over to her laptop. She tapped on a few keys and leaned in closer to the screen. Perhaps she needed glasses, but didn't want to put them on. 'Nothing in his calendar that I can see. Let me check his emails ... no, no mention of a Yuri Andronovitch.'

'What about Mark Hassleman?'

'He's the tech guy?' Sabine asked. 'Young?'

Hannah nodded.

'I was thinking about this last night — after the news,' Sabine said. 'And I think Harry met him at a dinner a few weeks ago. They were sitting at the same table. Apparently, he ate nothing and kept disappearing to the bathroom every five minutes, coming back more and more high, jabbering away like a madman to anyone and everyone.'

Markham glanced at Sarah, then back to Sabine. This was new. 'Are you sure?'

'Definitely. Harry was furious. He called me and said he never wanted to be within a mile of the man again. Harry hated drug addicts. He was contemplating reporting him to the police.'

'What date was that?' Sarah asked.

Sabine tapped away again at the laptop. 'The fourteenth of August.'

Hannah felt her pulse pick up. A connection. The first connection between victims. 'Where was the dinner?'

'It was ... It was at the Natural History Museum,' Sabine said. 'I think a company that wanted Harry to do some consulting for them arranged it.' She continued to search through her emails. 'Here we go. It was the European Economics Agenda. They're a think tank that advises the government and various corporations. A Terrence Swift invited Harry.'

'I didn't know they did dinners there,' Hannah said.

'They set up the tables in the main atrium, under the dinosaur bones. It can be quite "wow" when done right.'

'You don't know who else was there, by any chance?'

'No, but I'll give you Terrence's number. Perhaps he can give you the seating plans or the guest list.' She looked around, spotted a pack of post-it notes near the sink, took one and jotted down a phone number. 'Here you go.'

'Thank you,' said Hannah.

'But you should ask David. He was there,' Sabine said.

It took everything Hannah had to keep her face impassive. 'David?'

'David Smythe. Harry's son-in-law,' Sabine said.

'He's Harry's number two, isn't he?' Hannah said.

'He thinks so.'

'But Harry didn't?'

Sabine took a deep breath. 'David's a nice man. His heart's in the right place.'

'But?' Hannah asked.

'When he lost his job with the bank, he couldn't find anything else for ages,' Sabine said. 'Laura, his wife, was quite upset over it all, so Harry said he'd help and he made up a job for him. He said it was a bit like giving Laura some of her inheritance now because David didn't really do anything to earn his salary.'

'What does he do?'

'A bit of research here and there. Looking for some new investment opportunities and so on. Harry even let David buy some property a few times for the portfolio. And sometimes he would go along to functions with Harry too — like the thing at the Natural History Museum,' Sabine said.

'David's wife mentioned her husband was actually behind the PPE contracts,' Hannah said.

'And what a disaster that was,' Sabine said. 'The PR damage was almost catastrophic. Harry's reputation was everything to him. He'd been against the idea from the beginning, but David insisted. Harry was going to donate all the money he made to charity.'

'Was he?' Sarah asked. 'How much are we talking about?'

'I think it was about thirteen million pounds.'

'That's a lot of money to give away,' Hannah said.

'It would've stopped him from being called a "pandemic profiteer" though,' Sabine said.

'It must've caused tensions between Harry and David?' Sarah asked.

'Tensions? More like fireworks,' Sabine said. 'Harry was furious with David.'

'We were under the impression that David would take over the company,' Hannah said.

'Well, Laura will own the company, but the business was really Harry's connections and what they were worth to various corporations. That ... That ... That's gone with Harry.' Sabine started to cry. She snatched a tissue from a box to dab at her eyes. 'I suppose my job's gone too.'

Hannah glanced at Sarah. This was dynamite information. They had a link between two of the victims and David Smythe had been lying to them. Innocent people didn't do that.

'Ms Cricheaux,' Sarah said. 'Am I right in thinking you organised Harry's itinerary for his trip to the States?'

Sabine looked up, her enormous eyes glistening. 'Harry would tell me who he had to meet and then I'd arrange it all, so he had time for everyone. Harry ... Harry wasn't good with details like that. He needed schedules to get anything done.'

'David Smythe said Harry's schedule was common knowledge to quite a few people,' Hannah said. 'Is that right?'

Sabine thought for a minute. 'Not really. I mean he and Laura had a copy of it and I don't know if they told anyone else but otherwise his driver, Samir, knew when he was leaving and coming back, as did Tonya, his cleaner — but they've both worked with him for longer than I have. The people he met in the States only knew about their specific appointment time with Harry. He didn't even like people to know where he was staying in case someone tried seeing him unexpectedly.'

'So, if someone rang you and asked when he was travelling back, you'd refuse to give them that information?' Sarah said.

'Of course,' Sabine said. 'I wouldn't have been a very good PA otherwise. And with the crazies that seem to be everywhere these days, you have to be so careful about everything.'

'And Harry hadn't had any threats or anything like that recently?' Hannah asked. 'Any crazies?'

'Nothing serious,' Sabine said. 'Just the usual. It's difficult being successful in the world today.'

'What was the usual?'

'Not threats, really. Just abuse. A bit of name calling. Stuff like that.'

'And these came in the post or by email?'

'It's mainly Twitter these days. From someone with a load of numbers after a fake name, full of outrage that someone like Harry has made something of themselves. We ... We used to laugh about them.' Sabine let out a massive sob. 'God, do you think it could've been one of them who killed him?'

'We have to look at all possibilities,' Sarah said. She glanced at Hannah and gave a subtle nod towards the door.

'Thank you for your time, Sabine,' Hannah said. 'We'll let you get on. You've been a massive help.'

'My pleasure,' Sabine said.

Hannah stood up. 'If anything else comes to mind, please let us know.'

'D'accord,' Sabine said. She picked up another tissue and pressed it against her eyes.

'We can see ourselves out,' Sarah said, standing as well. 'Thank you.'

Hannah and Sarah left Sabine crying in her kitchen and made their way downstairs and out into the street. The moment the door was closed behind them, Sarah had a cigarette in her mouth and alight.

'Did you have that in your hand the whole time?' Hannah said as they headed back to the car.

'Don't judge me,' Sarah said. 'I get enough of that at home.'

'No judgement,' Hannah said. 'I was just impressed, to be honest.'

'It was interesting what she said back there,' Sarah said. 'About the dinner at the museum. That puts two of our victims together. It'd be great if Andronovitch was there too.'

'Tell me about it,' Hannah said.

'Should we call Smythe and ask him?'

Hannah thought about it for a moment. 'Let's talk to the Guv first. Maybe there's another way we can find out. I don't know why, but I don't want Smythe to know we know about the dinner.'

'Why's that?'

'Because he didn't tell us about it himself. It sounds like Hassleman made quite the impression on Sir Harry at that dinner. Smythe couldn't have been oblivious to it and yet he said nothing. In fact, he denied knowing Hassleman at all.'

'Maybe his father-in-law didn't confide in him the way he did with his PA?'

'If Hassleman was that out of his head, Smythe would've noticed.'

'So he lied to us.'

'Yeah, and I really don't like it when people lie to me,' Hannah said. Especially jumped-up Hooray Henries.

30

'Clarke and Hassleman were at dinner together?' Wise said in near disbelief. 'You're joking.'

Hannah smiled. 'On the fourteenth of last month. The night Hassleman took an Uber somewhere.'

'It was organised by a think tank,' Sarah added. 'The European Economics Agenda.'

'Not only that,' Hannah said, her eyes shining bright with excitement. 'They were on the same table together and Hassleman proceeded to get off his tits, pissing Clarke off.'

'You haven't told him the best bit,' Sarah said.

Wise looked from one to the other. 'What best bit?'

Now Hannah grinned. 'The wanker was with them.'

'David Smythe?' Wise said.

'Bingo,' Sarah said.

'He lied to us,' Hannah said. 'He bloody lied to us.'

The three of them were alone in MIR-One, a half-eaten pizza on the table between them. Everyone else had called it a night.

'Now, why would he do that?' Wise said. No wonder they were excited.

'Because he didn't want us to know there was a link between them,' Hannah said.

'What about Andronovitch?'

'Sabine had no record of Harry meeting him, but she didn't know who else was at the dinner,' Hannah said. 'She gave us the organizer's name, though. Terrence Swift.'

'Good work. Let's go see him first thing in the morning.'

'She also said Clarke wanted Smythe to resign for the PPE screw-up and that he was going to give all the profit Smythe had made to charity.'

'But now Clarke's dead, he gets control of the company instead,' Wise said. 'That's a damn good motive if ever there was one.'

'We thought that, too. But why kill the others?' Hannah said. 'He gains nothing from Hassleman and Andronovitch's death.'

'I know,' Wise said, 'but we have a link at last between two of the victims — this dinner. Maybe there's someone else there that they were all doing business with. Someone else Smythe was tied up with.'

'I looked up the event on social media,' Hannah said, 'but there's nothing from any of the guests and nothing on the museum's own feeds.'

'That's interesting,' Wise said. 'I would've thought there'd be loads of posts up from guests at such a swanky affair.'

'Not this one, Guv,' Hannah replied. 'It's as if it didn't happen.'

'We also asked about Clarke's schedule,' Sarah said.

'And?' Wise asked.

'Only Smythe, his wife, the driver, the cleaner, and Sabine knew when he was coming back,' Sarah said.

'Let's look at the driver and the cleaner some more,'

Wise said. 'Maybe they sold the information to someone or got chatty down the pub with the wrong person.'

'I'll get Jono and Hicksy on that first thing in the morning,' Sarah said.

'Thank you.' Wise looked over at the whiteboards. There was almost too much information up there now — and none of it connecting apart from Hassleman and Clarke attending the same dinner and Smythe lying about it.

He pulled out his phone and looked up Samson's number, aware that it was 10 p.m. on a Sunday night. He dialed anyway. If he was right, another murder was going to happen in approximately twenty-four hours. Bothering someone late at night on the weekend didn't matter compared to that.

'Yeah?' Samson answered after a good minute of his phone ringing, his voice gruff and aggressive.

'Sorry to bother you. It's DI Wise,' Wise said.

'Yeah?' he said again, less hostile this time.

'I don't know if you heard, but we've had another murder. Sir Harry Clarke.'

'Yeah, I heard.'

'Well, we have both Hassleman and Clarke attending an event on the fourteenth of last month at the Natural History Museum, hosted by ...' Wise glanced over at Hannah, who mouthed "the European Economics Agenda" back. 'The European Economics Agenda,' Wise repeated. 'And I was just wondering if you knew where Andronovitch was on that night.'

'I guess you're hoping he was there with them,' Samson said.

'Just a bit,' Wise said.

'This number your mobile?' Samson asked.

'Yeah.'

'Give me ten minutes and I'll call you back.' The line went dead.

Wise put his phone down on the table. 'He's going to call me back,' he told the others.

Hannah and Sarah picked up another slice of pizza each, but Wise wasn't hungry. All he could do was stare at his phone, willing it to ring with some good news.

Ten minutes crawled by, then another five. The pizza gone, Hannah and Sarah were both staring at the phone alongside Wise.

Another five minutes passed.

'Do you think you should call him back?' Sarah suggested.

The phone rang just as Wise reached for it. Samson's name was on the screen. Wise answered it on the second ring. 'DI Wise.' God, he sounded keen — or desperate. He wasn't sure which.

'Sorry it took so long to get back to you. Sunday night isn't a good time to get information,' Samson said.

'No problem. I appreciate you going to the trouble.'

'It's not good news, I'm afraid.' Samson's words punched the hope from Wise's heart.

'No?'

'I'm afraid dear Yuri was in Switzerland on the fourteenth. He returned to the UK on the twenty-third.'

'Shit.' Wise glanced over at the others and shook his head, even though they both knew it was bad news. 'You don't know if he had any connection to the European Economics Agenda, by any chance?'

'I asked about them and got shut down pretty quickly,' Samson said. 'They certainly share the same sort of friends and have the same sort of agenda. They should really be called the non-European Economics Agenda, though, if you get my drift.'

'Ah.' Wise did.

'If you're going to see them, be quick and tread gently. If they refuse to speak to you, you'll just have to accept it.' Samson sighed. 'To be honest, if they are involved, there's a good chance this will come back to me, anyway.'

'My big boss got hauled into Number Ten yesterday and was given a bollocking. They want this solved,' Wise said.

'Yeah, right — unless it upsets the wrong people. Look, good luck, eh? I hope you get the bastard. I really do.'

'Cheers,' Wise said, and hung up. 'Andronovitch was in Switzerland,' he told the others. He hated seeing the disappointment on their faces, so he kept the rest of Samson's message to himself. The last thing they needed to know was the entire case could get buried — but how the government could do that with all the press interest was another thing altogether.

'What do we do now?' Hannah said.

'Go home. Get some sleep,' Wise said. 'We'll start again in the morning. Hopefully, we can shake something out of this Terrence Swift bloke.'

'You sure?' Hannah said. 'I don't mind staying on.'

Wise shook his head. 'I need to get home myself.' Hopefully, Jean would let him in. It'd been two days since he'd last been back and he knew painfully well that he'd not called her all day, either.

Sarah squeezed his arm as she walked past. 'Night, Guv.'

Hannah lingered, but Wise nodded towards the door. 'Go on.'

'I'll see you tomorrow,' Hannah said and followed Sarah out the door.

Wise walked over to the window and looked down. A

few of the press were still out there, but he knew they'd be back in force tomorrow. And God help them all if there was another murder.

Wise didn't need to be a good detective to know that his career would be over if there were. He looked over at the board one last time and all the pictures of the motorbike messenger. 'Who the hell are you?'

Monday, 19th September

31

'Good morning, everyone,' Wise said from in front of the whiteboards. 'I'm pleased to say we have six new team members joining us today to help us with the investigation.' He nodded to a small group who were standing near the back of the room, officers brought in from other Major Investigation Teams from across London. 'We can do proper introductions later but for now I want to run over everything we know about the case to help bring everyone up to speed as quickly as possible.'

The door to the incident room opened, and Roberts entered with Detective Chief Superintendent Walling. Never a good sign. The rest of the team knew that too, and the atmosphere changed in a heartbeat. Everybody tensed up as they exchanged as nervous looks around the room. It was the last thing Wise needed.

'Morning, Simon,' Walling said with a furrowed brow that made him look like he was there for a fight. 'Don't mind us.' They headed over to the corner near Hannah, who sensibly moved out of their way.

Wise nodded, then turned to the whiteboards.

'Three days ago, someone murdered Sir Harry Clarke on the doorstep of his home in Hans Road, Knightsbridge,' Wise said, pointing to Clarke' picture.

'The murder has all the hallmarks of those previously carried out by the person who the media has christened "the Motorbike Killer."' Wise pointed to one of the blurry black and white pictures taken from the CCTV of a person dressed all in black and wearing a motorbike helmet. 'Sir Harry was extremely wealthy, living in a street full of billionaires' homes. He was shot in the head on his doorstep after returning from America. Nothing was stolen, and the killer made their getaway immediately after the murder. The motorbike drove into a public car park a few streets away and vanished off the face of the earth. This is exactly the same MO as the murder of Mark Hassleman, who was killed three days previously, and Yuri Andronovitch, who was killed three days before that.' Wise pointed to pictures of each man as he named them, even though most of the team knew their faces well.

'And you've found nothing to connect the men?' Walling asked, looking distinctly unhappy. 'No mutual business connection or membership to the same golf club, for instance?'

'Apparently Sir Harry was at a dinner at the Natural History Museum on the fourteenth of August and Mark Hassleman was also there. Sir Harry complained to his PA about the man being on drugs and asked her to make sure they never crossed paths again. Andronovitch was in Switzerland at the time, but we're tracking down a full guest list this morning it case there were other mutual connections,' Wise said. 'Sir Harry's son-in-law was also in attendance at the party.'

'What about forensics?' Walling said.

'Forensics haven't been able to find any physical evidence at any of the crime scenes,' Wise said. 'The killer is covered head-to-foot and they don't touch or interact with anything or anyone other than shooting the victim, and they pick up the bullet shell casing before leaving.'

'The motorbike he uses is a Honda PCX Scooter, the most popular messenger's bike in London, and they sell over three thousand new ones each year in the capital.' Again. Wise pointed to a picture on the board.

'That doesn't look very fast,' Walling said.

'It doesn't have to be with London in near constant gridlock all the time,' Wise said. 'It just needs to be nimble enough to weave its way between the cars — and it's about as anonymous as a bike can get. He uses stolen number plates, changing them for each new murder.

'We've searched mobile phone data to see if there's a common number that appears in the area at the time of the murders, but we haven't found anything there, either.

'We have CCTV footage of them going to and from each crime scene from a public car park but each time we've been unable to trace them back to their base. They're just there one minute and gone the next. We're tracking down vehicles that could have transported the bike to and from the car parks at the moment. Now we have extra personnel, we'll be able to fast track that avenue of enquiry.'

'Do you even know it's a man or woman?' Walling asked, not bothering to hide his frustration.

Wise went back to the photographs. 'Obviously, we can't be one hundred percent sure. The shooter is tall, between five foot ten and six two, and they have a slim build, so yes, we could be looking for a tall woman. However, eighty percent of all murders and ninety-two percent of known serial killings are committed by men, so odds are we're looking for a man.'

'It would be good to know something definite after all this time, Inspector,' Walling said. 'Some sign you've made progress.'

'I think it's safe to assume we're dealing with a person of great intelligence and control,' Wise said, doing his best to ignore Walling's rudeness. Reacting would only give the man the fight he was looking for. 'These killings have been well-planned and executed. They know where all the cameras are, so they've done plenty of reconnaissance in the areas. Considering the types of individuals who live in Eaton Square and Elgin Crescent and Hans Place, it seems likely that the killer can move about very comfortably without drawing attention to themselves.'

'You sound like you admire the bastard. No wonder you can't catch him,' Walling huffed, standing up. He turned to Roberts. 'I've got a call to make. Join me in my office after the briefing.'

'Yes, sir,' Roberts replied.

It was a miracle that Wise didn't call him a wanker as he left. How could the man think that the performance was going to help anyone in the room?

Instead, Wise waited until Walling had left the meeting before continuing, as nothing had happened. 'As it's our only potential link between the victims, the guest list for the dinner looked at and anyone on Clarke's table interviewed. We'll also have a word with David Smythe and see why he failed to mention the evening before.

'And now, we have some extra help, let's talk to more of the season ticket holders in the car parks our killer used and see if they saw anyone loading a bike into the back of a van. Jono, you can sort out the teams for that.'

'We've already been talking to quite a few people, Guv, but it's been pretty fruitless so far.' Jono looked around the room. 'No one's seen anything.'

'Well, hopefully the fact that there's a killer loose will help focus their minds,' Wise said. He glanced at his watch. 'It's 9 a.m. now. If we don't get lucky today, there's a good chance there'll be another murder tonight between the hours of 11 p.m. to 12 a.m. I want the entire team on standby in case that happens. Donut will coordinate everything out of the Despatch Centre, monitoring the emergency calls as they come in. Sarah will be with the CCTV teams in the Force Control Room. The rest of us need to be ready to move as fast as we can to the crime scene, to the car parks.

'So far, all the murders have taken place in this three-mile area around Hyde Park.' He circled the map from Ladbroke Grove down to Hans Place. 'This will be our area of focus. Hopefully, if we can react in real time, we might catch our friend here.' Wise tapped the picture of the motorbike rider again. 'Now, let's get to work.'

As the meeting broke up, Roberts walked over. 'I'm going to see what Walling wants. I'll call you if it's anything you need to know.'

'The man didn't look happy,' Wise said.

Roberts glanced over at the door. 'He's under a lot of pressure.'

'Aren't we all?'

Roberts raised an eyebrow in response, then left the incident room.

Wise stood by the whiteboards, feeling very much alone. He had thirteen, maybe fourteen hours before the motorbike killer struck again, and he didn't have any idea how he was going to stop him.

Even focusing their eyes on the current kill area was a hunch. The truth was the killer could strike anywhere in London and be long gone before any of Wise's teams got there.

It was times like these, he missed Andy more than ever. His friend would've had some ideas to toss in the ring or crack a joke to break the mood. When he was with Andy, Wise felt nothing was impossible.

But Andy was gone. His brains splattered across a Peckham rooftop. His reputation destroyed. Now Wise was dying a slow death alone.

'Guv,' Hannah said, walking over.

'Yeah?' Wise said, forcing his melancholy from his face.

'I was just speaking to Sabine Cricheaux again. She's Clarke's PA. Apparently, David Smythe informed her he was going to Birmingham for the night and he'd be back late tomorrow.'

'Did she say why he's going up there?'

'Apparently, his father's in a residential care home just outside the city centre and Smythe visits him regularly.'

'Was the trip planned? Seems odd to leave his wife alone three days after her own father's murder.'

'She didn't say.'

'Shit. Still, we didn't tell him he couldn't go anywhere.' He rubbed his face, utterly exhausted, and it was only the start of the day. 'Let's see Mr Terrence Swift. Maybe we can have some luck there.'

Of course Roberts had to grab him before they could leave. 'Simon, can you come to my office?' Roberts' voice sounded strained over the phone.

He glanced over at Hannah and mouthed 'Roberts' to her. 'Sure.' Wise ended the call. 'I'll meet you in the car.'

When he entered Roberts' office, his boss looked like the world was about to end. 'Walling's had another call with Downing Street and the brass over at the Embankment.'

'I take it they're not happy?' Wise said.

'That's the understatement of the year.' Roberts shook her head, not meeting Wise's eyes.

'And?' he said, even though he knew where this was all going. He felt sick, he felt angry, he felt worn out by the whole bloody thing.

'They're lining up people to take over the investigation.'

Of course they were. 'I'm surprised they're not already here. Walling had obviously made up his mind before he'd the DMM earlier. The man was gagging for a fight.'

'It's not just you, Simon,' Roberts said, finally looking up. 'I offered to take over as SIO, but that suggestion was declined as well. We're both on the out if things go against us.'

Wise found it hard to feel sympathy for Roberts, sitting as she was in her office, surrounded by her paperwork that she loved so much, waiting for Wise to go out on the streets and chase the thinnest of leads. 'How long have we got?'

'The new team will be ready tomorrow — if there's another murder.'

He knew then that there would be. Whatever luck he'd once had, whatever hope he had that things would go his way, was gone. He clenched his fists, wanting to hit something, hurt someone. They still ached from the fight in the stairwell, the bruises still visible. A reminder of what good his anger did. He stood up instead. Better to walk away. Prove the bastards wrong. Somehow. 'Thanks for letting me know.'

'I believe in you, Simon — it's just that they have dealt us a shitty hand on this case.'

'Yeah, well. It could be worse,' Wise said.

Andy tumbles forward, red mist leading the way, his brains and blood already splattered across the rooftop.

He left Roberts to her paperwork.

32

The European Economics Agenda had their offices in the Shard, that monument to London's financial clout and ambition. It was only two and a half miles from the station, but it still took Wise and Hannah almost half an hour to drive there, the traffic unappreciative of the urgency of their journey.

After parking near London Bridge, Wise climbed out of the car, his eyes already on the seventy-two storey skyscraper. Despite the stormy skies, the Shard cut an impressive silver slash into the grey clouds. Even so, Wise wasn't much of a fan of the place. Like the Gherkin and the Cheese Grater, the building didn't really fit into Wise's idea of London. Even the way they towered over the city irked him, as if they were screaming "look at me" to everyone who passed by.

And, if that was the case, what did it say about the people who called it home? Nothing good, that was for sure.

'Everything alright?' Hannah asked as they headed to the main entrance.

'Everything's wonderful,' Wise said. He'd not told her

about what Roberts had said. It'd just be another distraction in the way of getting the job done. But the fact was, unless he or someone on his team uncovered something sensational in the next twelve hours, there would be most likely be another murder that night and he'd be dragged off the case in the morning, his reputation in shreds.

Inside the Shard, a security guard directed them to an elevator, its doors magically opening as they approached. The doors shut behind them just as quickly once they were inside, and the elevator shot upwards without the need for any buttons to be pushed. Three seconds later, it stopped on the sixty-fifth floor, where a woman waited to greet them. Behind her, floor to ceiling windows revealed the north side of the Thames in all its glory. St Paul's poked up above the rooftops to the left and, to the right, there was the Tower of London, still looking magnificent.

'Detective Inspector Wise, Detective Sergeant Markham, welcome to the European Economics Agenda. I'm Claire Haynes, Terrence Swift's assistant,' she said. 'Terrence is waiting for you in the boardroom. This way.'

They followed her down a silent, wood-panelled corridor, past men and women bustling along dressed in suits and looking very serious about life. It was a very different universe to Sparks' office in Covent Garden.

Haynes needed both hands to push the massive door to the boardroom open and, as it swung silently open, Wise had to blink at the sudden brightness. The boardroom was the size of half a football pitch with a table that could have comfortably seated dozens of people. How anyone could concentrate on work in there though was beyond Wise, because the view was even more breath-taking than it had been in the reception area.

'Impressive isn't it?' a man said, stepping forward with

his hand outstretched. 'I'm Terrence.' If the rest of the office was full of people in suits, Swift hadn't seen the dress code. He wore baggy jeans, with filthy white Nikes, an unironed white shirt and what looked like his grandfather's cardigan, complete with a hole on one elbow. Half-moon glasses sat on his nose. It looked like a whirlwind had styled his hair, adding height to an otherwise diminutive man.

Wise and Hannah shook hands with him as they introduced themselves.

'Can I get anyone a drink?' Haynes said.

'Coffee please,' Wise said. It was the only thing keeping him going.

'Not for me,' Hannah said.

'I'll have one too,' Swift said. 'Not that I need it. I think if I was cut, I'd bleed caffeine.'

'I know someone else like that,' Hannah muttered, glancing at Wise with a hint of a smile.

Swift waved towards the meeting table. 'Please, have a seat. How can I help you today?'

'We're investigating a series of murders,' Wise said. 'We're hoping you can help us with our enquiries.'

'The ones on the news? Sir Harry and the others?' Swift interjected.

'That's right,' Wise said.

'A terrible business,' Swift said with all the emotion of a man discussing the weather.

'We're interested in a function you hosted on the fourteenth of August,' Wise said, 'at the Natural History Museum that Sir Harry attended.'

'That's right,' Swift said. 'Just a little thank you to our business partners and a way of saying hello to some prospective clients as well.'

'How many people were there?' Wise asked.

'About a hundred,' Swift said. 'Maybe slightly less. We had ten tables of ten. Everyone we'd invited had accepted, but there's always one or two no shows.'

'Did you invite Sir Harry Clarke to the event?'

'Yes, that's right. He came with David — David Smythe, his son-in-law.' Swift paused and shook his head. 'I still can't believe Harry's dead.'

'Was Sir Harry there as an existing client or a prospect?'

'Obviously, we knew Harry, but we'd not worked with him, but we had hopes,' Swift said. 'Harry was very connected and he could've opened a lot more doors for us.'

'In what way?'

'What do you know about the EEA?'

'Just that you are a think tank,' Wise said.

'I've always hated that term,' Swift said. 'It makes it sound like we spend our days rubbing our chins until inspiration strikes, when really it's quite the opposite. We use data to understand people's behaviours and use those insights to guide their responses in the direction our clients would prefer.'

'Right,' Wise said, none the wiser.

'For example, we worked with various Leave organisations during the Brexit referendum, working towards winning a yes vote and, since then, we've continued to help the various Conservative prime ministers get the right messages across to the voters,' Swift said.

'I thought that was Cambridge Analytica who worked on Brexit?' Wise said.

Swift laughed. 'They were amateurs. When we do our job properly, no one knows we even exist. They came in like a bull in a china shop and got everyone all worked up. We're a whisper in the wind.'

'And you didn't work with Sir Harry in his time in government?'

'Unfortunately not. Harry was old-school. His generation believed in knocking on doors and speaking to voters one-on-one, so he was very much against our methods. It was one reason he fell out with the party leadership. Of course he was also an ardent Remainer, so that put him on the opposite team to anyone who mattered.'

'So why did you invite him to the dinner?'

'Well, David had been in touch. He saw the value in what we do and there were several Harry's clients that he thought we could help with. We both thought a social setting like the dinner was a good way to open chats with Harry about working together at last.'

'And was it?'

'No. It was a disaster. First of all, David had told him they were attending a charity dinner for underprivileged children, so Harry was extremely upset when he discovered the truth. Then, another guest got rather the worse for wear quickly and caused quite the scene. In the end, Harry stormed out before the main course.'

'That guest was Mark Hassleman?'

'It was.' Swift put his hand to his mouth. 'God, Mark's dead too.'

'Yes, he is,' Wise said.

'And you think their murders could have something to do with the dinner?'

'We're just looking at everything at the moment,' Wise said. 'Why had you invited Hassleman?'

'Mark did quite a lot of work for us. The man was a genius. He understood human behaviour like no one else and the data he had at his disposal through his dating app was incredible. Once we included that into our modelling, it was a game changer.'

'Was that legal using Sparks' data?' Hannah asked.

'When someone signs up for Sparks, everyone has to give us permission to use their data,' Swift said. 'It's covered in the terms and conditions.'

'Who reads those?' Hannah said.

'People should,' Swift said, as if he was talking to a child.

'Who were the clients David wanted you to help with?' Wise asked, although it was feeling like a waste of their time being there.

'I'm afraid I can't say,' Swift said. 'We have to keep who we work with so very confidential. People can get very upset when they think we have manipulated them.'

'But that's what you do — you manipulate people into doing what you want them to do,' Hannah said.

'It's not as Machiavellian as that. We just give them a nudge or two in the direction they are already leaning towards,' Swift said. 'That's all.'

'If it's as harmless as you say, then why do you keep what you do a secret?' Hannah said.

'Oh, the right people know who we are,' Swift replied. 'It's just the plebs who are ignorant.'

'Will Hassleman's death affect your business?' Wise asked before Hannah could say anything else.

'Not really. We have his data and his algorithms already. If I'm being brutally honest, in the short term, his death actually helps us. We won't have to pay him his consulting fees now.'

'And how much was he being paid?'

'Twenty million pounds a year,' Swift said in a manner that made it sound like he'd said twenty pounds instead.

'That's quite a sum of money,' Wise said. Worth killing over, he thought.

'Not really. Not in the grand scheme of things,' Swift said. 'To work with us, our every client has to pay thirty million pounds in a signing on fee.'

'Thirty million pounds?' Wise repeated.

Swift waved towards the windows. 'The view doesn't come cheap.'

'And what do they get for the thirty million?'

'The view and my company while they enjoy it,' Swift said. 'Everything else after that comes with a separate bill.'

Wise let out an exasperated laugh. No wonder the man was arrogant.

'Oh, don't mock, Inspector,' Swift said. 'We give a tremendous value for money.'

'Did you have any dealings with Yuri Andronovitch?' Wise asked.

'That's the other man who was murdered?' Swift asked.

'That's right.'

'No, we did not invite him to the event, nor have we worked with him.'

The news was like a punch in the gut to Wise. The dinner connected two of the victims, but not the third. 'Are you sure? Perhaps he could've been dealing with one of your other colleagues?'

'Inspector, I work across all our clients' business. Consider me the conductor to our orchestra of data. Without me, there is no think tank or product to sell.'

Wise found he was clenching his fists again. The bloody clock was ticking, and he had up to put up with this smug git.

Just then Haynes returned with two coffees. She placed them on the table in front of Wise and Swift, while a man placed a jug of milk and a pot of sugar next to them. Both left without saying a word.

'Do you do any work with Russia?' Wise asked, ignoring the coffee.

'No. "We stand with Ukraine,"' Swift said, doing air quotes with his fingers. 'Once, perhaps, we had conversations with Vladimir, but not now, not in this current climate.'

Wise glanced over at Hannah and gave her a nod. They'd wasted enough time listening to this man's bullshit.

'Before we go, we'd like the guest list for the Natural History Museum dinner, please,' Hannah said.

Swift winced. 'I'm afraid I can't give you that either. Confidentiality and all that. As I said, we like to be invisible.'

'You do understand we're investigating three murders, don't you?' Wise said in disbelief. Even after Samson's warnings, the man's attitude shocked him.

'Of course,' Swift said, his smile looking uncomfortable on his face. 'That's why I've answered all your questions as best I can. But some things are just not possible.'

'I can get a court order and force you to give it to me,' Wise said.

'As is your right. We, of course, would appeal against it and our solicitors would win.' Swift glanced up at the ceiling. 'They are on the floor above if you'd like to chat with them now.'

Wise stood up. 'How about I arrest you for wasting police time and I drag you out of your fancy office in handcuffs in front of your clients? Your solicitors can impress me when they bail you out.'

Swift laughed. 'Please. If you do that, I'll sue you personally for every penny you have for wrongful arrest and defamation of character and whatever else we can think of.'

'You better pray that the next victim isn't another one of your guests,' Wise said, jabbing a finger at the obnoxious man. He headed for the door, Hannah following. He hauled the heavy door open, angry that it moved so slowly when all he wanted to do was to get the hell out of there. Haynes was waiting on the other side, but he ignored her and marched straight for the lift.

'These bloody people,' Wise said once he and Hannah were alone in the elevator. 'They think they operate in a different world to the rest of us, that the law doesn't apply to them.'

'I told you they're all wankers, Guv,' Hannah said.

'No wonder someone's killing them.' The moment he said it, Wise regretted it. He was being petulant just because he was frustrated.

'I know we've mentioned it before, but is that so hard to believe?' Hannah said. 'You saw that office? It's just pure affluence showing off and what about all that "I don't get out of bed for less than thirty million" nonsense? There are people in this country starving because they can't afford their groceries or they're freezing to death because the energy companies are ripping them off. Maybe someone had to listen to their bullshit and just had enough.'

'Some kind of Robin Hood figure? Doing their bit for the common people?'

'Well, I nearly hit him when he referred to the public as plebs.'

'Me too,' Wise said. 'And it's not that I don't agree with everything you said. It's just that I don't see any anger in these attacks. There's no hate in them. If anything, they're the opposite of that. Each killing is so dispassionate and cold.'

'It was interesting what he said about Smythe upsetting

his father-in-law,' Hannah said. 'They obviously had very different views on what to do — and he indirectly benefits from Clarke's death now his wife owns everything. And he lied to us about knowing Hassleman.'

'If it was just Clarke's murder we were looking at, I'd say he'd be a serious suspect but the man has no connection to the other two victims that we know of — certainly no reason to want them dead,' Wise said. 'Hassleman embarrassed him in front of Clarke, but is that a reason to kill him?'

It was raining by the time they were back out on St Thomas Street and night appeared to be quickly drawing in, despite the fact it was only just past 3 p.m. Just another reminder that time was running out.

'I've seen kids stab another kid for less,' Hannah said.

'Yeah, but we're not dealing with people worrying about street cred.' Wise looked up, feeling the September wind on his face. 'But maybe we are. Maybe the people who walk in this world worry about their reputations in the same way. Maybe it is about being a player.' Wise shook his head. 'It's almost like the killer has gone out of their way to confuse us.'

'Is it worth having another chat with Smythe's wife?' Hannah said. 'Especially now he's up in Birmingham.'

'Yeah,' Wise said. 'We might as well.' It wasn't like they had any other leads.

33

Laura Smythe-Clarke wasn't thrilled to find Wise and Hannah on her doorstep, but she let them in all the same. She'd tied her hair back tight against her head and knotted in a bun. She appeared to be wearing the same long black jumper as she had on when they'd visited her two days earlier. Her cheeks were hollowed out and her eyes were raw from crying.

Her children played elsewhere in the house, their laughter and shouts drifting through the building, contrasting with how miserable their mother looked. 'They don't know yet,' Smythe-Clarke said in explanation as she led them through to a small office. 'They should be at school, but I couldn't face sending them in today. The nanny can earn her money for once and look after them here.'

A desk, set up by the window, overlooked the street, a light blue iMac looking out of place in the classic decor of the rest of the room. Smythe-Clarke headed over to a small sofa against the other wall and sat down and waited while Wise and Hannah sat in the armchairs opposite. There was no offer of anything to drink.

'How old are your children, Mrs Smythe-Clarke?' Wise asked.

'Four and six,' she replied. There was a faraway look in her eyes that might be from medication.

'It's a tricky age. They're not babies anymore, but they still need you for everything,' Wise said, trying to find some common ground.

'You have children of your own?' asked Smythe-Clarke.

'One of each. Nine and seven.'

'Then you know,' Smythe-Clarke said with a sigh. 'I love them, but they are so demanding. It'd be easier if their father was around to help, but he's never here.'

'Your husband's job takes up a lot of his time?'

'Perhaps. Maybe. Sometimes I think he uses it as an excuse to avoid his responsibilities. The man is inherently lazy.'

'Mr Smythe is visiting his father at the moment,' Wise said.

'Of course he had to go now. He couldn't wait until his usual time to visit,' Smythe said-Clarke.

'The trip wasn't planned?'

'No. He said Daddy's death had upset him and made him realise he had to see his own father more often.' Smythe-Clarke's voice was taut, barely hiding her anger.

'How often does your husband visit his father?'

'He goes on a guilt trip every month or so,' Smythe-Clarke said. 'Sometimes he'll stay up there for a night, sometimes several nights. I couldn't tell you how much of that time is actually spent with his father. It wouldn't surprise me if he's just sitting in his hotel room watching television and enjoying the peace and quiet.'

'A guilt trip?'

'Yes, a guilt trip. He's certainly not going out of love.'

'Why's that?' Hannah said.

A look of irritation crossed Smythe-Clarke's face. 'He doesn't have a close relationship with his father like I do ... did.' She blinked furiously and put her hand over her mouth as if to hold back any emotions that might show. 'David's not that keen on reminders of his past.'

'No?' Wise said.

'It was all a bit working class for him.'

'How do you feel about him leaving you now to visit? I would imagine you could do with his support right now,' Wise said.

'Support? From David?' Smythe-Clarke let out a bitter laugh. 'He'd have to stop thinking about himself for once.'

'How did you and David meet?'

'We met at Oxford, back when we thought the world was ours,' Smythe-Clarke said. 'I saw myself as the next woman Prime Minister, a true daughter of Thatcher. David was there, trying to bury his northern roots.'

'I thought your husband was from Birmingham?' Hannah asked.

Smythe-Clarke fixed her a glare. 'That is the north.'

'Right,' Hannah replied. 'My mistake.'

'Why didn't you go into politics after university?' Wise asked.

'Oh, I don't know. We got married. I started playing the dutiful wife. Life happened. Children. And, of course, David didn't really like the idea of me working. He felt it was all so very embarrassing all of a sudden. I have no idea why I listened to him back then.'

'What about now that you own your father's business?'

Smythe-Clarke snorted. 'God. I could just imagine David listening to anything I said. No. He's already told me he wants me to stay out of things.'

'Will you?'

'Do I look like I have the energy to get involved? And life's miserable enough without fighting with David.'

'Have you ever thought about getting divorced?' Hannah asked.

Smythe-Clarke sat back, as if slapped. 'Why would you say that?'

'It's just that you don't seem very happy in your marriage,' Hannah said. 'Perhaps this is one of those moments when you get to change things.'

Smythe-Clarke glared at her through her red-rimmed eyes. 'Thank you for that observation, Detective. Let me know how that helps solve my father's murder.'

Wise gave Hannah a look to stop her from saying more. The last thing they needed was to upset Smythe-Clarke more. 'Could you walk me though a typical evening when you are both here?' Wise asked instead.

'Why do you need to know?' Smythe-Clarke asked.

'No particular reason,' Wise said. 'Just curiosity.'

'We're just like any other family. We have dinner — together if we can — around 6 p.m., then the children have their baths, the nanny puts them to bed between 7:30 and 8, and then I go to bed utterly exhausted at around 9.'

'Your husband said you take a sleeping tablet?' Wise said.

'Unfortunately, it's the only way I can sleep. My mind seems to think the moment I turn the light off that it's time to go over every little thing in minute detail.'

Wise nodded. He understood that feeling only too well. 'And your husband? What time does he go to bed?'

'Later than me.'

'You don't know a time?'

'I'm always asleep by then. Both of us prefer it that way.'

Smythe-Clarke leaned forward. 'I'm sorry, but I don't understand how any of this has anything to do with my father's murder.'

'You mentioned before that your father was very anti-Russian.'

'That's right. He first became a politician back in the seventies, when a nuclear war with the Russians seemed a real possibility. Of course, he was a World War Two baby as well, so he didn't like the Germans much either.'

'This animosity towards the Russians ... Could it have, perhaps, led to arguments or fall outs with anyone from that region who might have wanted to do business with your father?'

'Perhaps. He was never shy about telling people what he thought, and probably even more so as he got older. Daddy said he didn't have to play "the game" anymore, and he liked that.' Smythe-Clarke smiled. 'Not that many people took offence. He was always charming with it. Everybody loved him.'

'What about your husband? Did he respect your father's anti-Russia stance?'

'David? That man only cares about money and who has it. He'd do a deal with the devil if there was a quick profit to be made.'

'Did that cause problems between David and your father?'

'No. David knows what side his bread's buttered. He may have stupid ideas, but he's not stupid. He wouldn't have argued with Daddy.'

'We've taken up enough of your time, Mrs Smythe-Clarke,' Wise said. 'Again, we're very sorry for your loss.'

They all stood.

'Please catch my father's killer,' Smythe-Clarke said.

'We'll do our best,' Wise said. 'By the way, where does your husband stay when he visits his father?'

'It's a boutique hotel called The Dormitory or something stupid like that.'

'Thank you for your time,' Wise said. 'Take care.'

Smythe-Clarke shut the door in his face.

'I'm not sure the divorce comment was what she wanted to hear,' Wise said once he and Markham were back in the car.

'I'm sorry, Guv,' Hannah said. 'All that "woe is me. I'm miserable" stuff gets on my tits. The woman has enough money to do whatever she wants and, instead, she's acting like the world's taken a big crap on her.'

'Someone just murdered her father.'

'I know, I know. But you can't tell me she wasn't like that before they killed him?'

'No, I'm not.'

'Besides, you've met her husband. Who wouldn't want to get divorced from him?'

'Fair point,' Wise said with a smile. 'What did you make of all of it?'

'As much as I don't like David Smythe,' Hannah said, 'and he's obviously a shit husband, I think we can rule him out. Obviously, he gains by his father-in-law's death as it puts the company in his control, but there's nothing that ties him to the other two. It's like Emily Walker all over again.'

'Everything about this case is wrong,' Wise said. 'Normally, the more crimes means more evidence, but we've got nothing. Just lots of nothing.'

He glanced at the clock in the car. 4 p.m.

They were running out of time.

34

Tony Richardson looked at the clock when the doorbell rang. Ten past ten. 'Who the bloody hell is that, this time at night?'

His wife didn't answer. She was curled up on the sofa, asleep. It happened every time they tried watching a movie these days. Ten minutes in and she'd be snoring away. Aliens could blow up the world and she'd sleep through it. Not that he was much better most of the time. He hated growing old.

The doorbell rang again.

'Alright. I'm coming. Keep your hair on.' Tony struggled out of the sofa and headed to the hallway, passing the sideboard full of pictures from his younger days, when he was a manager to pop stars and on tour all over the world. People talked about the good old days but, in his case, it was true. How many can claim to have managed the first pop band to play behind the Iron Curtain? None of them. Everyone had said it was impossible, but he'd made it happen in the same way he'd made Wild into the biggest act of the eighties.

It was still hard to believe that Jack Andrew, the singer, was dead. Of all the people and bands from back then, Jack was the last person he'd ever have thought would end up a rock 'n' roll casualty. Jack didn't even leave a beautiful corpse when he popped it. Just a fat man with a rug on his head lying in his own vomit. It was no way for a star to go. What a cliche.

Just looking at the pictures made him depressed. Maybe he should swap some of the surrounding pictures around one of these days. Put something from now, not then. The grandkids perhaps.

Then again, silver, gold and platinum discs lined the hallway, so there was no avoiding painful memories anywhere in his house. Reminders that the last good thing he'd done wasn't even yesterday. He was decades past his best and he hated it.

The doorbell rang for the third time, just as Tony reached it. 'Hold on to your horses. I'm coming.'

'Is someone at the door?' called out his wife from the lounge, finally roused.

'Of course, there is — unless the door bell's on the bloody fritz,' he called back, not hiding his irritation. After forty years together, Sheila could get on his nerves just by breathing too loudly. 'Is there someone at the door?' he muttered to himself in a poor imitation of her. 'No, it's a bloody ghost.'

The front door was big and black with about a dozen bolts on it for security and, to the right, there was a video intercom. Not that Tony normally bothered with it. He might be seventy-eight, but he could still handle himself, still had the bulk he'd picked up from boxing during his university days. The six-pack was long gone, of course —

along with his hair — but few people could say that they'd even had abs in the first place.

Tonight, though, he used the intercom. It was late, after all. Ten past bloody ten. And there had been the killings that were all over the news. Some nutter murdering rich people. As if there weren't enough problems in the world. He pressed the button and a man in a motorbike helmet appeared on the screen. 'Yes? What do you want?'

The man in the helmet looked towards the camera. 'Package for you.'

'You can leave it on the step, thank you,' said Tony.

'I'm afraid you need to sign for it.' The helmet muffled the man's voice.

'It's very late for a delivery.'

'My bike broke down. I wouldn't be bothering you so late, but the order said it was urgent and needed your immediate attention.'

'It did?' Tony's mind raced through who could've sent him something important. He'd retired decades ago. He didn't even know if he knew anyone still in The Biz.

'Yes, sir,' said the man. 'Very important.'

It was silly but Tony grinned at hearing that, straightened his shoulders, feeling just a little bit like he did back when he'd been a Very Important Person. The sort of person who never waited in line, the man who everyone wanted to be friends with. These days, he could barely get the attention of the girl behind the deli counter in Waitrose. How many times had he wanted to shout at her 'Don't you know who I am?' But of course she wouldn't know. Not now, he was old and unneeded. Famous in the eighties? He might as well tell people he was a dinosaur.

'Give me a moment,' he said and unlocked all the bloody

bolts Sheila had put on the door. Always worried about getting robbed, she was. Ridiculous.

'Who is it?' she called out, as if on cue.

'It's for me,' he called back. 'Something important.'

Finally, he got the last bolt undone and Tony opened the door. 'Now, what is it—'

The man in the motorcycle helmet pointed a gun at his head.

35

They were all in the incident room. Silence smothering them. A bunch of grim faces watching the clock, watching Twitter and watching each other.

Wise picked up his phone for the hundredth time, checked it was still working and the battery was near enough full. The time was 10:15 p.m. If there was going to be another murder, it'd be in the next two hours. By God, he hoped he was wrong. He prayed the killer was done with the three already dead.

Pointless thoughts.

He rubbed his eyes, trying to get some life back into them, and thought about getting another coffee from the canteen, but his gut ached from the gallons he'd already drunk.

Hannah was by the window, staring out at London, as if she'd be able to see the murder being committed from there. Jono and Hicksy were playing cards, communicating by glares alone. Callum was on his phone, checking Twitter. Even the new crew were there, suffering with the rest of them, waiting for someone to die, jumping at every time the phone rang.

Only two of the crew were missing. Donut was over at the CAD Centre, monitoring the emergency calls as they came in while Sarah was with the CCTV crews at the Force Control Room. If something happened, Wise and the others would know about it as near as real time as they could get.

If something happened.

Walling would have a fit at the overtime costs if the night was a bust. Then again, he'd have a fit if it wasn't. Another murder and the Chief Superintendent would bring in his new team and he would cast aside Wise.

They'd even run out of things to say about the case while they waited to hear if there was a victim number four. Each murder had put back all the progress they made in-between, after all. There was no reason to think tonight's murder wouldn't do the same.

His eyes drifted to the whiteboards and the three victims already there. All the information gathered to get nowhere. Reset every three days with each new body.

Three days chasing their tails.

Wise stood up. What was it about the three-day gap? He walked over to the boards. 'Why wait?'

'Wait for what?' Hicksy said from behind him.

Wise turned and saw everyone was watching him. 'I was wondering why the killer waits for three days before killing again.'

'It's a classic serial killer cooling off period,' Callum said. 'When they go back to their normal lives.'

'But it's not much of one,' Wise said. 'And these aren't frenzied attacks that need recovering from.'

'What about researching the next victim?' Jono suggested. 'Preparing for the next murder?'

'Maybe, but these killings are so well-planned, it feels like there's been months of work put into it already,' Wise replied.

'What are you thinking, Guv?' Hannah said.

'I was just thinking how waiting three days lets us go chasing leads — good leads — and then there's another and we're back at the start again. Like a macabre game of snakes and ladders. It's as if—'

Wise's phone rang. He ran over to the table where he'd left it, saw Donut's name on the screen. This was it.

The murder call.

Wise snatched it up. 'Yes?'

'Guv, we've just had a call. Cottesmore Gardens, Kensington. A man's been shot on his doorstep. Sounds like our man.'

'We're on our way,' Wise said, grabbing his jacket, his team moving with him. 'Cottesmore Gardens everyone. Let's move it. You all know what you need to do.'

They bundled down the stairs, a herd of elephants in an otherwise quiet station, and out into the dark night, rain spitting down.

The moment they burst through the station's front doors, the press waiting by the gates perked up, sensing a story. Camera lights went on and reporters started shouting questions. 'Get them out of the way,' Wise shouted at the uniforms. 'Be quick.'

It was like throwing bloody meat to sharks.

Wise and Hannah dived into the Mondeo. On went the blues and twos, washing the car park in strobing light, and then they were off. Wise gunned the engine and shot out the station car park, wheels screeching past the press and onto Kennington Road.

'Come on,' he said, squeezing the car through a gap that

was only wide enough by a hair's breath. Behind him, flashed more blue lights, the team following.

Please let luck be with them.

'All units, eyes out for a Honda PCX Scooter,' Hannah shouted into the radio. 'Stop with caution. Driver might be armed.'

Through Lambeth, over the bridge, through Westminster. Traffic was light enough, and most people had the sense to get out of their way.

'Hornton Street Car Park all clear,' a woman said over the radio. 'No sign of the suspect.'

'Kensington High Street clear,' another officer called in.

'Come on,' Wise hissed through clench teeth. 'Don't let them get away.' He accelerated past Westminster Cathedral, tore past the back of Buckingham Palace, then slung a hard left at Hyde Park Corner, then straight along the park. Wise had the Mondeo up to seventy, eighty and it still wasn't bloody quick enough.

More calls came over the radio. 'Holland Park all clear.'

'Copthorne Hotel is all clear.'

'How many car parks are there?' he said to Hannah.

'A dozen within a mile of Cottesmore Gardens. Over twice that number within two miles,' Hannah replied.

'That's too many. Too fucking many.'

Wise glanced at the clock. How much time had passed since the murder? Fifteen minutes? The killer would be long gone by now. They'd—

'RTC at the junction of Lexham Gardens and Marloes Road,' a voice crackled over the radio. 'Motorbike and an SUV. Ambulance on its way. Need police assistance. Any nearby units, please respond.'

Wise glanced over at Hannah. 'Motorbike?'

'Yeah, and it's close to the murder scene.'

'Tell the others we're taking a detour and call Sarah. Tell her to check the CCTV around the RTC.' Wise accelerated once more, past the Dutch embassy, past the turn for Cottesmore Gardens and onto High Street Kensington, his heart racing. Finally, luck might be with them. Maybe the killer was—

A bus pulled out into the Mondeo's path.

He slammed down on the brakes. The tires squealed and shrieked. He swerved out to the right, into the oncoming traffic. He held his breath, arms rigid, as a van rattled towards them. Instinct took over. He put his foot down, aiming for a gap that wasn't big enough to fit through.

'Shit,' Hannah shouted, her arms braced against the dashboard, expecting impact. Time slowed as Wise fought the wheel, steering into space, blue lights washing everything around him, hoping, praying that they'd make it.

Tires screeched next to them, the bus breaking, allowing Wise to overtake it and get back on the left-hand side of the road, and on they went. 'Fuck,' whispered Wise as they turned by the tube station, into Wrights Lane, the road narrowing, cars parked on either side, everything darker now they were away from the neon of the high street, down residential streets, full of people tucked in for the night, into Marloes Road and then they saw the ambulance, lights flashing, back doors open, paramedics in their high-viz jackets standing nearby. There were a few bystanders too, gawpers attracted by the lights and the drama.

The SUV was sideways across the road, a motorbike wedged under its left front wheel.

Wise stopped the Mondeo. Both he and Hannah were out in a flash, leaving the Mondeo's doors wide open, warrant cards in hands, and sprinted to the accident.

'What happened?' Wise shouted as he reached the

crashed vehicles, trying to see the make of bike, hoping to see a body. Dear God, if it was the killer, let them be squashed like a bug.

'Is it a scooter?' he shouted. 'Is it ours?'

'Yeah, looks like it,' Hannah said, bending down. 'Same make. Black, like ours.'

There was no rider, though.

'It wasn't the driver's fault,' said a man with a small little dog on a lead. 'The motorbike should've stopped — there're double white lines for a reason — but he didn't. He went straight across as if it was his right of way. The car didn't have a hope.'

'Where's the rider?' Wise said, looking at the ambulance, but the person wrapped up in a foil blanket was a woman, middle-aged, small and plump. Not their man.

'He ran off that way,' said the dog walker, pointing down towards the Cromwell Road. He looked like he was in his sixties, white hair poking out the side of his flat cap. 'Didn't even bother to see if everyone else was alright.'

Wise ran, even though he knew it was pointless. The rider had a ten-minute head start on him. Enough time to get away even if he had two bloody, broken legs.

Hannah was with him, God bless her, shouting on her phone to Sarah as they ran, hoping to get some help from the CCTV.

They stopped when they reached the Cromwell Road. Too many options for the motorbike rider. There was a bus stop right next to them, a dark alley on the other side of the traffic crossing, dim lighting down the main road in either direction. He could've gone anywhere.

Hannah looked at Wise, phone still clamped next to her ear. 'It was definitely him, but they've lost track of him.

Sarah's trying to pick him up again, but she's not having any joy at the moment.'

'Shit. Shit. SHIT.' God, Wise wanted to smash something. Couldn't anything go their way? 'I want every bloody cop car in London looking for a motorbike rider without a bloody bike. Search every bus that left that stop. I want this bastard found!'

Wise stood in the middle of the Cromwell Road, staring down one end of the road then the other as cars swerved around him, honking their horns and shouting abuse. He wanted to run on, keep chasing, keep searching — if only he knew what way to go.

'Guv.' Hannah touched his shoulder, pulled him gently. 'You need to get out of the road, Guv.'

He ignored her, still searching for a sight of the killer. To the left were the museums. To the right was the road out of town. All the airport hotels were there. Too many options. 'Shit.'

A car stopped right by him and honked its horn, trying to assert its right of way.

Wise turned on the driver, mad with anger, and slammed his fists down on the bonnet of the SUV. 'What's your fucking problem?'

The driver pressed down on his horn, not letting up.

'Get out of the fucking car,' Wise shouted over the noise. 'Come on, then!'

Other cars started pressing their horns, adding to the cacophony of madness, but Wise didn't care. He wanted to hurt someone and this twat of a driver had fucking volunteered. He stormed over to the driver's door, tried yanking it open. 'Come on, big man. Out you get.'

The driver shouted something at Wise through the window, but he didn't move. He certainly didn't unlock his door. Wise glared back, desperate for the idiot to get out. He punched the window. 'Come on!'

'Guv.' Hannah pushed her herself between Wise and the car, her eyes full of worry. 'He just wants to get home. Let's get back to the bike, eh? Maybe there's a fingerprint or some DNA on it we can use.'

For a moment, Wise thought about pushing her out of the way. The twat in the car deserved a kicking. Then he blinked and saw the man's scared face, saw Hannah's concern. Dear God, what had he nearly done?

He let Hannah lead him over to the pavement. 'SHIT.'

'We'll get them, Guv,' Hannah said, her voice calm. 'We will.'

'I'm sorry,' he said. 'It's just …' Damn. He didn't know what to say. He was out of excuses.

'It's okay.'

He shook his head. It was far from okay.

They walked back at a good pace to the site of the RTC. Wise was grateful for the time to get his thoughts back in order. Get back in control. He couldn't let the cracks tear him apart. Not now. He had a job to do. A killer to catch. The bastard.

How could they have gotten away?

36

A marked police car had parked up next to Wise's Mondeo and two uniforms were taking statements. Wise and Hannah went straight to the motorbike, both bending down to get a better look.

The SUV had scrunched the bike's front wheel, but it had barely damaged the main body of the bike. The make was clear to see, too, the badge on the tank that said 'Honda PCX.'

'Right make,' Hannah said.

'That's something, at least,' Wise said. That was progress. There had to be something on the bike that could point them towards the killer's identity. There had to be. 'Call in forensics. Let's get this taken in straight away.'

Wise stood up and looked around for the man with the dog. He was still there, watching the commotion, the dog pulling on the lead, eager to get away from the blue lights and the noise. Wise walked over to the man.

The man nodded a greeting. 'You didn't catch him then?'

'No,' Wise snarled. 'But we will.' He had to. He looked

around and saw a reporter loitering, camera man just behind. Great.

'This seems a lot of fuss for a road accident,' the man said

'Yeah, there's a bit more to it than that. Can you take me through the accident again?'

'Well, it was as I said: the motorbike came down the road here.' He pointed to Marloes Road. 'But he didn't stop at the double white lines like he should and the big car was coming the other way.' He pointed off to his left, down Lexham Gardens. 'It had the right of way, obviously, so it's not stopping. The motorbike must've seen it at the last minute and it went into a skid. The rider went tumbling away, and the bike ended under the big car. Me and Daisy were standing right here when it happened — Daisy's my dog — and before we could help, the man was up and off towards the Cromwell Road. I shouted after him 'cause it's illegal to just scarper, but he didn't stop.'

'And how was he moving, this man? Was he hurt when he came off the bike? Limping? Bleeding?'

'I don't know about that,' said the man. 'He certainly wasn't running. You wouldn't after something like that, would you? I mean, it has to hurt, coming off a bike like that, even if you had on some padding and a helmet. But I didn't see any blood and I can't really say if he was hobbling or anything — but he might've been.'

'Thank you,' Wise said. 'You've been a great help.'

'Always happy to do my bit,' said the man. 'I hope you catch the rascal.'

Wise returned to Hannah. 'I'm going to head over to the murder scene. You wait here for forensics. Make them check the road for blood. Maybe he cut his leg up when he came off the bike.'

'Will do, Guv,' Hannah said. She glanced up at the sky, at the spits of rain falling down. 'Hopefully, the weather won't get any worse before they get here.'

'Check if you can get some blankets off the ambulance crew, then cover the bike up and anything you see on the road, just in case.'

'I'll catch up with you at the murder scene,' Hannah said.

Wise looked down at the squashed bike. 'Shame he didn't get trapped along with his bike. Would've made all our lives easier.'

Hannah didn't disagree.

Wise walked back to the Mondeo. The reporter came over, but he ignored her and shut the passenger door.

'Inspector Wise! What's going on? Was that the killer's bike?'

He gave a glare in reply and climbed in behind the wheel. The reporter came to the car window, shouting more questions, but Wise turned the engine on, drowning out anything she had to say. Then she had to jump out of the way as he began manoeuvring a three-point turn so he could head back the way they'd come.

He drove slower this time, the blue lights turned off, the need to rush long gone, the murder done, the killer escaped, his mind on what he was going to find at Cottesmore Gardens. Who was the poor fool who'd had his brains blown out? What new direction was this murder going to send the case?

Of course the bloody press had to be waiting for him, as Wise pulled up at the corner of Stamford Street and Cottesmore Gardens. At least a dozen reporters crowded around the barrier that stopped traffic entering or leaving the street. They'd probably followed his team all the way from Kennington. Great.

It was the last thing they needed. The last thing he needed. He tightened his grip on the steering wheel. He had to stay calm. Stay in control. No cracks.

And, of course, the vultures had to swarm around his car the moment Wise stopped.

'Is it him?' one shouted. 'Is this murder number four?'

'Is this the Motorbike Killer?' called another, shining a light into the car, so Wise had to shield his eyes with his hand.

'Who's dead, Inspector?'

'Have you got a clue?'

'Do you know what's going on?'

At least one of the uniforms moved the barrier quickly so Wise could drive through and leave them behind.

Of course, it was even more of a circus on the other side. Police vehicles filled the street, blocking in all the Bentleys and Mercedes. Wise even spotted a McLaren outside one house.

Flood lights illuminated a white awning over the entrance to a house two-thirds of the way down on the right-hand side of the street. SOCOs darted in and out of the awning, already hard at work. At least, no one was wasting any time in processing the crime scene.

Hicksy came over as Wise got out of the Mondeo, his face all hopeful that Wise would have good news by the looks of it.

'Bastard got away,' Wise said instead. 'We've got their bike though and maybe some blood if we're lucky.'

Hicksy shook his head. 'Wanker.'

'Who's the victim here?' Wise asked, nodding to the house.

'Tony Richardson, aged seventy-eight. Retired. Used to be a lawyer for some big pop bands back in the day, including Wild. They had a few big hits back in the day.'

'Yeah, I've heard of them.' Wise looked the building up and down. It was a four-story Victorian terrace — the sort of place that was only owned by Russian Oligarchs and Middle Eastern royalty these days. A few of the houses in the street had lights on in their windows, but most were pitch black and looked empty, properties bought for their investment value rather than to be a home.

'According to the wife, Shiela, they were watching television when the doorbell went,' continued Hicksy.

'What time was that?'

'Ten past. Tony went to answer it. Next thing his wife heard was a crash, sounded like someone falling down in the hallway. She thought Tony must've tripped on the carpet or something and rushed out to see if he was okay. She found the door open and her husband's brains splattered across the wall. The wife called 999, then collapsed.'

'Where's the wife now?'

'We've had her taken to Kensington Hospital for a check-up. She's pretty shaken up as you can imagine and she's not young. I sent one of the newbies along with her. The Richardsons have two grown-up children who live out of town. We've sent their local plod to break the bad news.'

'And she didn't see anyone or hear anything other than her husband falling?'

'No, Guv.'

'Right. He's made his first mistake with the RTC,' Wise said. 'Maybe there's more to come. Let's go see.'

'I bloody well hope so.'

They walked over to Forensics van and got kitted out with overalls and shoe coverings, then moved onto the house where another PC signed them in. Neither of them spoke as they walked under the awning to the front steps.

Wise paused before going up the steps to the front door. For the first time that he could remember, he didn't want to enter a crime scene.

The case felt like a curse. A damn curse that was breaking him a bit more each day. How long had it been since he'd had a decent night's sleep? He was running on fumes, his temper frayed, doubting everything and everyone, especially himself.

But he couldn't quit. Couldn't give up, no matter how much he wanted to. Stubborn to a fault he was. Wise by name, dumb by nature.

So, he stood at the bottom of the steps, taking in a few deep breaths, fighting the tiredness and the despair, trying to find the courage to go on.

'You alright, Guv?' asked Hicksy.

He glanced over, saw his concern, and did his best to smile. 'Yeah, I'm okay. All things considered. Come on, time to get to work.'

They walked up the stairs to the front door. SOCOs were crouched over the doormat, trying to discover something that probably wasn't there. After all, the killer hadn't left so much as a drop of sweat at any of the previous crime scenes, let alone their name and address, to make things any easier for the police.

A SOCO moved aside to let Wise and Hicksy into the house to see the bloody mess the killer had made of Tony Richardson.

Blood and brains had splattered over the right-hand wall of the hallway, covering some framed records that bands get when they had a million sales or something equally impressive. The murder victim lay on the hardwood floor a few feet further in from the door, as a SOCO took pictures of the body.

He looked down at the mat in front of the door, the spot where the killer had stood a few hours earlier, gun in hand, waiting for the door to open, getting ready to commit murder. What was going through the mind of the motorbike rider? Was he nervous? Excited? Bored? Was he killing these people because it turned him on, or was it a bloody crusade against the rich in the country? Was he striking a blow against the 0.1% on behalf of the other 99.99 or was there a real genuine grievance against each of the victims?

Murder number four and Wise still didn't have a clue.

Maybe this would be the one to make the difference. Maybe they'd find a clue that would put a stop to the madness.

Maybe.

With one last deep breath, Wise stepped into the house.

37

Wise stared at the body. A big man, Richardson was wearing grey slacks and a white formal shirt, a style of dressing ingrained into his very being, no doubt from a very young age, that need to look smart when there was no need to. Probably didn't even own a pair of jeans. His Dad's sort of man.

Of course, Richardson didn't look so smart now. Blood stained the white shirt and most of the left side of his head was missing. The next time he'd be all dressed up would be for his funeral. No doubt in his best suit and crisp white shirt. Definitely with a tie.

Wise looked back at the door and counted the locks and bolts. 'Someone in the house was security conscious,' he said to Hicksy. 'When we speak to the wife, let's find out if there was a reason behind all the locks. Maybe someone threatened them before.'

Hicksy scribbled notes down in her book. 'Will do, Guv. But if it is the Motorbike Killer, then it's really just bad luck, isn't it? He got killed for no other reason than he had money.'

'We investigate each case by the numbers. If we take shortcuts because we're making assumptions, we'll never catch him.' Wise pointed to the security monitor. 'Is there any footage from this?'

'No, Guv. Apparently it doesn't record anything. Just shows you who's outside when you press the button,' Hannah said.

'Fat lot of good that is then.' Wise moved into the hallway, stepping from plate to plate, his eyes drifting to the records on the wall. Little plaques in each of the frames noted five hundred thousand sales here or a million sales there of some of the biggest hits of the eighties. 'My mum used to be really into this band,' he said. 'The singer died a few years back, didn't he?'

'Yeah. Jake Andrew. He had a heart attack on New Year's Day two years ago,' Hicksy said.

'Was the victim still managing him at that point?'

'I'll find out, but I don't think so. He last had a record out a decade ago, as far as I know.'

'He was in the papers a lot, though.'

'A few drunk driving incidents here and there. Crashed his car a few times under the influence. He got done for possession of class A drugs as well and there was an indecent exposure charge from when he got caught on Hampstead Heath with his trousers down. Claimed he was caught short while walking the dog and that's why he was waving his microphone about for the world to see. The court found him guilty and Andrew got a fine and community service.'

'I remember now. There were all the pictures of him picking up litter in a high viz jacket.'

'That's the one.'

Wise turned into the living room. Everything in the

room looked like it cost a fortune. A highly polished wooden antique sideboard was by the door, its surface covered with pictures of the rich and famous in silver frames, all taken a long time ago, judging by the mullets and shoulder pads on display. It looked quite the life though. Wise recognised Jake Andrew, of course, and the guitarist bloke — whatever his name was — who made up the band. He picked up one picture, taken backstage at a packed Wembley Stadium. They had their arms around an older man, big grins on all their faces, the crowd stretching out behind them.

'This Richardson?' he asked Hicksy, pointing to the man in the middle.

He peered over his shoulder. 'That's him.'

Wise put the picture back. There was a drinks cabinet in the corner of the room, the bottom half full of high-end spirits and the upper half filled with crystal glasses of every shape and size. There was a giant marble fireplace in the middle of the opposite wall, with a mirror in an ornate silver frame hanging above it. Silver candlestick holders sat on the mantle piece surrounded by more pictures, including one of Richardson with Princess Diana and Jake Andrew sporting matching hairstyles.

The far end of the room was where the Richardsons spent most of their time by the looks of it, on sofas and armchairs with gold tassels dangling off the bottom, positioned around a fifty-inch Sony television with a Sky box and DVD player underneath. The Richardsons certainly enjoyed watching TV, judging by the well-worn sofas, with dents where they sat all night long, the material worn smooth, his and her spots. There was a half-drunk glass of scotch on one of the side tables, with an iPad next to it.

It was easy to imagine them both sitting on their sofas, watching a soap or a film, content with life in their own way, enjoying their golden years, until someone knocked on their door to destroy it all. Why? Just because they had money? It couldn't be that simple.

'This place is like something out of the bloody Antiques Roadshow,' Hicksy said, following him in.

Wise glanced over his shoulder at him. 'Not your cup of tea, then?'

'The only antique I've got is a second-hand toaster. I'm more of an IKEA man when it comes to interior design.' He looked around the room. 'Besides, you could probably fit my whole flat into this room with space to spare.'

'Very different from Hassleman's place.'

'I don't know,' Hicksy said. 'Sprinkle a bit of coke over the coffee table, pop on some porn on the wide-screen, and you'd not be able to tell the difference. Come to think of it, it'd look like my place as well.'

Wise smiled despite himself. 'You'd need a bendy straw to get the coke up that broken nose of yours.'

'You'd be surprised what I can do with this nose,' Hicksy said.

'I don't want to know,' Wise said, holding up a hand, enjoying the banter. It'd been too long since they'd all had a smile together.

They continued to walk through the downstairs. There was a dining room that could fit a dozen people around the table with a chandelier dangling above it and a full chef's kitchen with a double oven and six burners. They'd lined every sort of gadget up along one of the long white marble counters. 'Rice cooker, air fryer, bread maker, slow cooker, expresso machine,' Wise said, walking past them all. 'Someone likes their toys.'

'They're not worried about paying their electricity bill, are they? And the place is spotless,' Hicksy said, not hiding his disgust. 'There's not even a dirty dish in the sink.'

Floor to ceiling windows overlooked the garden. Wise flicked a switch that was next to the back door. Spotlights blazed into life, illuminating a sizeable plot of land that looked well-maintained. 'That garden's probably worth a few million on its own.'

'Cheesy pop songs pay well.'

'Maybe,' Wise said. 'Maybe the Richardsons had other sources of income.'

Hicksy looked at him with a raised eyebrow. 'Illegal sources?'

'I expect you to get to know a few gangsters in the music business,' Wise said. 'That singer bloke was getting his drugs off someone and I doubt it was a bloke down the pub.'

'I'll pull their bank statements and see if they were living above their means,' Hicksy said. 'Maybe all the victims were borrowing money off loan sharks and couldn't pay them back.'

'Hassleman had his drugs. Andronovitch might be a gunrunner. Clarke was a politician who could've been into all sorts. Maybe Richardson was mixed up with something dodgy, too.'

Callum was on his way down the stairs just as Wise and Hicksy were about to head up. 'Guv,' he said in greeting.

'I had a nose around Richardson's office, but I didn't see any threatening notes or anything like that. From the amount of crossword books in there, he seemed to have spent a lot of time doing puzzles,' Callum said.

Wise waited for Callum to get to the bottom of the stairs. 'Well done, Call. There's an iPad next door. Bag it, and any other computers in the house, so Digital Forensics can have a look at them. After that, call it a night. It's going to be another long day tomorrow.'

The lad nodded. 'Cheers, Guv.'

Wise and Hicksy spent another hour going through the house together. Callum was right — there were no signs that anything had been disturbed or stolen. All the rooms were in a similar style to the living room — all old-fashioned and costing a fortune. No sign either of any sort of secret life or a reason someone had killed Richardson. He and his wife were just a wealthy couple who enjoyed the good life as far as Wise could see. But maybe that was all the Motorbike Killer needed to target him. Maybe the sick bastard really did just hate rich people.

'I'm surprised the DCI didn't show,' Hicksy said once they'd returned their forensics suits and signed out.

'Roberts knows when to keep her head down,' Wise said, glancing over at the reporters at the end of the street. 'She can sniff out bad press a mile away and she's not keen on being told she's useless. She's happy to delegate that honour.'

'Lucky us.'

'Don't worry about it. You'll be fine. The buck stops with me.'

'That's not right.'

'What is it they say? Success has many parents, while failure is always an orphan.' Wise looked at his watch. 12 a.m. Was this the start of another three-day cycle before another murder?

But what did it matter? Wise was off the case the moment he stepped into Kennington tomorrow.

And what did that leave him?

Tuesday, 20th September

38

The new murder had brought even more journalists to Kennington Police Station. More, their vans blocking up the road, not caring if they got tickets for illegal parking or not. *Sky News,* BBC, ITV and Channel Four were all there, along with that chap with the beard from LBC, and the press mob from the *Mail*, the *Express*, the *Mirror*, the *Sun*, *Telegraph* and *Guardian*, plus a few other morbid sods from overseas stoking up sensationalism about the murders.

They'd drafted more uniforms into Kennington by the looks of things, playing crowd control, keeping the hordes back as best they could, and making sure all the vehicles could get in and out without too much hassle.

Wise parked up at the station with half an hour to go before the DMM, full of dread and dog tired. He'd barely slept, his mind going over and over the case, analysing what he'd done, what he could've done differently, trying to see if he'd made mistakes or overlooked facts. The only thing keeping him sane was his belief he'd done everything right. It was as if the case was designed to confound them all.

He got out of the car, slipped his suit jacket on, ignored the shouts from the press and marched straight up to the front door, where another uniform buzzed him in.

'Thanks,' Wise said.

'DCI Roberts asked if you could go straight to her office,' said the police officer.

'Great,' Wise said. No one intended to waste any time before dishing out the bollocking, it would seem.

When Wise got to her office, Roberts was behind her desk, a folded newspaper in front of her.

'Boss,' Wise said in greeting.

'Simon,' she replied. 'I hear we had another one last night.'

'Yeah. Someone shot Tony Richardson on his doorstep over in Cottesmore Gardens.'

'Number four.'

'Yes, boss.' As if he needed reminding.

'We're not not looking good, Simon. Not good at all.'

'I know. I'm sorry, boss.'

'We've increased your team, and we're fast-tracking all the forensics through the system for you, but you've still got nothing to show for it.'

Wise noted the way she said "your team" and "for you." Never a good sign.

'And have you seen this?' Roberts unfolded the newspaper so he could see the front page. It was the *Mail*. The headline said, "Top cop hasn't a clue what to do." Beneath it was a picture of Wise from last night in his car, shielding his eyes.

'Ah,' Wise said. That didn't look good either.

'I've always been a fan of yours, Simon,' Roberts said. 'Seeing you do well over the years has been a source of pride for me. Even with all the business with DS Davidson, you

stood tall and carried on and I admired that. But there's
nothing wrong in saying you're out of your depth, that you
need help. It can happen to the best of us.'

And there it was. His out if he took it. His escape from
this nightmare of a case. And the end of his career too. He'd
never recover if he gave up now, never get a big case again.
Christ, he'd be lucky to be asked to give out parking tickets
on the Isle of Skye. He'd never make up for what happened
to Sellers that night or find who was behind Andy's death.
God. He was a crap husband, a terrible father and now The
Job was going to be taken from him. 'I'm not out of my
depth, boss.'

'I'm glad you still have confidence, Simon,' Roberts said.
'Now, we have to see Detective Chief Superintendent
Walling.'

'Time to meet the replacements. Eh?'

'You're still on the case for now,' Roberts said. 'Don't get
me wrong — he wanted to kick you into touch, but I
convinced him that the investigation would suffer if
everything stopped while they brought a new team up to
speed and we all know the clock is ticking once more.'

'Who's the new team?'

'A DCI from the Yard. Doug Riddleton.' Roberts winced
as she said the man's rank, the same as her own. Making
sure Wise knew her neck was on the block with his own.

'I know him,' Wise said. The man was a self-serving
careerist. A total prick, if Wise was being honest.

'He's going to be looking at the case with fresh eyes.
Perhaps he'll see something you've missed.'

'Right,' Wise said.

Roberts looked at him. 'And you'll work with him?'

'I'll do anything if it means catching the killer, boss.'

And Wise meant it, too. He might not like the idea, but what choice did he have?

'Then let's say hello,' Roberts said, rising from her seat. 'And don't forget to smile.'

Wise recognised Riddleton straight away when they entered Walling's office. They'd been on a course at Hendon once when they'd both been the same rank and Wise disliked him on the spot. Whereas Wise was useless when it came to politics, Riddleton was a master at it. He kissed the right backsides when he had to, made sure he belonged to the right clubs and lodges. Even on the course, the man was so over-eager to impress, it hurt. Wise and the others on the course had taken the piss out of the man, but it was Riddleton who held the higher rank now.

Wise was pleased to see Riddleton had lost a lot of hair since then they'd last met, despite his best efforts to comb over what was left to hide the fact. He hadn't lost the smug look on his face, though. If anything, that had gotten even more pronounced over the years.

'Here they are,' Walling said, from behind his desk, as if no one had noticed Wise and Roberts enter. 'We were just talking about you both.'

'Wonderful,' Roberts said. She nodded at Riddleton. 'Doug. Good to see you.'

'And you, Anne,' Riddleton replied.

'Hello, Doug,' Wise said, offering his hand to shake and smiling like he was happy to see the man. 'Or should I say, "sir?"'

Riddleton shook his hand, his grip overly tight, his smile just as fake. 'Been a while, Simon — and Doug's fine.'

'We've not met,' the other man said, standing up and flashing white teeth through a thick beard. He had a runner's physique and skin that positively glowed from self-care. Any man that moisturised wasn't a copper.

'This is Detective Chief Inspector Roberts and Detective Inspector Wise,' Walling said. 'They've been running the investigation into the Motorbike Killer so far.'

'Pleased to meet you,' the man replied.

'I didn't catch your name,' Roberts said.

'Where are my manners?' Walling said. 'This is Doctor Kenneth Cheil. He's a psychologist, helps now and then with the more specialised cases out of the Embankment. I thought it was way past time we had a proper profile worked out.'

Wise said nothing. Cheil was obviously very well connected. He wondered who'd asked him to get involved. Probably wasn't Walling.

Cheil sat back down, but there weren't any other chairs, so Roberts and Wise remained standing. Another sign of who was in and who was out of favour.

'Now,' Walling said. 'We all know the case isn't going anywhere at the moment, so I asked if Doug and Ken could help, give us some fresh thinking. Ken can develop a profile of this Motorbike Killer chap so we can narrow some options down and, perhaps even predict where he'll strike next.'

'That's a fantastic idea,' Roberts said. God only knew how she faked the excitement. 'I'm so glad you can help, Doctor.'

'Doug's here to help the team too,' Walling said. 'Add his expertise and perspective to the task. A fresh pair of eyes. Perhaps he can see the wood from the trees.'

And there it was. No wonder the man looked smug. Here to help, then take over.

'Welcome on board,' Roberts said, sounding like she meant it, as good a politician as her boss.

Riddleton held up both hands and smiled. 'Anything to help the cause.'

'Give him five or six of your best troops, Simon,' Walling said. 'Make sure one of them can walk him through the case from the beginning. I want him up to speed by the end of play tonight.'

'I can do that myself,' Wise said, even though it was the last thing he wanted to do.

'No need to trouble yourself,' Riddleton said. 'I'm sure you've got more important things to do.'

'It was time we were all getting on anyway,' Walling said. 'Take Doug and Ken up to the pit and get them set up. We need to get a result on this one, ladies and gentlemen. Fast. The Powers That Be are watching and they do not have the patience of saints. Far from it. They were tetchy before last night's murder. They'll be even worse now.'

'We will get him, sir,' Roberts said.

'I expect no less,' Walling said before giving Wise the dirtiest of looks. Did the man think Wise hadn't cracked the case on purpose or something? It wasn't as if he could just pull clues out of thin air or make them up like they did back in the day when Walling was a rising copper.

He waited for Roberts, Riddleton, and Cheil to leave before he followed them out the door.

'I'll try not to step on your toes,' Riddleton said, as they walked up the stairs.

'I'm sure you won't,' replied Wise, thinking quite the opposite. The man was there to find out where Wise had messed up, discover what he had missed, and flush Wise's career down the toilet in the process.

They all stopped outside MIR-One. 'Let me know if you need anything,' Roberts said.

'We will,' Riddleton said.

Roberts went to leave, then stopped. 'Oh, Simon. Pop in to see me before you go out.'

'Will do, boss,' Wise said.

MIR-One was quieter when Wise, Riddleton, and Cheil entered. Most of his crew weren't in yet after the previous night, but Sarah was at her desk, talking to Callum, and a few of the newbies were still milling around. Wise called them over. 'This is DI Riddleton and Doctor Cheil. They've come over to help us with the investigation. I'd like you all to take them through where we've got to so far and help them moving forward.'

Sarah gave Wise a look as if to say 'what the fuck,' but he ignored it. She was a smart girl, and she'd been a copper long enough to work out what was going on.

'Nice to meet you all,' Riddleton said, stepping forward, full of smugness. Wise resisted the urge to punch him in the side of the head.

'I'll catch up with you later, Doug,' he said instead. 'It was nice to meet you too, Doctor.'

Cheil gave a nod back, but his eyes were focused on the whiteboards.

Wise left them and headed toward his office.

Hannah came into MIR-One, stopping him. 'Singh wants us over at the morgue at midday, Guv,' Hannah said, doing a double take on Riddleton and Cheil as she passed them.

'Ok. I've just got to make a call and I'll be with you,' Wise said and entered his office. It felt smaller than ever, the walls so close he felt like he could barely turn around. He pulled his phone out, wanting to speak to a friendly voice, to hear someone who cared about him to say everything was going to be okay. But who could he call? Not Jean — they'd not spoken since the argument about the kids at the weekend.

God, he even wished he could talk to Andy and listen to his stupid jokes, but that ghost only had one thing to say to Wise.

'Don't come any closer,' Andy cries, his eyes wide and bulging, burning cocaine bright. He presses the revolver against Morris' head.

There was his dad, but Wise knew that if he called, his father would only worry. He couldn't do that to the man. He thought about calling Doctor Shaw. She'd understand. She'd help. She'd ...

Tears sprung in his eyes. A hollow, sick feeling spread in his gut. It was all over. He was all over.

He shook his head, getting angry with himself for feeling so pathetic. He needed it now. Needed the fury. Let it burn the misery away. Show those bastards that he could still do it.

'Pull yourself together,' he hissed through clenched teeth. This was no time to stop. No time to fall apart. The bloody clock was ticking. The killer was out there, planning another murder.

Wiping his eyes, he picked up his jacket and went to get Hannah. 'Come on. Let's go.'

She said nothing until they were out of the incident room and on the stairs. 'What the bloody hell is going on?' she whispered the moment they were out of earshot.

'We can talk about it in the car,' Wise said. 'I've got to stop at the DCI's office on the way out. I'll meet you outside.'

He could feel the temper sitting nicely in his gut when he knocked on Roberts' door. It made him feel strong. Confident. Even the sight of her grim face didn't bother him.

'This isn't good, Simon,' she said. 'That shit Riddleton is one of the top brass' blue-eyed wonder boys. His fast track to glory is paved with the bodies of fuck-ups, and I will not be one of them. Is that clear?'

'Crystal, boss,' replied Wise. He already knew he was on his own.

'And as for that stuck up ponce of a doctor! We might as well give Mystic Meg a bloody call.'

'I'll keep you updated on our progress,' Wise said, only wanting to get out that room and get to work.

'You bloody better, Simon. Because if you fuck this up, I'll happily throw you to the wolves so they don't feel the need to eat me too.'

'Appreciate the honesty, boss. If there's nothing else, I've got to get to the morgue.'

'Go.'

39

Hannah watched Wise come charging out of the station, looking like he wanted to murder someone. The moment he stepped outside, the press vultures started shouting their questions again but, Wise ignored them. Instead, head down, he marched over to the Mondeo, where Hannah waited in the passenger seat, arms crossed.

'You don't fancy driving?' Wise said as he climbed in. She'd put the keys in the ignition, so he turned the engine on.

'I figured you were having a bad enough of a day without me making it worse for you,' Hannah said, trying to lighten the mood. 'I drive a bike for a reason.'

'You have a point there.'

The uniforms cleared a path through the press contingent outside the station so Wise could drive through. Even so, the press did their best to blind them with all their lights as they passed by. Hannah had to cover her face as Wise turned right onto Kennington Road.

She saw Wise glancing in the rear-view mirror.

'They following?' she asked.

'No,' Wise said.

'Thank God for that,' Hannah replied.

She let him continue down Kennington Road saying nothing, aware that he was strangling the steering wheel to death with those enormous hands of his, aware too of the bruises on the knuckles, more pronounced now than they had been the other day. He'd been in a fight at some point. Who with though? And when? She'd been with him almost non-stop since the beginning of the week.

But did it matter? She had a feeling whoever had been on the receiving end had deserved it — or she hoped they did, at least. Wise certainly had a temper on him. She'd seen it brewing more and more since the murders had begun, as their frustration with the case had grown. In fact, she'd thought Wise was going to throttle that idiot in the SUV the previous night. Maybe he would've done if she wasn't there.

A part of her told her she should be worried, that Wise was a bomb waiting to go off, but the other part of her liked the fact that the case was getting to him. It showed he cared. He really cared about what he was doing. The Job wasn't just a job to him. God only knew she'd worked enough with people going through the motions, burnt out by the twenty-four-hour crime cycle in London.

'So?' Hannah said in the end when they were halfway down Kennington Road. 'Are those twats taking over the case?' It was a risk being rude about senior officers, but she hoped Wise would appreciate the support that went into the question.

Thankfully, Wise smiled. 'Is there anyone you like?'

'I like you well enough.' Hannah didn't add that he was part of a very select group of people.

'Cheers. Appreciate that,' Wise said. 'As for those twats,

as you so eloquently called them, the chief's brought DCI Riddleton in "for a fresh pair of eyes," along with a shrink to work up a profile of our killer. However, if we don't make some progress soon, they made it perfectly clear that I'll be out and dear old Doug will come charging to the rescue.'

Hannah thought as much, but that didn't make hearing it any less annoying. 'What a bunch of wankers. We're busting our balls to catch this freak.'

'Easy now. You're talking about our senior officers,' Wise said.

'Am I wrong?' Hannah said.

'No comment.'

Hannah shook her head. 'It's not right.'

'It is what it is,' Wise said, but his manner suggested anything but acquiescence.

'Okay — what's the plan?'

Wise sighed. 'We carry on doing what we've been doing. We work the case and look for the evidence that will help us catch the bastard. There are no shortcuts. We just work hard until our luck changes.'

Hannah winced. 'Not been doing us much good so far.'

'It's the only way I know.'

'You know what the definition of insanity is, Guv?' Hannah spared him a glance. 'Doing the same thing over and over again and expecting a different result.'

Again, she saw the hint of a smile on his lips. That was good. 'You're not quoting Einstein at me, are you?'

'You're not the only educated person in the force, Guv,' Hannah said.

'Apparently not,' Wise said.

By the time they pulled up outside the morgue, they were fifteen minutes late. Normally, the morgue at the back of King's College Hospital in Camberwell was only ten minutes away from the nick on a good day. Straight down Kennington Road to Denmark Road and onto Coldharbour Lane and you were there. Of course, London traffic didn't do good days anymore. There were just bad days and utterly horrific days, and this was the latter.

'Next time I'll drive — my motorbike. You can go on the back,' Hannah said. 'London and cars don't go.'

'I'm not riding pillion with you,' Wise said. They walked up a ramp to a set of grey doors. 'I'd rather be late than dead.'

'Either way, you'd end up here,' Hannah said, pushing the doors open.

Wise looked at her and shook his head. 'You're alright, Detective Sergeant Markham.'

'Cheers, Guv. You're not bad yourself.'

Singh's assistant met them, took them to get suited up with gloves, face masks and gowns and then escorted them through to the examination suite.

'You're not too late for once, Inspector,' Singh said when she saw them. 'Perhaps one day you'll be on time?'

'Miracles can happen, Doctor,' Wise said.

'Well, today seems to be your day, Inspector,' Singh said. 'I have some interesting things to tell you today.'

'You do?' Wise said, sounding surprised. Hannah stepped forward, eager for some good news.

'I do,' Singh said. 'I'm not sure if you know, but all the other victims were shot from various angles. Hassleman was shot through the hand and into the face, Sir Harry was turning, and Andronovitch wasn't a tall man, so the bullet entered at the top of the man's forehead.'

'Right,' Wise said. 'We know that.'

'This is the first time the killer was standing directly in front of the man he killed,' Singh said. She picked up a metal rod and inserted it into the bullet hole in Richardson's head. Even from where Hannah and Wise were standing, it was clear that the rod was completely upright. 'We know this because the bullet has entered Richardson's eye with a zero-degree divergence.'

'That's a straight line,' Wise said.

'Very good, Detective.'

'And?'

'The killer shot the victim directly in the right eye, suggesting the killer was left-handed,' Singh said. Hannah felt a surge of excitement. For once, they had a clue that could help focus the search.

'Why's that?' Wise asked.

'If they were right-handed, the bullet would have entered the eye at an angle as the killer would have been shooting across the body as it were — or they would have shot the victim in the left eye as that would have been directly in front of a gun in the right hand.'

Images of Richardson being shot flashed through Hannah's mind; the surprise of seeing a pistol in front of him, the shot being fired, his body falling back already dead.

'And I'd say we're looking for someone who's slightly taller than the victim,' Singh continued. 'Again, the bullet has gone straight in through the eye. If the killer was shorter, they'd have to aim up and the bullet would've gone in at an angle. The same is true if they were much taller; the bullet would've gone in at angle and exited through the lower part of the skull.'

'Richardson was five foot ten,' Hannah said. 'When you say "slightly taller," how much are you talking about?'

'If they were the same height,' Singh said, 'and the killer pointed the gun straight at the victim, the bullet would have entered just below the eye — about here.' Singh pointed to the bottom of the eye socket. 'But it's entered here — two inches higher.'

'So, we're looking for someone who's left-handed and six feet tall,' Wise said.

Singh smiled. 'Wonderfully summed up, Inspector. The only proviso I'd add is to check where Richardson was standing when he died. There might be a slight difference to consider if the inside of the doorstep was slightly higher than the outside. Then you just add that into the calculation.'

'Christ, that's more information than we've had since all this started,' Wise said.

'And you're one hundred percent sure about that, Doctor?' Hannah asked.

Singh shifted her gaze to the sergeant. 'Nothing's ever one hundred percent unless we're matching DNA, but I'm as sure as I can be with the information we have. Perhaps if the killer was standing to one side of the door so their right hand was in line with the victim's right eye, then that changes things. Something to check with the crime scene — footprints, boot marks, even if there is enough room to stand off to one side.'

'Thank you,' Hannah said, with more than a touch of ice to her voice. 'I wouldn't have thought of that.'

'Nothing else on the body?' Wise asked. 'Anything that could belong to the killer?'

'I'm afraid not,' Singh said. 'He's as clean as a whistle — apart from his own blood and brains, of course.' She looked up, focusing her attention on Wise.

Hannah glanced over at Wise, saw the gleam in his eye.

'You weren't joking when you said you had something interesting,' Wise said. 'Our killer's left-handed and six feet tall. That's amazing news, Doctor. Thank you.'

'Glad to be of service, Inspector,' Singh said. 'I hope it helps.'

'It just might, Doctor. It just might.'

'You can buy me a drink sometime as a thank you if it does.'

'It'd be my pleasure,' Wise said. He turned to Hannah, all the darkness gone from his face. 'Let's go check the house one more time before we see Mrs Richardson.'

'Right, Guv.' For the first time, Hannah felt the buzz of a lead. Suddenly, the thought of catching the killer didn't seem impossible.

'Thanks again, Doctor,' Wise said. 'Hopefully, I won't see you again with another dead body for a while.'

'Just for that drink, then?' Singh said.

'We catch this killer. I might even buy you two,' Wise said.

Singh was chuckling as Hannah and Wise left the examination suite.

'Over to Richardson's then, Guv?' Hannah said. 'Confirm the height?'

'Yeah, let's go.' Wise grinned.

They all but ran to the Mondeo and were soon on their way back over the river to West London.

'Something at last,' Wise said. 'Something definitive.'

It was amazing to see the difference in Wise. He was so full of energy and looked so positive after Singh's news. That look of his, like he wanted to murder someone himself, was gone from his eyes. 'That was worth the trip to the morgue,' Hannah said, feeling pretty damn happy herself.

'Yeah, it certainly was,' Wise said. 'We can stop chasing ghosts and being pushed in every direction. This gives us a real start point to discover the killer's identity.'

For once, the traffic gods were on their side and they

were at the Richardson's house in just over thirty minutes. Cottesmore Gardens was open once again to traffic, but police tape stretched across the access to the murder scene itself as SOCOs continued to work under the awning, looking for evidence.

Once more, they put on the protective overalls. Hannah had to smile as Wise struggled to get himself into the one-size-fits-all suit. 'You'd think they'd make an extra-large by now.'

'Yeah, well, every time I crouch down, I'm petrified I'm going to split the thing in half,' Wise said.

'Let me do the measuring then, eh?' Hannah said.

'It'll be my pleasure.'

After borrowing a tape measure from the SOCOs' van, they moved on to the house. The front door was open and, as they approached, it was clear that there was a slight difference in height between the last step and the inside of the door. 'Looks like we're in luck,' Hannah said as she bent down to check what the measurements. 'It's one inch lower.'

'That could make the killer six foot one,' Wise said. 'Do we know what type of shoes or boots they're wearing? That might make a difference.'

'Yeah, but not much,' Hannah said. 'I can't remember what they had on, but I know it wasn't anything unusual.'

'Say they've got biker boots on, then that would add maybe half an inch to their height. Sneakers and shoes slightly less than that. It still gives us a pretty tight height to work on,' Wise said. 'Now, let's check the left-hand theory.' He stepped over the threshold and into the house and turned to face Hannah. 'We know Richardson was standing square in the doorway.'

Hannah nodded and stood up, facing him. Wise was four or so inches taller than her, but they were close enough in height to act out the murder well enough. She raised her right hand in the classic gun pose, two fingers extended. The gun pointed at Wise's left eye. Hannah then moved her aim to target where the bullet had entered Richardson's head. 'The bullet wouldn't have gone straight in like it did. It would've gone in at an angle through the eye and out near his ear.'

'That's good,' Wise said. 'Move to your left so you can shoot straight on.'

Hannah did as she was told, but her left foot ran out of step before she could get into position, and it was impossible to get a direct aim on Wise's right eye without half-falling off the steps.

'Swap gun hands,' Wise said.

Hannah moved her imaginary gun to her left hand. The moment she stuck out her two fingers, the 'barrel' pointed directly at Wise's right eye. 'Bingo.'

'Singh was right,' Wise said. 'She was bloody well right.' He grinned. 'Let's see Mrs Richardson now.'

40

'Thank you for taking the time to see us,' Wise said, sitting down. 'We're really sorry for your loss.'

Sheila Richardson sat opposite him, her daughter by her side, clutching her hand. They were in a suite at the Langham Hotel in Portland Place. The room was just as ornately decorated as the Richardson's own home. It felt like somewhere out of a BBC period drama, like *Downton Abbey* or *Brideshead Revisited*, the sort of shows that Wise's mother loved to watch back when she was alive. Apparently, the suite even came with its own butler. Wise hadn't seen the man, but someone had set up a tea service on the coffee table with a silver teapot and some very delicate cups and saucers. There was even a plate of cucumber sandwiches alongside untouched sponge cake.

'Do you mind if I smoke?' Sheila asked. 'I gave up years ago. Tony hated it — the smoke. He was always complaining I'd give him second-hand cancer.' Despite decades of good living, her Essex roots still showed in her accent. 'But a cigarette is all I can think of now. It's stupid. I keep telling myself I don't need it, that I don't smoke, but then I remember Tony—'

'It's fine,' Wise said, even though Sheila wasn't really asking his permission. She'd already pulled a Dunhill out of a packet with shaking hands and was trying to click her lighter into life. In the end, her daughter, Helen, took the lighter and lit her mother's cigarette. Sheila took a deep drag as if her life depended on it, the tip glowing bright and furious.

Sheila Richardson was seventy-two years old, but she had that well-preserved look that the only truly wealthy could ever aspire to. Her face was taut and wrinkle free, her hair a silver blonde artfully crafted to just brush her shoulders, and her physique was either sculpted by dieticians and personal trainers or excellent surgeons — perhaps even a combination of them all. She was, despite her age, still a very attractive woman. She would've been quite something when she was younger.

Her daughter, in her fifties, looked almost identical. In fact, if Wise were to see them only in passing, it would be easy to assume they were sisters rather than mother and daughter.

'Let us know if at any point you feel unwell or need to take a break,' Wise said. 'I'll do my best to be brief as possible.'

'I'm fine,' Sheila said, not too convincingly, the cigarette wobbling in her hand.

'Do you want me to get you a G&T?' asked Helen with an accent that came from only the very best private schools.

'Make it a large one, darling,' replied Sheila, patting her daughter's hand.

Helen jumped out of her seat and headed to the room's minibar.

'You don't want one, do you?' Sheila asked. 'Drinking on duty's a bit of a no-no still, isn't it?'

'We're fine,' Wise said, forcing a smile. 'If I may take you back to last night …'

Shiela's hand went to her mouth as if to hold back a sob. Then she must've remembered the cigarette in her hand because she took another drag from that instead and then exhaled. 'Yes.'

'You were watching television?' Wise asked. It was always good to start with the simple questions, the uncontroversial ones.

'Tony was watching one of those sci-fi shows on one of the streaming channels,' Sheila said. 'Binge-watching it. Hour after hour. "Just one more," he'd say, but he'd never let me say what I wanted to watch — and he wondered why I always fell asleep.' She gave a sad little laugh. 'Bloody Tony. I always said I'd have to snatch that remote control from his cold, dead hands.'

'Mum!' said Helen, bringing the drink over. She set the tall, crystal glass down on the table next to the teapot, ice chinking along with a slice of lime. 'You can't say that.'

'It's true. You know it is,' Sheila said as her daughter returned to her place by her side. 'He always had to be the one in charge, the one running things. Once he couldn't boss those silly little pop stars around, he had to order us around instead. That's why you left home as quick as you did.' Sheila took a gulp of her gin and tonic, emptying half the glass in one go. 'These dear police men — police people — police …'

'Officers,' Hannah said.

'Officers,' Sheila continued, 'want us to tell the truth. We shouldn't make your father to be a saint. He wasn't. Far from it. I should know — I've lived with him all these years.'

'When you say he wasn't a saint, Mrs Richardson,' Wise said, 'what do you mean by that?'

'Please, call me Sheila.'

Wise smiled. 'Sheila.'

'As I said, he was a selfish man with the TV remote and did I ever hear him apologise for anything he did wrong in the forty-eight years we were married? No, I did not. He had to be right about everything, even if it meant trying to convince you that night was day and vice versa.' Sheila finished the gin and tonic in another swallow.

'Forty-eight years is a long time to be together,' Wise said. 'How did you meet?'

Sheila gave a big sigh. 'It was like in that song. You know the one — the Human League. I was working as a waitress in a cocktail bar when I met him and all that. Well, Tony was managing this band back in the early seventies. A dreadful band. All big hair, makeup and glam rock high heels. Trying too hard to be David Bowie or Marc Bolan, but not a shade on either. It wasn't a surprise they had no hits.' She waved her cigarette about as if turning back the clock. 'I was working in this dive hole of a club in Grays. Mystique, it was called. Tony's band was playing there one Saturday night, and he came in, blond hair down to his shoulders and his shirt open to his belly button, leading his band in like they were about to play Wembley. It was love at first sight for him and, well, I didn't think he looked too ridiculous. So, when he asked me out for a drink, I said yes and that was that.

'We barely spent a day apart after that. I even used to go on tour with him. All the others used to love being away from their wives and partners for months at a time, but not Tony. We'd laugh at them all chasing girls young enough to be their daughters — or in Jake's case, any boy with pretty eyelashes.' Sheila took one last, long drag of her cigarette, then stubbed it out in an already full ashtray. 'Happy days.'

'Must've been quite exciting mixing in that world,' Hannah said.

'Oh darling, you couldn't imagine,' Sheila said. 'It could be amazing and terrifying all at the same time. I struggled sometimes with it all. I mean, I was a cocktail waitress from Essex. What did I have to say to Princess Di? But Tony? He didn't care. "They all have to wipe their arses the same as you," he'd say. It wouldn't matter where he was or who he was with. And if he didn't like you? You better watch out. He even told old Charlie boy to sling his hook once.'

'Charlie boy?' Wise asked.

'His Majesty himself,' Sheila replied. 'He was being a right arse to Di at this charity concert at the Hammersmith Odeon, and Tony wasn't having any of it. He was old-fashioned like that. Chivalrous.'

'Father could be a bit opinionated, though,' Helen said. 'He wasn't one to sugarcoat how he felt about something.'

'He never mellowed, either. You should've heard what he had to say about that poor girl from Waitrose. Just because she hadn't heard of Wild. I said to Tony, "She was born fifteen years after they broke up. Why should she have heard of them?" But of course, that made it worse. It didn't help that she was ...' Sheila glanced at Hannah, 'not from here.'

Wise glanced at Hannah and gave her a raised eyebrow in support. Why did money and racism seem to go so well together? Or was it just that generation? 'Did you ever consider getting a divorce from Tony?'

'Oh God, no,' replied Sheila. 'I loved the man for all his faults. He could make me want to strangle him one minute, then have me rolling about laughing the next.'

'The "strangle him" is just a figure of speech,' Helen said. 'He could make you grumpy, but that's all. No one wanted to kill Dad.'

'What about other people?' Hannah asked. 'Could he make them want to "strangle him?"'

'Everyone used to put up with Tony's eccentricities and opinions back in the eighties because they had to,' Sheila said. 'He was making them all so much money. Now though? We didn't really talk to anyone these days, let alone argue with anyone. It was just us. Tony didn't like that — the quiet life — but it suited me. The last people Tony had words with were the bin men. I don't think they'd want to hurt him — not over mixing up his recycling.'

'Tony didn't stay in touch with anyone from the old days?' Wise asked.

'No. The Biz doesn't like it when people get old. It's all about the Now, the New, the Shiny. Unless you're the Rolling Stones or the Beatles, no one cares what you once did. Tony hated that. Hated being left behind.' Sheila wiped a tear away. 'What did he know about streaming and downloads? You can't bung an algorithm five hundred quid to play your record and get it into the charts. Or maybe you can? We wouldn't know.'

'And no one had made any threats against Tony? Nothing in the mail? Odd phone calls?' Wise said.

'You only ever get nuisance calls on the phone these days,' Sheila said. 'People trying to sell you this or that or convince you to hand over your bank details. Even the kids seem to have forgotten how the phone works. It's all texts and emojis these days.'

'Can you think of any reason anyone would want to murder your husband?' Hannah asked.

'No,' Sheila said. 'Not at all.'

'Did your husband know Mark Hassleman, Yuri Andronovitch or Sir Harry Clarke?' Wise asked.

'They're the other victims of the Motorbike Killer, aren't they?' Helen asked.

Wise nodded.

'Was my father murdered by him?' Helen said with a shiver. 'By the Motorbike Killer?'

'That's one possibility we're looking at,' Wise said.

'He was killed because he'd made a success of himself? Is that it?' Helen's voice was rising, her eyes wide. She shifted closer to her mother and grasped her arm.

'The Motorbike Killer has targeted wealthy men like your father, but we don't know if that's the reason he's committing these murders. That's why we need to know if there's a connection between the other victims and your father,' Wise said.

'Tony didn't know them,' Sheila said, her voice a whisper as she fumbled for another cigarette.

'Are you sure?' Wise asked.

'We talked about them when they were killed — when they were on the news. We were both outraged, but that was the first time either of us had heard their names,' Sheila said. She clicked her lighter into life on the first attempt this time and sucked another lungful of smoke. 'We never thought we would be targeted. We were well off, but we weren't rich like those other poor sods.'

'Really?' Hannah said. 'I would've thought your house alone was worth millions.'

'About twenty-two, actually,' Sheila said. 'But you can't spend that. Not without selling the place and there wasn't any point mortgaging it at our age.'

'So you weren't struggling financially?' Wise asked.

'We're not starving, if that's what you mean. We

could still enjoy a meal out at San Lorenzo's when we wanted to or enjoy a couple of weeks in the sun now and then. But the others that died were billionaires, weren't they? Private yachts and houses all around the world?'

'Yuri Andronovitch probably fitted that category, but not the others,' Wise said. 'But, perhaps, to someone who has nothing, you all look like billionaires.'

'Well, maybe they should check everyone's bank balances before shooting them then,' snapped Sheila. 'We're hardly the one percent that everyone hates.'

Wise glanced at Hannah just in case she was about to disagree with that comment, but Hannah kept her opinions to herself.

'And your husband didn't have any business dealings in Russia?' Wise asked.

'Tony didn't have any business dealings anywhere. He was as retired as a person can get.'

'What about the Conservative party?' Hannah asked. 'Was he a member or did he donate money to them?'

'Dear God, no,' Sheila said, eyes wet with tears. 'He hated the Tories. Even back in the eighties, when everyone thought the sun shone out of Maggie Thatcher's arse, Tony thought she was a wrong 'un. God knows he had enough arguments with the bloke next door about bloody Boris and the rest of them.'

Wise stood. 'Well, thank you for your time under these awful circumstances. We'll be in touch if we have any more questions.'

Hannah rose to her feet, too. 'Thank you.'

Sheila didn't respond. Her head dropped as she stubbed out her cigarette, then she reached for another straight away, her shoulders bobbing as the tears came.

'When can my mother return home, Inspector?' Helen asked.

'Not for a while,' Wise said. 'We still have teams looking for evidence at the house. And even when they are done, it might be best to stay away for longer. The press can be quite painful to deal with in cases like this. Perhaps your mother would be better off staying with you.'

'Of course,' Helen said, slipping her arm around her mother.

'We'll speak soon,' Wise said and headed to the door, Hannah on his heels.

'Poor thing,' Hannah said as they walked down the corridor to the lift.

'Wait until we're in the car, eh?' Wise said. 'You don't want the butler to overhear.'

As if on cue, a man in tails and a white bow tie appeared. 'Good afternoon, sir, madam,' he said.

'Right you are,' Hannah said. 'I think Mrs Richardson might want another gin and tonic.'

'I'm on my way,' the butler replied with a curt nod.

'I wouldn't mind having one of those at home,' Hannah muttered, watching him go. 'I bet he's a dab hand at the housework.'

The ancient lift opened, and they climbed inside. Its wooden panels had been polished until they positively shone. A muzak version of Do You Want To Hurt Me played over tinny speakers. No wonder Sheila Richardson liked it here. The hotel was stuck in the past.

Hannah's phone pinged. She checked the screen. 'Sarah's wondering when we'll be back.'

'Tell her we'll be back in about half an hour,' Wise said.

Wise's battered Mondeo couldn't have looked more out of place amongst the Mercedes and the Lamborghinis outside the front of the hotel, but he didn't care as he climbed behind the wheel. In fact, he quite enjoyed the looks of curiosity and mild disgust from the hotel's clientele.

'What are you thinking?' Hannah asked as they got into the car.

'Just that it's easy to get angry at people like the Richardsons. It's easy to see the money but not the person. The Richardsons worked hard to earn their lifestyle. Maybe there was a bit of luck in it, but you heard her — she was a cocktail waitress. There were no pictures of her ancestors hanging on their walls,' Wise said.

'So was Andronovitch to a point,' Hannah said. 'Even though some of it might've been illegally gained.'

'Hassleman must've come from some sort of money for private boarding schools.'

'Clarke seems pretty old money, though.'

Wise shook his head. 'Money is still the only thing they all have in common.'

'So we're back to an angry man striking out at the rich?'

'Yeah — but it's like we're meant to think that,' Wise said. 'God knows most of the country's got reason enough to be furious at anyone with cash right now, but this guy's actions aren't impulsive. There's no rage in the murders. If anything, they're the opposite of angry. They're patient, calculated, prepared. Even the means of killing is efficient, precise.'

'I'd agree with that,' Hannah said.

'That tells me there's something else behind these murders,' Wise said. 'I don't even think it's the work of a real serial killer. Serial killers normally like to play with their victims. They enjoy the pain, savouring the moment during the kill and afterwards. They don't just execute people. Our killer hasn't even tried to take any sort of souvenir from his victims. He's just shot them and left.'

'Like he was doing a job,' Hannah said. 'A professional?'

'Only in so much as he's cold and detached from what he's doing but I don't think he's a hitman — that would suggest that someone else is paying for these murders and we've not found any connection between the victims to place one person behind that.' Wise flicked the indicator, then tuned left at Notting Hill Gate. 'This guy is something different. Something we're not seen before. And that frightens me.'

41

It was late by the time Wise and Hannah returned to Kennington, but Wise didn't care — he was in a good mood for once. They'd checked the Richardsons' doorstep. It would've been impossible for the shooter to be standing anywhere other than directly in front of Mr Richardson when he killed him, so that confirmed Singh's left-handed theory. There was also a one-inch height difference between the inside and the outside, so that put the killer at six foot, six foot one.

It wasn't much, but it was something at long last. Some facts to put on the board. It was progress.

The news crews were still loitering outside, desperate for anything to talk about, but Wise ignored their shouts and cries as he entered the station.

'One of these days, I'm just going to give them the finger,' Hannah said, 'and see if they'll put that on the TV.'

'I'd rather you didn't,' Wise said with a smile. 'Walling disapproves of that sort of thing.'

'He's lucky I don't —'

'Don't say it. Whatever it is, don't say it.'

'Spoilsport.'

'That's what everyone says,' chuckled Wise.

Naturally, his good mood didn't last. It vanished the instant he walked into MIR-One. 'What the hell?'

The room was still busy despite it being well past 7 p.m. but that was to be expected on a murder enquiry of this size, and the clock ticking before the next murder. However, most of the officers were watching Riddleton and Cheil. They stood in front of the whiteboards — whiteboards that had been wiped clean of all the evidence that Wise and his team had gathered — and were busy cherry-picking information to put back.

They'd stuck an image of the killer, grabbed from CCTV, in the centre of the board, with the words "THE MOTORBIKE KILLER" scrawled above it in big, red letters. To the left were the pictures of Hassleman, Andronovitch, Clarke and Richardson, under the title of "VICTIMS."

Sarah rushed over. 'I'm sorry, Guv. I told them you enjoyed having everything up in a certain way, but they insisted.'

'It's alright, Sarah,' Wise said, gritting his teeth, burying his fury. 'They're just doing their job.'

'Even so ...' she replied. Yeah, even so. Wise stared at the performance in front of him, feeling redundant in his own incident room. He'd known this moment was going to happen no matter what Walling had said in the morning, but the progress of the day had pushed it from his mind. Now it hurt even more.

He clenched his fists, reining himself in, keeping control.

As the others noticed Wise and Markham had returned, the babble of chat faded until even Riddleton and Cheil noticed.

Riddleton turned, saw Wise and that smug smile of his

magically reappeared on his face. 'Simon. You're back. I hope you don't mind, but we were just trying to sort out what was important and what wasn't. As the Super said, it was hard to see the wood for the trees with all the information you had up, especially as so much of it didn't seem ... relevant.'

Wise ignored the dig and walked over, forcing a smile, arms locked by his side. 'Think nothing of it. I appreciate the fresh pair of eyes.' He nodded at Cheil. 'What did you think was ... irrelevant?'

'Because we're dealing with a serial killer,' Cheil said, as if talking to a classroom, 'we've removed everything about the victim's relationships with their families, friends, etcetera, along with information about their business dealings. Our killer isn't from their world — he hates it — so we won't find him lurking in their lives.'

'Right,' Wise said. He didn't agree. He believed the killer was entirely comfortable with the world of Belgravia — but he wasn't stupid enough to argue the point. Riddleton and Cheil were Walling's team. Fighting with them would be like fighting with Walling himself.

Riddleton looked like he was enjoying himself, though, playing the clever clogs with Wise's team looking on. 'It's easy to get distracted with unimportant stuff. You can look busy, with your wheels spinning like crazy but, if you're not moving, you're going nowhere. We're just releasing the brakes on the investigation with what we're doing here.'

Again, the urge to punch the man in the face reared up in Wise's gut. The younger him — the teenage tearaway, the football hooligan — would've done it in an instant, but Wise couldn't be that person anymore. Still, he clenched his fists so tight they hurt. 'Right.'

'The only thing we need to know is that the victims were

rich, well-known figures, living affluent lifestyles that make the ordinary person jealous,' Riddleton said, his voice loud like an actor on stage. 'It didn't matter who they were. They are symbols of social injustice. They are the one per cent.'

'Right,' Wise said again, thinking of Sheila Richardson and what she'd say to that.

'The killer is someone who's used to getting his hands dirty. Doing it himself instead of ordering others around. In fact, he hates being ordered around,' Cheil said. 'Authority figures fuel his anger, his jealousy.'

'And the killer knows the streets of London,' Riddleton said. 'And his confident use of the messenger bike shows that's where his comfort level is. That's his world.' He jabbed his finger against a picture of the killer on his bike. 'That's who he is.'

'He's a motorbike messenger?' Hannah asked, barely hiding her sarcasm.

'Exactly,' Riddleton said. He uncapped a red pen and wrote "MESSENGER" on the whiteboard under the image with a flourish.

'But what's put him over the edge? What's turned resentment into a killing rage?' Cheil said. He looked around at the other officers, but he wasn't asking their opinion. 'He's lost his identity. Someone with power, with money, has taken away the only tiny thing he has in his life, and now he's no one. He's anonymous.'

'That's why he's doing this,' Riddleton said. 'To be someone again. To have us find who he is and give him his identity back.'

'Right,' Wise said.

'We're looking for someone who was recently fired or, more likely, was made redundant,' Cheil said. 'Perhaps he's even lost his home as a result and all he has left is his bike.'

'And a gun,' Hannah muttered, but no one, except Wise, was listening. Riddleton wrote "UNEMPLOYED" and "HOMELESS?" with his big red pen on the board.

'If he were angry about losing his job, why not take it out on his employers?' Wise asked. 'Why attack people he doesn't know? That has nothing to do with his change in circumstances?'

'This is all about taking back control of his life,' Cheil said. 'Balancing the books, as it were. Striking back on behalf of the whole of the working class. In his mind, he's Robin Hood, he's Zorro. A hero to be applauded.'

'If that was the case, why hasn't he made any statements to that effect? Surely he'd want the attention, the ... Applause as you say?' Wise said.

'This man is probably uneducated,' Cheil said. 'He's letting the violence spread the message because he doesn't have the words.'

Wise nodded, but his gut told him that this was all wrong. It was all nonsense. He saw the murders as the act of someone very intelligent, capable of misdirecting everyone until they didn't know which way was up. Or did he just want to believe that because he was jealous that they had worked this all out within a day of being on the case? Was he really not up to the job anymore? Was he lying to himself about keeping all those cracks inside him from tearing him apart?

'Finally,' Cheil said, 'there's the man's expertise with the gun to consider. The man knows what he's doing. He's experienced in this, and he's organised despite his anger. He believes in preparation.'

'He's ex-military,' Riddleton said. How he avoided adding a 'ta-da' to the statement was beyond Wise. His right fist bunched as if it had a will of its own. Riddleton didn't notice, though. He was too busy writing "EX-MILITARY" on the board. The DCI turned back to the room. 'Now, we know who we're looking for.'

He tapped the board from one point to the next. 'Motorbike messenger. Unemployed. Homeless. Ex-military.' Like a schoolteacher giving the correct answers to an exam.

'This is all guesswork,' Wise said. 'There's no proof to back it up.'

Riddleton's smug look turned to one of condescension. 'It's called deduction, detective.'

Wise really wanted to knock him down. All he had to do was take one step forward and drive his right fist into the bridge of the man's nose. Bone would break, blood would spill, and down he'd go. God, it'd feel good. If his career was going to be over, he might as well go out swinging.

But was his career over? He wasn't off the case yet. Not officially. But if he struck a senior officer?

Wise would certainly enjoy the moment, but there'd be definite consequences if he did; suspension pending an enquiry, then demotion if he was lucky, dismissal if he wasn't — and face it, he and luck were pretty much strangers these days. The pleasure of knocking the twat down wasn't worth all that.

While he was still on The Job, he had a chance of catching the actual killer.

Hannah stepped forward, putting her body between Wise and Riddleton, as if she sensed what he was contemplating. 'We have some new information ourselves that you can add to the board.'

'Oh yes?' Riddleton said. He leaned forward.

'We were at the autopsy this afternoon and Doctor

Singh informed us that the killer is between six foot and six foot one and left-handed.'

'Excellent,' Riddleton said, not even bothering to ask the hows and whys behind that bit of information, turning back to the board. Up went "LEFT-HANDED" and "6'1" next to his other declarations. 'This really narrows things down even more.'

Wise stared at the words on the board in disbelief. It was all so simple, so ... obvious. Had he really missed what was staring them all in the face? Had he been over-complicating things? Looking for connections and patterns when really it was the work of an angry, homeless soldier?

Wise's gut said the killer was pointing them in the wrong direction yet again, and Riddleton and Cheil were jumping at his beck and call. Maybe the killer was ex-military, but there was even more of a chance he wasn't. As for the motorbike messenger angle? Wise just saw a man who wanted to be invisible. It was a disguise to blend in, not a declaration of identity or a lack of one.

Could he trust his instincts? He'd been so wrong about Andy, so blind to what he was doing.

'You don't know what I am!' Andy says, a gun in his hand. The red dot dances ...

'Tomorrow, we'll start hitting all the messenger firms in London,' Riddleton said. 'Starting with the ones that service the areas where our victims lived. We'll get names of anyone that's recently been fired or let go, anyone who's ex-military and ...' he winked at Wise, '... left-handed. It won't be a long list. We'll then bring the lucky ones in here for questioning. If we're smart about this, we could have our man by the end of the day.'

Everyone cheered in the incident room — everyone except Wise, Hannah, and Sarah. Even Jono and Hicksy were cheering with the rest of them. Wise could understand why everyone was happy — it did feel like progress — but was it a false hope Riddleton was feeding them? Not to mention he was railroading over Wise's investigation. So much for just lending a fresh pair of eyes.

'I think we should run this past the boss first, Doug,' Wise said. 'Get her opinion on what's best before we send everyone off any running.'

'Of course, of course,' Riddleton said. 'I'm sure she'll be delighted with our progress today.'

Wise forced a smile. 'I'm sure she will.'

'I'll call her, Guv,' Hannah said. 'See if she's still here.'

'Thank you, Hannah,' replied Wise. He looked around, saw Sarah loitering by a desk, looking his way. 'Well done, Doug,' he said, patting the detective on the arm. 'Back in a minute.'

He weaved his way through the desks, and the other officers until he reached Sarah. 'You okay?'

'I'm really sorry about all this, Guv,' she replied. 'I feel like I've let you down.'

'You couldn't do that if you tried,' Wise said.

'Still. It's not right what he's doing. Not right at all. This is still your investigation.'

'We all serve at the whims of our bosses and they want results, not headlines saying we haven't got a clue.'

Sarah winced. 'I saw that this morning. Bastards don't know what they're talking about.'

'That's never stopped them before. How did you get on with the CCTV?'

'Nothing new, I'm afraid.' Sarah sat down behind her desk and pressed a key to kick her computer into life. She called up the footage on her monitor. 'It's the same as before; here he is driving up to Richardson's house, calm as can be. Then he walks up to the steps of the house, but you can't see the actual doorstep or the murder. But here he comes, down the steps like he's just dropped off a letter and not put a bullet in someone's skull, hops on his bike and he's off.'

Wise watched the jittery black and white footage, a time stamp running in the corner. From getting off his bike to leaving took all of five minutes. 'He's bloody efficient, isn't he?'

Sarah played more footage. 'He potters through the streets, sticking to the speed limit, even passing one of ours going the other way, and then he has the crash. Luckily, neither of the vehicles were going too fast. Our man skids along the road a bit, then gets up and hobbles off.'

'That must've hurt all the same. Might even have lost some skin.'

Hannah came over to join them. 'The boss is tied up with something, but she said you and the big man can see her first thing in her office.'

'Okay,' Wise said. God, he felt exhausted. No sleep, and the ups and downs of the day had all taken their toll on him. 'Can you let Doug know?'

'Will do, Guv,' Hannah said.

'I'm going to call it a day and head home,' Wise said. 'I really appreciate all the hard work.'

'Before you go,' Sarah said, 'there's one more thing.'

'What's that?' Wise said.

'I've found how the killer is getting his bike to and from the carparks.'

'Oh yes?' Suddenly, Wise wasn't so keen to leave.

'Yeah.' Sarah tapped away at her keyboard. An image of a white van appeared on her screen. 'This van went into the car park the killer used for the Andronovitch murder half an hour before the murder. It came out twenty-five minutes after the murder. It has stolen number plates.'

Wise nodded. 'Okay.'

Sarah moved her cursor, and another image of a white van appeared. 'This one turned up at the car park the killer used for Hassleman's murder half an hour beforehand. Again, with stolen number plates. It left fifteen minutes after the bike returned there.'

Another click and another picture of a van appeared on the screen. 'And this is at the car park the killer used for Clarke's murder. Like the others, it has stolen number plates, and it arrives within thirty minutes of Clarke's murder and departs fifteen afterwards.'

'That's his magic trick,' Wise said. 'Now our unemployed, homeless soldier has a bike and a van.'

'And somewhere to hide both vehicles,' Sarah said. 'I've checked ANPR, but it disappears just like the bike.'

'That means the killer's not driving the van far,' Hannah said.

'But if they're parking the van in West London, that costs money,' Wise said. 'Serious money.'

Sarah glanced over at Riddleton. 'Do you want me to tell the others?' she whispered.

'Yeah. Let's not hide anything. We're all on the same team,' Wise said, even though it made him feel sick to do so. 'Good work again. I'll see you both in the morning.'

'Night, Guv,' Hannah said. For a moment, they shared a look, hers full of sympathy for the way the investigation had turned. She probably meant well, but it was a kicker all the same. She was the new member of the team and she was feeling sorry for him?

Wise headed for the exit, doing his best to ignore the excitement buzzing around the room. After all, Wise had his team trying to find one person from among the nine million who called London home each day. Riddleton and Cheil, with their "deductions," had narrowed it down to maybe a dozen people.

Were they right, though?

To Wise, all the evidence said no, but Andy had proven how fallible he was.

Wednesday, 21st September

42

The news crews weren't outside Kennington Police Station when Wise arrived the next morning — or rather their vans and cars were there, further along the road, all parked up, lights and engines off, but there was no sign of the reporters and their cameramen. Then he saw Hannah waiting outside the main entrance with a face like thunder, and he knew something bad was happening. She walked over as he parked his car, arms crossed against her chest.

'You won't believe what's happened, Guv,' she said as he got out the car.

'What now?' Wise asked, but he didn't really want to know. Not without a coffee first. Maybe two coffees.

'Our friend talked to Walling last night,' Hannah said. 'Him and his boyfriend. Told him all about their wonderful breakthrough, apparently.'

Wise felt sick. Of course they did. He closed his eyes for a moment, took a deep breath. 'Tell me he hasn't called a press conference.'

'Oh, he has.'

'When's it starting?'

'Fifteen minutes ago.'

'Shit. Is the boss with them?'

'No. She wasn't invited to the party, by the looks of things.'

Wise couldn't believe it. 'Walling is having a press conference without Roberts?'

'He's got Tweedledum and Tweedledee with him. He doesn't need anyone else.'

'Where is she?'

'In her office, waiting for you.'

'Great.' Wise marched into the station, dreading what Walling telling the press at that precise moment. He'd spent another sleepless night going over the case, checking his notes, looking at Riddleton and Cheil's hypothesis over and over again, trying to find the truth in what they were saying, but he couldn't. No matter how much he wanted to, he couldn't accept what they suggested was right.

Hannah followed as he took the stairs two at a time to the second floor. He stopped for a moment on the landing. 'I'll see you upstairs,' he told her. 'Thanks for the heads up.'

'Least I could do,' Hannah said before stomping up the stairs in her boots.

The sound of ringing telephones leaked out from the offices on either side of the corridor as Wise made his way to Roberts' office. Even so, he could hear the press conference broadcast from within Roberts' office as he knocked on the door.

'Yes.' If her voice sounded stern, Roberts' face was even grimmer when he entered.

'Boss,' Wise said.

'Shut the bloody door and come and watch these idiots,'

she said. She turned her laptop so he could see the live stream from the media suite on the ground floor.

Walling sat behind a large desk with Riddleton on one side and Cheil on the other. 'That bloody shrink has just told the world we're looking for an angry, left-handed, ex-soldier who was working as a motorbike messenger. Dear old Doug has asked the public to call with the names of anyone who fits that description. He gave this station's telephone number. They couldn't even wait for me to get a dedicated line set up and the personnel to service it.'

Her own phone rang. Roberts picked up the receiver and promptly dropped It back in its cradle.

'I'm sorry, boss. I specifically told Riddleton we needed to speak to you before we acted on any of his ... deductions,' Wise said.

'Well, he spoke to Walling first, who then spoke to me.'

'And?'

Roberts hit mute on the conference. 'Walling is taking personal charge of this case now, as he believes an arrest is imminent. My oversight is no longer required. And,' Roberts wagged a finger towards Wise, 'Doug is now the Senior Investigating Officer. You're out as well.'

'Out as in "not in charge" or out as "off the case completely?"' Wise sat down in one of the chairs in front of Roberts' desk even though she'd not said he could sit.

'Come on, Simon. You're not dumb,' Roberts said. 'I've been warning you that this was going to happen. They don't bring the likes of Riddleton in because they're happy with the way things are going or just for a "fresh pair of eyes." Especially now his golden boys have come in and cracked the case in one day.'

'They haven't cracked it,' Wise said, unable to keep the

bitterness out of his voice. 'They've just made some poorly judged guesses.'

'Like?'

'This killer isn't angry because he's lost his job. If anything, he's one of the coldest, calmest killers I've ever come across. He plans everything. He does only what's necessary. No more. No less. He's a professional.'

'I thought you said he wasn't a hitman?'

'He's not. What I mean is that the killer treats this like a job. He has an objective, works out how to make it happen and then does it. Those aren't the actions of a madman pissed off at losing his job. He's been leading us on a merry song and dance since day one.'

'Well, Riddleton and Cheil say otherwise and Walling trusts them.' Roberts' eyes flicked back to the screen, her lips curling in disgust. 'My opinion doesn't matter. Yours definitely doesn't.'

'But they're wrong.'

'Well, if they are, you can gloat afterwards. For now, we see how it plays out. In the meantime, I think you'd better take a couple of days off. Get some sleep,' Roberts said. 'You look like shit.'

Wise's temper growled from somewhere deep inside him, but he pushed it down as he stood. 'Ma'am.' He headed to the door.

'Simon.'

He turned, his hand already on the door handle.

'For what it's worth, I'm sorry,' Roberts said.

'So am I.' He left the office, the ringing telephones mocking him as he headed down the corridor, the cacophony cheering him on his way.

How had it ended up like this? From the moment Andy betrayed him, everything had just got worse and worse. Jean wasn't talking to him. He hadn't seen the kids. And now, Walling had taken his case, his job, away from him.

What was he going to do?

Just to make things perfect, the press conference ended as Wise reached the ground floor and reporters spilled out around him. Wise kept his head down, but they spotted him anyway.

'Inspector Wise! Why weren't you at the press conference?'

'Are you off the case, Inspector?'

'Why couldn't you solve the case, Inspector?'

Wise didn't look up to see who was calling out to him. Camera flashes popped around him. They shoved phones in his face, recording video. Bodies pressed against him as he headed for the door, not stopping despite the media's best efforts.

Their numbers seemed to double, then triple once he was outside, coming from everywhere, sensing blood, hoping to catch his fall from grace. Even getting in his car offered no respite as they swarmed around him, faces pressed against the windows, hands thumping on the bonnet.

'Inspector Wise! Talk to us! Inspector Wise!'

'Inspector!'

'Inspector!'

'How did you miss these vital clues?'

'Inspector? Did your mistakes allow the killer to claim so many victims?'

He started the engine, but it had no effect on the press. No one moved. No one cared. They were too busy trying to capture his failure, his breakdown. They banged on his car door, on the bonnet, on the roof. Each time, he could feel the cracks getting bigger and bigger inside him.

God, all he wanted to do was get away and he couldn't. Not without running the bastards over? That really would make a bad day worse. It would make good TV, though, and Wise wouldn't put it past some of them to hope that would happen.

He stared at them through the window, trying to hold his composure, trying to appear unfazed by the madness, by his failure, by his dismissal, but he could feel it all slipping. The cracks becoming fractures.

'Please let me out,' he whispered. 'Please.'

In the end, some uniforms came to his rescue and moved the reporters and cameramen to one side so he could drive out of the station. Not that he could make a quick escape, not in London traffic, but it was moving at least and the station disappeared from sight quick enough in the rear-view mirror.

Only then did he let his mask fall.

'Shit.' He slammed his hand against the wheel. 'Shit. Shit. Shit.' How could this have happened? What a mess. What a disaster. He could imagine it now, his entire team's time being wasted looking for messenger riders, the hours that would go into interviewing them and processing them, and, all the while, the clock was ticking.

It was day two after Richardson's murder. Tomorrow someone else would die. And he was off the case. Sent home in disgrace.

He smashed the steering wheel again. His anger rising. His fury boiling. He wanted to turn the car around and go back and smash the smug smile off Riddleton's face. Maybe visit Walling too. Leave him bleeding on the floor.

He wanted to go home and hide away. He wanted to throw his warrant card in the bin. Walk away from everyone and everything.

God, he even wanted to just go drive the car into the bloody Thames and put an end to it all.

He pulled the car over to the side of the road, ignoring the double yellow lines, ignoring the honks of the surrounding traffic, and screamed. He screamed with all the anger, frustration, humiliation and despair of the past few weeks.

Why hadn't he been the one who'd got his brains blown out on that rooftop? Better he was dead.

The body tumbles forward, red mist leading the way, brains and blood already splattered across the rooftop. He lands on the concrete with a wet thud and lies unmoving, his eyes open. But it's not Andy lying there. It's Wise with a hole in the side of his temple where the red dot had been. Wise dead on the rooftop.

He closed his eyes, trying to breathe, but there was no hope. He'd never felt so alone and lost. What the hell he was going to do?

43

Wise sat in Doctor Shaw's office, picking at the lip of the Starbucks cup in his hand. 'Thank you for finding the time to see me.'

Shaw gave him her best, kindly smile. 'You sounded like you needed a friendly ear.'

'Yeah. I did.' He barely remembered calling or the drive over to Shaw's office. It was as if he'd blinked and he'd gone from crying in the car to sitting in her office. Even now, he felt a ghost of the person he once was. Empty. He looked at the coffee in his hand. Even that had lost its appeal.

'What's upset you?' Her voice was almost hypnotic in its calmness.

'The case I was working on ... It's been challenging and I ... er ... they took me off it and told me to go home.'

'I saw the press conference earlier,' Shaw said. 'The Motorbike Killer — that's was your case, wasn't it?'

'Yeah,' Wise said. 'But I wasn't getting results, you see.'

'And how did that make you feel?'

Wise looked up, almost smiled at the question. Surely, the answer was obvious. 'Not good. That's why I'm here.'

'Angry? Sad? Happy?' Shaw paused for a heartbeat. 'Suicidal?'

'Certainly not happy.'

She nodded. 'So unhappy then. How unhappy?'

'I thought driving into the Thames was looking like a good idea.'

'I'm glad you called me instead,' Shaw said. 'Is it the first time you've had such thoughts?'

'No. But not seriously. Not like this.'

'Why did it seem such a good idea?' Once, Shaw's continual questioning annoyed the hell out of him but, as a detective, he appreciated how she got him to open up despite his misgivings. After all, he'd not exactly grown up in an environment where he sat around discussing his feelings with his dad and Tom. Then again, maybe if they had after his mum had died, things would've turned out differently.

'I'm just tired. Tired of all of it. Being haunted by Andy's death. Hiding from my family. Failing at work. I thought, maybe it'd be easier to just give up. For good.'

'Did you think it was fair for you to be taken off the case?'

'Nothing in life is fair,' Wise snapped.

Shaw raised an eyebrow. 'Okay. Do you think they were right to take you off the case?'

Wise glanced at the grey slate skies outside Shaw's window. Miserable weather for a miserable day. 'I don't know. I knew it was going to happen and yet I hoped it wouldn't. We were finally making progress on the case, but everything I'd put together was binned out for this new angle — which I don't agree with. No one trusts me after what happened with Andy, and I can't blame them for that because I don't trust myself, either. So maybe they're right and I'm wrong but, if that's the case, where does that leave me? The Job is all I have at the moment. If I can't do that ...'

'Why don't you trust yourself?'

'For the same reason the top brass don't — Andy.'

Shaw nodded. 'But Andy wasn't your fault. He did what he did by himself.'

'I should've spotted it before things ended up on that rooftop, though.' Before he ended up dead.

'Why's that? What makes you any different from the rest of your team? Or your senior officers? None of them realised what Andy was doing.'

'Because he was my friend. He was my partner.' Wise's voice was rising, the emotion threatening to get the better of him. He stopped, swallowed, took a breath. 'I spent nearly every minute of every working day with him. I thought I knew him.'

'Simon, accept that Andy fooled everyone — not just at work, but at home, too. His wife didn't know what he was doing. You didn't. Your colleagues didn't. And that's because he was an expert in hiding it from you all. He just showed you the side of him you knew. He wore a mask that stopped you from seeing the darkness in him.'

'Even so ...'

'How many people know what you're going through right now?' Shaw asked.

'I'm sorry?'

'How many people know you're struggling? That you don't sleep at night? That you're plagued by nightmares of Andy dying?'

Wise took a breath. 'No one — apart from you.'

'And I suspect even I don't know how much you're suffering.' She smiled as if to say that's all right. 'What about your team?'

'No. I don't think so, at least.'

'Because you hide what's inside so well. You put on your nice suits and go to work and pretend everything is good in your life,' Shaw said. 'And it's normal to do that. We all do it. No one ever shows all of who they are,' Shaw said. 'This Motorbike Killer isn't walking around with a gun in their hand ninety-nine percent of the time, are they?'

'It'd make my job easier if they were,' Wise said.

'Quite — but they're having dinner with their family, just like everyone else. The reason you're good at what you do is because you can see past the masks we all wear most of the time — but even you're not God. You don't get to be perfect. You're just human.'

'You make it sound so simple,' Wise said. He felt like laughing. He had a mountain on his back, crushing him, and Shaw made it sound like it was something he could just walk away from.

'Most things are — we just like to make them difficult for ourselves, often by holding ourselves to impossible standards and then berating ourselves when we can't reach those heights.'

'What should I do?' Wise asked.

'Apart from stop beating yourself up?'

Wise smiled. 'Yes, apart from that.'

'What do you want to do?'

'Be a good husband. A good father. A good copper.'

'What's stopping you?'

'Me,' Wise said with a sigh. 'What happened to Andy. The stuff that happened with Tom. All my fuck-ups.'

'Guilt from the past.'

'Yes.'

'Then the question really is this: are you going to let something you can't change destroy you or are you going to use it to learn from and become an even better version of who you are now? Are you going to drive into the Thames or are you going to be a good husband, a good father and a good copper?'

'Well, when you put it like that, it seems a simple choice,' Wise said.

'Most things are,' Shaw said.

'And yet it feels impossible.'

'I know you think it does right now, but let me ask you this: Did you think you were a good husband, a good father and a good copper before Andy died?'

'I think so.' Wise took a breath. 'No. I know I was.'

'Then be so again,' Shaw said. 'Don't give up what you're good at because of other people's mistakes. Don't let Andy's flaws ruin your life. You've got a wife and two kids who love you, who are probably waiting for the good husband and father that you are to come home to them. You've got a killer out there who needs the good copper that you are to stop them from killing again.'

'I'm off that case,' Wise said.

Shaw's eyebrow shot up. 'Are you?'

44

Hannah leaned back in her chair in MIR-One and just watched the surrounding chaos. Every phone was ringing non-stop all over the building. No one could action anything because they were all too busy answering the next call. And it wasn't as if the calls were coming up with anything productive. Hannah herself had people tell her that everyone, from a gym teacher in Camberwell with funny eyes to a shopkeeper in Edgeware with a shifty appearance, was the Motorbike Killer. That Walling, Riddleton and Chiel had specifically said they were looking for someone who was a motorbike messenger, unemployed, homeless, ex-military and six feet tall seemed to make no difference whatsoever.

The interview rooms downstairs were also fit to burst. They had sent teams out first thing to messenger companies across West London to bring anyone who was remotely a close match to the profile.

What was worse was that she'd gone from being in the heart of the investigation with Wise to just being a body answering telephones under Riddleton. Not that the man knew who she was. He'd not bothered speaking to any of the team one-on-one.

Maybe Wise was the lucky one being kicked off the case because what Hannah was witnessing was a shit show on an epic scale.

Ignoring the phone ringing on her desk, Hannah pulled out her mobile and dialled Wise.

'Hannah,' Wise said, sounding chirpy. 'What's going on?'

'Guv?' she said, turning her back on the main part of the room, even though no one was paying her a blind bit of notice. 'You okay?'

'Yeah, actually I am. Thanks for asking. What about where you are?'

'You really don't want to know,' she said, keeping her voice low. 'It's a madhouse here. That press conference has sent everyone crazy. The phones won't stop ringing. Tweedledum and Tweedledee have got us interviewing every messenger in London and all I can think is that someone's going to die tomorrow while we're on this stupid goose chase.'

'Well, I'm glad you called. I was about to ring you myself. Do you think you can slip away with no one knowing?'

Hannah laughed. 'I don't think they know I'm here, let alone notice if I disappear.'

'Do you know the Crooked Billet pub on Cosser Street?'

'No, but I know how to use Google Maps.'

'It's a five-minute walk from the station. Fancy meeting me there?'

'It'll be an absolute pleasure. When?'

'I'm there right now.'

'See you in five.'

Wise hung up, and Hannah put the phone back down on her desk. Well, that little chat had perked her up. What was Wise up to? Not that she cared. Anything had to be better than sitting in MIR-One playing answering machine.

She looked around. There was no sign of Riddleton or Chiel and everyone else was on a call, wrapped up in their own little worlds, so Hannah stood up, slipped her phone in her pocket and headed out to the stairs. Sarah passed her on her way up her way, but Hannah ignored her and trotted down as fast as she could without drawing anymore attention to herself.

She used the rear exit of the station so she could avoid the press and then, after a quick check of her phone, strode off to meet Wise.

She found the Crooked Billet pub easily enough and had to approve of his choice. It was a good, old-fashioned, neighbourhood boozer that hadn't been taken over by a chain and had its soul destroyed. It was quiet for a Wednesday lunchtime, just a few serious drinkers at the bar and a couple who were old enough to know better but couldn't stop sticking their tongues down each other's throats at one of the tables.

Wise had tucked himself away at a corner table, a glass of coke in front of him, still all suited up and looking immaculate. She slipped into the chair opposite him. 'Fancy meeting you here.'

'You were quick,' Wise said.

'I had nothing else on.'

'You want a drink?'

'I'm good for now.'

'Okay.' Wise smiled, a gleam in his eye. Whatever had happened between him leaving the station and meeting Hannah had done him the world of good. 'Let's pick your brain instead.'

'Go for it,' Hannah said, excited that Wise trusted her to help.

'Well, for a start, I've been thinking about how nothing in this case makes sense.'

'It doesn't.'

'I was talking to someone a little earlier, and she made this comment about how everyone hides who they really are and we only let other people see what we want them to see,' Wise said, 'and that got me thinking some more.'

Hannah leaned in. 'And?'

'Walling was right about one thing — we can't see the wood for the trees. We've got too much information and none of it's any good. It's as if the killer wants us running around in circles, looking for connections that don't exist and getting more and more confused with each new murder.'

'It's certainly chaos up there now.' Hannah said.

'I've been going over everything again,' Wise said. 'For a start, I don't believe this is the work of an ex-veteran, motorbike messenger who's pissed off at the wealthy. There's not enough rage in these attacks. They're too calm, too calculated. Too smart. There's no hate involved at all.'

'Yeah, you said that the other night.'

'And even if it was, how is the killer picking these victims? Of all the wealthy people in London, why these four in particular?'

'We don't know. There's no connection between them.'

'Exactly — they have nothing in common except their money and even that isn't consistent. Andronovitch and Hassleman were billionaires, but Clarke and Richardson, while very rich, weren't in their league. And Richardson was retired and not even in the public eye anymore.

'However, serial killers don't work like that. There's

always a pattern to how they pick their victims. They either know them personally — Shipman and his patients — or they hunt them in the same areas — red-light districts, for example, like the Yorkshire Ripper. Whatever it is, there's always a pattern. Always. But not here. In fact, these killings are too random — that's why I think they were chosen to be like that.'

'To confuse us,' Hannah said, smiling with excitement. 'To keep us chasing our tails.'

'Exactly. That's why I don't think we're dealing with a serial killer either.'

'Okay.' It was thrilling to see Wise like this. It was as if he were a completely different person. 'So where does that leave us?'

'Someone very clever carefully orchestrating everything to confuse us. Like a magician distracting you so you don't see what they're actually doing,' Wise said. He took a sip of his Coke. 'That's why I think there's only one victim that matters to our killer. The rest of the murders are just a distraction to stop us from working out who they are.'

'Bloody hell,' Hannah said. 'That's ... that's smart. Evil but smart.'

'Yeah, I know,' Wise said. 'But it's the only thing that makes sense to me.'

Hannah sat back, going over what Wise had said in her mind. She couldn't fault his logic. 'I think you're right.'

'Normally, if someone is murdered,' Wise said, 'we always look at family and friends first because nine times out of ten, the killer is someone they know. We started doing that with Hassleman, but the moment other bodies started cropping up, we stopped exploring that avenue because we were looking for a common link between the victims.'

'And we couldn't find it because it didn't exist,' Hannah said.

Wise nodded. 'Right. Now, when you consider the main motives for killing someone are money, power, sex and vengeance, it gets really interesting, because the question I keep asking is, who benefits from one of the victim's deaths?'

'Sheila Richardson gets her husband's money,' Hannah said, even though that wasn't the first name that sprung to her mind.

'But you saw her. She's devastated by his death and she already had his money, really. And I don't think she hired a hitman to kill her husband because he hogged the remote control.'

'David and Laura Smythe get everything from Harry Clarke — his company, his properties, his personal fortune, his house in Hans Place,' Hannah said.

'Bingo,' Wise said. 'Money and power. A lot of money and power.'

'But Laura has been in pieces since her father died. She wasn't faking that.'

Wise's smile grew wider. 'And she's not interested in the business, either. So really, it's just David who gets all the benefits.'

Now Hannah was smiling. 'I never liked him.'

'I know. Now, let's look at David Smythe. How tall would you say he was?'

'About your height but half your size.'

'Six foot, six one. And he's thin.'

'Just like our killer,' Hannah said, then bolted upright as another thought crossed her mind. 'He's left-handed too.'

'You sure?'

'Yeah. I watched him sign the paperwork identifying Clarke's body like he was a famous or something. I remember at the time thinking how pretentious it was. Definitely left-handed.'

'He's suddenly ticking a lot of boxes,' Wise said.

'But he was at home with his wife when Clarke was murdered. We woke him up.'

'Did we? His wife takes a sleeping pill every night at 9 o'clock. If she's out cold, then he could easily slip out, shoot his father-in-law and then get home before we turned up at his door. His wife wouldn't notice and she'd swear he was at home with her.'

'That's the same with Hassleman and Andronovitch — but he was in Birmingham the other night when Richardson was killed,' Hannah said. 'That puts him in the clear.'

'Does it?' Wise said. 'We don't know he went anywhere for sure.'

Hannah pulled out her notebook, started flicking through pages. 'We know he told his wife and Sabine that he was going to see his father and he was staying at ... The Dormitory Hotel.'

'No harm in giving the hotel a call, eh? See if he checked in?' Wise's eyes gleamed.

Hannah tapped away at her phone, googling the hotel's contact details, feeling the same rush Wise must be feeling, and made the call, desperately praying that the answer wouldn't kill this breakthrough.

'Dormitory Hotel, how may I help you?' a man answered with a thick Brummie accent.

'Hi, my name is Detective Sergeant Hannah Markham of the Metropolitan Police,' Hannah said. 'Who am I speaking to?'

'Er ... my name's Craig. I'm the day manager,' the man replied. 'I'm sorry. You said you were the police?'

'That's right. I just wanted to check if someone stayed with you this week. A David Smythe.'

'We don't normally give out that information.'

'We're investigating some very serious crimes,' Hannah said. 'This will help eliminate someone from our enquiries.'

'Right ... er. I suppose there's no harm in telling you ...' Hannah heard the man tapping away on a keyboard. 'David Smythe you say?'

'That's right.'

'Ah yes,' Craig said, sounding like he'd won the lottery. 'Mr Smythe checked in on Monday and left Tuesday.'

The news was a punch to the gut. Still, she wasn't ready to give in yet. 'Have you any way of checking if he stayed in his room or went out at all?'

'Well ... the door locks are all electronic so we know when the guest opens the room to go in, but I can't tell you if they went out at all because the key card's not needed for that.'

Hannah smiled. 'That information would be wonderful.'

Craig tapped away on his keyboard. 'It looks like Mr Smythe checked in at 3 p.m. and went into his room ten minutes later. The next time it's unlocked is at 7:30 a.m. The next morning.'

And, just like that, hope blossomed again. 'Thank you. I don't suppose you have any CCTV footage of the car park or elevators?'

'I'm sorry,' Craig replied. 'Someone vandalised the cameras. I remember because we had to get the repair company out and they cost a fortune. You'd think they were fixing a spaceship for the money they charge.'

'That must be very frustrating,' Hannah said. 'I'll let you get back to your day now, sir. Thank you for your help.' She ended the call.

'And?' Wise said.

Hannah told him the good news.

'So, at some point, he left the room, but we don't know when,' Wise said.

'And the hotel's CCTV went down while he was there.'

'What a coincidence,' Wise said. 'Birmingham's only an hour and a half, two-hour drive away. He could easily have checked in, then driven back down here, done the murder, and taken his time getting back.'

'He was up visiting his father, right? That's what he'll say. He left to go to the care home.'

'Check with the care home,' Wise said. 'If they have a record of him visiting on Monday night and then leaving, we know he doesn't go back to the hotel, so that makes it really doable to get back here and kill his father-in-law.'

'What about an ANPR check?' Hannah suggested. 'If Smythe drove up and down the M1 to Birmingham, they'd have pinged him multiple times.'

'I'll call Sarah,' Wise said. He picked up his phone while Hannah called Sabine Cricheaux.

'Allo?' Sabine said.

'Hi, Sabine,' Hannah said. 'This is DS Markham. We met the other day.'

'Ah, oui.'

'I was just wondering if you knew the name of the care home where David Smythe's father lives?'

'I think I have it somewhere. One minute.' There was silence on the phone. Hannah watched Wise as he spoke to Sarah, amazed at how the case was suddenly opening up. Maybe he should get kicked off cases more often if it did this to him. She could almost see his mind whirring away.

'Allo?' Sabine was back.

'Yes, I'm here. Any luck?'

'His father lives at the Clearacres Retirement Home in a place called Headley Heath,' Sabine said.

'Headley Heath,' Hannah confirmed.

'Oui. That's right.'

'Excellent. Thank you. You've been a massive help.'

'My pleasure.'

Hannah ended her call just as Wise finished talking to Sarah.

'She's on it,' Wise said.

'And I've got the name of the care home,' Hannah said.

'Make the call,' Wise said. 'Let's destroy David Smythe's alibi once and for all.'

45

I t took just under two hours to reach the care home where David Smythe's father lived in Headley Heath, a small village to the south of Birmingham. The journey had been necessary because, when Hannah had rung the home, the administrator had refused to give out any details over the phone.

'How do I know you are really the police?' a Miss Imra Sahin had said. Hannah had offered to do a video call to show their warrant cards, but Sahin was having none of that either. 'How would I know if they're fake?' she'd said.

It was a point neither Wise nor Hannah could really argue with, even though making the journey north had been the last thing Wise had wanted to do. So off they went in the Mondeo up the M1. They used the time to push and prod their theory about Smythe but, no matter which way they looked at it, everything suddenly made sense.

To kill four people to get away with killing one was devilishly clever. Too bloody clever. Maybe if Wise had been in a better head space when the killings had started, he might've spotted what Smythe was up to earlier, but he was on him now and there was no way the man was going to get away with it.

And to think only a few hours earlier, Wise was contemplating driving his car into the Thames. Thank God, he'd called Doctor Shaw instead.

When they pulled into the Clearacres Retirement Home, the place looked more like a village than any care home Wise had seen before. Once they'd been let in through the large cast iron gates, they drove up to a small square, surrounded by houses and apartments. Perfectly maintained trees and hedges gave the place a country air that matched the rolling hills on the other side of the perimeter walls. Wise noticed two nurses in blue uniforms entering one home as he slipped the Mondeo into a visitor parking spot.

'This is very fancy,' Hannah said.

'It certainly doesn't look a terrible place to end up,' Wise said as they got out of the car. His nose twitched as the scent of roast chicken wafted past from the main building.

'My Nan refused to go into a home. She said they were glorified prisons,' Hannah said. 'Stalag Seniors, I think she called it.'

'Maybe everyone here prefers it that way?' Wise noticed two security cameras watching over the car park.

'Or they're digging tunnels to escape.' They headed into the main building. Hannah pointed to a sign that said "art class – 3 p.m., Tuesday." 'That's where they're forging the passports.'

'Maybe Smythe's dad is in the cooler right now with his baseball glove,' Wise said.

'Wouldn't surprise me.'

The reception area certainly didn't look like the inside of a prison. In fact, it looked like something out of a boutique hotel rather than a hospital, with its oak desk and discreet computer monitor tugged away in one corner, and the Laura Ashley style sofas and armchairs scattered here and there, around tables with vases of flowers, that matched the walls covered in floral wallpaper. The weekly flower bill alone had to run into several hundred pounds a week.

A middle-aged woman, in a black skirt, white blouse and suit jacket, smiled as they approached. 'Welcome to Clearacres. How may I help you?'

They both held up their warrant cards. 'Miss Sahin is expecting us,' Wise said.

The woman acted as if she saw police badges every day and smiled again, her perfect white teeth positively gleaming. 'Just one moment.' She picked up the phone, press a button, waited a heartbeat and said, 'Imra, the police are here.'

The receptionist had barely put the phone back in its cradle when another woman appeared through a door off to the right with a waft of efficiency. She was a small lady, perhaps not even five feet in height, dressed in the same black suit and white blouse as the receptionist, but her smile was even broader, with a manager's air of superiority. 'Detective Inspector Wise?'

'Hello,' Wise said, holding out his hand. 'Miss Sahin?'

The woman shook it. 'Sorry to drag you all this way, but we have security protocols we have to follow. I'm sure you understand.' There was a hint of a Brum accent to her voice, but the edges had, no doubt, been polished away as Sahin's career had advanced.

'Of course,' Wise said. 'This is my colleague, Detective Sergeant Hannah Markham.'

'Pleased to meet you,' Hannah said.

Sahin smiled awkwardly. 'May I see your IDs, please?'

'Of course,' Wise said, and held out his warrant card. Hannah did the same.

Sahin took them and examined them carefully, even though Wise doubted she'd ever seen a real warrant card before. Satisfied, she returned them to Wise and Hannah. 'Would you like to chat here or somewhere more private?'

'Perhaps, somewhere more private,' Wise said, smiling despite himself.

'There's my office if you don't mind a mess ...' Sahin said.

'I'm sure it's fine,' Wise said, even though he wasn't so sure once she'd led them back the way she'd come. For starters, it made Wise's office back at Kennington feel positively spacious. There was a small desk with just enough room for a laptop, a lamp, and a precarious pile of paper with two chairs for visitors wedged tightly together in front of it. Sahin had to manoeuvre herself sideways to get to her own chair that was pressed against a radiator under the room's sole window that overlooked a delivery area.

'Please, sit down,' Sahin said, indicating the chairs opposite.

Wise let Hannah take the chair pressed against the wall, then perched himself on the outside edge of the other. Even then, it felt like they were sitting on top of each other, and the room grew even more claustrophobic. 'Hopefully, we won't take too much of your time,' Wise said, eager to be out of that room as quickly as he could.

'Normally, I'd not be able to speak to you with any detail because of patient confidentiality,' Sahin said. 'But I called David Smythe, and he's given me permission to answer any questions you may have about his father and his visits here.'

Wise sat forward, unable to believe what he'd just heard. 'You did what?'

'I rang David Smythe after you called and asked his

permission to speak to you,' said Sachin, sounding very pleased with herself.

Wise glanced at Hannah as he tried to contain his frustration, who shook her head at what Sahin had done. Smythe now knew they were checking up on him. Damn.

'Right. David Smythe,' Wise said. 'His father is a resident here.'

'That's right. Michael Smythe has been with us for about three years now,' Sahin replied.

'And does his son visit often?' Wise asked.

'David does, yes. He's very good like that, even though it must be very difficult for him.'

'Why's that? Because he has to travel up from London?' Hannah asked.

'Oh no,' Sahin said. 'I mean, that must be tiring but, really, I was referring to his father's condition. Michael has very advanced Alzheimer's. He's not really aware of anything anymore. It must be heart-breaking for David.'

'How bad is Michael's Alzheimer's then?' Wise asked.

'About as bad as it can get,' Sahin said. 'His brain has almost shut down completely. Soon, he'll forget how to swallow, then eventually how to breathe. Alzheimer's is a very cruel disease,' Sahin said. 'I don't think he be with us for more than another six months.'

'Would Michael know if his son came to see him or not?'

'Well, one hopes it makes a difference, but, in all probability, no. Not in the slightest. But still David keeps returning to see his father, once or twice every month. He'll even sleep over to look after his father personally while he's here. Their relationship is quite special. We have other residents that suffer from similar ailments and their children rarely visit and, even then, you can tell it's only out of guilt.'

'Was Michael Smythe ill before he moved here, or is his Alzheimer's a recent thing?' Hannah asked.

'Unfortunately, he was ill beforehand — but that's why he and his family chose Clearacres. We specialise in medical assistance for seniors who can no longer look after themselves,' replied Sahin, slowly gathering her composure again.

'Do you know if David Smythe visited his father on Monday?' Wise asked.

'Yes, he did. Absolutely. I spoke to him myself. He arrived shortly before dinner at 5:30. He stopped by the office to say hello to me before heading over to his father's house. David then helped feed his father and stayed overnight so he could read to Michael and keep him company until he had to leave the next morning.'

'He was here all night?' Wise could feel all his excitement of earlier turn bitter in his gut. No wonder Smythe was happy for Sahin to tell all. He would appear to have a perfect alibi for the last murder, after all.

'I wasn't on earlier that day but I spoke to Delores, who was on duty, and she said David spoke to her just before he left at 7 a.m.'

'What did he speak to her about?'

'He was just asking about the week's menu, whether we were taking his father out for some fresh air — that sort of thing.'

'Does David often check up on these things?'

'Sometimes, but the menu is the menu. I don't think we've changed it since Michael moved here. Wednesdays are always roast chicken and mashed potatoes, for example.'

'When David visits, does he park in the visitors' spots outside the front or can he park nearer to his father's residency?' Hannah asked.

'All visitors must park in the allocated bays,' Sahin said. 'We insist in case there's an emergency and we have to call an ambulance. If that happens, there's no time to track down the owner of someone who's parked inconsiderately.'

'I noticed you have security cameras overseeing the car park,' Wise said.

Sahin nodded. 'That's right. Most of the public areas have cameras and we have full-time security operators who monitor the feeds — just in case someone has a fall or something like that.'

'Could we see the footage from Monday night?' Wise asked, even though he didn't want to. Not if it confirmed Smythe was there all night and not in London killing Richardson.

'Normally, I'd say no...' Sahin said. 'We have to respect our residents' privacy ... but ... you've come all this way.' Sahin rose stiffly from her seat. Because of the size of her office, both Wise and Hannah had to leave the office before Sahin could even manoeuvre around her desk. She joined them in the reception area, then pointed to a set of double doors. 'It's this way.'

As Sahin led them down a corridor decked out in the same floral wallpaper as the reception area. The security office was three times the size of Sahin's, with two large computer monitors showing the feed from a dozen cameras. The operator jumped up from his chair as Sahin entered, then did a double take at the two officers behind her. 'Miss Sahin,' he said, somehow managing not to snap off a salute despite looking like he wanted to.

'Hello, Donald,' Sahin said, her air of superiority back again. 'Detective Inspector Wise and Detective Sergeant Markham would like to see some footage from Monday evening.'

Donald was in his late fifties, overweight, and had that worn out look that life so happily dished out, but he perked up at the mention of Wise and Hannah's ranks. 'Any specific area and time on Monday?'

'The visitors' car park,' Hannah said. 'At 5:30 p.m.'

Donald nodded. '1730 hours,' he said. 'Right. Give me a moment.' He tapped away at his keyboard. One monitor started playing a video clip in full-screen mode. Wise recognised the area where he'd parked earlier. The visitor spots were empty apart from the one where a Lexus was parked. Then Smythe's Porsche zipped into a spot beside it. A minute later, out popped Smythe with his wax jacket on and he jaunted up to the reception area. From the position of the camera, they had a perfect view of his face. It was definitely him.

'There you go,' Sahin said. 'Just as I said.'

They carried on watching as Smythe exited the main building a few minutes later and headed towards his father's residence, only to stop by his car, turn and look at the main building again, offering another perfect view of his face to the camera, before carrying on. He moved like a man who was very happy with life.

'He's not camera-shy,' Hannah muttered.

She wasn't wrong about that. The man looked like he was doing his best to be seen. It didn't seem right.

'Can you fast-forward to when the car leaves, Donald?' Wise asked, not ready to give up yet. His gut still told him he wasn't wrong about Smythe.

'No problem, sir.' The man clicked on the double arrow icon on the screen. The images sped up. A woman got into the Lexus, reversed backwards, and then sped off, leaving the Porsche alone. There were various other comings and goings, but the Porsche remained where it was. The sun rose

Tuesday morning at 6:55 a.m. and then there was Smythe again at 7:30.

'Go to normal speed,' Wise said, and the screen slipped back into real time. They watched Smythe approach, stop again by the car and look up at the camera yet again. He wasn't as spick and span as he'd been the night before and the spring had gone from his step. Was that because a car had hit him in London or he'd just slept badly? 'Is there a spare bed at his father's residence or does he have to sleep on the sofa?'

'Michael has one of our premier residences,' Sahin said proudly. 'It has a fully equipped guest suite for when David stays over.'

'Is he limping?' Hannah said, peering closer at the screen.

'I'm not sure,' Wise said. Maybe Smythe was. Maybe he and Hannah were seeing what they hoped to see, not what was really there.

On the screen, Smythe headed into the main building. Ten more minutes went by before he reappeared, got into his car, and drove off. It was exactly as Sahin had said. The car was there all night. Smythe had gone nowhere.

Shit.

'Michael doesn't have a car here, does he?' Wise asked, even though it felt like he was clutching at straws. Another car would still give Smythe the means to get to and from London, and his father wouldn't know he was gone.

Sahin laughed. 'We don't allow residents to have cars here, Inspector. It'd be too dangerous. Michael can't even eat by himself, let alone drive.'

So much for that theory. So much for that hope. Wise was just as bad as Riddleton, making desperate, wild guesses and passing it off as intuition. A fool. Wise wanted to be sick, the day's adrenaline bitter in his gut.

Again, he shared a glance at Hannah and saw her disappointment, too.

Wise shook his head. Shit. Shit. Shit.

'Is there anything else you would like to see?' asked Sahin.

'No, that's all,' Wise said. 'Thank you for your time.'

Sahin smiled. 'I'll show you out.'

'Thank you, Donald,' Wise said to the operator.

'An absolute pleasure, sir' said Malcom.

Once more, Wise and Hannah followed Sahin back down the corridor, through the double doors, and into the reception. She stopped by the main doors to the car park. 'I'm sorry for making you drive up here, but I hope the journey was worth it.'

'It certainly was,' Hannah said.

Sahin shook their hands. 'We could all do with a few more David Smythes in our lives.'

'Quite,' Wise said. 'Have a good evening.'

Wise and Hannah stepped outside into the cold, late afternoon air.

'What I don't understand, Guv,' Hannah said, 'is why did Smythe book a hotel room in town if he was planning on staying here? Seems a waste of money to me.'

'Yeah, it was.' Wise stared out over the car park and drive, running his gaze over the houses and apartments. Most had lights on as it was getting darker and he could see movement here and there behind the odd window.

Hannah walked to the car, but Wise didn't move. He couldn't shake the feeling that something wasn't right. Yet again, nothing made sense. Why book the hotel? Why ham it up in front of the cameras at every opportunity? Every opportunity Smythe had to be seen, he took. All irrefutable evidence proving he was innocent.

'Almost if he wanted a paper trail proving he was here, and plenty of witnesses to the fact,' Wise said, more to himself than to Hannah.

'Innocent people don't need that,' Hannah said, returning to his side.

'No, they don't,' Wise said and turned on his heels, heading back inside. This wasn't over yet. There was something Wise hadn't seen yet. Smythe's alibi was too perfect. Too deliberate.

Sahin was talking to the receptionist. She looked up as Wise entered the reception area. 'Inspector? Is something wrong?'

'No,' Wise said. 'I was just wondering why David and his father chose somewhere so far from London. As lovely as it is here, I'm sure there must be somewhere closer to his home that's easier to visit?'

Sahin laughed. 'You couldn't get anywhere closer to their home than here.'

'I don't understand,' Wise said.

'Come, I'll show you.' Sahin set off through the doors and out into the car park. Wise and Markham had no choice but to follow. She strode off towards a set of houses to the right of the main drive.

She stopped by a small house with its own little front garden set off to one side. There was no perimeter wall running behind it, only a row of trees and bushes separated Clearacres from what looked like farmland. 'This is David Smythe's house,' Sahin said proudly. 'And over there is the Smythe's family home.' She pointed to the farmland. It was hard to see in the encroaching darkness, but Wise could just make out a building in the distance.

'When you say the Smythe family home ...' Wise said.

'That's where Michael used to live before he came to stay with us. David grew up there as well, so it made sense to move his father here when he became unable to look after himself,' Sahin said. 'It kept any disruption to a minimum. Of course, when he was still mobile, Michael wandered off back to the old house a couple of times — but he was easy enough to find before he had an accident.'

Wise stared at the house in the distance. 'How far away is that?'

'Less than a mile as the crow flies,' Sahin said. 'But about ten minutes' drive by car. It's all windy roads around here.'

Wise looked around. 'No cameras here.'

'No, this is one of the more private areas and Michael has a nurse with him twenty-four hours a day,' Sahin said. 'Apart from when David visits.'

Suddenly, Wise could feel his mood lifting. Maybe Smythe's alibi wasn't so perfect. 'Who lives in Michael's old house now?'

'No one, as far as I know. The family still owns it, but I think they only use it if the whole family comes to visit Michael.'

Wise smiled. No cameras to record if Smythe sneaked away and a house less than a mile away where he could store who knows what? Like a car to drive to London? Suddenly, Smythe's perfect alibi wasn't as perfect as it was. Suddenly, the hunt was on again.

46

Wise told Sahin that he and Markham were going to drive back to London, thanking her yet again for all her help. 'You've really helped David,' he said, just in case she called Smythe with an update on their visit.

'He is such a lovely man,' Sahin replied.

Wise couldn't keep the smile off his face when they were out of sight of the care home. He turned to Hannah. 'How about that?'

'His alibi is bullshit for Tuesday night,' Hannah said. 'No wonder he was smiling at all the cameras and saying hello to everyone. It was all too bloody perfect.'

'I agree,' Wise said, his excitement back. 'He could've easily left his father after dinner, left Clearacres, driven back to London, killed Robinson and returned in plenty of time to wave to all the cameras again. After all, his father won't know if he was there for five minutes or five hours, let alone all night. We just need to know how he got back to London, because he certainly didn't use his Porsche.'

'What if Smythe's here?' Hannah said. 'We know he

checked out of the Dormitory on Tuesday but we don't know if he headed back to London right away.'

'Then we'll smile sweetly and just say we popped around to say hello,' Wise said. 'He knows we're in the neighbourhood.' But, by God, he damn well hoped the man wasn't at the family home.

Sahin had been right about the windy roads to the Smythe family home. The lane was barely big enough for one car to pass along it. God only knew what they were going to do if another car came from the opposite direction. Still, Wise had to fight to keep his speed down, before his eagerness to get to the house got them both killed.

He watched the sky too. They were running out of daylight and neither he nor Markham had any kit to do any real nosing around in the dark — not to mention they didn't have a search warrant for the premises. But, finally, it felt like luck was with them. They had a break, a crack to pry open. He wouldn't stop now.

Still, they found the house without getting killed. It was called Hurstwood according to a carved wooden sign, rubbed raw by the elements, that stood guard by an entrance that looked like a break in the hedge. Turning in, Wise followed an equally narrow and twisting driveway another half mile until they reached the main building, a black shadow against the darkening sky. It wasn't a mansion, but it seemed odd to call something that size a house. Smythe may have married into money, but he came from a good amount of it himself, whatever he thought of his roots.

As they drew closer, the car crunching on the gravel drive, details came out of the shadows; the thatched gable roof, the asymmetric Tudor beams set into white stucco, and the tall, narrow casement windows overlooking the drive with enough space for a dozen cars to park comfortably and not get in each other's way.

'Doesn't look like anyone's home,' Hannah said as Wise parked by the front door. 'Not for a long time.'

'We'll knock anyway,' Wise said, and they both got out of the car. 'Just to be safe.'

It was quiet in the driveway, the leaves barely rustling in the wind as if they were too scared to break the silence. The September chill added to the sense of unease. Perhaps, with lights on and a fire burning in the hearth, it might be more welcoming, but now, it felt like a ghost lingering in a world where it no longer belonged.

Hannah used the brass knocker in the centre of the door to hammer away three times, then stepped back, waiting. They both watched the windows for any sign of life, but no light came on, no footsteps sounded. There was just the wind pinching at their skin and darkness staring back at them from the house. 'He's not in.'

'Try again,' Wise said.

Hannah knocked even louder, enough to wake the dead, but even then no one stirred. Wise scanned the windows for movement. It didn't mean Smythe wasn't there, because no one answered the door.

Hannah tried the door handle. 'Locked.'

Wise stepped into the flower bed so he could get a closer look through the window. Cupping his hand against the cold glass, he peered inside, but it was impossible to make out anything other than the most basic shapes. He moved along to the next window and the next, but still saw no sign of life. Satisfied, Wise stepped back onto the driveway, the crunch of the gravel loud under foot.

'Might as well have a look around while we're here,' Wise said.

'It's all very grim,' Hannah said. 'Can't imagine it was too much fun growing up here.'

'I've seen worse places,' Wise said. How many times had he found kids with junkie parents, left to fend for themselves in crack dens or squats? 'Maybe it was well-loved when old man Smythe lived here. Maybe this was where the country set came for their swingers' parties and their barbecues.' He ran his finger over a dirty windowpane, leaving a streak of almost clean glass behind. They followed the driveway as it curved around the side of the house and saw a free-standing garage tucked away out of sight from the front of the house. 'And what do we have here?'

It was big enough to house at least two cars, if not more. Hannah tried to lift the main door. It rattled, but that was all. 'Maybe it's electric and needs a clicker.'

They moved around the side where Wise tried to peer through small windows set at head height along the garage's wall. They were as filthy as the rest of the house, though, and he couldn't see anything.

Hannah reached the back of the garage before Wise. 'There's a door here,' she called out. 'But it's padlocked.'

Wise joined her. The padlock was small, cheap and rusted — except around the keyhole. That looked well-used.

He sighed.

Wise knew he should call this in. He should apply for a search warrant, do things by the book, but getting one could take weeks. After all the cutbacks, nothing happened as fast as the police needed it to these days — even if his trip up north was sanctioned. But, as he was on an unofficial fishing trip, he'd have no hope of fast-tracking anything. Plus, there was the matter of the new codes introduced back in 2015, that said notice had to given to the homeowner of the intention to search their property with forty-eight hours before the time of entry. It was a nightmare ruling that took all the advantage out of police hands. There were ways around it, of course. If that notice could hinder the reasons for the search, for example, but reasons for circumventing advance warning had to be given in writing and justified in triplicate before a judge would sign the warrant off. In this case, Wise wasn't even sure he had enough evidence to justify the search in the first place. Just because Smythe had lied about his whereabouts wasn't enough.

There was only one other way to see what was inside, and that was to break the lock and go in without permission. Wise didn't want to do that though. He believed in following the rules, no matter how dumb they seemed. Following the rules stopped mistakes from happening.

A memory of a fight in a stairwell flashed through his mind. If he'd followed the rules then, that wouldn't have happened. It shouldn't have happened. If Andy had followed the rules, he wouldn't be dead. He'd be next to Wise instead of Hannah.

Andy wipes his free hand across his face, rubbing the snot from his nose, blinking tears of his own away. 'I have to do this.'

What choices caused Andy to be on that roof? Did he cross the line bit by bit until he was so far gone he couldn't be saved?

'What do you want to do, Guv?' Hannah asked.

Shit. He needed to know what was in that garage. Somehow, he sensed it could make or break his case. Damn it.

He didn't want to break the law but ...

'I have to do this.'

Wise closed his eyes and took a breath. This would not be the start of a road to ruin. He'd just crawled out of one abyss. He wouldn't dive into another. This was a one-time thing. A necessity for now. 'I hear the local kids around here are always getting into trouble.'

Hannah raised an eyebrow. 'I imagine they're real troublemakers. Must be bored with nothing to do ...'

Wise picked up a good-sized rock from the flowerbed. 'An old lock like this must've been tempting.'

Hannah smiled. 'I imagine it was. I wonder if they stole anything when they smashed it.'

'Best we check,' Wise said.

'Yeah, we should,' Hannah said, giving her blessing.

The lock gave way on the third strike. Wise put on a pair of disposal gloves before removing the remains of the padlock from the latch. The door creaked as he pulled it open.

Inside, Wise found a light switch just to the left of the door and flicked it on. A strip light spluttered to life and Wise smiled. 'Jackpot.'

There was a black Volvo estate in the centre of the garage while a tarpaulin covered lumps and bumps of something off to the right that looked distinctly motorbike shaped.

He walked over to the Volvo, then reached inside his jacket pocket for his phone and dialled Sarah.

'Guv, I was just about to call you,' she said on answering. 'ANPR finally got back to me. It's not good news, I'm afraid.'

'It's all right,' Wise said. 'I know Smythe drove up to Birmingham on the Monday and came back the next day — but I need you to check another vehicle for me. It's a black Volvo. It's probably registered to a Michael Smythe, judging by the age of it.' He read the car's number plate to Sarah, then walked around the car. As opposed to everything else at Hurstwood, the car was in perfect nick, despite its age. He peered through the windows, but there were no guns left lying around on the back seat or a schedule with all the murders on it stuck to the steering wheel, unfortunately. 'Tell them to get back to you as quickly as possible.'

'Will do, Guv. By the way, Riddleton's been asking where Hannah is,' Sarah said.

'Tell them she's chasing a lead.'

'She with you?'

'She's chasing a lead.'

'You two on to something?'

'I think so.'

'Thank God for that,' Sarah said. 'We've got sweet FA here.'

'Listen, if the car was in London on Monday, try to find out where it went. The cameras would've pinged it somewhere.'

'I'll find it. Good luck,' Sarah said.

'Cheers.' Wise hung up.

'Look at this,' Hannah said, pulling back the tarpaulin. There was a motorbike underneath. 'It's a Kawasaki dirt bike. A good one. Someone's a rider. You don't get this sort of bike if you don't know what you're doing.'

Wise bent down to examine it. 'It looks almost new. Registration's from last year.'

'It's definitely not his father's,' Hannah said. 'That's good to know.'

'I wouldn't have thought Smythe was into dirt biking by looking at him.'

'He probably grew up riding a bike over the farmland and woods behind the house,' Hannah said. 'Navigating the streets of London would be a piece of cake compared to that.'

Wise stood up, feeling happy at long last, the mountain lifted from his shoulders. 'He's our man. I know it.'

'We've got nothing to link him though that will hold up in court,' Hannah said. 'We don't even know if this car has left this garage in years. Knowing our luck, he just comes over to give it a polish.'

'I know it's him,' Wise said. 'Tomorrow's day three and we will not let him out of our sight. We'll get him.'

'What if he's killed enough? What if Sahin's phone call spooked him and he stays home, playing the innocent?'

'We'll still nick him. Look, I know he's a smart bastard, and he won't take any unnecessary risks but, at some point, he'll slip up. He must have somewhere else we don't know about yet. Somewhere he was storing the Honda and whatever he was using to move it to the various car parks. Somewhere he's keeping the gun too and his motorbike gear. We find that and we'll have all the proof we need to put him away for a long time,' Wise said.

'I bloody well hope so,' Hannah said.

His phone rang. It was Sarah.

'That was quick,' he said, answering.

'Sometimes the ANPR gods favour you,' Sarah said.

'Tell me.' Wise had to resist crossing his fingers.

'We have the Volvo on the M1, heading south. The cameras picked it up three times — at 7:15 p.m., 8:05 p.m. and 8:45 p.m.,' Sarah said. 'We also have it returning the following morning with the first ping at 2 a.m. and the last at 3:15 a.m.'

'Yes,' Wise said, clenching his fist. 'We've bloody got him. Well done.'

'I have got no results yet of where he went to in town yet, Guv,' Sarah said, 'but the tech boys have promised to get me that for first thing in the morning.'

'You star. You absolute star,' Wise said. 'I owe you a bottle of something. I'll see you tomorrow.'

After he'd hung up, Wise told Hannah the good news. 'We better head back to London and call the boss on the way. We're going to need more than the two of us working on this if we're going to catch Smythe.'

'What about Smythe himself?' Hannah said as they left the garage. 'He knows we were up here, checking out his alibi. What if we've spooked him and he does a runner?'

'Call him too. See where he is right now and tell him we'd like to update both him and his wife on the investigation tomorrow morning if we can.'

'What if he asks about our visit up here?'

'Tell him it was a box ticking exercise. Then we'll get some people staked out in front of his house if we can. If not, then you and me might have to do an all-nighter — if you're up for it.'

'Of course. If we can catch this bastard, it'll be worth it.'

Wise and Hannah climbed into the Mondeo. The dashboard clock said 6:30 p.m. Not the best time to hit the M1. They'd be lucky to reach London by 9. Still, Wise didn't care. It'd been worth it. If Sahin hadn't insisted on a personal visit, they'd never have found out about the father's car. That jobsworth had cracked their case for them.

Now they just had to get enough evidence to arrest David Smythe.

47

Wise hammered the Mondeo down the M6, eager to get back to London, eager to get Smythe behind bars.

'Call Sarah and put it on speaker,' he asked Hannah. She got her phone out and dialled. The chirp of the ring tone was loud in the car.

'Hannah! Where the fuck are you?' Sarah said on answering. 'Riddleton is pissed that you didn't turn up for his evening debrief.'

'Sarah,' Wise said. 'It's me. You still in the nick?'

'Yeah, Guv.'

'Jono and Hicksy around too?'

'Yeah — and everyone else. We're drowning in suspects and making no progress fast, so you can imagine the mood.'

Wise smiled despite himself. 'Can you get the pair of them and then call me back from somewhere private? Got a bit of a favour to ask of you all.'

'I take it you want me to be sneaky with it?'

'Too bloody right I do.'

'Give me five,' Sarah said and hung up.

True to her word, Hannah's phone rang just as Wise switched from the M6 to the M40. She answered, putting it on speaker once again.

'Hi, Guv,' said Sarah, 'I've got Jono and Hicksy with me in one of the interview rooms. You're safe to talk.'

'You been up to no good. Guv?' Hicksy asked. 'This is all a bit clandestine.'

'Oh, we've been up to all sorts,' Wise said, 'and I need your help if you're up to it.'

'What do you want us to do?' Sarah asked.

'Let me tell you what me and Hannah have found out first.' Wise updated them on what they'd discovered in Birmingham.

'And you think this David Smythe bloke whacked three others as camouflage?' Hicksy asked. 'That's fucking cold.'

'His late father-in-law was worth four hundred and fifty-five million pounds,' Wise said. 'That works out about a hundred and ten per head. He probably reckons that's good business.'

Someone whistled. 'Seems like a good deal if you put it like that,' Jono said. 'What do you want us to do?'

'I need bodies to help me keep eyes on Smythe — especially tonight. The manager of the care home told Smythe we were on our way up to see her, so he knows we're nosing around in Birmingham. We've just spoken to him and said it was a box ticking exercise. He seemed to buy it and we've made an appointment to update him on the case tomorrow,' Wise said. 'But this guy is smart. We don't want him doing a runner tonight or sneaking off to destroy evidence.'

'And you want us to keep an eye on him tonight?' Hicksy said.

'Bingo — and for bonus points, it'd be great if we can track his phone as well,' Wise said.

'Do we know where he is now?' Sarah asked.

'He said he was at home when Hannah called him ten minutes ago but we can't trust a word this man says,' Wise said, 'so let's make sure he's at home, without giving the game away, before we spend all night sitting outside.'

'I'll get his phone's location,' Jono said, 'then I'll call and ask to speak to some random name. If he's at home and he answers, he'll think it's a wrong number and we're good to go.'

'What if the phone's at his house, but he doesn't answer?' Hannah said. 'He could've left it at home and gone out.'

'If he doesn't answer, knock on his door with some excuse and check that way,' Wise said. 'If he's not home, we might have to get more official in tracking him down.'

'Why don't we go to the boss and Walling now?' Jono asked. 'Go all out now?'

'The evidence we have at the moment is good, but it's still only circumstantial,' Wise said. 'I want something more concrete before going to the pair of them, especially Walling. He'll go apeshit after his song and dance of a press conference this morning.'

Hicksy chuckled. 'I can't wait to see his face if we crack this.'

'All right, we're all on the same team, remember?' Wise said with more than a hint of sarcasm.

'If you say so, Guv,' Jono said.

'Right. We're still about two hours from town,' Wise said. 'Keep me updated on your progress and we'll see you when we get there. We can take it in shifts keeping watch tonight because tomorrow's going to be a busy day, no matter what. It's day three, so there's a good chance he might kill again.'

'Bloody hell, Guv,' Sarah said. 'You don't think four murders are enough for him?'

'I hope so,' Wise said. 'But we've got to be ready for the worst. Who knows? Maybe he's got a taste for it now.'

'Fuuuuuuuuuccccckkkk,' Hicksy said.

'Listen, we know who he is now,' Wise said. 'Let's get busy and make sure no one else dies.'

'You can count on us,' Sarah said and, for the first time since Andy died, Wise really believed he could.

Enough people had died. Now it was time to put a stop to it all.

Thursday, 22nd September

48

Wise stared at himself in the mirror. He was in a hotel's toilets around the corner from the Smythe's house in Cadogan Gardens, where he'd shaved and replaced his old shirt with a fresh one that he kept in the boot of his car. There was no escaping the fact he looked tired — no amount of cold water was going to hide the black rings under his eyes — but, at least, he didn't look like he'd spent the entire night camped out in his car. In fact, he almost looked his old self.

Knotting his tie, he nodded to his reflection. It felt good not to feel haunted.

Now it was time to get Smythe.

He walked briskly back to the car, where Hannah watched the house, at one end of Cadogan Gardens, tucked away just around the corner from Smythe's house but with a good enough view of the front door. Jono and Hicksy had set themselves up at the other end. Sarah was back at Kennington, monitoring Smythe's phone, just in case he gave his observers the slip somehow.

Thankfully, though, Smythe was at home, waiting for Wise and Hannah to pop round.

When he reached the Mondeo, he tapped on the passenger side window, startling Hannah. 'Bloody hell, Guv. You gave me a fright,' she said, getting out of the car.

'Sorry,' Wise said, smiling.

She looked him up and down as she pulled on her motorbike jacket. 'How come you always look so smart and I must look like something the cat dragged in?'

'It's all smoke and mirrors,' Wise said. 'And a clean shirt. You ready?'

She nodded. 'How do you want to play this?'

'Like I'm an incompetent idiot who's been taken off the case?'

'Sounds good to me.'

They walked around the corner and headed up the street towards Smythe's house. Wise had his shoulders slumped, all but dragging his feet. The door opened when they were still a few yards away, and Smythe beamed at them from the doorway. 'Good morning, detectives.'

'Good morning, sir,' Wise said, keeping his face impassive as his mind raced. Smythe had obviously been keeping an eye out for them, but why open the door early? Was it to let them know he was aware of what was going on in the street, or was he just eager to get the meeting over with? Was he suspicious of why they were there? 'Thank you for seeing us.'

'No problem,' Smythe said with complete friendliness. He looked like he was welcoming family friends around for a chat, not a pair of detectives in a murder enquiry. 'My wife is waiting for you in the office.' He led them through to the small room where Wise and Hannah had last spoken to Smythe-Clarke. Wise watched Smythe walk, trying to spot if

there was a limp from the motorbike accident on Monday
night. The man certainly moved awkwardly, but was it from
an injury? Whatever it was, it wasn't pronounced enough for
him to ask, and Wise didn't want to mention anything that
might arouse the man's suspicion, because he certainly
didn't appear concerned or nervous right then.

Smythe-Clarke was once more on the sofa, still stony-
faced. She didn't welcome them, barely lifting her head to
acknowledge their entrance.

'It's good to see you, Mrs Smythe-Clarke,' Wise said.

'Is it?' she replied.

Smythe, hovering near her shoulder, smiled awkwardly.
'Please, sit down. Can I get you a cup of tea or coffee?'

'We're fine, thank you, sir,' Wise said. 'We just wanted to
let you know that a Detective Chief Inspector Riddleton has
taken over the enquiry. I'm not sure if you saw the press
conference yesterday?'

'We did,' Smyth-Clarke said. 'Have you arrested anyone
yet?'

'Not yet,' Wise said, 'but the team is confident that we're
very close to finding the person responsible.' He glanced
over at Smythe. Seeing him once more in the flesh, it was
hard to imagine the man as a cold-hearted killer, standing
so meekly next to his wife. But it was all a mask. The man
was cunning. Wise had to give him that.

'Why did it take so long for you to discover the killer's
profile?' Smythe-Clarke asked. 'Surely, you've known since
the first murder that you were looking for a motorbike
messenger?'

'I'm afraid that it didn't appear as straight-forward as
that,' Wise said. 'However—'

'Why wasn't it straight-forward?' Smythe-Clarke
interrupted. 'I've seen the videos, the pictures. It couldn't be

any more straight-forward. Who did you think did it? Father Christmas?'

'Mrs Smythe-Clarke, I—'

'Or did you not see it?' Smythe-Clarke said. 'Is that why they have taken you off the case? Because you've screwed up everything?'

'Laura, you can't say that,' Smythe said.

'Of course I bloody can,' she snapped back. 'Perhaps Daddy wouldn't be dead if this lot had been better at their jobs.'

'I'm sorry,' Smythe said. 'My wife's—'

'Stop bloody apologising!' his wife shouted, tears forming in the corner of her eyes.

'We didn't mean to upset you,' Wise said.

'Just go and don't come back until you have some actual news,' Smythe-Clarke said.

Wise stood, holding his hands up. 'Okay. We'll leave you now.'

'I'll show you out,' Smythe said. Wise and Hannah followed him back to the front door as his wife struggled to keep her sobs to herself. 'I'm sorry about Laura. She's not really taken any of this well.'

'And how are you holding up, sir?' Hannah asked.

'It's been tough. I must admit. It reminds you of how fragile life is,' Smythe said. 'As you know, it made me rush up and see my father. I had to tell him I loved him, even though he wasn't aware of anything. It made me feel better, though.'

'Thank you for giving Ms Sahin permission to tell us about your father,' Wise said.

'It surprised me you were interested in my trip to Birmingham,' Smythe said. 'I couldn't understand what it had to do with the investigation.'

'Just box ticking,' Wise said. 'So much of what we do is eliminating the obvious from our enquiries — and, I must admit, I think the higher ups just wanted me out of the way while the new team took over the investigation so sending me to Birmingham was a perfect opportunity for them.'

'In my day, you were "sent to Coventry,"' Smythe chuckled. 'Anyway, I'm sorry they have taken you off the case.'

'It is what it is,' Wise said. 'It happens all the time. With the sensitivities of this case, it's not surprising they'd want a more senior officer on board.'

'Well, thank you for everything you've done,' Smythe said, opening the front door.

'Good day, sir,' Wise said. He and Markham set off back to the Mondeo. Wise again, walking like a man about to lose his job.

Hannah glanced back over her shoulder. 'He's still watching us from the door.'

'It's okay,' Wise said. 'I don't think he suspects anything. He's just being cautious.'

Hannah's phone rang just as they got to the car. 'Sarah, what's up?'

Wise walked around to the driver's side and unlocked the car. Smythe was no longer watching them from the doorstep, but that didn't mean he wasn't watching from a window in the house somewhere. Wise climbed into the car and started the engine.

Hannah finished her call and joined him inside. 'We going somewhere?'

'Yeah,' Wise said. 'I think we should move in case he's watching us still. We could give the game away if we just sit here. What did Sarah want?'

'She just wanted to pass on the good news.'

'Good news?'

'Yeah.' Hannah grinned like she'd just won the lottery. 'We've got lucky on the ANPR check on the Volvo. It entered the Ultra Low Emission Zone at just before 9 on Monday night. Straight off the M1 via Cricklewood. He drove straight down the A41 towards here. The last ping we've got was around 9.30, halfway between Smythe's place and Sir Harry's house. The next hit is in the early hours when he's heading back up north.'

Wise drove out of their parking spot and headed along Draycott Place, looking for another spot to stick the car, but, at that time of morning, every space was taken. 'So he parked up somewhere, swapped the Volvo for whatever he's driving the scooter around in, goes to a car park, gets the bike out, and then heads to Cottesmore Gardens to kill Richardson by 10:10 p.m.'

'That's a forty-minute window, Guv.'

'Considering how organised he is, that's plenty of time.'

'Sarah's checking the street CCTV around where the car was last pinged to see if she can eyeball the car.'

'If we can find his little hideaway, maybe we won't have to wait until he tries killing anyone.' Wise turned left into Blacklands Terrace, then left again into Culford Gardens.

'But where could he be hiding vans and bikes and God knows what else? Everything around here costs millions. Even a garden shed would cost a fortune.'

'Sir Harry was a property developer, wasn't he?' He turned left again into the lower end of Cadogan Gardens. An Amazon delivery truck pulled out of a space on the left and Wise nabbed it for himself.

'Yeah. Big time.'

'Call your friend, the PA, Sabine whatever-her-name-is,

and find out if the company owns any property around here. Maybe that's how he's managed it.'

As Markham started scrolling through her contacts, Wise's phone rang. It was Jono.

'Guv, where are you?'

'We had to move the car,' Wise said. 'We're further down from where we were. What's up?'

'Our man's left the house. He's heading up towards us on foot,' Jono said.

Wise felt a rush of panic. 'He's not seen you, has he?' He could just imagine Smythe storming down to confront them or rushing off to escape.

'Nah, he's got a flat cap on. Looks like he's out for a stroll. We're going to follow on foot once he goes past.'

'Just don't let him see you,' Wise said.

'Don't worry, Guv. We'll be fucking ninjas.'

Wise tuned to Hannah, who was on the phone to the PA. This time, it was his time to grin. 'He's on the move.'

49

W ise listened to the silence on the phone, waiting for Jono to speak again. Seconds passed as a million fears played through his mind. Was Smythe aware of what they were doing and playing a game with them? What if he gave them all the slip? Or was he really just out for a walk?

'Right,' Jono said at long last. 'He's just gone past us. We're going to follow on foot. Hold on.' Wise heard the car doors open. Jono huffed as he got out of the car and then slammed the door shut. Wise heard a beep as the locks were engaged. 'You still there, Guv? I've got my AirPods in.'

'Loud and clear,' Wise said.

'All right. He's crossing over, heading to the roundabout.'

Wise glanced over at Hannah, saw she'd finished her call, so he put his own phone on speaker and then started the car. 'We're following.'

'He's turned up Cadogan Square,' Jono said.

Wise pulled out of his parking spot and followed Smythe's route. 1 p.m. on a Thursday and the traffic was slow going but, at least, it was moving.

'Sabine's going to call me back,' Hannah said. 'Most of the properties they own are commercial buildings, but there were a few residential ones, too. Apparently Smythe was telling everyone that office buildings were all going to become obsolete after everyone started working from home during lockdown. The old man didn't agree, but he let Smythe pick a few places up.'

Wise nodded as he tried to spot Smythe walking. 'Let's hope one's around here.'

'He's still on Cadogan Square,' Jono said over the speakerphone. He already sounded out of breath. 'I'm about twenty yards behind him. Hicksy's cut down Clabon Mews to try to get ahead of him.'

'Good job,' Wise said. 'Is he limping?'

There was a pause. 'I'm not sure, but if he is, it's not much of one.'

'Where's he bloody going?' Hannah muttered.

Wise turned onto Cadogan Square but took his time following. Even if Smythe wasn't aware of his car, his beaten up Mondeo stuck out like a sore thumb among all the Range Rovers and BMWs.

Jono's voice cut in again. 'He's crossed over the road and walking alongside the gardens. I'm going to stay on this side of the road.'

'Be careful,' Wise said.

'Should've come dressed as a nanny with a pram.'

'That I'd like to see.' Wise could see the gardens up ahead on the right, but there was no sign of Jono or Smythe.

Markham's phone rang. 'Hicksy,' she said, answering it. She listened to what he had to say. 'Don't kill yourself, all right?' She disconnected the call. 'Hicksy's about to have a heart attack, by the sounds of it.'

'Where is he?' Wise asked.

'He's run up the road parallel to us,' Hannah said. 'It turns back to Cadogan Square up ahead. He's going to take over from Jono from there.'

'You hear that, Jono?' Wise said.

'Yeah, I can see him. Smythe's heading towards him on the opposite side of the street. He's fifteen yards away ... ten ... seven ... wait ... fuck. Now, he's stopped dead opposite Hicksy. He's looking around.'

'Has he spotted you?' Wise asked. He stopped the car as he listened to silence over his phone. Dear God, don't let them have screwed it up already. Wise could feel the panic stirring in his gut. 'Jono, talk to me.'

'He's not seen us. He's turned right into Shafto Mews, but we can't follow him in there. There's about ten or twelve houses there — max — and a dead end,' Jono said. 'I'm going to walk past, but Hicksy's got eyes on him, I think.'

'All right,' Wise said. 'We're nearly there.' He spotted Hicksy standing by some black railings on the corner of Clabon Mews and Cadogan Square, smoking a cigarette and pretending to look at his phone. Opposite him was a red brick archway leading through to a cobbled street. As Wise drove past, he peered into the mews and saw white brick houses with black doors and garages, but there was no sign of Smythe.

A Mini pulled out of a parking spot up ahead, so Wise manoeuvred the Mondeo into the space. Jono jogged over, opened the rear door, and climbed in. Sweat peppered his brow. 'Alright, Guv.'

'You did well,' Wise said. 'How did he appear as you followed him? Do you think he's suspicious?'

'He seemed as calm as you like,' Jono said. 'He certainly didn't look like he was up to no good.'

'And he definitely didn't spot you?'

'Didn't even so much as look in my direction. I told you — I'm a ninja.'

'The big question is, what's he doing here?' Wise said.

Hannah had Google Maps open on her phone. 'Er ... I hate to say this, but that mews might not be such a dead end.'

That got Wise's attention. 'What?'

'There's a gate at the end, connects to the other side of Cadogan Square,' Hannah said, showing him the map. 'What if he's using the mews to flush and dump any tail and he hops out the back way?'

Jono puffed out his cheeks. 'Right. I'll go check.'

'Cheers, Jono,' Wise said, reaching for his phone. He dialled Hicksy as Jono climbed out of the car. 'Did you see where Smythe went?' he asked when the other detective answered the phone.

'He disappeared into a house on the left, but I couldn't tell you which one,' Hicksy said.

'Are you alright where you are to keep watching?'

'Not where I am, but there's a doorway with some fancy trees outside it further back along the road. I should be okay there.'

'Okay, well done. We're parked a few yards up from you. Stay in touch.' Wise ended the call and turned to stare at the mews. What the hell was Smythe doing in there? Visiting a friend? A lover? Or was that his home away from home, where he planned his murders? Where he stored his vehicles? Was he destroying evidence in there?

If only they had a bit more concrete to go on, they could drag him down to the station. They were close but not close enough, damn it. He turned to Hannah. 'What do you think?'

'I don't think we've spooked him,' Hannah said. 'But he's

a bloody good actor. You saw him back at his house, all meek and mild, wouldn't say boo to his wife.'

'I agree.' Wise rubbed his face. 'So, let's find out about where he is exactly. Call Sabine back and give her the address. It might help her search.'

'On it.'

Wise's phone rang. It was Jono. 'Talk to me.'

'Hannah was right,' Jono said. 'There's a green gate connecting this road to the mews, but it's locked. Residents might have a key, but the door's pretty grungy. I don't think anyone has opened it in a long time.'

'Keep an eye on it,' Wise said. 'I don't want Smythe getting away because we assumed anything. We've got the front covered.'

'I'll call if anything happens,' Jono said.

Hannah dialled Sabine and put it on speaker.

'Allo,' the PA said.

'Hi Sabine, it's me again,' Hannah said. 'We were wondering if the company owned any properties in Shafto Mews in SW1.'

Wise kept his eyes on the entrance to the mews as he listened.

'Hold on, let me check,' Sabine said. 'Shafto mews?'

'That's right.'

Wise felt his pulse quicken. They were so close.

'Oui. I've found it. Shafto Mews. David bought it for the company six months ago. Two bedrooms, a double garage. It is a nice place.'

'Excellent,' Hannah said. 'How much did the company pay for that?'

'Five million pounds,' Sabine said.

Wise's eyes nearly bulged at that.

'Is it rented out to anyone at the moment?' Hannah asked.

'No. Not yet. David said it needed some work doing on it, but there were other properties that he wanted updated first.'

'You wouldn't have the keys for the place, would you?' Hannah asked. 'We'd like to see inside.'

'You do? Why is that?'

'Unfortunately, we can't tell you why — only that it's important.'

Wise raised an eyebrow, aware that he was holding his breath as they both waited for Sabine to reply.

'D'accord. We should have the keys somewhere here in the office. I'll have a look.'

'That's beautiful, Sabine,' Hannah said. 'Thank you. Can you call me when you find them?'

'Of course,' Sabine said. 'Au revoir.' She ended the call.

Wise's eyes were back on the entrance to the mews. 'A double garage gives him plenty of room to stash vehicles.'

'It really is him, isn't it?' Hannah said.

'It sure looks that way,' Wise said. He checked the time. 2:35 p.m. There was still a way to go before it got dark, before Smythe would kill again. He thought about calling Roberts and updating her, perhaps even asking for more bodies to help keep track of Smythe when he reappeared. If he came out of the mews in a vehicle or on a bike, they'd be in trouble — especially if he headed in the opposite direction to where the Mondeo was facing. By the time Wise could get the car turned around, Smythe would be long gone. Then again, he knew what Roberts would tell him — he still had no actual proof.

Wise's phone rang. It was Hicksy. 'He's come out. He's holding a duffel bag.'

Wise craned his neck, watching the mews, aware that Hannah was doing the same. There was no sign of Smythe yet.

'He's coming towards the arch, towards me,' Hicksy said.

'Okay, I'm going to dial Jono into the call,' Wise said, secretly cursing they hadn't nabbed some radios from Kennington last night. Putting Hicksy on speaker, he started tapping away at his phone, dialling Jono and merging everyone together.

'What's going on?' asked Jono.

'Smythe's on the move,' Hicksy said. 'Just at the arch now … and he's turning left. Maybe he's heading home. I'm going to follow.'

'I'm on my way,' Jono said. 'I'll stay on the other side of the gardens.'

Wise watched Smythe head back down Cadogan Square, a brown leather duffel bag now in his left hand. He was walking just as casually as before, with no urgency whatsoever. Was that because he'd disposed of whatever evidence was in the mews house? Or did he have it all with him in the duffel bag? Was his gun in there?

'I'm going to pull the car around,' he told the others. 'I'll be on Jono's side of the street.'

'Got it,' Hicksy said.

When Wise saw the detective step out onto the road about twenty yards behind Smythe and follow the suspect, he turned on the Mondeo's engine and pulled out of his parking spot. He turned right, slipping into the narrow road that ran along past what was once Lord Cadogan's manor house and then turned right again, past the back of Shafto Mews and down towards the gardens. He slowed as he spotted the other detective. 'Passing you now, Hicksy.'

'I can see him. Looks like he's out for a Sunday stroll. You sure about this, Guv?'

'If he dumps anything out of the bag, I want you to pick it up, no matter how innocent it looks,' Wise said.

'Will do,' Hicksy said.

'What if he has his gun in the bag?' Hannah said. 'Maybe we should nick him now while we can.'

Wise pictured the white boards back at Kennington, before Riddleton had stuck all his wild hypotheses all over them. The first two sections, "What do we know?" and "What do we think?" were full now, but it was that last section, "What can we prove?" that remained elusive. They had Smythe's father's car in the vicinity of the last murder, they had Smythe's height and build matching that of the murderer, and the fact he was left-handed, but none of that would convict him in a court of law. He'd amble up, all stooped shoulders, playing the hen-pecked husband with the best solicitors money could by next to him.

The bastard would get away and Wise couldn't allow that to happen, no matter how much he wanted to grab him right then.

'Nothing's changed,' he said through gritted teeth. 'What if he's just got his gym gear in there? We have to leave him alone for now. We can't risk screwing this up now.'

The words stung in his throat, but he knew it was the right thing to do. The only thing to do.

A second later, he spotted Smythe crossing the road thirty yards away, his head fixed straight ahead, bag in hand. A minute later, Hicksy crossed too on the other side of the street, followed shortly by Jono.

'He's heading home, Guv. He's just crossed over to his side of the street and picking up the pace,' Hicksy said. 'I'm going to get back in our vehicle and watch from there.'

'I'm right behind you,' Jono said. 'Get the heating on. I'm bloody frozen.'

'Alright. Well done, the pair of you. I'll see if I can find a spot down the other end to park up,' Wise said. 'Shout if he moves again before we're settled.'

He ended the call, deflated. But what did he expect? That Smythe was going to go out and start shooting people in the street? The man was too smart for that. Too cunning.

'What now?' Hannah said. 'We wait again?'

Wise nodded, feeling sick. 'We wait.'

Markham's phone rang. 'It's Sabine,' she said before answering it. 'Hello ... uh huh. We can do that.' She looked over at Wise and mouthed, 'She's got the keys. Wants to meet us there in about twenty minutes.'

Wise grinned. The game wasn't over yet. It wasn't even half-time. 'Let's go meet her.'

50

Hannah and Wise headed straight back to Shafto Mews. Wise had called Sarah Choi on the way and told her to join Jono and Hicksy over at Cadogan Gardens to watch Smythe. Sarah had agreed and said she'd bring Callum for company.

'You better watch out, though,' Sarah had said. 'Most of our team's AWOL. They know something's up and Riddleton is stomping around like a bear with a sore head, looking for someone to growl at.'

Sarah's words had made Hannah nervous. For all her bravado of the previous day, she didn't really want to screw her career up a week after getting promoted. Especially if they didn't get a result.

'Are you going to call DCI Roberts and let her know what's happening?' Hannah said, feeling disloyal for even suggesting it.

'I will. Soon,' Wise said, his eyes fixed on the road, his jaw set. 'Right after we've seen inside his little hideaway here. Hopefully, we'll find enough here to lock him up and not have to worry about him getting away, no matter how good his briefs are.'

'Right,' Hannah said, and tried not to think of all the ways things could go wrong. At least Wise was confident, and that made her feel better.

'Listen,' Wise said, looking her way. 'I'll take all the crap on this if things go that way. I'll tell everyone that I didn't inform you I was off the case and, as far as you were aware, you were following official actions.'

Hannah's phone went before she could say anything. She looked at the caller ID, but there was just a telephone number. Even so, they both knew it was Kennington.

'Maybe you don't answer that, though,' Wise said with a smile. 'Let it ring out.'

'You're the boss.' Hannah silenced the call and slipped her phone in her jacket pocket.

They didn't bother hiding the car this time. Wise drove straight into the mews and parked outside Smythe's house. They got out of the car and walked over to the front door.

Like most of the houses in the mews, the white building had black framed windows, a black front door and black garage doors. A small bench sat weathered and worn under the windows, with two pot plants on sentry duty on either side. It was beautiful, sitting alongside its neighbours along the cobbled, private street. A calm oasis, straight out of the past in the heart of a bustling city. No wonder it had cost millions.

But what lurked behind its frosted windows?

A black cab pulled into the mews, making them both turn and watch as it pulled up alongside the Mondeo. Sabine Cricheaux climbed out, wearing a bright red coat. She smiled when she saw Hannah. 'I hope I didn't keep you waiting long.'

Hannah smiled back. 'We just got here ourselves. This is Detective Inspector Simon Wise.'

Wise stepped forward and shook Sabine's hand. 'It's nice to meet you, Miss Cricheaux. Thank you for coming down here so quickly.' His London accent mangled her name, but Sabine didn't correct him.

She glanced back at Hannah instead. 'Anything to help catch Harry's killer.'

'Have you been to the house before?' Hannah asked, once the cab had gone.

'No. David handled everything,' Sabine said. 'Harry was sceptical about all this. The property had gone up in value from three hundred thousand to five million in just under twenty years, but he felt that there wasn't much more room to increase after that. Harry thought the whole London property market was on the verge of plateauing out.'

'I take it David didn't agree?' Wise asked. There was an intensity about him now as they were closing in on Smythe, that Hannah liked to see. She'd been worried a few days back as a darkness seemed to hover over him. She'd been worried when they'd taken him off the case. A lot of coppers would've shrugged, taken the time off and forgotten all about the case — or they'd wallow in a pit of self-pity and gone off to sulk with a bottle of whisky. But not him. Not Wise. He was a stubborn bastard, and Hannah liked that.

'No, David didn't like it,' Sabine said. 'It was one of the things they argued about. David thought the property market was easy money, but Harry told him there was no such thing.'

'But he still let David buy this place,' Wise said.

Sabine shrugged. 'Harry might've disagreed about the potential profit, but it wasn't as if he'd lose on the deal. If he was proved right, it would not cost him any money.' She delved into her handbag and dug out a handful of keys. 'We are supposed to have two sets of keys, but I could only find this one.'

'As long as it opens the door, that one's enough,' Wise said, sparing a glance at Hannah. They knew who had the other keys.

Sabine smiled. 'Let's see.'

Sabine selected a key from the bunch in her hand and slid it into the lock. A loud clunk announced to them all she'd got lucky on the first attempt. She pushed the door open, but Wise stopped her from entering. 'I'm sorry, but I think we need to take over from here. Is it alright if we keep the keys for now? We'll get them back to you the moment we're finished here?'

'Sure. Go ahead,' Sabine said, stepping back. 'I'll go then.'

'Thank you ever so much,' Hannah said. They watched Sabine walk to the end of the mews before turning their attention back to the house.

After putting on their blue latex gloves, they entered the silent house. Immediately inside was a small corridor with a set of stairs directly ahead of them. To the left, through a doorway, Hannah could see the main living room. It was completely bare, with traces of dust visible on the hardwood floor. No one had used it in a long time. Certainly not Smythe. Wise still stuck his head around the doorway to double check. When he turned back, he gave Hannah a shake of the head. One room down.

Neither spoke as Hannah followed Wise to the kitchen at the back of the house.

That too was a bust. There wasn't even a kettle on any of

the dusty countertops. Wise opened a few of the cupboards to look inside but found nothing and he slammed them shut, each time louder than the last.

Wise stood in the kitchen and looked around at the space once more, that dangerous look in his eyes again, like he wanted to break something — or someone. 'Fuck.'

Hannah knew how he felt. Everything was riding on what they could find here. There was a niggle of doubt in the back of her mind, but she did her best to pay it no mind. There was still plenty more to explore. Someone as clever as Smythe wouldn't make it easy on them, no matter how much she wished he would.

He looked at her, his eyes dark with menace. 'Upstairs.'

This time Hannah led the way, aware of her boss stomping along behind her, his presence filling the space. A once white carpet covered the stairs, now worn and grubby. Each step creaked under their weight, the sound echoing through the house, carrying their expectation. Hannah never considered herself religious, but she found herself muttering a quick prayer that this wouldn't be a waste of time and, if it was, what that would mean for their investigation. What it would mean for her? She'd joined Wise's team against everyone else's advice because she was ambitious and sick of being held back. That ambition made her go rogue with him plus, if she was being really honest, because she was just flattered he'd asked her. Would she have gone if Riddleton had given her something more worthwhile to do instead of just answering phones?

Probably. Her ambition had always overruled her common sense. She just hoped it wouldn't cost her everything she'd worked so hard for.

The stairs came out onto a small landing with three

doors leading off it. One was open and Hannah could see the sink and bath. The other two were shut. The bedrooms. If they were empty like downstairs, she and Wise were up shit creek without a paddle.

Hannah reached for the first door handle.

51

Wise's frustration had been growing with every empty room they found. He knew this was the place. There was a reason Smythe had spent twenty minutes in this house and left clutching a holdall. Something had to be here. There had to be evidence — but so far he didn't have enough to justify calling in the SOCOs to tear the place apart to look for more. Every room they'd looked in had contained nothing but dust.

He followed Hannah up the stairs, resisting the urge to push past her, forcing himself to be patient.

If they found nothing, he'd have to convince Roberts, somehow, to make the surveillance on Smythe official with multiple teams watching him twenty-four hours a day and taps on all his phones. He just wasn't sure he had enough on Smythe to sway her to authorise the action and the expense involved. He wasn't exactly the golden child anymore, and Walling had already gone all in on Riddleton's theories.

But he wasn't about to give up hope. His eyes scanned the ceiling in case there was an attic that might hold the treasure he sought, but, of course, there wasn't a door that he could see.

However, there were two rooms off the landing and a garage to search still. One of those would give them the evidence they needed. He damn well hoped so, anyway.

The door handle creaked as Hannah opened the door to the first room. Wise peered over her shoulder, holding his breath, hoping, praying that this would be the room.

The door swung open with a groan, revealing ... white walls and bare floorboards. Another damn room full of nothing but disappointment.

Wise's heart sunk. Shit.

He wasted no time and moved to the second room. The last room. Their last hope.

He opened the door, already convinced that this was going to be like the others, that Smythe had played them for fools. He'd known they'd been watching him and this was just another part of his game, another misdirection to hide his guilt.

Another bloody waste of time while he was doing God only knew what.

Wise wasn't even really looking as he barrelled into the room, already convinced he'd find more bare walls and bare boards to taunt him.

Then he looked up and had to stop himself from going further into the room.

For once, he was glad he was wrong.

So very wrong.

There was furniture for a start; a foldout table and a chair set up in the middle of the room. Set up to face the main wall. Set up to face a multitude of pictures, newspaper clippings and maps that covered it from one side to the next. The portraits of people Wise knew very well. After all, he'd had many of the same pictures on his evidence boards back in Kennington.

It was Smythe's murder wall.

Andronovitch was there, first in line, the words "criminal' scrawled over one image in a red pen. Next, there was Hassleman, marked with "addict" and underneath that "wanker." He'd scrawled "bully" over Richardson's picture, taken from a magazine article on Jack Andrew and Wild. On the largest picture of Sir Harry Clarke, he'd drawn a target over the man's forehead, but that was all. There was nothing derogatory written on the image, though. No label. As if Smythe didn't need reminding why his father-in-law had to die.

There was one other man on the wall. A fifth man Wise didn't recognise. He looked old, maybe in his sixties, with sharp eyes staring out over a beaked nose and a grey goatee. Was he tonight's intended victim? Another billionaire destined to be murdered? Smythe had marked the portrait: "polluter."

'Jesus Christ,' Hannah said from behind it.

'We've struck gold,' Wise said, unable to take his eyes away from it all.

He pulled his phone out, found Roberts' number, and made the call.

'Simon,' Roberts said, sounding cautious. 'Where are you? Half your team has gone missing.'

'I'm in Knightsbridge, boss,' Wise said. 'I know who the motorbike killer is.'

'What are you talking about? You're supposed to be on leave,' Roberts said, caution replaced by confusion. 'And what do you mean, you know who the killer is?'

'It's David Smythe, boss. Sir Harry Clarke's son-in-law. He killed them all for the money. Clarke's money.'

'David Smythe? You're joking, aren't you? Is this some sort of joke?' Roberts was angry now. 'What are you playing at?'

'We're at a house in Shafto Mews in Knightsbridge. He's been using it as a base to plan the murders. I'm looking at all his plans now. I'll tell you all about it when you get here, but I need the property secured ASAP and a full forensics' team down here ASAP.'

'You're being serious, aren't you?'

'He's got another target he's planning to kill tonight.' Wise walked over to the picture of the fifth man, taking care of where he put his feet, and read the information Smythe had stuck next to the portrait. 'Benedict Clime. Lives in Ovington Street. CEO of the Burlington Group. Owns one of the water companies that's been dumping sewerage into the rivers and sea. We need to get him to safety right away.'

'You are being serious.'

'David Smythe is the Motorbike Killer, and he intends to kill Clime tonight,' Wise said.

'Shit,' Roberts said. 'Right. Okay. Where's Smythe now?'

'He's at home. I've got four of my team watching him, but he might have his gun with him. He came to this house earlier and left carrying a holdall. Picking up the gun is the only reason for coming here that I can think of. We need to do a risk assessment before we arrest him. He's got a wife and two children living in the house with him. Maybe a nanny, too.'

'Hostages? Bloody hell, Simon. And you're sure about this?'

Wise stared at the picture of Benedict Clime. 'One hundred percent.'

'Okay. Okay. I'll start making calls. Good work,' Roberts said. She took a breath. 'You know there's going to be a

fallout from this? Walling went on TV and told the world
that the motorbike killer was a pissed off courier. He's had
half the Met dragging possible suspects in for questioning
for the last two days. He's going to go apeshit, especially
since you're supposed to be on leave.'

'I know, but we can't let Smythe get away because
Walling went rushing off, half-cocked. I told you his theory
was wrong.'

'Yeah, well, you might be right about all this, but the
man won't appreciate being made to look an idiot — even if
we get an arrest out of it.'

'We can pass the courier nonsense off as a ruse to give
Smythe a false sense of security while we gathered evidence.
Walling can still save face,' Wise said. If he was being
honest, he didn't give a shit what happened to Walling but
he was smart enough to keep that opinion to himself. He
just wanted Smythe behind bars.

'Alright,' Roberts said. 'I'll be with you as quick as I can.
Hang on.'

'Cheers, boss.' Wise ended the call.

'The boss happy?' Hannah asked.

Wise smiled. 'Not sure I'd call it happy, but she's coming
straight down with the SOCOs.'

'What do we do now?'

'We wait for backup to arrive and then we go and nick
Smythe,' Wise said. And he couldn't bloody wait to put the
cuffs on the man.

52

Wise and Hannah waited outside the house so as not to contaminate the crime scene. There was a chill to the air but, at least, the rain was holding off and the cold was helping him stay focused. The adrenaline of earlier was wearing off and he could feel the toll of the last few days clawing away at the edges. When this case was over, he hoped he could get a decent night's sleep at last. Then he could start rebuilding his life. He could start apologising to everyone he'd hurt and pushed away, especially Jean and the kids.

Forty minutes passes before the SOCO van pulled into the mews. It pulled to a stop beside Wise and Hannah. Two SOCOs climbed out.

'You Morecambe and Wise?' said one, a bearded officer.

'Yeah,' Wise said. 'She's Eric and I'm Ernie.'

The SOCO went bright red. 'Sorry, sir, I ... er ... must've misheard when they gave me your names.'

'I'm Detective Sergeant Hannah Markham,' Hannah said, stepping forward. 'We believe the house behind us is where the Motorbike Killer has been planning his murders.

We want everything photographed, everything checked and everything sent for DNA checks.'

'Have you been in the house?' asked the other SOCO, a small, plump woman in her late thirties.

'We have,' Hannah said. 'Only to ascertain that this was his base, then we called you in and came out here.'

'Nice gaff.' The bearded officer looked up at the house. 'I thought the killer was a homeless, unemployed messenger rider?'

'He's not,' Wise said, and he couldn't help a small smile of satisfaction.

Another SOCO van arrived, spilling out another three more officers plus a uniform. She walked straight over to Wise and Markham. 'I'm Sergeant Janet Arble. I'm the Crime Scene Manager. We're just getting set up, then we'll get to work on the inside.'

'Thank you,' Wise said, but the arrival of a third vehicle, a marked police car, distracted him. Once it had parked, DCI Roberts got out the back on one side and DCI Riddleton clambered out on the other side, without his usual smug look on his face.

Wise saw Hannah slink back to stand amongst the SOCOs, but he walked over with no hesitation, shoulders square and head back, flashing a smile of his own, vindication in his heart. 'Boss. Doug. Thanks for getting here so quickly.'

'I must admit I was a bit surprised,' Riddleton said, his cheeks red, 'when I heard you'd been running your own rogue operation.' His eyes flicked over to Hannah. 'With DS Markham no less.'

'It wasn't intentional,' Wise said, enjoying the shoe being on the other foot. 'I didn't want to waste anyone's time if the lead turned out to be nothing.'

'It sounds like it wasn't,' Roberts said, glancing over at the house as the SOCOs got ready to enter.

'No. It's like Aladdin's cave in there,' Wise said. 'We haven't even searched the whole place yet.'

'I've sent some troops over to look after Clime and his family,' Roberts said. 'How did you access the building? We won't have problems with that in court, are we?'

'Smythe bought it on behalf of Sir Harry Clarke's company,' Wise said. 'Clarke's PA gave us the keys and permission to enter the premises.'

Roberts gave both Wise and Hannah a nod of approval. 'Well done, you two.'

'Yes,' Riddleton said. 'Well done.' He looked like he was about to choke on the words.

'Thank you,' Wise said, feeling good now he had all the answers. He could forget all the doubts and the setbacks. He'd vindicated himself, and now it was all about getting the result.

'Smythe's at his home at the moment?' Roberts asked.

Wise nodded. 'We've got two teams watching the house — but his wife is there with him and his two children. Maybe even a nanny.'

'And you believe he's armed?' Riddleton said.

'Unless the SOCOs find it in there,' Wise said, nodding towards the house.

'Well, that's the first thing we need to find out before we call Armed Response,' Riddleton said. He called over the scene manager and told him to prioritise the weapons search.

It didn't take long before they were called over to the garage.

In forensics suits, Wise, Roberts and Riddleton followed a SOCO inside. A white builder's van took up most of the space and the air was thick with the smell of oil.

'Sarah's mystery van,' Wise said. 'That's how he got his bike to and from the car parks.'

'What I want to show you is at the back of the garage,' the SOCO said. She led them to the rear, where there was a small table near the door into the house. A black motorbike helmet lay on it and, to its right, there was a small, metal cash box, open with the key still in its lock. 'It smells heavily of gun oil. This is probably what he used to store the weapon.'

The three detectives exchanged looks.

'Thank you,' Roberts said to the SOCO. 'We'll leave you to it.' She left the garage, and Wise and Riddleton followed. Once they were outside, Wise waved Hannah over to join them. He gave her a nod. 'They found an empty gun box.'

'We should arrest him now,' Riddleton said. 'We've wasted enough time.'

'If he's got the gun, we should call in Armed Response,' Roberts said. 'Let them deal with the situation.'

'Or that could make everything worse,' Riddleton said. 'Turn it into a hostage situation.'

'Hannah and I visited the house this morning,' Wise said. 'I could call him and ask if I could return with some updates to the case. As long as he suspects nothing, I could arrest him before he knew what was going on.'

'Or we could give him another hostage,' Riddleton said. 'I don't like it.'

'We could always wait for him to leave the house,' Roberts said, 'and grab him on the street.'

'If he's outside, he'll be on his way to Clime's. He'll be armed and prepared to kill,' Wise said. 'Inside the house has to be better. I can't believe he's walking around, waving his gun around.'

'Unless he knows we've rumbled him,' Roberts said. 'Then who knows what he'll do? He could plan to kill his family before killing himself.'

'Smythe thinks he's cleverer than all of us,' Wise said. 'He probably doesn't think we can work out what's going on. We should go in.'

'I don't know,' Roberts said. 'It seems risky.'

'I can go with him,' Hannah said. 'Between the two of us, we can subdue him. Besides, it'll look strange if I don't.'

'I agree,' Riddleton said. 'We'll get Armed Response ready. Simon and DS Markham can go knock on the door.' He looked at Wise. 'Tell him you need to speak to him in private, and separate him from his family. Then, if you can arrest him without threat to the family, then do it. If not, the Shots can go in hard and heavy.'

Wise glanced at Hannah. 'Hannah, you sure about this?'

Hannah chewed on her lip for a moment. Wise could see a flash of fear in her eyes, but she nodded all the same. 'Yeah, I'm in.'

'Let's go make some calls,' Riddleton said.

53

Smythe sat at his desk in his home office on the second floor, thinking about his next murder. An unneeded bedroom, his office had none of the glamour of Laura's "workspace" downstairs. None of the expense lashed out on comfort that she'd happily spent on herself. All he had was a crappy Scandinavian build-it-yourself thing of a desk for his laptop and an uncomfortable chair to sit on — although he was the only one in the house who actually worked for a living. All Laura did was arrange playdates and activities for the kids. He couldn't think of a single good reason she needed one of the best rooms in the house and a five hundred-year-old antique desk to sort out Claudia's dance lessons.

It was just her way of saying he was unimportant. Unnecessary. Another way to demean him, the bitch. If he'd known she'd end up a nasty piece of work, he'd never have married her, but oh, no, she had him fooled back then. She'd been all sweetness and light and all that bullshit. Back then, away from Daddy, she'd loved him — or at least he thought she did.

But then she changed. Especially after he'd lost his job through no fault of his own. She couldn't cope with a husband who was out of work. Heaven forbid the morning coffee girls found that out. So, she'd got him a job with Daddy. Smythe didn't mind. He was good at it and he knew a good opportunity when he saw it. He knew which way the future was going.

But Daddy? Old Harry was stuck in the past. Living by old rules that no one cared about anymore, especially not Smythe.

And then he had the cheek to suggest Smythe move on. 'To other pastures.'

Move on? The old fool couldn't see the future was Smythe's, not his. He was past it. Smythe had done him a favour by putting a bullet in his head. Just like he wanted to put one in his own father's head.

Smythe rolled his neck, listening to Laura cry in the bedroom next door. Who'd have thought it would be such a turn on to hear her so miserable? He could feel himself getting hard at the sound, knowing her pain was because of him and what he'd done.

He glanced down at the duffel bag by his desk, saw the back of the Sig P365 just visible, nestled in amongst his murder clothes. It'd be so easy to take the weapon next door and show Laura who he really was, let her see the man she'd really married.

She'd not think him weak then. She'd not mock him or scold him or tell him what to do.

No, she'd beg and plead and scream.

Smythe put his hand on his groin, feeling the pressure, enjoying the thrill.

Who'd have thought killing people was so arousing? So fun?

Smythe smiled, thinking about each murder, remembering the power he'd felt each time he pulled the trigger. How happy he'd felt.

It was a shame he'd had to use a silencer each time. The gun spat out bullets with a cough when really he'd wanted a roar, a boom to tell the world what he'd done. It was the only disappointment, taking some of the fun away from the moment. Some, but not all.

Everything after that happened in slow motion. The bullet left the barrel of the gun, chased by the briefest of flames to punch a hole out the back of their skulls, painting the walls red and black. Like Jackson Pollock at work. A modern masterpiece created by him.

God, it turned him on. He thought about masturbating, especially with the sound of his wife crying, but he dismissed it just as quickly. He had things to do. Plans to go over.

There would be a time to show Laura the gun. A time to kill her. It wasn't far off, but it wasn't right then. He had to be patient.

It was a shame he'd not had time to get another bike, but he didn't see why that should stop him from killing Clime. He just needed to be more careful. That was all. There was no need to deprive himself of the fun. Not now.

Smythe remembered when he'd come up with his plan. It had seemed madness. Impossible. But he knew it was the right thing to do — the only thing to do. He would not let that old fool rob him of his rightful prosperity. And God, Laura. If he had lost his job, she would have been even more unbearable. She'd have known that Harry had forced him to quit. She's blame Smythe and harangue him more than ever. Maybe she'd even kick him out of the house and divorce him, leaving him nothing.

There was no way he could've allowed that to happen. No way. He didn't care about Laura, but he would not lose his lifestyle, his position, his respectability.

So, he had no option but to carry out his plan. Killing Harry secured his wealth. Killing the others hid his culpability. Little did he know that executing the plan — executing the people — would set him free. It had made him who he truly deserved to be.

In fact, picking his victims had been the hardest part of his plan to begin with. He'd liked the idea of doing some good for society, so that had helped guide him. Bumping off one of Putin's pals was almost a righteous act. And that drugged out tech head was just an embarrassment to himself and to others, especially after that atrocious dinner at the Natural History Museum. That old music mogul might as well have waved his hand around, shouting 'Pick me!' after he'd been so rude to that girl in Waitrose a few weeks back and then was even ruder Smythe when he'd asked the man to apologise. People with no class deserved to be taught a lesson. And, of course, Benedict Clime was happy making billions pumping muck into Smythe's favourite fishing spot, so that was a straightforward choice, too.

He'd only picked five victims because five seemed enough of a distraction when he first came up with his plan. Five seemed plenty. But now, though? It felt like he was only getting started, only now hitting his stride.

And, of course, it was all made so much sweeter because the police had no clue. They were off chasing angry homeless people like the fools they were. He'd manipulated them perfectly. That another pleasure he'd not expected.

He walked over to the window and looked up and

down the road. It'd be dark soon. Time to feed the children and put them to bed, dear old Laura to pop her sleeping pill and then he'd have some peace to do what he had to do.

The Grenshaw's nanny strolled down the other side of the street, pushing a pram with her two charges in it. The nanny was from eastern Europe somewhere but was nice enough all the same. Good looking, at least. Certainly a major upgrade to the old hag Laura had hired to look after his own children. That would be something else that would change after he'd killed his wife. There'd be no more hags in his house. Only hotties that appreciated Smythe being in charge.

He watched the Grenshaw's nanny walk past a Chinese woman at the end of the street, standing by a car, puffing away on a cigarette, forcing the nanny to push the pram through her clouds of smoke. It was disgusting. If Smythe had his way, he'd ban smoking everywhere.

He'd always hated smoking. When the boys at his prep school had all started stealing cigarettes off their parents to smoke, he'd not joined in with them down the end of the rugby pitches. They'd made fun of him, but Smythe hadn't cared. His father had told him that smoking was something poor people did and, even at that age, Smythe hadn't ever wanted to look poor, let alone be poor.

With Harry dead, though, Smythe never had to worry about that again. Especially not when Laura was in the ground with him. He was rich, rich, rich.

His phone rang, breaking him from his thoughts. Detective Inspector Wise's name came up on the screen. Why was he calling now he was off the case? They had probably given him another pointless task to do. The poor sod. Washed up and on his way out.

He had to force the smile from his face. He didn't want to sound too happy after all. 'Inspector? Is everything okay?'

'Good afternoon, Mr Smythe,' Wise said. 'I'm really sorry to bother you yet again today but I hoped that DS Markham and myself could pop over for five or ten minutes.'

'Of course,' Smythe said. 'Can you tell me what it's pertaining?'

'I'd like to show you some photographs. Someone's come up in our enquiries and we were wondering if, perhaps, you'd seen them loitering around your office or Sir Harry's house.'

This time Smythe didn't bother trying to contain his glee. The police had a suspect. Smythe would be more than happy to identify whoever it was as someone he'd seen lurking around. 'Of course, of course. I'd be delighted to help in any way I can.'

'Thank you,' Wise said. 'We'll see you shortly.'

'I'll look forward to it,' Smythe said. He disconnected the call, feeling even better about everything. It was all working out so well. Almost as if it was his destiny to succeed.

He walked back to the window as he listened to Laura cry. Life really couldn't get much better.

The street was quiet outside. No cars. No nannies. No nothing. It was as if the world was waiting, too. Waiting for Smythe to go out once more, gun in hand, and put another rich waste of space into the ground.

Sudden movement caught his eye. A car door opened at the end of the street. The interior light snapped to life, illuminating a black man sitting behind the wheel and ... The Chinese woman climbed out. The Chinese woman from earlier. She pulled out a cigarette and lit it.

Smythe watched her smoke furiously. After the first few

inhalations, she looked up at Smythe's house, almost as if she sensed him watching. He took a step back from the window, but he knew she couldn't see him. So why was she watching his house? Why was she sitting in that car with the black man? How long had they been there?

She stubbed the cigarette out and climbed back into the car. This time, as the light came on, Smythe saw that the black man was watching his house, too. Then the interior went dark as the Chinese woman shut the door.

Smythe waited, hoping that they'd turn the engine on and drive off, but he knew they wouldn't. Not now.

They were police.

They were watching his house because they knew.

They knew he was the killer.

Wise wasn't coming around to show him pictures of a suspect. He was the suspect. How had they'd worked it out? What had given him away?

A shiver of fear ran through him, but he pushed it aside. He'd planned for this moment too, like he'd planned everything else.

What was it they said in the army? Follow the seven Ps? "Proper Planning and Preparation Prevents Piss Poor Performance." It had stuck with him when he'd heard it mentioned on that TV show with the ex-SAS guys. Knew it made sense. Knew it was how he'd do what he had to do and walk away afterwards scot-free.

Laura hadn't, though. She'd been too busy laughing at the idea of him taking part on the show. 'You wouldn't last an hour if they had you on,' she'd howled, tears of a different sort running down her face then. 'Maybe not even a minute.'

As if her mockery could hurt him. He knew he wasn't a soldier type. He wasn't built for obstacle courses or living off the land. But it turned out he had a soldier's mind, a soldier's instinct.

He knew how to plan. He knew how to prepare. And, by God, he definitely knew how to kill.

He closed his laptop and placed it inside his duffel bag. As long as he had that, he could access the bank accounts later that evening and transfer everything to his Cayman Islands accounts.

He left his phone on his desk and took out the anonymous burner from his desk drawer, registered under a fake name in some pop-up store in a Birmingham shopping centre. Smythe checked the power bar, happy to see it was at ninety-eight percent. Even so, he popped the power cable for the laptop and the charger for the phone into his duffel bag as well. The last thing he needed was flat batteries slowing things down.

Satisfied, Smythe pulled out the gun. It still amazed him what you could buy on the dark web if you looked hard enough and had the cash. He checked the cartridge. Five rounds left. More than enough.

54

Wise paced up and down Shafto Mews, impatient to be off. They were running late but the powers-that-be insisted on going over everything again and again, looking for better ways of arresting Smythe where they'd be little or no risk in anyone getting hurt but every route they explored ended up at the same place — Wise and Hannah knocking on his door.

Wise watched Hannah adjust her leather jacket, trying to get comfortable with the bulletproof vest she had on under her clothes. He was wearing one too, along with a wire, stretching the fit of his shirt and making his suit jacket feel tight but, even he had to agree, it made sense to have them on. Better to have it and not need it than need it and not have it, as someone had once said.

Despite the other day, Wise didn't want to die. Not now.

His mind drifted back to Jean and the kids and the mess he really needed to fix.

'Is this on?' Wise said, tapping the mike on his chest, to the tech who'd fitted him up with the wire along with an earpiece that was all but invisible.

'Not yet,' replied the tech.

'Cheers.' Wise glanced over at the others. 'I just have to make a call.'

Taking his phone out of his pocket, he walked away from the others to a corner at the far end of the mews. He scrolled through his contacts, found Jean's name and hit dial before he could change his mind.

'Simon?' Jean answered almost immediately. Her voice was full of concern. 'Where are you? Are you all right?'

'Hey. Sorry — I'm working. We've cracked that case I was on,' Wise said, looking down at his feet. 'But ... have you got a minute?'

'I'm just getting the kids' tea ready, so you have literally a minute.'

'I just wanted to say sorry for everything. For not being the best husband or the best father lately. I know I've let you all down more times than any of you deserve.'

Silence answered him. Seconds passed.

'You've certainly not been easy to be around,' Jean said.

'My mood has nothing to do with you and the kids. It's just ... since Andy died ... nothing's made sense. Everything's hurt.'

'We all understand, but we can help you. We want to help you — you have to let us.'

'I know. And I am sorry. I've been an arse.'

'You've always been an arse, but we still love you.'

'I love you too.'

'When are you coming home?'

Wise glanced around, saw everyone was watching him, waiting for him. He had to go.

'Soon,' Wise said. If he made it through the next few hours alive. 'But I want you to know that marrying you was the best thing I've ever done. It really was. We've had some pretty good years together, haven't we?'

'We sure did.' He could hear Jean's smile, and that made him feel like he could do anything. If he got through this, he'd do his best to make her smile more.

'And we made two beautiful kids.'

'Yeah, we did that too,' Jean said.

'They make all of this worthwhile. They really do,' Wise said. 'Tell them I love them for me, eh?'

'Do you want to speak to them? Tell them yourself?'

'I can't right now. I'll speak to them later if I can.' Wise winced the moment he said it.

'"If you can?" What do you mean by that? Jesus, Simon, you're not going to do something stupid, are you?'

'Me? Do something stupid?' Wise laughed. It sounded fake even to his ears. 'Not if I can help it.'

'Be careful,' Jean said. 'Come back to us.'

'I love you.' Wise ended the call, hoping he'd made a promise he could keep.

'Are you ready?' asked Roberts, seeing him put the phone away.

He walked back over. 'Yeah.'

Riddleton gave him a nod. 'Don't fuck it up and don't get killed. There's too much paperwork involved when that happens.'

'I'll do my best to spare you that chore,' Wise said. The two men exchanged glances, any animosity gone now the end of the chase was in sight and lives were at stake.

'Good luck,' Roberts said.

'Thanks, boss.'

'You remember what you say if it all goes tits up and you need the AROs to rescue you?'

'Help?'

'I'm being serious,' Roberts said.

'Marmite,' Wise said. 'I'll say "marmite."'

Roberts turned to the tech team. 'You got everything up and running?'

'All turned on now,' said the tech. 'We'll be able to hear everything.'

'The Armed Response team is in place, too,' Riddleton said.

'Good. Now go nick that wanker, Simon,' Roberts said.

'Will do, boss,' Wise said.

With that, he and Hannah walked over to the Mondeo. 'How you feeling?' he asked.

She shook her head. 'Nervous. I've not faced a gun before.'

'Hopefully, we won't have to this time,' Wise said, unlocking the Mondeo.

'What about you?' Hannah asked, opening the door.

'I'm nervous too,' Wise said. 'Only fools don't have nerves in situations like this.' They both climbed into the car. 'By the way, I'm glad you joined the team when you did.'

'Are you?' Hannah said.

'I am. I like the way you think and I like the way you make me think. We wouldn't have solved this if not for you.' Wise started the car and pulled away. 'It's not been easy for me since Andy died. You've helped me see the future as a good thing.'

'Let's hope we have one, eh?'

'We'll be fine,' Wise said.

'I can't wait to arrest the bastard. I always thought Smythe was a wrong 'un.'

'That's because you've got a copper's intuition.'

'Yeah? My girlfriend says I just don't like people.'

'Sometimes that's the same thing.'

They passed the Armed Response team's van, parked where Jono and Hicksy were earlier. Inside were six men and women, ready to charge in, if and when necessary. They did a job Wise could never do. Some said AROs weren't right in the head, but they were just wired differently. They didn't freeze when things got heavy like most people would do. They could charge towards someone firing a gun instead of ducking for cover. Maybe they were crazy, but it was a good crazy if they were.

'Everyone hear us?' he asked as he parked the Mondeo.

'Loud and clear,' Roberts said in his ear.

'And no sign of the suspect?'

'He's not left the house,' Sarah said.

'Where are you, Sarah?' Wise asked.

'At the end of the street with Callum,' Sarah replied. 'Jono and Hicksy are around the corner.'

'Good to know.' Wise and Hannah got out of the car and crossed over the road to Smythe's house.

'Don't be a hero,' Roberts said. 'Call for help if anything looks bad.'

'Will do.' They climbed the three steps to the front door, and Hannah rang the intercom. With his jacket on and a tie covering the space between the jacket lapels, he knew Smythe wouldn't spot the vest. Even so, Wise still ran his hand down the front of his chest, trying to flatten the vest a bit more.

A minute passed, and no one came to let them in. Wise glanced over at Hannah. 'Ring the bell again.'

She did so and, this time, they heard footsteps clumping down the stairs.

'Who is it?' Laura Smythe-Clarke's voice crackled out from the intercom.

'It's Detective Inspector Wise and Detective Sergeant

Markham,' Wise said. 'We have an appointment with your husband.'

The door opened, revealing Smythe-Clarke, all red faced and bleary-eyed. 'Come in then.' As Wise and Hannah entered, Smythe-Clarke hollered up the stairs. 'David! The police are here.'

Smythe didn't answer.

'Jesus Christ, that man,' muttered Smythe-Clarke. 'David!' She called again, louder this time. 'David! The police are here!'

Smythe still didn't answer. That wasn't good. Wise glanced over at Hannah and saw her concern, too.

'Where is your husband?' Wise said, moving further into the house, dread building in his gut.

'He's working in his office upstairs,' Smythe-Clarke said. 'He's probably just got his headphones on. The man lives in a world of his own.'

Wise pushed past her and ran up the stairs, Markham following. 'Mr Smythe! It's the police.'

'Where are you going?' called Smythe-Clarke after them, but Wise ignored her. She was the least of his worries right then.

The first door he opened revealed the main bedroom. Smythe wasn't there. Hannah opened the next door. It was the office. They both saw the empty desk, the empty room.

'The suspect is not here,' Wise said into the radio as he checked the next room on the landing. A guest room. Empty. 'Repeat. The suspect is not on the premises.'

'What do you mean, he's not there?' Roberts said in his ear.

'He is not fucking here,' Wise snapped. He couldn't believe it. How had he got away without being spotted? He had two teams watching the front door, for God's sake.

The last rooms on the floor belonged to the children. They looked up and screamed as Wise burst in. He held up his hands and said sorry, before backing out.

Hannah was on the third floor, banging doors open. 'He's definitely done a runner.'

'Shit,' Wise said.

By the time he'd made it back down to the ground floor, more police had arrived and the street outside was awash with blue flashing lights. Smythe-Clarke was standing bewildered as officers streamed in, tears streaming down her face. 'What's going on?'

'Where's your husband?' Wise demanded as Hannah and the others set off to search the rest of the house.

'I don't know! He was upstairs,' Smythe-Clarke said. 'What's going on? I don't understand.'

'We believe your husband murdered your father and three other men,' Wise said, in no mood to be nice. 'Now, where is he?'

'I don't know. I swear.' Smythe-Clarke looked around. 'I ... I ...'

Wise gave up on trying to get anything out of her. He saw Sarah and Callum bounded up the front steps of the house.

'I'm sorry, Guv. I don't know how he got—' Sarah said, but Wise cut her off.

'Get Ms Smythe-Clarke here and the children and take them down to the station for now. We sort out somewhere for them to stay later.'

'Yes, Guv,' Sarah said.

Hannah was back then. 'There's a ladder against the garden wall. Looks like he used that to climb over and slip away with no one seeing.'

'You hear that, boss?' Wise said into his mic.

'I did. I'll get the Force Control Room on it. He'll be on

camera somewhere,' Roberts said. 'I'll get an all-ports warning out too in case he's trying to skip the country.'

'We spoke to him here thirty minutes ago,' Wise said. 'He could be at St Pancras and on the bloody Eurostar by now.'

'We'll get him, Simon,' Roberts said, but Wise wasn't so sure. Smythe had always been a hundred miles ahead of them. He was still too damn clever for them.

'What do you want to do, Guv?' Hannah said.

Wise took a breath. Panicking would not get them anywhere. Smythe definitely didn't do panic. He planned. He prepared. He wasn't going to wander the streets without a destination in mind. Smythe would have an escape route all carefully planned.

'Guv?' Hannah said again.

'When you spoke to Sabine earlier, she told you Clarke let Smythe buy a few properties. The mews was one of them. Where were the others?'

'She didn't say.'

'Call her and find out. If he's used one of them as a base, he could've got the others set up as well.'

Roberts' voice came through in his ear. 'CCTV has him going into Sloane Street tube but we lost him there. We're checking other stations.'

'That's the Circle and District line,' Wise said as he watched Hannah make the call to Sabine. 'He could be anywhere on that.' He got his own phone out and pulled up a tube map, following the green and yellow routes of the Circle and District line, but nothing jumped out at him as a possible destination. If he changed at Piccadilly, he could almost be at Heathrow by now or on his way to the south-coast and the ports.

'Guv,' Hannah said, putting her hand over her phone. 'Sabine says he bought two other properties; a flat in

Canary Wharf and a house in Chiswick Park. I've got the addresses.'

Wise looked at the tube map again. Both were on the Circle and District line. He told Hannah what Roberts had told him. 'He could be at either by now.'

'Or neither,' Hannah said.

Wise shook his head. 'I think he'll be at one of them. Maybe not for long, but knowing Smythe, he'll have an escape plan ready. Clothes, money, maybe another passport, a car even.'

'Canary Wharf is busy all the time,' Hannah said. 'Plenty of CCTV. It's an apartment building so they'll be other residents, shared parking. Not a great place to hide.'

'Sabine said he'd been renovating one of the properties. Which one was it?'

'The one at Cambridge Road North. Chiswick Park.'

Wise switched to Google Maps on his phone and typed in the address. 'Big house, quiet residential street, plenty of parking.'

'The sort of place where people mind their own business,' Hannah said.

'That's the one,' Wise said. He called Roberts and told her about the addresses.

'We raid both,' said the DCI.

'Me and Hannah are going to go to Chiswick. We think that's where he's going,' Wise said.

'Go,' Roberts said. 'Take the AROs with you.'

55

'Come on!' Wise shouted as he tried to force his way through the evening traffic. Even with the blues and twos going, London's rush hour just didn't care. Cars packed both lanes, leaving no space for anyone to get out of the way. No wonder Smythe took the bastard tube!

They passed Earl's Court, charging through the red lights at the junction, somehow finding a gap that hadn't existed seconds before. The road widened into three lanes, not that it made any difference. Wise pushed his way out into the outside lane, then crunched his tires up and onto the pavement that separated the incoming and outgoing lanes until his car only had its left tires on the road and accelerated, honking his horn to add to the wail of the siren. The cars in front swerved out of his way, leaving just enough room to squeeze by.

Hannah had her hands braced against the dashboard, arms locked. 'Shit. There's a fucking lamppost.'

Wise saw it, forty yards ahead, but he didn't slow down. He kept going, jerking the wheel to the left at the last moment, and heard the scrape of metal on metal as they passed. Another dent in the car to add to the collection.

On he went, repeating the trick, up onto the pavement, jerking back down before he hit the next lamppost, the time ticking away loud in his head.

'Local police report a light on in the house and movement,' Roberts said over the radio. 'I've authorised closing off the street around the house. We can't risk him getting away again.'

'Roger that,' Hannah said into the car mic.

'No. Tell them to keep the house under covert observation only,' Wise shouted as he bumped back down into traffic. 'We don't want to spook him. Only shut up the place up once we know it's definitely Smythe inside.'

Hannah relayed the message as Wise banged the car back into the outside lane. Trees and bushes had replaced the central reservation, so it forced him to continue on the actual road.

Somehow, some space opened up as more cars inched out of his way and Wise pushed his foot further down on the accelerator. The car sped up to seventy, eighty, ninety miles an hour.

The ARO van was right behind him as they stormed up the flyover, but already Wise could see more brake lights up ahead. More stationary cars. Railings ran along the central reservation so he couldn't go onto the wrong side of the road. Shit. He braked, one eye on the road in front of him, one eye watching the van so close behind.

His tires screamed in protest at the rapid deceleration and then he was back to nudging his way forward.

'This is taking too long,' he hissed through clenched teeth. 'Come on.'

The railings suddenly ended and Wise went up on the

pavement again. The strip was narrow, though, not even the width of his car. As he drove, he had one half of the car in both outside lanes. Cars on both sides that couldn't make enough room for a whole car to pass, pulled aside just enough to let Wise's Mondeo and the AROs' van through. He was back up to forty miles an hour, fifty miles an hour, and making progress again.

'Have they got a visual yet on Smythe?' he demanded down the radio.

'Negative. Negative. Still one light on, upstairs. Definite movement inside,' the message came back.

'It could be anyone in there. Anything! Shit.' Wise prayed he wasn't wrong.

The railings were back, so he crunched back down into the outside lane. They'd gotten ahead of the rush hour traffic just enough, though, that there was room to move. He drove on, the world awash in strobing blue lights, the siren screaming above his head.

He saw the M&S on the left and the Hammersmith Flyover ahead. It'd only taken them thirty minutes to do a fifteen minute journey so far. Even though the flyover narrowed down to two lanes, it was kinder to them, at least, and they made real progress, passing St. Paul's church and St. Peter's in good time.

Wise could feel the sweat soaking his back and wished he'd been able to take his jacket and his vest off before they'd hared off.

The radio crackled away as they drafted more police in to help. More AROs with dog support, more uniforms getting ready to lock Cambridge Road down the moment they knew Smythe was there. But they still had no confirmation of that.

The road widened again to three lanes as it turned into

the A4 proper. They passed a construction site, promising London's new tech hotspot. Trees replaced concrete. Warehouses and office buildings took the place of terrace houses. But it still wasn't good enough. Wise wanted to be there now. 'Come on!'

Then up ahead, he spotted the Fuller's Brewery. He could smell the hops. That meant they were nearly at the Hogarth roundabout. They were close.

Cars and vans were pulling aside, letting the Mondeo and the van through, but it wasn't fast enough for Wise. As they reached the roundabout, he yanked the wheel to the right, into the oncoming traffic. The exit he needed was the last one, and he was taking the most direct way to it.

'Fuck!' Hannah shouted as a van nearly sideswiped them, but Wise didn't slow down. They'd made it to Chiswick Park.

They killed the lights half a mile from the house and slowed down to the speed limit, even though it felt too painfully slow after the mad dash to get there. Wise's heart was going ten to the dozen as he blinked sweat from his eyes. 'Still alive?' he asked Hannah.

'Only just,' she said, trying to unwind her body from the brace position.

'We're here,' Wise said into the radio as they turned into Cambridge Road North. 'What's the situation?'

'No confirmation yet,' the operator said.

'Where's the house?' Wise said, looking left and right, checking the numbers. The road was similar to Smythe's home in Cadogan Gardens, except here the Georgian houses were semi-detached rather than in a terrace. BMWs, Mercedes, Range Rovers, Audis and the like, favoured by bankers and CEOs the world over, lined both sides of the street.

'On the right,' Hannah said, pointing to a red brick building. Unlike the rest, there were no lights on, despite the day being long gone.

'Keep going,' the radio operator said. 'We have the house under observation.'

'You've got to be joking,' Wise said. 'This is my arrest.'

'You do not have operational command, DI Wise,' the operator said. 'AROs are in position. Now move — before you blow everything.'

'Shit!' Wise hissed, but he knew they were right, damn them. He drove on another hundred yards from the house and then pulled the Mondeo over, partially blocking someone's driveway. The AROs van that had followed Wise from Knightsbridge drove past and parked another ten yards down the side of the street.

It took an effort to unclench his hands from the steering wheel so he could turn and look over his shoulder. 'See anything?'

'Nothing,' Hannah said.

Wise waited, staring back towards the house, doing his best not to worry that he'd got it all wrong, that the bastard was going to get away.

Smythe had to be in there. He had to be.

56

Wise and Hannah sat in the dark of the Mondeo, the engine still ticking after its mad dash from Knightsbridge, staring back towards Smythe's property. The only noise came from the radio as the AROs watched the house.

'The light is still on in Black Two Two,' a man said, the code for the rear of the house, second-floor, second window.

'Do you have a visual of the suspect?' a woman asked.

'Negative. Negative.'

'White team?' the woman asked.

'All dark. No movement,' another man replied.

'He is in there, isn't he?' Hannah asked.

'I bloody well hope so,' Wise replied. God, he wished he had some water. His mouth was dry from all the adrenaline from the drive there and now he had to sit on his bloody hands, listening to the radio. 'Why don't they just go in?'

Suddenly, a light came on, illuminating the driveway that Wise had partially blocked with the Mondeo. A second later, the front door opened, and a man stomped out of the house and marched towards the car, a v-neck jumper stretched across an impressive belly, like he was about to storm the beaches.

The man tapped on the car window on Hannah's side.

'Fucking hell,' Hannah muttered before winding down the window.

'I'm afraid you're going to have to move your car,' said the man in that terribly polite way middle-class people use when they're really pissed off. 'This is a residents' only parking area and you're blocking my driveway.'

Hannah showed the man her warrant card. 'Can you go back inside your house, sir? For your own safety.'

The man didn't know what to say. He started spluttering. 'But this is my driveway. My house.'

'Go back inside ... NOW,' Hannah said. The man took the hint then and retreated inside, with only a couple of indignant looks back.

'We have movement. Black Two Two,' the ARO said over the radio. 'A man is at the window looking out over the garden. IC One. Tall. Thin.'

'Is it the suspect?' the woman asked. 'Confirm.'

'Confirm, it is the suspect,' the ARO said. 'Repeat, confirm. It is the suspect.'

'Yes,' Wise said. Thank God for that.

'Containment teams go,' the woman said over the radio. 'Stop all traffic in and out of the target area.'

The quiet street erupted into life. Blue lights stormed down the road towards the house from both directions. A van and a squad car drove past Wise and Hannah and blocked the road off fifty yards away. Officers in uniform and high-viz jackets spilled out of the van. The AROs that had followed Wise from Kensington exited their vehicle in full combat gear, black helmets on, Heckler and Koch MP5s slung across their chests and Kevlar shields on their arms.

Wise and Hannah got out of the Mondeo and walked towards the blockade. A similar two vehicle barrier shut off the road a hundred yards away further down. A uniform came to stop them from approaching, but they showed their warrant cards and they waved Wise and Hannah on. The main group sheltered behind the safety of the van, directing the AROs into position around the front of the house. Nearby, another ARO stood waiting, with an Alsatian, the firearms support dog, on a leash by his side.

'All units, confirm you're in position,' a uniformed officer said into her radio. The crown on her epaulettes said she was a superintendent. She glanced over at Wise and Hannah. 'Don't get in the way.'

Wise nodded and listened to the various teams confirm they had the area completely contained. Smythe wasn't going anywhere. That was something, at least.

'Control,' the ARO, who had observed Smythe at the window, said. 'Light has gone off at Black Two Two. Repeat, light has gone off at Black Two Two.'

'Received,' the superintendent said. 'Sounds like our man's trying to hide. Time to let him know he's got nowhere to go and, hopefully, if he'll come out without a fight.' She picked up her hat and put it on, then straightened her hi-viz jacket.

Another officer handed her a megaphone. The Superintendent moved to the front of the van so the bonnet still covered most of her body. 'David Smythe. This is the police. I repeat, this is the police. We have you surrounded. You have nowhere to go. Come out now, with your hands on your head, and surrender. I repeat, come out now, with your hands on your head, and surrender. No one wants you to get hurt.'

Her words echoed through the neighbourhood as the

blue lights washed over all and sundry. Wise watched the house, looking for movement, a sign that Smythe was going to give in peacefully. He'd be a fool not to. He could end up dead if he tried to fight his way out. The AROs wouldn't hesitate if they thought anyone's lives were at risk.

A red dot dances across Andy's shoulders, seeking his head, finding its spot, stopping on his temple, dead still.

Wise blinked. Now wasn't the time for those thoughts. That ghost.

'When this is over, I'll find out who got you killed,' he whispered to himself.

'What did you say?' Hannah asked.

'Just hoping he'll come out,' Wise lied.

'Do you think he will?'

Wise stared at the dark house. 'I really don't know. He's smart and devious, but he must realise he has no way out.'

Nothing moved in the dark house. The door remained closed.

The Super repeated her message. There was no way Smythe couldn't hear her from inside the house. He had to realise it was all over.

So why didn't he come out?

'What if he kills himself?' Hannah said.

'He's too clever to give up like that,' Wise said. 'If he doesn't walk out, it's because he thinks he can still get away still.'

'He's not going anywhere,' the Super said, her face set in grim determination. 'I'll give him one last chance, then we'll send the troops in.'

Wise nodded, but already his mind was racing. What had they overlooked? Smythe had always planned everything so meticulously. He'd even given the slip back in Knightsbridge easily enough, the ladder set up at the back of his garden to help him climb over the wall when the time came. Smythe knew then the police would discover his identity at some point, and he had prepared his escape.

Smythe had run to Chiswick, to this house, but this wouldn't be his last stop. Only a temporary resting place. There'd be somewhere else. Somewhere safe. And the police were simply giving him more time to get away.

'I think we should go in now,' Wise said. 'He's up to something. We should go now.'

The Super looked at him as if he was mad. 'I've surrounded the house with armed officers. We have every exit covered.'

'There'll be another way out,' Wise said. 'Something we don't know about. Something hidden.'

The Super laughed. 'Next, you'll tell me he's digging a bloody tunnel.'

The words were like a slap across Wise's face. 'You need to go in NOW.' He looked over at Hannah. 'This was the property he spent money doing up, right? That's what Sabine said.'

'That's right,' Hannah said, eyes going wide.

'What's he built?' Wise said. 'Why would he build anything?'

'To get away,' Hannah said.

The Super grabbed the radio mic. 'White team. Force entry now. Repeat, force entry now.'

57

Hannah watched the video feed on a small screen set up in front of the Super. A picture came to life, showing the front of the house. The viewpoint was low down and she could see to the left of the frame a leg of an ARO. She looked around, trying to see where the camera was, and realised the firearms support dog wore it.

'White team. Good to go,' an ARO said over the radio.

'Go. Go. Go,' the Super said.

Hannah was aware of Wise tensed up just behind her as five AROs moved forward, Kevlar shields covering their bodies. Some had MP5s in the raised position ready in case Smythe opened fire on them from the house. The forearms support dog went with them, while another carried the big, red key — the one-man battering ram used by police forces across the country to open any door.

Her eyes flicked from the Super's screen and the dog's point of view and what was happening in front of her. Suddenly, everything felt surreal, like she was watching a video game taking place, but this was as real as it got.

The officer with the battering ram was first up the stairs to the front of the house, closely followed by the dog handler and the Alsatian. When they reached the front door, he slammed the sixteen kilograms of reinforced steel into the door, just above the handle.

The locks splintered with a crack and the door broke open, creating a gap for him to shout through. 'ARMED POLICE! ARMED POLICE!' the officer called out. 'Show yourself with your hands on your head NOW!'

Silence.

'ARMED POLICE! ARMED POLICE! Come out with your hands up NOW!'

There was no reply.

Next thing Hannah knew, the Alsatian was off into the house, moving fast, looking for Smythe. All eyes went to the Super's screen then as the dog raced down the hallway, into one room, scurrying around, through another room, into the kitchen, all empty, just like Shafto Mews. There was no furniture inside. Nothing that said anyone had been there.

'Go upstairs,' Wise urged the screen in a whisper.

The dog raced on, searching rooms in the house, then it was up the stairs like Wise had wished for, the camera showing it bounding up two steps at a time, weaving in and out of doors, empty room after empty room, finding nothing, finding no one.

Wise was shaking his head as he watched the screens, his fists all balled up, growing in size as his frustration grew. Like the Hulk, Hannah thought. Ready to smash.

The dog ran into another room. This one had furniture. A folding table. A camp chair. Just like Shafto mews. The dog started barking, but there was no sign of Smythe.

'That's his room,' Wise said. 'He was there. He is there.'

'White team, commence slow search contact,' the Super said. 'Repeat, commence slow search contact.'

Instantly, the door got another whack, smashing it wide open this time. The AROs went in, all with their MP5s raised and ready.

'ARMED POLICE! ARMED POLICE! Come out with your hands up NOW!'

Hannah could hear the shouts and could only imagine how terrifying it must be if those officers came through the door after you. The thought made her smile. She wanted Smythe to be shitting himself.

'ARMED POLICE! ARMED POLICE!' the shouts went on.

Then, over the radio, there were other voices. 'No change. No change.' That wasn't what they wanted to hear. They wanted to hear 'Contact. Contact.' That meant they'd found Smythe.

The flashlights that were strapped to the barrels of the MP5s were visible through the windows of the house as the officers moved through the building.

'ARMED POLICE! ARMED POLICE!' the shouts went on.

'No change. No change,' the radio squawked.

'Shit. Shit. Shit,' Wise said. 'Where the fuck is he?'

Hannah said nothing, too scared to say what they all had to be thinking. That Smythe wasn't there. He'd got away. God, she wanted to be sick.

'No change. No change.' Each time she heard the words, her anxiety rose.

'No change. No change.' How was it possible?

The AROs were upstairs now, clearing the rest of the house room by room, sweeping their guns from left to right, checking every hiding place before moving on to the next room, the next possible point of contact.

'No change. No change.'

'No change. No change.'

'He has to be in there,' Wise said. 'He has to be.' He started moving towards the house.

'Inspector,' the Super snapped. 'Stay where you are!'

'He's bloody getting away,' Wise snarled back.

'You rushing into the house and getting shot by one of my officers won't prevent that,' the Super said. 'Now, stand down.'

For a moment, Hannah thought Wise was going to ignore the order, tensed and bunched up as he was, but then she saw him visibly deflate and accept the command. He shook his head and stared at the house. 'Bastard.'

An ARO appeared at the front door. 'The house is empty,' his voice said over the radio. 'Repeat, the house is empty. The suspect is not in the house.'

The shock rippled through all of them. After everything, Smythe had gotten away again. Somehow, he'd done the impossible.

'No,' Wise said, and ran straight to the house. Up the steps, past the ARO, and inside.

Hannah glanced at the Super.

'Go on,' the senior officer said. 'We might as well all have a look.'

Hannah followed Wise into the house, aware of the Super on her heels. The AROs had the inside lights on; the bulbs shining naked in a hall, all bright and freshly painted white. It contrasted against the AROs' black combat gear, their faces anonymous with their Kevlar helmets and goggles on.

'Have you looked everywhere?' Wise asked the senior officer.

'We've been through every room,' he replied, 'and checked the attic. The house is empty.'

'But one of your lot saw him here,' Wise said.

The ARO shrugged. 'Maybe he made a mistake.'

'What about the garden? A shed? A garage?'

'There are four officers out the back. No one went past them.'

'FUCK!' Wise roared and wheeled away from the officers into one of the empty rooms.

'Calm yourself down, Inspector,' the Super said. 'Losing your temper will not help anyone.'

Wise turned to face her, but Hannah got in front of him first, scared he'd say or do something that there'd be no coming back from. 'We'll get him,' she said in the voice she used to reserve for talking drunks down on a Saturday night.

'I don't bloody believe it,' Wise said. 'I just don't believe it. Not after everything we've been through. How can he not be here?'

'We'll find him, Guv,' Hannah said.

'Fuck.' Wise had his fists clenched again, and Hannah could sense the violence emanating from the man. 'Fuck.'

Hannah looked around. The AROs were conversing with the Super, the dog sitting patiently to one side, all of them all dressed up with no one to arrest. Their radios spat out the progress of the search teams — or lack of progress.

The house itself was big and impressive and obviously expensive. Wooden floorboards gleamed under a fresh varnish and polish. The walls were spotless. The work on the place had been well done. It was so different from the place in Shafto Mews. That felt forgotten.

'Do you want to check out the room Smythe was in, Guv?' she asked Wise. 'Maybe there's something there that will tell us why he came here and how he got away.'

'You go up first,' Wise replied. 'I'm going to speak to the Super.'

Hannah winced. 'You're not going to do anything stupid, are you?'

Wise smiled. 'Me? No. Not now. Smythe's not won. The game's not over. We're just going into extra-time.'

'Good. I wouldn't want you to get sent off when we need you.'

'Go. I'll be up in a minute.'

Still, Hannah hesitated. The darkness in Wise's eyes worried her. There always seemed to be an element of danger lurking below the surface with him. She watched him head back to the others, but there was no outburst of anger and he didn't punch anyone with those big slabs of meat that he called hands. That was something, at least.

Hannah headed upstairs, passing an ARO on the way down. Unlike Shafto Mews, with its two rooms and a bathroom, the Chiswick house had multiple doors leading off the landing. A ladder reached up to an attic that the AROs must have searched, but Hannah ignored that. If Smythe had hidden up there, the officers would've found him.

Instead, she took her time, starting from the opposite end of the floor from where Wise had been working, going from room to room, not really looking for anything but letting her eyes get a feel for the place, wondering what Smythe had been doing there, why he'd come here and not just run off into the unknown.

For someone, the Chiswick house would be a family home of their dreams, a symbol of life's achievements, hard work and success, but, for now, it was an empty shell waiting to be more.

The bathroom looked new and very modern. Perhaps that was part of the work Smythe had done on the place? There was no towel though or toiletries that suggested it was being used, but there was toilet paper in the holder. Was that there for the builders or for Smythe?

Hannah thought about calling Sabine to check what exactly had been done on the house but decided that could wait till later.

The bedrooms were clean and well-decorated, and only the faintest smell of fresh paint lingered. All the bedrooms had built-in wardrobes and were of a good size. In fact, most were much bigger than the one she had at home in her flat, and would fit a double bed with ease, as well as desks and drawers and other stuff people need.

The master bedroom was twice the size of all the other rooms and had its own ensuite bathroom, fully fitted out.

Finally, she came to the room Smythe had been using. It was half the size of the other rooms, which surprised her. Why pick such a tiny room as a base? It had furniture, though; the same table and chair set up he'd had in Shafto Mews, in the middle of the room, just like before. Here, though, the walls were white and bare. There were no pictures, no plans. They had built a wardrobe along the wall to the right. Half the doors of which were still open from the AROs' search. Behind the desk were windows that overlooked the garden. Hannah walked over and looked down into the darkness of the garden. Was she standing where Smythe had stood?

She tried to imagine his reaction when he knew the police were there. Maybe he'd spotted someone in his garden but, somehow Hannah doubted that. The AROs were all ninja'd up. So, it would've been when the cavalry had turned up lights and sirens blaring. Even if he'd run straight away, he'd not have gotten downstairs and out of the house. The house was contained, all exits watched.

She thought again about the attic. He could've run and gone up there before anyone had entered the house, but it was a dead end, a place to be trapped and quickly found.

The Super had joked about him digging a tunnel and, for a moment, that kind of made sense. It'd be a way out that was out of sight. But where would a tunnel go? Not out the front of the house. And not to either side. There were neighbours that would've noticed if someone had dug a tunnel through their property. So that left the back garden.

Hannah looked again out the window, looking properly this time. The garden was about a half-acre in size, but the grass looked immaculate and well-cared for. It would be impossible to dig anything under it and maintain how good it looked. Unless he'd installed a brand new garden over the work, had rolls of mature grass brought in to cover up the damage done.

It was a mad thought. But one that made sense because Smythe had gotten out somehow.

Hannah ran from the room and headed down the stairs. The game wasn't over.

58

W ise was still with the Super when Hannah came clomping down the stairs in her boots in a hurry.

'What's up?' he asked, feeling a burst of hope. 'What have you found?'

'Nothing,' she said, her eyes bright with excitement. 'But, if Smythe was here, there's no way he got out of this house without being spotted unless he had a way out that couldn't be seen.'

Wise and the Super listened as Hannah explained her thinking about a tunnel into the garden. 'I can't fault your thinking,' he said once she was finished, 'but a tunnel? It'd be a massive job — expensive — and it'd be impossible to keep hidden from the neighbours. I don't see Smythe taking that sort of risk.'

'We've spoken to the neighbours too,' the Super added. 'They mentioned months of work inside the house, but nothing outside.'

'Right,' Hannah said, the spark dying. 'Sorry.'

'Don't be,' Wise said. 'Because you are right. Smythe was

here. An officer saw him, identified him. So, if it's impossible to get out of the house, then he must still be here.'

'But we've searched everywhere,' the Super said.

'Have we?' Wise said, looking around once more. 'How many rooms does this house have? How many potential hiding places are there?'

'We're not children playing hide and seek here,' the Super said. 'We know what we're doing.'

'Yes, but this man ... he's smart. He plans. He prepares,' Wise said. 'Smythe came here for a reason. And why did this house need months of work? A paint job doesn't take that long.'

'The upstairs has new bathrooms,' Hannah said. 'That would've taken a while. The bedrooms all have built-in wardrobes that look new.'

That perked Wise's interest. 'There's been construction upstairs?'

'Yeah. Nothing major but some.'

'What are you thinking?' the Super said.

'That Smythe is still here in some hidey-hole we've not seen,' Wise said. 'I think we need to have a look around upstairs again.'

The Super turned and called over two AROs. 'You two come with us. Bring the dog too.'

A group of six of them went upstairs. Wise, Hannah, the Super, two AROs with their MP5s and the dog handler with his Alsatian. It was more than Wise liked, but if Smythe was upstairs, he had a gun and the AROs and the dog were better equipped to handle that.

The first thing he saw was the ladder leading up to the attic. 'What about up there?'

An ARO shook his head. 'There's nothing up there. Not even floorboards. All the joists are exposed. There's nowhere to hide, nowhere to go and one wrong step and you're falling straight through the ceiling.'

They checked the bathrooms first, but there was nothing there. They even pulled off the panelling around the tub. Nothing.

They moved into the bedrooms, checking cupboards, floorboards and anywhere they could've been a hiding spot and again found nothing. The last room was the one Smythe had been using.

Again, they found nothing. Wise stared at the wardrobe with its doors open and drawers all pulled out.

'He's gone,' the Super said.

Wise said nothing. He couldn't accept that. Wouldn't accept it. Smythe had to be somewhere.

He sighed. The room felt claustrophobic with everyone in it. It was so small compared to the other rooms. He walked back out onto the landing, growing frustrated yet again. He could feel the clock ticking. Extra time running out. Soon, they'd have to pull everyone out. There was no way anyone could justify keeping a road blocked off and all these officers on duty much longer. Not for an empty house.

The others joined him. Wise could see the look in the Super's eyes. She was about to call it a bust officially. Send everyone home. Leaving an empty house. Maybe there'd be an officer outside. But maybe not even that. It wasn't as if Smythe would come back.

Not to an empty house.

But it wasn't empty. Smythe was here, waiting for everyone to give up and go home, leaving him alone to escape in his own sweet time, feeling ever so bloody impressed with himself. So very, very clever.

His phone rang, Roberts' name on the screen. Wanting an update, no doubt. He declined the call.

'We're heading back down,' the Super said as expected. 'It's time to call it a night.'

Wise nodded but didn't move. He watched the others head back down the stairs. Only Hannah stayed.

He walked over to her and whispered in her ear. 'He's here, waiting for us to go.'

Hannah nodded, not saying anything.

They stepped apart, both looking around the landing once more. Hannah's words played through Wise's mind that Smythe wouldn't have had time to go anywhere without being seen. They'd even had eyes on all the windows. If he'd gone downstairs or into another room, the AROs would have spotted him. Windows overlooked the landing on one side as well. Maybe if he'd come out in a crouch, they wouldn't have noticed him, but then where would Smythe have gone?

There was nowhere to go.

That left the room he'd been in. The one smaller than the others.

And yet the doors on the landing were equally spaced apart.

Wise went to the far bedroom and looked inside, mentally measuring the size of it. He moved onto the next room. As far as he could tell, it was of an equal size. Finally, he headed back to Smythe's room, tracing his hand along the landing wall as he walked, counting steps. Ten.

He went back to the first bedroom and, this time, he counted the steps between the first and second room. Ten steps again.

He entered the room, walked to where the wall separated it from the second bedroom. Nine steps.

He repeated the count in the second bedroom. Nine steps. That all made sense. Nine plus one for the wall itself.

'What?' Hannah mouthed as she watched him return to the landing and count the distance from the third room's door — Smythe's room — to the end wall, where the master bedroom was. Ten steps again.

So why was Smythe's room smaller? There was only one answer. It wasn't. He was using the difference for a hiding place.

He walked over to Hannah and whispered in her ear again. 'Smythe's room is smaller than the others, but it shouldn't be. Get the AROs back up here, but be quiet.'

Wise stood staring at the wall while he waited for Hannah. Smythe was probably feeling so, so clever right then. Making fools of everyone yet again.

Hannah returned with two AROs. They came up the stairs, making minimal noise. Wise pointed to the smaller room. They entered, and Wise pointed to the wardrobe. 'He's in there,' he mouthed.

The AROs took up position, MP5s raised and aimed at the wardrobe.

'Mr Smythe,' Wise called out. 'This is Detective Inspector Wise. I have armed police with me with weapons aimed at your hiding place. We know you're in there, so you might as well come out. The game's over.'

No one answered.

Wise glanced out at the landing. The Super was there with more AROs, listening and watching.

'Mr Smythe, if you don't come out, we're going to have to dig you out,' Wise said. 'And if we have to use an axe, I can't promise you won't get hurt, and no one wants that.'

Again, there was no answer, but there was no doubt in Wise's mind. Smythe was in there.

An ARO looked over at him. 'What do you want to do, sir?'

'Get someone to bring an axe or two up here,' Wise said, loud enough for Smythe to hear. 'I'm done waiting.'

Before anyone could move, there was a loud click and the back of the wardrobe swung open, revealing David Smythe sitting in a little hidey-hole, on a cushioned bench, a hold-all tugged in beside him.

Immediately, the AROs had their MP5s raised and aimed at him. 'ARMED POLICE! Put your hands on your head NOW! Put your hands on your head!' one of them shouted.

Smythe looked petrified at the shouts and the guns and the helmeted men facing him. Slowly, he did as he was told.

'Keep your eyes on me,' the ARO commanded, 'and come out with your hands on your head.'

Smythe swung a leg out, glancing at Wise as he did so.

'DON'T LOOK AT HIM! LOOK AT ME!' the ARO screamed. 'KEEP YOUR EYES ON ME!' He had the barrel of his gun aimed directly at Smythe's head. 'Come out with your hands on your head.'

Smythe swivelled around so he could swing his other leg out and then he slowly stood in front of the ARO.

'Get on your knees,' the ARO said. 'Keep your eyes on me and get on your knees.'

Smythe did as he was told. The second ARO stepped forward and slammed Smythe down so he was now lying on the floor.

'Look at me,' the first ARO said. 'Keep your eyes on me.' He still aimed the gun at Smythe's head. 'Slowly move your hands behind your back. I repeat, slowly move your hands behind your back.'

God, it felt so good to see the man meekly comply and watch the second ARO cuff him.

'David Smythe, I'm arresting you on suspicion of the

murders of Yuri Andronovitch, Mark Hassleman, Sir Harry Clarke, and Tony Richardson,' Wise said. 'You do not have to say anything, but it may harm your defence if you do not mention when questioned something you later relay on in court. Anything you do say may be given in evidence.'

'Did you tell her?' Smythe said, not taking his eyes off the ARO.

'Tell who?' Wise said.

'Did you tell Laura that I killed her darling Daddy?'

'Yes,' Wise said.

'And? What did she say? What did she do? Did she cry?' Smythe grinned.

'You're pathetic,' Wise said, and left the man with the AROs.

Out on the landing, the Super gave him a nod of approval. 'Good work, Inspector.'

'Thank you,' Wise said. 'Your team was great.'

He headed downstairs, Hannah following, eager to get out into the night and breathe the night air. He felt too tired to be elated, but he was damn glad it was over. They finally had the bastard.

'What's next, Guv?' Hannah asked.

'We'll take him back to Kennington and get him processed,' Wise said, 'then we can get some sleep before all the fun starts again tomorrow.'

'Sounds good,' Hannah said, a big smile across her face. 'I can't believe we got him.'

'What do you think?' Wise asked. 'Now your first murder case is all done? You don't regret joining us?'

'No. Not in the slightest,' Hannah said. 'To be honest, I loved it. It was everything I could've hoped for.'

Wise grinned. 'Good, because you're a skilled detective. I'm glad you're on the team, Hannah.'

'Guv?' Hannah said, a little sheepishly.

'Yes?'

'I wouldn't mind if the next one's a bit more straight-forward.'

Wise laughed. 'No promises.'

59

It was nearly midnight when Wise parked his car outside his house with its bright red door, feeling very happy with himself. Smythe was in a cell at Kennington where he could stew until the morning when the teams would begin interviewing him. Meanwhile, Forensics were bagging and tagging everything at Shafto Mews so they had all the evidence to put Smythe away for the rest of his life.

They'd found a pistol and silencer in his hold-all in Chiswick, as well as a passport and his laptop. Wise knew that the gun would match the bullets that had killed the four victims.

Considering they had taken him off the case less than forty-eight hours before, it had been a good couple of days' work.

He turned the car engine off, but he didn't get out of the car just yet. Instead, he leaned back and closed his eyes.

It was done. It was over.

He'd got a result and made a good start in restoring the damage done by Andy.

Even his friend's ghost seemed a distant thing for once, instead of a bloody memory torturing Wise day and night. Still, with Smythe in a cell, he could start working on finding out who Andy was working for. That was someone else Wise would see behind bars.

But tonight, Wise was going to sleep.

He rolled his neck, grabbed his jacket and phone from the passenger seat, and got out of the car. He walked up to the house and let himself in, doing his best not to make any noise.

It was quiet inside, the central heating ticking over enough to keep any chill at bay but not so hot that the bill would bankrupt them. There was the customary glow from the bathroom light that was always left on, shining through the half-open door.

He hooked his jacket over the newel post and kicked his shoes next to the pile near the door, smiling at the sight of Ed and Claire's little trainers and Wellington boots. He stopped in the kitchen to drink a glass of water and then headed upstairs.

Wise stuck his head into Ed's room first. It was all neat and tidy. Chelsea posters covered the walls. A framed shirt, signed by Thiago Silva, that Wise had won in a raffle at a police federation charity dinner, took pride of place.

Ed's head was just about visible, poking out the top of his CFC duvet. His little boy dreaming away. Wise crept in and kissed his son, his heart swelling with love and pride.

Next door, Claire's room was a complete contrast. It looked like a bomb had gone off in there with toys, books, and stuff everywhere. Her night light was on and an army of stuffed toys guarded the base of her bed. It was more difficult reaching her, as he had to watch out for whatever things she'd left lying around. Tripping over a box of beads was not something he wanted to do. He reached her though without mishap and kissed her on the forehead too, enjoying the little snuffle sound she made as she slept. Claire was so much like her mum and he loved her all the more for that.

Finally, Wise headed into his own room, feeling like a stranger trespassing for a moment after so long hiding in the spare room. But Jean was fast asleep on her side of the bed and there was his spot on the other side of the bed waiting for him. He slipped out of his clothes, folding his trousers and placing them over the back of the chair by the dressing table.

He climbed into bed carefully, not wanting to wake his wife. She slept on her side, turned towards him, a frown on her face, making the same snuffle sounds Claire made, her long, brown hair tied loosely back.

Wise settled down next to her, watching her sleep, feeling at peace for the first time in an age. Happy to be home. Happy to be there. Happy to feel himself at long last.

Wise closed his eyes and slept.

FRIDAY, 23RD SEPTEMBER

Friday, 23rd September

60

Wise drove into Kennington police station, feeling better than he had in ages. He'd had a decent night's sleep for one thing — nearly a solid six hours. He'd woken to a kiss from his wife a second before the kids had pounced on him and he could still feel their laughter ringing in his ears. Why had he spent so long hiding from them?

The press were waiting en masse, word of the previous night's arrest having summoned even more than before. After parking, Wise ignored their shouts and cries for information as he made his way through them and out into the street. He crossed Kennington Road and headed straight to Luigi's Cafe, enjoying the bright, early morning sunshine and the cold, fresh air.

The cafe was its normal hustle and bustle as Luigi, his wife, and daughters served caffeine and pastries to all who needed it.

'Detective Inspector,' said Luigi when Wise reached the counter, a big grin on his face. 'How are you today?'

'I'm good, thanks,' Wise said, and it felt good to actually mean it. There was no need for a mask today.

'I hear you make an arrest,' said Luigi. 'This motorbike killer.'

'We have someone in custody,' Wise said.

'Good man, good man. I can sleep safely at night again because of you.'

'It wasn't just me,' Wise said. 'It was the team.'

'Well, thank them all for me,' said Luigi. 'In the meantime, your coffee is on the house.'

'I've actually come to get coffee for the entire team,' Wise said.

Luigi glanced at his wife, who gave him a brisk shake of the head, topped off with a glare that could curdle milk. His smile faltered only for a second. 'Well then, that is one less you have to pay for.'

'Thank you, my friend,' Wise said. He gave his order and then pulled his phone out of his pocket. Opening WhatsApp, he sent Jean a message. *Love you x*

A message dinged back almost immediately. *Good to have you back X*

Wise smiled. He'd got lucky marrying Jean. He wouldn't screw things up with her again.

Even Maria's death stare as he paid for the drinks on his card didn't bother him. Today was going to be a good day. Carrying a tray full of coffees, Wise headed back to the nick, aware that he was grinning from ear to ear.

MIR-One was already full and buzzing when Wise entered, and an enormous cheer greeted him. There was no sign of Riddleton and his pet shrink and someone, most probably Sarah, had rearranged the white boards back to the way he liked it. A picture of Smythe had been stuck in the centre of the 'what do we know' section. Someone had drawn vertical bars over his face and scrawled NICKED underneath it.

His team swarmed over, relieving him of the coffees and offering their congratulations. Backs were slapped and tales told and Wise loved standing there amidst his team, back to winning ways, that lingering air of doubt and suspicion gone at long last. No matter how tough the Smythe case had been, it had succeeded in bringing them all together again.

He made a point of going over to Hannah. 'Well done again.'

She smiled. 'Thanks for your trust in me. It means a lot.'

'Well, I'm sorry if I wasn't as welcoming as I should've been to start with. You didn't exactly join at a good time.'

'It's okay,' Hannah replied. 'Your mood swings weren't that bad.'

'They probably were, but I'll try my best not to be like that anymore.'

Hannah was going to say something, but stopped herself and nodded towards the door. 'The boss is here.'

Roberts had appeared as if by magic, no doubt sensing the free coffee in the air. 'Good morning, Simon.'

'Good timing, boss,' Wise said, walking over with a cup for her. 'How are the powers that be after last night's excitement?'

'Walling wasn't happy about looking foolish, but the arrest made up for that,' Roberts said, taking the coffee. 'He's off to the Embankment to claim all the credit.'

'That's his job, after all.'

'Quite.' Roberts looked around as if to check no one was listening. 'Sorry to drag you away, but can you come to my office for a minute?'

'Something wrong?' Wise asked.

'I hope not,' Roberts said, but there was something unsettling in her face.

'Right,' Wise said. Bringing his coffee, he followed her out the door, a sense of unease stirring in his gut. What the hell was this about? Roberts should've been over the moon. They'd bagged the Motorbike Killer and Riddleton and the shrink looked like a bunch of fools.

Roberts didn't speak as they walked down to her office. She stopped and opened the door to her office, and then stepped aside to allow Wise to enter. That was when he saw two people sitting in front of Roberts' desk. They stood as he walked into the room and nothing about them said they were there for a friendly conversation. He recognised one of them, a short man with Richard Gere's eyes.

'I'll leave you to chat,' Roberts said, and shut the door behind Wise.

'Detective Inspector Wise?' said the woman. 'I'm DCI Rena Heer from Specialist Crime and Operations 10. This is my colleague, DS Brendan Murray. We're part of an interdepartmental task force investigating organised crime in London.'

'I know DS Murray,' Wise said. He'd been the man Jono had called about Andy.

Murray didn't seem to want to be friends, though, judging by the grunt he gave Wise in return.

'Sorry to drag you away from your work, but we'd like to ask you a few questions if that's okay?' Heer said. Nothing in her tone suggested it was a request he could turn down.

'Do I need my federation rep with me?' Wise asked.

Heer shrugged. 'That's up to you, but this isn't a formal interview. We can make it one if you want, but I'm hoping we can avoid that.'

A part of Wise wanted to walk out and find Roberts to let

her know exactly what he thought of her little ambush, but that would only delay the inevitable. Instead, he walked around Roberts' desk and sat down in her seat, grateful he'd brought his coffee. He noticed there was a brown folder on the desk in front of Heer, turned face down. 'I'm all yours.'

Heer glanced at Murray, then both sat back down. 'Do you know a man called Barry Lawrence?' said Heer.

'No,' Wise said.

'What about Sokol Manaj?'

'No.'

'Georgi Mostovoy?'

'No.'

'Tiago Dursun?'

'No.'

'Clarence Wu?'

'Look, why don't you tell me what you really want instead of just running through a list of random names?' Wise said.

'What about Elrit Selmani?'

'Yeah, I know him,' Wise said. 'I put him away for twenty years.'

'He was the one your partner was trying to get off,' Murray said. 'By killing the only witness.'

'If I don't do this,' Andy says, 'he told me he'd kill them.'

'Who did?' Wise takes another step forward.

'I'm sorry, Si,' Andy says. 'I'm sorry for ev—' His head lurches forward a heartbeat before Wise hears the crack of the gun. Time slows as Andy tumbles forward, red mist leading the way, his brains and blood already splattered across the rooftop.

'I don't think Andy was working for Selmani,' Wise said. He picked up his coffee and took a gulp, his hand shaking just a little.

'Then why were you getting people to ask what's happening with our investigation?' Murray asked.

'Because I want the bastard who is responsible behind bars as well,' Wise said.

'Do you?' Murray said.

'Yes, I do,' Wise snapped, his good mood a distant memory now. 'Look, what's this about?'

'Six families run organised crime in London,' Heer said. 'The Albanians, like Selmani, run prostitution and human trafficking, the Turks handle the majority of the heroin trade, the Chinese the gambling and so on. They might not like each other but, as long as they don't interfere in each others' business, they left each other alone.'

'Until two years ago,' Murray said.

'This is fascinating,' Wise said, 'but what's it got to do with me?'

'Two years ago, a local gang took on the families,' Heer said. 'They started grabbing territories off the other gangs, stealing businesses, snatching merchandise and happily killing anyone who got in their way. A kind of criminal Brexit, if you will. Taking back control. They made the Russians look like peace-loving snowflakes.'

'They left dead bodies everywhere,' Murray said.

'Obviously, we wanted to know who this new gang was, but no one would talk — and I mean no one,' Heer continued. 'So, we put a Covert Operative into their operation.'

'I'm assuming it didn't go well,' Wise said.

'Oh, it went very well,' Heer said. 'Our CO got in and worked their way up through the ranks — except they still didn't know who the top man was. The gang didn't trust anyone with that information. It took them a year to get a name — just a first name, but it was progress. Then, it was another six months before they had time to meet the boss.'

'Eighteen months undercover?' Wise said. 'That's hard graft.' Still, he was interested now. Was this gang leader the man who'd turned Andy?

'Yeah, it was. Unfortunately, two days ago, someone hit our CO with a car and killed them,' Heer said.

'I take it you don't think it was an accident?'

'The car that hit the CO reversed and ran over them at least three times.'

'Shit.'

'Before our CO was killed, they sent me a photo with a message — identifying the big boss.'

'Right.' Wise didn't know why, but he felt anxious — like he was in a car about to crash and there was nothing he could do to stop it.

Heer picked up the folder and turned it over. Opened it. 'This is what they sent us. This is what they got killed for.'

There was a single picture inside, taken from a distance, of a Caucasian man, early forties, short blonde hair, well-built. There was a date in the corner — 21/09/22 — and a time, 1705HRS. Wise knew the man's face as well as his own.

Murray leaned in. 'That *is* you, isn't it?'

Wise stared at the picture, mouth dry, heart racing, his mind full of a thousand thoughts, a million fears. 'It looks like me, but it's not me,' Wise said. He pointed to the date and time. 'At that time, I was with DS Hannah Markham in Birmingham, interviewing someone at The Clearacres Retirement Home. I was with her all night, watching a murder suspect, accompanied by DS Jonathan Gray and DS Roy Hicks.'

Heer and Murray exchanged looks.

'But you know that,' Wise said. 'Otherwise you would have arrested me already.'

'Then how do you explain this?' Murray stabbed his finger down on the photograph.

'It's someone who looks like me,' Wise said. 'That's all.'

'He doesn't just look like you — he's your bloody twin,' Murray snapped.

Wise couldn't argue with that. The man was right, after all. It was his twin. 'What was the name you were given?'

'Our CO said his name was Tom,' said Heer.

Wise stared at the picture of the most dangerous man in London.

His brother. His twin.

Tom Wise.

Was he the man who'd destroyed Andy's life?

'If I don't do this,' Andy says, 'he told me he'd kill them.'

'I'm sorry,' Wise said. 'I can't help you.'

THANK YOU

Thank you for reading *Rich Man, Dead Man*, the first Detective Inspector Simon Wise thriller. It means the world to me that you have given your time to read my tales. It's your support that makes it possible for me to do this for a living, after all.

So, please spare a moment if you can to either write a review or simply rate *Rich Man, Dead Man* on Amazon. Your honest opinion will help future readers decide if they want to take a chance on a new-to-them author. Click here to let people know what you think.

Leaving a review is one of the greatest things you can do for an author and it really helps our books stand out amongst all the rest.

This book was only made possible by the help of some very wonderful people. I'd like to thank Rebecca Millar for her incredible editorial advice, Graham Bartlett for his expert advice on police procedure, and Dawn Ferguson for proofreading the book. Any mistakes contained within this book are despite their best efforts.

Thank you once again!

Mike (Keep reading to get a free book)

GET A FREE BOOK TODAY

Sign up for my mailing list at www.michaeldylanwrites.com and get a free copy of Dead Man Running, and discover exactly how DS Andy Davidson ended up on that rooftop in Peckham with a gun in his hand.

Plus by signing up, you'll be the first to hear about the next books in the series and special deals.

Join DI Wise in The Killing Game. Order it today.

THE DI SIMON WISE SERIES

Out Now:

Dead Man Running

Rich Men, Dead Men

The Killing Game

Coming soon:

Into The River Dead (January 2024)

Printed in Great Britain
by Amazon